BASIC TRAINING
OF THE HEART

Visit us at www.boldstrokesbooks.com

BASIC TRAINING OF THE HEART

by
Jaycie Morrison

2016

BASIC TRAINING OF THE HEART

ISBN 13: 978-1-62639-818-4

This Trade Paperback Original Is Published By
Bold Strokes Books, Inc.
P.O. Box 249
Valley Falls, NY 12185

First Edition: September 2016

CREDITS
Editor: Ruth Sternglantz
Production Design: Susan Ramundo
Cover Design By Jenna Albright

Acknowledgments

My undying appreciation first to Joanie, Marti, and Casson, my loyal beta readers. Without your encouragement, this book would never have been anything but a file on my computer. The support of my special group of "flat tire friends" and others as this process has moved from dream to reality has been incredible. Thanks to Len and Sandy of Bold Strokes Books for taking a chance even after hearing the worst pitch in the history of pitches, and a special thanks to Ruth, possibly the world's most patient editor.

On a serious note, this story began with the intention of honoring two groups that I greatly admire: those who have served and are serving in the armed forces, especially those trailblazing women, and the long-suffering members of Native American communities. While I have tried to do my research, I do not claim to be an expert on either and sincerely apologize in advance for any offense I may have given. Even though this is a work of fiction, in both cases, an honest effort was made to remain respectful and not break any taboos. Any errors are entirely mine, but I would like to acknowledge the dedication of Mr. Jack Luskin of the Ft. Des Moines Museum and Education Center and the invaluable assistance of Ms. Renee Woodruff, who came on board as my consultant on Lakota language and customs after my early missteps but hopefully in time to save me from additional ones—philámayaye, mitȟámaške.

Dedication

To my wonderful family, who first taught me about love,
and to Sandy, who makes me believe in it every day.
Without you, my beloved wife, there would be no romance,
no music, no stars. You are my match, my one and only.
And for Gambo, and that other book we always
meant to write. Your brave heart and beautiful
spirit will always be with us.

In honor of
Oveta Culp Hobby
(1905–1995)
First director of the Women's Army Corps

CHAPTER ONE

August 11, 1944

"Well, it looks as if you girls are in for a rough eight weeks." The perspiring driver's words vibrated like the bug-smeared windshield as she peered out at the robust figure standing stiffly ahead. "You've drawn the meanest sergeant in the service." Braking hard enough that Bett's shoulder briefly brushed the woman next to her as they both swayed along the benches of the converted cattle truck, the uniformed woman turned around to confront the assortment of faces before continuing her explanation. "Her name's Sergeant Moore, but I've heard they call her Sergeant Less, 'cause she grinds her recruits down to a lot less than they start out with." She chortled as the truck ground to a stop. The damp heat of a late Iowa summer promptly filled in the spaces where the air had been moving.

As if in confirmation of this assessment, the sergeant's booming voice pierced the flapping back cover of the truck. "Get your asses out of that truck, ladies, and give me a line right here, right now!" Jolted into action, Bett and the other occupants began quickly gathering their possessions. The faces around her showed a variety of reactions: some were clearly terrified, others appeared determined, a few suppressing a smirk at the use of the word *ass*. Bett had to agree that it was almost funny to hear the words *asses* and *ladies* in the same sentence. Judging from the urgency of the sergeant's tone, it was more important that everyone move the former than the obvious fact that several in the truck didn't fit into the latter category. *Clearly there's a good reason this isn't called the Ladies' Army Corps*, she thought.

"Move it, move it, girls!" the voice insisted as the truck lumbered away, leaving a blast of well-worn dust that settled warmly around the young women's ragged line. Once the movement had subsided, the group silenced as the ruddy, narrow-eyed Sergeant Moore began to speak. "You are officially members of the Women's Army Corps now. That means you will look Army, act Army, think Army, and be Army! And for right now, I am the Army. So that means you will do what I say, when I say it, how I say it. Are there any questions?" She waved a clipboard threateningly in their direction.

A general shaking of heads followed. Raising her voice a pitch, Moore added, "You are the sorriest bunch of recruits I've ever seen. I guess pickings must be getting mighty slim out there. Where did they find you?" She fixed a glare on the fourth girl in line, a stick-thin waif in a shapeless shift dress who, at first glance, looked as though she might blow over in a strong wind. "Skid row?" The girl ducked her head, her short hair not quite hiding the rise of color coming into her cheeks. She clenched her fists, hiding dirty fingernails and causing the wiry muscles in her arms to bunch.

"I am a sergeant," Moore resumed. "That means you will answer my questions with 'Yes, Sergeant' or 'No, Sergeant.' Do you understand?"

"Yes, Sergeant," a few brave souls mumbled.

"What?" Sergeant Moore almost screamed.

"Yes, Sergeant!" they replied together, loudly.

Moore's skeptical gaze came to rest on a tall, fair-skinned redhead who had been regarding her almost pleadingly. Taking a step closer to the girl, she shouted, "Are you looking at me?" As the redhead shuddered, her eyes moving wildly around for anyone or anything else to look at, the segeant directed, "When you are being address by a superior, you hayseeds will look straight ahead, not at the officer." Everyone tried to assume this expression as Moore looked down the line. Her critical inspection settled on a brown-complexioned young woman standing toward the end of the line on

Bett's left. The sergeant's thick brows lowered and her voice was heavy with disgust as she snorted, "I can't believe they keep letting mutts like you into my Army."

Although her breath shortened, the girl remained still, looking at nothing.

Widening her contempt to encompass them all, Moore looked down at her clipboard as she barked her next order. "Sound off! For today that means you will give me your first and last name and where you're from." Moore stepped to the first girl in line, a young, pleasantly plump girl with streaky brown hair who managed to comply after a quick swallow.

"Charlotte Jackson," she stated nervously, adding, almost unnecessarily to Bett, who was quite familiar with the soft, drawling notes of the South, "Montgomery, Alabama." Moore made a notation on the paper.

The next girl in line was shaking visibly with her head bowed, and several of the others dared to glance at each other. Riding just the short distance to the base in the noisy truck, Bett had only heard a few words from the soft-spoken young woman, but she'd detected a significant stammer. She assumed the others had become somewhat better acquainted since they'd all been on the train for some time before she'd joined them at the station in Des Moines. Still, no one seemed to know what to do as Moore stepped in front of the frightened girl and demanded, "Well? Are you waiting for a personal invitation?" The girl's mouth opened but no sound came out. She seemed unable to breathe. "Are you deaf?" bellowed Moore.

The girl swayed just a bit, as though she might faint. After a few more anguished seconds, Bett took a breath and called out in her most imperious tone. "Wait."

In unison, the whole line turned toward the sound. Sergeant Moore's head snapped around angrily, and Bett moved forward a step as she continued in her most pronounced British accent. "I wonder if you might indulge me, Sergeant. I'm an alumna of Oxford University"—she paused to offer a somewhat sheepish grin at her fellow recruits—"which is why I sound a bit like the Queen."

At that, her fellow recruits began murmuring to each other.
"Sure does."

"Like one of those characters on the radio."

"That's right."

Before Sergeant Moore could recover from the surprise of being interrupted, Bett pushed a strand of blond hair behind her ear and continued. "My degree was in linguistics, but I presented on regional accents and colloquial dialects of the United States, so I was wondering if you might allow me a conjecture as to the geographical location from which each of these young ladies originates? Give my studies a bit of a tryout?" She ended with what she hoped was a winning smile, and the group stirred with relief and anticipation.

"What did she say?" the thin girl wondered in a whisper.

"She wants to guess where we come from," the Alabama intonation replied quietly.

"Shut the fuck up." If Sergeant Moore's face was red before, it was now almost purple. The recruits were shocked and frightened into silence as Moore strode down the line. "What part of doing it my way did you not understand?" she snarled into Bett's face.

"But aren't you the least bit curious to see if she can do it, Sergeant Moore?" A new voice, clear and almost melodic somehow, cut through the sweltering tension. No one had noticed her approach, focused as they were on the drama unfolding at the other end of the line. Even Sergeant Moore appeared startled as she whipped around and then nodded briefly in acknowledgment.

"So is it Master Sergeant now, Rains? I was told you might be gone for half a day." From her vantage point, Bett could clearly see Moore's thinly veiled hostility as she eyed the stripes on the newcomer's sleeve. "They're letting you try out the new uniform, I see." Though they both wore a stiff-brimmed, rounded khaki hat with the WAC insignia on the front, Rains's long-sleeved khaki shirt and tucked olive green tie disappeared at her narrow waist into a pair of pressed khaki pants. While Moore's stomach strained at the straight line of her skirt and the buttons of her top, the cut and drape of the uniform fit Rains's form flawlessly and complemented the tight lines of her thin figure. In further contrast to Moore's red-faced, threatening appearance, Bett's first impression was that Sergeant Rains looked every inch the military model of command—concentrated, competent, and completely in control.

Seemingly unaffected by Moore's antagonism, Rains's voice was calm. "Yes, just now. But it's still First Sergeant. Until we get this group through." Facing the group, she stiffened to attention. "Good day." Spontaneously, they all mirrored her position as she continued, "My name is Sergeant Rains and I will be your drill instructor until you graduate from basic training. I had a meeting at headquarters today and Sergeant Moore was kind enough to cover for me." Turning back to Moore, she gave a curt, dismissive nod. "I know you're due to rotate out for some R and R today, Sergeant. Thank you for your time." They saluted each other at the change of command.

"Good luck with this bunch, Rains," she said unkindly, handing Rains the clipboard as she got off one final comment. "I've been trying to teach them the fundamentals, but they're dumber than a box of rocks. They might even cost you that promotion." Turning back abruptly, she added, in a low, menacing tone, "And I'll have my eye on you, Your Highness."

Bett flinched, but more with distaste than fear.

Sergeant Rains surveyed the group again with a serious expression. As Moore's retreating back grew smaller, they gave an almost unison sigh of relief. Rains focused her dark eyes on Bett as she began to speak. "So, Private…?"

"Smythe." Bett filled in after the briefest hesitation.

As Rains gave another quick, almost imperceptible nod, there were some hoots and giggles from the rest of the line, apparently at the distinguished pronunciation the young woman gave to the common name. The sergeant silenced them quickly with a sharp look. "One thing the Army expects us to teach you is how to work as a team. More than that, the women in this squad will become your sisters." Her tone was firm but pleasant, taking on an almost hypnotic cadence as she moved noiselessly down the line, looking at each girl. "So no matter how things are with your relations on the outside, you have a new family now. One that we will build together. We will look out for each other, learn to count on each other, trust each other, and respect each other. We will be making vital contributions to the war effort, and we will demonstrate something important about the abilities of the American woman. So to the outside world, we present a united front. We are together. We are one. Because your family, and now this Army family, is a big part of who you are and what you will become. Added to whatever else you have been, a daughter, a sister, the youngest, the prettiest"—two or three of the girls giggled slightly at this—"from this moment on, you are also a WAC." She turned and went down the line. "But we are part of a larger family, too—the Army family. And there are rules for our larger family as well. We do things a certain way, because we know they work. What makes these rules fair to the whole family is that since everyone follows the same procedures and has the same experiences, we can understand each other more easily."

Ending up again in front of Bett, she continued her lecture to the group. "Doing things differently can be a risk, because new ways may not get the results that we want. But sometimes a new thing is better and its success rewards us for trying it. Private Smythe here has taken a risk by speaking out. She wants to try something that is not the Army way. So we will try, and see if her risk is rewarded. But should she fail, you will all run one lap for each one she gets wrong"—she quickly swept her gaze over Bett—"to help us remember the pitfalls of questioning an officer's instructions." She turned to the group again. "Understood?"

The young woman on Bett's left whispered, "I hope you're really good at this stuff, girl, cause I hate runnin'."

The rest were nodding as Sergeant Rains repeated, with slightly more volume, "Understood?"

"Yes, Sergeant," came the unison, obedient reply.

Satisfied, Rains looked back at Bett, her head cocked slightly with curiosity. "Can you really tell where someone comes from, just from hearing them say their name?"

"Well," Bett allowed, "since you've put such high stakes on it, I would like a little more opportunity to hear each person speak. Perhaps if they could also state, in one sentence, why they volunteered for the WAC?"

"Fair enough." Rains moved back up the line, and instructed the group, "You will give your name"—she stopped and then added—"and what you prefer to be called, along with your reason for joining up. Private Jackson has already given her origins away, I believe," the sergeant continued, and Jackson nodded. Rains stopped in front of the second girl, who had stopped shaking, although the long thin curls of her hair were drenched with sweat. The tall sergeant leaned away from her slightly, taking a nonthreatening pose, and said softly to the girl, "You may look at me, Private." Teary eyes opened but did not look up. The sergeant's voice gentled. "Can you tell your new family your name and why you volunteered?"

"Te-Te-Te...," the girl began, in an almost sobbing voice, but kept her eyes open. Bett wondered if anyone else heard Sergeant Rains making a soft hushing sound, almost like what a rider would make to settle a skittish horse, that seemed to draw the frightened girl's eyes upward. As she met the sergeant's eyes, she took a breath.

"Teresa Owens," she abruptly shuddered forth, almost surprising herself. "But everyone j-just calls me Tee, c-c-cause that's usually all I c-c-can get out." Then she added, "I volunteered b-b-because..." She trailed off, trying to catch her breath again. "Because we lost the farm and...if I'm not r-running the plow, I'm just another m-mouth to feed. No one in town would hire m-me and there warn't nowhere else for me t-to go."

Some of the other girls were looking at the ground, embarrassed, but Bett saw Tee relax a bit when Rains gave an encouraging nod. Then the sergeant turned to her with a questioning look as the rest of the group waited anxiously.

"Oklahoma," Smythe said with some certainty, thankful that the stutter had not covered up the twanging vowels of the southwest. "Perhaps near Tulsa?"

Owens's eyes opened wider. "She's right!" A cheer went up and Bett breathed a sigh of relief.

The third recruit was a pleasant looking auburn-haired woman in her late thirties. "Barbara Ferguson," she said clearly, "but you can call me Barb." Her face turned solemn. "My husband got called up last month. He's going into the Air Force and I thought there must be some way I could do my part, too. I know we all wanna do whatever we can to get our men home soon as possible."

While the others nodded sympathetically, Bett smiled. Barb's broad *a*'s and dropped *r*'s could only mean one thing. "Massachusetts. Boston, or perhaps Cape Cod," she announced and the group cheered again as Barb smiled.

"Boston, Hyde Park," she confirmed.

The thin girl gave her name as Helen Tucker. Still unwilling to look up, she mumbled angrily into the ground, her shoulders slumping. "My daddy was a miner. He got killed last month. My brother's already in the Army so there wasn't no one else to work for us. My auntie says the Army's givin' three meals and a bed, along with money each month. So I figure I need to learn me a trade." Her head turned toward Tee and her voice seemed to strengthen. "Maybe just 'cause we're girls don't mean we hafta always be dependin' on somebody else. Maybe not anymore." Tee managed a small grateful smile, drawing in another shuddering breath.

A few of the other girls murmured in agreement and everyone seemed to stand a little straighter. The sergeant's expression softened. "My brother is in the Army too, Private," she said, her voice low. "That means our brothers are brothers, as we will be sisters."

Helen's head came up slowly. Her light green eyes met the sergeant's dark ones defiantly for several seconds. What passed between them, Smythe couldn't see, but when Rains offered no reprimand, Helen's gaze finally shifted into the distance. In the silence, Smythe cleared her throat. "Kentucky. Western Kentucky."

By then, Helen herself had straightened almost to attention. "Damn right," she said, startling the line into a laughing applause.

Waiting for the enthusiasm to die down, Rains turned to study Smythe. She was surprised to see Smythe looking directly at her, although when their eyes met, Smythe dropped hers at once. Sensing some kind of discomfiture, Rains turned back to the group.

"Now, ladies." Her tone was sterner now. "Tell me the truth and we will stop this now with no laps to run. Did you make this up as a prank on the train on the way here?"

Rains listened closely for signs of deceit, but the group denials were instantaneous and sincere.

"No way."

"No, Sergeant."

"Absolutely not."

"No, ma'am."

The tough-looking dark-haired girl standing to the right of Smythe joined in, jerking her thumb in Smythe's direction as she spoke. "Queenie here wasn't even on the train with us, Sarge. She got in the truck from some big fancy car. I saw it."

When one or two of the others began nodding in agreement, Rains jumped in quickly. "You're out of line, Private."

"Yeah, but, I'm just tryin' to explain how this couldn't be no setup, see?" insisted the speaker, turning back to Smythe. "Go on, Queenie, do your magic. Jo Archer. Here to defend the good ole US of A. From...?"

Getting the slightest affirmative motion from Rains, Bett finished in a fair imitation of Jo's strong accent. "New York, New York." More laughter and cheers followed as Archer shook her fists triumphantly, and Bett thought she might have seen the corners of Rains's severe mouth turn up just a bit.

After Norwegian-looking Phyllis Kendrick, who had a nephew in the Navy and wanted to do something positive while waiting for a teaching job to open up, was correctly identified as being from Minnesota, the brown-haired, brown-eyed girl on Bett's left introduced herself as Maria Rangel who was following the example of her cousin, a nurse who was already stationed in the Pacific. "Texas," Smythe said after a few seconds' thought. "South Texas?"

"No," Maria said, a bit sadly. "I live in New Mexico." A chorus of groans cut off when Rangel brightened as she added, "But I was born in Texas."

Private Smythe turned to her sergeant. "Once a Texan, always a Texan?" she tried, her eyebrows raised persuasively. Rains folded her arms across her chest and responded with a kind of grunt that everyone seemed to take as a yes, and the cheering resumed.

In the entire row, Bett's only miss came on Irene Dodd, a tired-looking older woman who rejected Bett's guess of Illinois as incorrect but declined to give a specific right answer, only saying, "I'm from all over. We moved a lot."

"And why are you here?" asked Rains, over the girls' sighs of disappointment. Dodd had not volunteered this information either.

"I don't know," Dodd replied, almost disinterestedly. "Some guy give me a paper to sign outside the grocery where I worked. Said it would help end the war faster. A couple of weeks later, I get a notice in the mail to report here."

There were a few seconds of silence, as if no one knew how to respond to this.

"Okay, Queenie, it's your turn, anyway," crowed Jo, flushed with their success. "And I'll do the guessing," she added with certainty, puffing her chest a bit.

"Well, my name is Elizabeth Frances Pratt...Smythe," she began, her clipped British accent bringing the group to a courteous silence. "My friends at boarding school used to call me Pratt, because it sounds so much like *brat*, I think." The group laughed easily. "But my family calls me Bett. My mother wanted it to be Beth, you know, from Elizabeth, but my little sister couldn't say the *h*, so she called me Bett, and it just stuck." She looked imploring at Jo and then took in the rest of the group. "But please, not Queenie. I admire Her Majesty, of course, but in spite of my accent I am an American—a proud American."

Her patriotic assertion was met with scattered applause and some ragged cheers. "And your reason for being here?" prodded Rains.

Pushing her wavy blond hair back behind her ears, Smythe replied, "I had just left England when the war broke out there. I still have many friends and colleagues who are suffering through this terrible struggle." She sobered as she added, "My father sent me away to school so I would learn to think for myself. When I came back to the US five years ago and begin doing just that, he was horrified. I was briefly employed as a teaching assistant at a local college, but enrollment dropped so dramatically once we entered the war that I was let go. So my father began trying to introduce me to polite society through endless boring parties, but I was able to dodge most of that drudgery, partly by volunteering in at the Red Cross and with the USO." She looked down for a moment, and her voice softened. "I—I actually know…knew…someone who was killed recently in one of those horrible rocket attacks on London, so the war has become more than just news to me." There were some sympathetic murmurs and nodding of heads. Her voice strengthened. "Shortly after that news I was taking a different route to the USO, trying to avoid a terrible traffic jam, and I saw the WAC recruiting office. It just seemed to call to me. I guess my family still thinks I've lost my mind, but there it is. And here I am," she added, with the slightest curtsey.

Most of the group was smiling as they turned to Jo for her assessment, but Jo looked completely lost. "How do you do this again?" she asked Bett, who only smiled and put a finger to her lips. Jo turned to the rest of the company. "I give up. Youse guys go figure it."

Names of numerous cities were suggested, but to each Bett only shook her head. "Why don't you guess, Sarge?" Jo asked, when the calls had died out.

Rains shook her head slightly at Jo. "Here is one important thing for you to understand, Private Archer. Your sergeant will never guess. Your sergeant will always know. Los Angeles, California."

She shifted her eyes to Smythe, whose expression had turned to one of complete surprise, and the group applauded at her reaction. Before the blonde could recover, Rains spoke again. "All right ladies, it's time to get your gear and get you settled into your barracks. Let's move."

Rains formed them into two columns and began leading them across the compound at a brisk walk. Trying to keep her mind off the effort of breathing in the heat, Smythe focused on the sergeant's lean form ahead of her. She walked with a graceful stride, but her long legs covered ground almost as if she were at a run. Bett had already seen that the sergeant had very black hair by the almost too-long bangs that draped above her eyes. From the back, a thin line of straight hair barely covered her neck. Bett was glad that she'd gone to her own beauty salon for a new shorter hairdo after she'd enlisted.

She had no intention of letting some Army barber create some severe style with her hair as they seemed to have done to Sergeant Rains.

Bett heard the soft vowels of the Kentucky accent—Helen, wasn't it?—whispering behind her. "Look at this place, Tee. It's really somethin'. We're gonna have us a time here!" She supposed that Tee, with her stutter, wouldn't make much of a response, but she thought she heard a soft "uh-huh." She took a quick glance at her new surroundings and was pleasantly surprised. The stately buildings on either side of the roadway stretched ahead almost as far as she could see. An intersecting street not far away stretched out to her left and right, with more of the deep red-brick and white-trimmed structures on either side. The Fort Des Moines grounds were much larger than she had expected and much more attractive. With its large shade trees and expanses of well-maintained grassy areas and numerous buildings in a pleasant neoclassical style, it almost resembled a college campus or even the business district of a town. Lines of women marched smartly in one of the fields; in another area, small groups were gathered in circles for what looked like some kind of instruction. The distant strains of a military band drifted across the warm air. She glanced to her right where Barb was wiping the perspiration off her brow.

"This place could use a visit from one of our nor'easters," she whispered to Bett, who nodded agreeably.

Sergeant Rains halted at a large, low building and the squad fell in behind her, most of them breathing hard and wiping their faces. Dozens of other young women were in lines or milling about. "This is where you will get your gear and be directed to your barracks," she called over the noise. Bett joined the group clustered tightly around their sergeant, wondering if her expression was as apprehensive as some of the other squad members'. Sergeant Rains looked over the scene around her and nodded thoughtfully, as if seeing it through their eyes. She raised one arm to shoulder height, almost as if safeguarding them from the surrounding chaos and gestured with her other hand, palm up. "Don't be concerned about this process. The people inside have done it thousands of times and they will walk you through each step. We all want you to be the best soldier you can be, and this is just the beginning. I will meet you at your barracks when you are finished." Bett felt herself relax at the clear confidence in Rains's tone, and she exchanged quick smiles with Barb and Jo who were closest to her.

As the new recruits began to press up the stairs and into the building, the sergeant positioned herself near Bett. "A word please, Private." They stepped into a shady spot on the side of the building. "Very impressive magic back there," Rains began, not unkindly.

Bett tilted her head up to meet the officer's eyes, wishing for her sunglasses. "Really, Sergeant, I'm sure you're aware it was not magic at all. It was years of study, hours and hours of recordings, poring over US maps. It was my university degree, after all. And the girls gave me marvelous clues with their explanations of why they joined."

"Hmm." Rains made her little grunting sound again and looked away, across the compound. In the silence Bett felt compelled to go on. "But I would never have even thought of attempting such a thing if it hadn't been for that horrible Sergeant Moore, screaming at little Teresa. What a brute."

"Sergeant Moore was in the first officers' class ever here at Fort Des Moines, back when we were the Women's Army Auxiliary Corps and not eligible for protections or benefit of the regular Army," answered Rains, sounding somewhat defensive as she focused on a stand of trees in the distance. "She has guided hundreds of women through this program, including me." She hesitated. "But she's tired. And I believe she recently got some bad news from home."

"That may be, Sergeant, but being a bully will not make things better for her," Bett replied, determined to make her point.

"This is not what I wanted to speak to you about." Sergeant Rains tried to begin again. She turned her eyes back to Private Smythe. "I know who you are. Details of your enlistment were discussed in the meeting I had at headquarters today."

"Oh," Bett said and shifted her train of thought. She smiled approvingly. "So that's how you knew where I was from."

"It was my understanding that you were to avoid drawing unnecessary attention to yourself," Rains continued, with a slight accusation in her voice. "If this is your idea of how to accomplish that—"

Bett cut her off. "No, of course not. But you didn't hear how awfully Sergeant Moore was talking to everyone."

"I heard."

"And were you not going to do anything about it?" Bett demanded, an accusation of her own.

Rains crossed her arms. "Hasn't anyone told you that you are not supposed to argue with your sergeant?"

Bett duplicated her gesture. "Hasn't anyone told you that changing the subject does not win an argument?"

The two women stared at each other for a few seconds. Bett had the thought that she had never seen eyes as bottomlessly black as Rains's. Finally, she thought that ghost of a smile might have flitted across the sergeant's mouth again.

"Get your gear, Private. And try to keep in mind that is what you now are," she said, turning sharply and striding away.

Bett almost called out a sarcastic, "Thank you for the advice," before remembering that this was a place where she was probably not going to have the last word. At least not with Sergeant Rains.

❖

By the time she got into the building, the crush of bodies had thinned out a bit, and the girls from her squad were being combined with three other newly arrived squads into what would become their platoon. This group was separated into two lines—those whose hairstyle already fit the Army's requirements, and those who would have to have their hair cut. Bett was able to move into the line where she was issued her supplies: two skirts, one olive and one khaki, with a matching hip-length jacket for each, five shirts, or waists, as the WACs called them, two neckties, service and athletic shoes as well as overshoes, cotton and wool hose—no silk was available, as "there's a war on, you know," a purse, gloves, underclothes, an exercise suit, pajamas and a bathrobe, a raincoat, a winter coat, a toothbrush, comb, a hat, and the Pallas Athena insignia of the

Women's Army Corps. They had also been told that certain supplies could be brought from home, so naturally Bett had brought all of those as well: her grooming and personal supplies, along with a sewing kit, pen and pencil and stationery, a bathing suit, a mirror, several selected pieces of her jewelry and, of course, her books. When they reached the barracks and she saw the small wall unit and footlocker in which her possessions were to be stored, Bett wondered if she had the spatial skills to organize everything. She began making some progress, but quite a few items were still piled on her bunk when Jo Archer interrupted her sorting process.

"Better get dressed, Queenie," she said with a grin, modeling her uniform. "You can't be out of that uniform for the next seven weeks, except at bedtime." She held up her plain cotton WAC pajamas and added, "And even then, we're all Army now."

Ten minutes later, Elizabeth Smythe examined herself in the mirror and sighed. *What have I gotten myself into?* Army khaki wasn't exactly the type of fabric she was accustomed to wearing, and although the various measurements that had been taken ensured that the uniform fit her fairly well, it wasn't anything that anyone she knew would consider stylish. And the shoes were even worse. She opened her mouth to complain to the person next to her, but before she made a sound she saw that it was Helen, the girl from Kentucky. Helen was looking at herself in the mirror also, but her expression was one of pride and great satisfaction. *I wonder how long it's been since she's had a new outfit of any kind,* Bett thought, and instead of complaining, she smiled. "You look very nice, Helen."

Helen's smile was just a bit shy as she took a breath. "Uh, Bett, I got some room in my footlocker if you need a place to put some of your things." Bett realized that her packing dilemma must have been obvious to everyone. *I guess most everything in our lives will be common knowledge for the next few weeks.* It also occurred to her that Helen had room to offer because she probably hadn't been able to bring as many items from home.

"Thank you, Helen," she responded gratefully. "And do let me know if you need anything." She gestured at her suitcase. "As you can see, I always seem to overpack, so—"

Bett's offer was interrupted as those who had gotten their new Army haircuts began to trickle in, some making faces and moaning and some jostling for position among the remaining narrow bunks. Among them was Tee, the girl with the stutter. Bett was pleased to note that Helen had saved the little Oklahoman a space on the bunk next to hers. Helen whistled playfully at Tee's new haircut, making Tee blush. The company had pretty much finished unpacking their bags and making their beds when Sergeant Rains entered the barracks.

Bett's bed was closest to the door, and Jo Archer had claimed the bunk below her where she was stretched out, filing her nails. "Hey, Sarge," Jo said companionably.

"When a noncommissioned officer enters," Rains began patiently, "you are to call out *Attention!* so that your squad knows to stand at the foot of their beds and be prepared for instructions."

"Okay," Jo acknowledged pleasantly.

Sergeant Rains waited.

"I mean, yes, Sergeant," Jo tried again.

A small sigh escaped Rains.

"Oh—you mean, like, now?" Jo asked. Rains nodded. "Attention!" Jo tried to stand as she spoke, the top of her head narrowly missing the top bunk rail. That, and perhaps her sudden responsibility, made her so jumpy that only a squeak came out.

Hopping down from the bunk across the aisle, Minnesotan Phyllis Kendrick came to her rescue. "Attention on deck!" she called out loudly. "Officer on board."

Rains paced quietly down the length of the barracks as the girls scrambled into position and held their poses of attention. Returning to Phyllis, she said, "Very good, Private Kendrick, but this is not the Navy. A simple *Attention* will do."

"Yes, Sergeant," Phyllis replied, and was rewarded with a slight nod.

"Ladies, your next activity will be to dress in your exercise clothes and meet me on the parade ground in fifteen minutes." As they started to move, Rains froze them with the sharpness of her single word, "Not"—everyone waited and she continued—"until you are dismissed. And before you do that, your first order of business is to elect your squad leader. This private will be the spokesperson for your group, and the person to whom I will sometimes give orders for your behalf."

"Queenie!" Jo called out, and a murmur of assent swelled in the room.

"Oh no," Bett said, barely daring to sneak a glance at her sergeant whose message of discretion had been clearly delivered only a short time before.

"I'll leave you to your democratic process," Rains remarked, not meeting Smythe's eyes as she left the room. As she stood outside, Rains tried to figure out which was the best solution. She could already tell that Smythe was going to be augmentative and problematic. *Spoiled*, Rains thought, *or willful. Or both. Whatever it is that too much money does to people.* Whatever the case, she would be hard to manage as she was probably accustomed to giving orders, not taking them.

Just then, Jo appeared. "Sergeant Rains, we need to know what other duties the squad leader has," she requested. Rains gathered that the election was not going smoothly. Perhaps Smythe was attempting to remain inconspicuous after all.

"This is the private who will meet with me weekly or as needed," explained Rains, "to discuss the problems and progress of your squad. There is also talk of possibly forming a kind of council, on which she would be your squad's representative."

"Got it," Jo nodded. Rains cleared her throat. "I mean, thank you, Sergeant," Jo amended, and turned to leave.

"Private Archer?" The firmness of Rains's tone held no criticism. Archer turned back immediately. "We haven't gone over this yet, but when your conversation with an officer has ended, you are to salute before withdrawing." As Archer's shoulders slumped a bit at this latest gaffe, the sergeant added reassuringly, "If you wouldn't mind demonstrating with me when I show the rest of your squad, I'll teach you the procedure now." Steadily, Rains taught her the correct form for saluting and they practiced twice. Then she drew herself to attention and announced, "Dismissed, Private."

"Yes, ma'am," Archer said saluting proudly. "Thank you, ma'am."

A good one, that, Rains thought as she watched Archer return to the barracks. *Kindness inside, and willing to be taught. We'll see if she has the ability to teach others. With that and a little more confidence, she could become a good leader.* She had met several recruits from New York, and most of them had a proud kind of boldness that she appreciated. She felt it in Archer as well and thought that the young private would only need a bit of reassurance to make a good way for herself in the WAC.

Sergeant Rains turned her thoughts back to the matter of her new squad's leader. Should the recruits select Smythe, those weekly meetings would give Rains a chance to make sure that Smythe's cover was holding and to try to handle any problems before they got bucked up the line. When Colonel Issacson had given her this assignment, her contemptuous tone for this incoming private had not led the sergeant to expect the very attractive, confident woman whose image now came fully into her mind: a genuine smile and those amazing eyes—a blend of blue and green that Rains didn't think she had ever seen before. Did they show her true spirit? In that moment Rains could hear her mother's voice: *Certain things may catch your eye, but pursue only those that capture your heart.* Then Rains shook her head briskly. This was the Army. They didn't care about spirit. And there was no place for her heart here. Why were her thoughts wandering this way? She began pacing, trying to refocus. She had a feeling that these were going to be the hardest eight weeks of her career.

Inside the barracks, Jo was in full election mode. "Yes, Queenie," Jo insisted. "You can talk better than the rest of us put together." Others chimed in with shouts of agreement.

"No, Jo," Bett objected. "I simply can't do it."

"Why not?"

"Well for one thing, I don't think Sergeant Rains likes me," Bett suggested, groping for a plausible excuse.

"Oh, come on. You don't know that," Jo countered. "She let you play that game of figuring out where we were from. Can you imagine Sergeant Moore letting that go on?"

The room filled with various moans and shudders at the mention of Moore's name. "We sure were lucky to get Sergeant Rains instead," Maria commented and there was agreement all around. After a few seconds she added, almost in a whisper, "But Sergeant Rains is kinda scary too, only in a different way. Not 'cause she's harsh and mean like Sergeant Moore, but she just seems so..." She groped for a word while several of them supplied their own description for the tall, dark-haired woman who would control much of their lives for the next seven weeks—intimidating, forceful, commanding, decisive, strong—but Maria finished for herself, nodding slowly. "Like—like a superhero." There was an almost equal reaction of agreement and laughter to Maria's musings and she blushed and smiled, her hand measuring with descending heights as she added, "What can I say? I have three little brothers who read those crazy comics all the time."

Archer jumped in again. "Well, hey, Queenie has her own superpower. She can see...well, hear where people come from, so she's the right one to meet with our Super Sergeant."

Bett tried to speak over the sounds of approval. "But she told me after you all went in to get your gear that I'd better not try any stunts like that again."

"Oh, really?" questioned Phyllis. "I wondered what she was talking to you about."

"Well that's okay. You won't be doing anything like that anyway," Jo persisted. "You'll just be speaking for us and meeting with her sometimes. And you can do whatever she wants then."

Looking at the faces around her, it seemed obvious to Bett that no one else wanted the responsibility of facing their formidable sergeant on a regular basis. She threw up her hands in defeat and the room cheered.

CHAPTER TWO

On her first Sunday afternoon in camp, Bett spent her free time writing to her friends. Her decision to enlist had been so spontaneous that no one outside of her immediate family knew she had signed up for the WAC. The idea of their friend Bett in the military service was so absurd that none of her friends were likely to believe it without hearing the news directly from her. She couldn't begin to predict the responses she would get by return mail.

As she was finishing her outgoing letters, faint shouting drifted in the windows from the parade grounds. Bett had noticed that there weren't many people in the barracks, but she had been enjoying the relative quiet. Standing to stretch, she decided to walk over to see what was happening after finding her way to the PX where she could drop off her correspondence. On a grassy section of the field, an impromptu baseball game was under way between two groups of officers, and fans of each team were cheering from the reviewing stands. Bett scanned the faces and found Jo Archer sitting in the second row. She squeezed in next to her and asked, "Who's playing?"

Just then Sergeant Rains came up to bat. Like the other women, she was wearing her exercise clothes, but unlike some who were playing bareheaded, Rains still wore her khaki uniform hat. Jo pointed at her and said, "I don't know if these are official teams, but we're rooting for Rains's group. She stood and yelled, "Smack it, Sarge!" The noise level all around increased. "Notice how the outfield has faded back?" Jo pointed out as she sat back down. "Sarge must be a good hitter."

Bett had no idea what Jo was talking about, but she was interested in watching her new drill instructor in such a different environment. After taking a couple of practice swings, Rains did not move as the first pitch came in very low. "Good eye, Sarge," Jo yelled.

"Is there a score?" Bett asked as Rains stepped back into the batter's box.

Jo shook her head. "This is the bottom of the first with two outs. Rains is the cleanup hitter," she added as Rains's bat cracked against the ball. Bett followed the long arc of it with her mouth open. But the ball seemed to be curving away from the field and bounced well away from the left field player who was running to get it. The player who'd been on first trotted back to her base.

"Foul ball," the umpire yelled.

"Does that mean she's out?" Bett asked.

Archer looked at her with disbelief. "Don't you know anything about baseball?"

"No, not much, actually."

Indulgently, Archer began to explain. "Well, a foul ball counts as a strike until the third one. Then it would have to be a swing and a miss or a tip that the catcher gets."

"So she gets another chance?" Bett asked.

"Yeah. That's only one strike and one ball. It sure traveled though, didn't it?" Jo added, admiringly.

On the next pitch, Rains adjusted her swing and connected with another solid hit that went well over the head of the center outfielder and almost into the road. Rains circled the bases quickly, but without much effort. Archer and at least half of the bleachers were on their feet cheering. "Home run!" she yelled to Bett, who stood, too. "And an RBI." After Rains crossed home plate, Bett saw her glance into the stands. Archer was pumping the air with her fists and yelling. Without fully turning in their direction, Rains touched the bill of her hat very briefly and went to sit with her team. One more run was scored and then the inning was over.

When they took the field, Jo pointed out Rains's position and explained to Bett, "Some people think you can't win a baseball game without a good shortstop."

"How do you know so much about this game, Jo?" Bett asked.

Again, Archer appeared astonished as she looked Bett full in the face. "Are you kidding me, Queenie? Haven't you ever heard of the New York Yankees?"

Bett smiled. "Yes, I suppose I have."

"Well, there you go." Archer returned to watching the game while keeping up a running commentary on the players and their skills for Bett's benefit.

Bett had never been a big fan of sports but she did appreciate grace and form, and watching Sergeant Rains move around the infield was more than enough to keep her entertained. She was amazed by the way the sergeant seemed to have absolute control of her body, leaping to catch a ball hit in the air, charging a ground ball and pivoting in midair to make a throw, or sprinting into the outfield for a cutoff. Rains was clearly the leader of her team, and she showed uncanny accuracy at repositioning the outfielders to make an easy play on the ball as each new batter came up.

There were two outs in the top of the second inning when Sergeant Moore came up to bat. Bett suppressed the desire to boo, although she heard some rumbles from her squad mates. Clearly some of Moore's friends or previous squad members were sitting on the other side of the bleachers, as they cheered and yelled encouragement for a hit.

"Those are all veterans," Jo murmured to Bett, glancing admiringly at the group opposite them. "We talked a little as the teams were warming up. They all made it through basic and are working on the base."

Bett looked over at the uniformed women, reflecting on whether anyone would ever point to her and say the same. Thinking of the eight long weeks stretching ahead of her in this place, she asked herself, *Will I be able to do this?* She'd always asserted her independence, fought for it—even against her own family members at times—and now her impulsive decision to join the WAC had led her back to a situation where her life was not her own, where she was subject to the commands and control of others. She looked for Rains on the field, watching as her sergeant signaled to the outfield players, all of whom then moved back a few steps. Sergeant Rains was very much the unknown element in this equation, but Bett felt quite sure that had Moore remained as their sergeant, her chances of making it through basic training would have been greatly reduced. But it was also true that once genuinely committed to something, she'd always followed through, even if she did make a point of putting her own stamp on things as she'd done when they arrived for their squad formation. *So is this really what I want?*

She swept her eyes past the players, across the well-manicured field, to a line of elegant, two-story Colonial structures with wide verandas. "That's Officers' Row." Jo had followed her gaze. "Those houses have upper and lower apartments. Some of the male officers and their families live there and the rest are for WAC officers."

Bett tried to imagine herself as an officer, living in one of those apartments, working on the base. Her ambivalence wasn't due to the unfamiliarity of it all. She'd lived away from home for more than half her life, starting new courses each year, classmates coming and going, and at her all-girls boarding school they'd worn uniforms, too. She sighed pensively. *And what if I don't make it?* Even though her family's wealth gave her more opportunities than most other young women had, her options were still quite limited. Besides, her country was at war. In fact, the whole world was at war. If she did indeed want a part to play, then perhaps this was the place for her.

Jo sensed her mood and patted her shoulder a bit awkwardly. "Don't worry, Queenie. That's gonna be you and me in just a few short weeks."

They both looked back over at the other group, and one sergeant, whose nameplate said Edwards, caught the serious expressions on their faces. Boisterously, she chided, "What's wrong, rookies? Worried you're rooting for the wrong team?"

Unaccustomed to sports banter, Bett looked to Jo. She needn't have worried. Jo had already turned to face the big talker on the other side of the bleachers. "Nah, we're just thinking how boring it's going to be when Sergeant Moore strikes out." Thinking of one last taunt she added, "As usual."

The sergeant leaned toward Jo. "I don't suppose you wanna put your money where your mouth is?"

Her friends laughed, and one commented, "Oh no, Mae. You know these babies won't have anything to bet with, other than some nasty cotton stockings."

Bett tugged on Jo's sleeve. "Go ahead, Jo. I'll cover whatever you think is right," she whispered.

After studying Sergeant Moore for just a few seconds, Jo turned back to their antagonists. "Whatcha got in mind?" she asked coolly.

Edwards's friend hooted. "You got a live one here, Mae. Don't hurt 'em. Just make 'em pay."

The sergeant looked around cautiously, then huddled with her fellow veterans. Several offers and counteroffers were made before the two sides settled on their wager. If Sergeant Moore got on base, the recruits would pay for the veterans' drinks at Sweetie's, a local club in town that was famous for its hospitality toward WACs. Of course, they wouldn't be able to accompany them, since they wouldn't be allowed off the base for another eight weeks. But if Moore stuck out or was thrown out, the veterans would spring for an equal number of drinks at the NCO club on base—and provide escorts so the recruits could get in.

"Good." Bett turned back to Jo after they'd sealed the deal with a handshake. "Feel like doing some drinking tonight?"

Jo grinned. "Now you're talking."

Rains had been speaking to the third baseman while Moore took a few more practice swings. The umpire called, "Batter up!" and Moore stepped in.

"She's a power hitter, Queenie," Jo explained. "Just look at her swing and her stance. But power hitters strike out more often, too, so we've got a good chance here."

Bett didn't particularly want to look at Sergeant Moore, but she did notice that the catcher for Rains's team had a wrap on her right ankle.

After Bett pointed it out to Archer, the New Yorker commented, "Oh yeah, I wondered why she had such a weird stance. She probably won't make any plays at the plate."

After taking two balls, Moore got off a long hit to right field, which dropped in just over the glove of the right fielder. The first baseman went out to be the cutoff and Rains headed to home, waving the injured catcher aside. As Moore came charging around third, Rains got the throw. Bett watched things happen as if in slow motion. Moore continued coming hard and Rains braced for a collision. At the last moment, Moore went down to slide in, but Rains dropped in time to tag her leading foot before it hit the base. They were both engulfed in a ragged screen of dust as the umpire yelled, "Out."

For a moment, the noise from the stands drowned out almost everything else. Sergeant Moore's fans were voicing their objections to the call as Rains's squad and the others cheered loudly. Moore jumped up and began to argue the call with the umpire as Rains started away with the ball in her hand. As the noise from the bleachers was dying down, Moore continued her protest with a gesture at Rains's departing back, yelling something that ended with "that motherless half-breed."

Rains stopped walking. After about five seconds, she turned slowly and started back toward Moore. The stands got very quiet. The umpire stepped back, out of the way. When Rains and Moore were face to face—Rains a good four or five inches taller—Bett could see that the color had drained from Moore's face. Unable to meet Rains's eyes, Moore dropped her head and muttered something that might have included the word *sorry*.

Rains put the ball in her chest, perhaps a tiny bit harder than necessary and repeated, "You were out." One of Moore's teammates came up with her glove and pulled her out into the field. Rains went back toward her team's bench. Bett began to clap and the rest of the spectators joined in.

By the time Rains was up to bat again, the other team had changed pitchers and was trying a lefty. The sergeant approached from the other side of the plate.

"And Sarge is a switch-hitter, too," Archer said in an almost reverent tone. Then she grinned at Bett. "Just what you'd expect from a superhero."

"Isn't she supposed to be on the other side?" Bett asked, confused.

Archer began to explain about batting positions, but Rains hammered the first pitch into another home run.

Rains's team won the game, 14–4.

"Don't run off, ladies," Jo teased Moore's fans as the game ended. "Our throats are dry from all the cheering. We'll be expecting our escort to the NCO club real soon."

Good-natured grumbling sounded from Sergeant Edwards's group as they gathered on their side of the stands, checking purses and pockets for extra change.

Bett was still absorbed in watching Rains as she joined her team to shake hands with the other players. When she got to Sergeant Moore, Bett could tell that Moore was still conscious of her outburst, but Rains simply nodded a bit and shook her hand like everyone else. *Apparently she doesn't hold a grudge. That's good to know,* Bett thought, wondering if they were allowed to speak to the players now. She gestured to Jo. "I'd like to congratulate the sergeant on her play."

"Oh yeah. Good idea. I'll go with you," Jo said.

Rains was standing near home base, helping to collect the equipment, but she turned as they approached, several bats tucked in the crook of her left elbow. "Great game, Sarge," Jo extended her hand for a congratulatory shake. "You bat like DiMaggio and field like Rizzuto."

Their sergeant seemed relaxed and was as close to smiling as Bett had yet seen. "Thank you, Private Archer, but I think you must be missing your Yankees a lot to make those comparisons." They shook hands. Rains's face was a bit darker with exertion, her skin glistened with sweat, and her exercise clothes were quite dirty. Bett had never really been attracted to the athletic type, but something about having watched Rains's body all day made her interested in knowing more. To her surprise, Rains turned to her, making eye contact. "Did you enjoy the game, Private Smythe?" There was something adorably cocky in her tone.

She knows how good she is, Bett thought, *and she's proud of it.* Bett knew something about these sporting types. At Kent and at Oxford they all hung together, acting superior, but it was a different story when their prowess on the grounds or the court didn't always translate to the classroom. And those field hockey players were the worst, Bett recalled, usually confident that their physical skills on the field would translate into something desirable off it. And she did seem to recall that one... Somewhat self-conscious as she dismissed the memory, Bett leaned slightly toward Rains, whose dark eyes drew her quickly back to the present. "I'm afraid I had to ask Jo for a lot of explanation about what was going on, but even I could tell you were the best player out there."

Rains's color heightened, and Bett detected some surprise in her response. "That's very kind of you, Private."

Bett thought she'd see how Sergeant Rains responded to more of a verbal challenge. "But then, you didn't need me to tell you that, I'm sure. Your ability so clearly surpassed some of the other girls' that it made the game somewhat unfair, really. I mean, look at the score."

"We were born to succeed, not to fail," Rains quoted calmly. "If you don't bring your best to whatever you do, there is little point in doing it. A contest such as this one appears to pit one group's effort against another's and for some, that's all it does. But as I see it, the true challenge is to improve oneself at each attempt. To strive for a personal goal, not merely to be superior to one's opponent. Can I hit farther the next time? Can I throw more accurately?" Rains brushed her arm across her face, clearing away a glint of perspiration before leaning down to pick up another bat. "By your argument, should I assume that you sometimes deliberately missed questions on your school exams, just so your level of intellect wouldn't be unfair to the other students?"

Bett was taken aback, quickly realizing that she had completely underestimated Rains's intelligence and embarrassed that she had taken such a weak position. She shifted her stance slightly and tried again. "Of course, I've always felt that sports are overly glorified. There's really not much contribution to society in sweating and heaving a ball around, wouldn't you agree?"

Archer's mouth dropped open and she leaned back, apparently trying to distance herself from her squad leader. Rains set the bats down and straightened, ticking off points on her fingers as she took up the argument. "At this level of play, Private Smythe, I think participation in certain games can teach us a great deal about sportsmanship and teamwork, as well as about ourselves. The hand-eye coordination required in batting and fielding is good preparation for some of our specialized jobs. Many of our women are unfamiliar with the intensity of competition and they need to learn how to perform successfully under such pressure, as well as learning how to work well with others, which is also an important facet of sport." The sergeant moved her hands apart and stood with her palms out, softening her expression. "I was taught to view someone more skilled than myself as a role model, not as a competitor. Wouldn't you agree that a community such as this functions better when the achievement of one becomes the possession of all?"

Rains paused for her reply, but Bett's thoughts were too unsettled for a quick comeback. The idea that a community would benefit more from accomplishment by many instead of by the benevolent domination and informed control of a few was the exact opposite of what her father had preached at her for her entire life. Yet in this environment, it seemed to make sense. Jo was nodding in agreement.

Seeing that Bett had no ready response, Sergeant Rains added, "Plus, for some of the officers, the physical release of sweating and heaving a ball around helps us rechannel energies that otherwise might be misdirected at our more difficult recruits." Her gaze sharpened on Bett, and Archer let out a short laugh.

"Okay, Queenie. I think that's your third strike." She put her arm around Bett's shoulder as if to lead her away. "Let's go celebrate"—she gave Bett a little shake—"or drown our sorrows."

Seeing that Rains was again retrieving the equipment, Bett stepped away from Archer and deliberately slid her arm along

Rains's, reaching for the bats. "May I help you carry these?" she asked sweetly. The contact of their skin seemed to shock Rains and she took a step back as the bats spilled out of her arms. "Oops," Bett said. *Should I consider that a foul ball or a home run?* She wondered if Rains had detected the same electricity that she had in their touch.

"No, Private," the sergeant's voice was almost harsh. "But thank you anyway."

Archer jumped in, helping Rains pick up the bats. "Hey, Sarge, some of us are going over to the NCO club for a little liquid refreshment. Wanna join us?"

Rains did not look at Bett. "Thank you, Archer, but no. I'm not allowed to fraternize with enlisted personnel under my command and I..." Her voice trailed off for a few seconds. "I need to get cleaned up."

Bett thought she detected something else in that hesitation but decided not to press it. "Well, thank you for providing the afternoon's entertainment, Sergeant Rains."

Rains made a funny little bow. "Glad to be of service, Private Smythe." She turned back to Archer with a caution in her tone. "Watch your time. You must be back in the barracks before lights out. And"—she glanced at the veterans who were waiting—"leave no one behind, Archer."

Archer straightened to attention. "You can count on me, Sarge."

Rains mirrored her position as best she could without dropping the bats again. "I *am* counting on you, Private."

Sergeant Edwards led the way over to the NCO club. There was no problem finding a table, and Sergeant Riley, another member of Edwards's group, explained why. Sweetie's, the bar in town, was *the* place to go. "Some of the local establishments aren't particularly welcoming," a corporal named Davis told them. Another veteran, Sergeant Patterson, added how she'd been deliberately ignored by the saleswomen in a downtown department. The antagonism apparently stemmed from the locals' fear that the WACs were going to take their jobs, their men, and generally take over their town. Some places, the other veterans admitted, were okay. But Sweetie's was the preferred hangout, where the owner always made them feel at home, and the food and drinks were as good as it got. Sergeant Riley went on at great length about how the walls were covered with pictures from all over the world where soldiers had renamed their commissary Sweetie's or had constructed signposts with mileages to various hometowns, with Sweetie's included.

Bett understood. Sweetie's was a reference point, a touchstone for all those who came through Fort Des Moines, and it was probably one of those shared experiences to which Sergeant Rains had referred. Being there was common ground that gave them all a way to relate to each other a little better.

After they were served, the baseball game, and by extension Rains, was the next topic of conversation. Once the complaining about Sergeant Moore's being called out at the plate had subsided, Corporal Davis informed the group that Sergeant Rains had never played baseball before she signed up with the Army.

"No way," Jo said authoritatively. "No one could have her instincts for the game unless they'd been coached for years."

"It's true," Riley joined in. "Sergeant Moore told us she taught her everything. Said Rains didn't even know which end of the bat to hold or which hand to put the glove on at first."

"Sergeant Moore strikes me as the type who would claim credit for teaching the sky to be blue," Bett observed, bringing equal parts laughter and grumbling from the assortment of WACs at the table.

"Well, according to Moore, Rains could hardly write her own name when she upped," another of the veteran WACs chimed in, turning to one of her squad mates. "Remember that girl—I think her name was Cindy—who got transferred from Rains's squad to ours because she was so obsessed with Rains? The base shrink said it was unhealthy." A few of the girls at the table laughed uncomfortably at this. The speaker didn't seem to notice and went on. "Sergeant Moore spent a full week telling her every bad thing about Rains she could think of. None of it helped, though. One night Rains came back to her quarters and found Cindy in her bed. Moore said Rains came out of that room as if it was on fire. In the end they discharged Cindy with other-than-honorable."

A quiet moment of drinking followed this story. That kind of discharge was every WAC's nightmare. Besides the indignity of having to explain why you were suddenly out of the service, a blue ticket often meant difficulty in finding other work after being considered undesirable by the Army. Then Bett broke the silence by asking what she had really wanted to know. "So is Sergeant Rains married or dating or anything?"

Everyone looked at her for a second. Then one of the veterans said, "She's MTTS."

Bett and Jo looked at each other. They were already learning a lot of acronyms but hadn't heard that one. Finally they both shook their heads and all the veterans laughed. "Married to the service!" They toasted each other.

Bett and Jo joined in the laughter, and Sergeant Patterson went to get the next round. Soon they were all the best of friends, swapping life stories and tall tales about basic training. Bett had to explain again about her accent. Jo made her guess where their new friends were from and Bett got four out of six right, causing Patterson to assure her that with a skill like that she could significantly supplement her pay once she could go off base to Sweetie's or could make appearances at the NCO club if she got promoted.

After the fourth round of drinks, Bett began to notice that one of the veterans was making prolonged eye contact with her more frequently. She noted that the woman was wearing a pinkie ring on her right hand. In Bett's experience in the scene, that meant someone who was looking. Looking for another woman. Bett felt fairly sure that the veteran, whose name tag said PFC Covington, was only window-shopping. Even though Bett also wore a pinkie ring, she was wearing several other rings as well, which seemed to confuse the issue for most women. Bett's appearance was such that she was always assumed to be heterosexual, even by those who might know that not all women were. It wasn't a deliberate cover-up on her part; she dressed the way she'd been brought up to dress since that was how she felt most comfortable. In her experiences among lesbians in London and in Los Angeles, she had noticed that there was much more role-playing among the working-class types. The trend among those women was to look extremely masculine or extremely girly—butch or femme. The butches acted tough and stoic; the femmes were flirtatious and solicitous. Having slept with both types, Bett knew that once the lights were out these roles didn't necessarily hold true at all.

Bett was what those girls sometimes called *kiki*. They seemed to find it confusing or even offensive that girls like Bett didn't identify as either butch or femme. Since she was often shorter than her partner, Bett was often led around the dance floor, but was more than willing to ask a woman to dance, in which case she could lead quite well. And in bed? Well, she didn't believe in roles there either, although if she was with a woman who did, Bett was fine to oblige her companion for the night.

By the time they left the NCO club, Bett hadn't yet had enough to drink to make Private First Class Covington her type. She was stocky and somewhat masculine looking, although she had a nice smile. As they began walking back to the barracks, Covington positioned herself close enough to Bett that she reached out to steady Bett when she stumbled over a curb. Yes, those hands definitely lingered just a bit longer than necessary, Bett acknowledged to herself. *Hope springs eternal, I suppose.* This was a sport she knew very well. All it would take would be some meaningful eye contact in return, along with a few smiles and carefully worded innuendoes on her part. As a veteran, Covington would certainly know a place to go. She gave it a moment's thought and then decided she really wasn't interested just now.

Leaving nothing to chance, in the event that Archer had trouble getting everyone back, Sergeant Rains waited in the guardhouse, having showered and changed, when the group came giggling along the sidewalk that ran past the gate. She ended her conversation with the MP on duty and trailed them unseen as they made their way to the barracks. The veterans were teaching Charlotte and Phyllis one of the WAC songs, singing its newly rewritten and amusing lyrics to the tune of "The Marine's Hymn."

She could hear Smythe laughing at the ending and she appeared to be the slightest bit unsteady. PFC Covington, who worked in the mail room, seemed to be unnecessarily close by, but she was not singled out in the good-byes that were exchanged when the two groups made their way to their separate barracks, so Rains dropped back from the group.

Charlotte and Phyllis were also a bit wobbly as the squad stood at the foot of their beds for Rains's inspection, but she moved through quickly before announcing, "Lights out," and leaving without any other comment.

❖

For a time after they were all in bed, Bett's mind was still working, proof that she really hadn't had that much to drink. The veterans had turned out to be quite pleasant, almost gracious, once they'd accepted their loss. After replaying some of the more interesting conversation from the NCO club, Bett decided she was glad that she hadn't tried to make any further arrangements with Covington. There was no reason to start that up again. Not yet, anyway. She ran over her losing argument with Rains, almost ready to laugh at herself for being so soundly overcome. She was intrigued by the sergeant's comments about competition and success, so opposite of her own upbringing. But she kept coming back to how Rains had reacted to her touch. *As if it was on fire*, the veteran WAC had said of the other incident. Maybe officers were trained to be like that.

Not exactly homesick but not completely comfortable in her surroundings either, Bett drifted through thoughts of England, of home, of her friends and what they would be doing right now. She was almost asleep when she felt a brush of air as the barracks door opened. Her anxiety level jumped. Who could it be, coming in at this late hour? Her father's relentless warnings about threats to her safety began playing in her mind like a broken record until they stilled as Sergeant Rains's form moved soundlessly past. Relief flooding through her, Bett pretended to be asleep as her sergeant walked through the barracks. *Will she check up on us so late like this every night?*

She peeked ever so slightly as Rains slowly made her way to the far end of the barracks, retrieving Tee's ragged teddy bear from the floor and returning it to her arms and taking a book out of Barb's sleeping hands and setting it on the floor nearby. *She's not really so tough.* Bett smiled to herself, quickly closing her eyes and holding very still as Rains began moving back toward the door. The sergeant paused at her bunk and said softly, "You had better get some sleep, Private Smythe. I'll be running you tomorrow." Bett was so stunned that she didn't know what to do, so she just lay there with her eyes shut. Maybe Rains did have superpowers. She thought she heard her sergeant breathing out a chuckle as she went through the door.

CHAPTER THREE

True to her word, Sergeant Rains started her squad out with a morning trot after a stretching routine, taking them on a course which helped familiarize them with certain locations on the base. Along the same road where the quartermasters were located, she ran them past the theater, a chapel, tennis courts, various administrative offices, classrooms, and the PX which, in addition to a well-stocked store for toiletries and cosmetics and magazines, also housed a beauty salon, soda fountain and grill, and a dry cleaners. It was also the place to send and receive mail, so there was always a crowd there. This was only a small portion of the base, but Bett suspected that Rains had chosen to point out the places that would be most visited by the new recruits. While they recovered from their exercise, sitting on the bleachers of the reviewing stand, the sergeant went over various aspects of military courtesy, including where, when, and how to salute an officer. She called on a well-prepared Private Archer to help demonstrate, which obviously pleased the New Yorker, and appeared satisfied when most of the girls already demonstrated the correct form. The lecture continued with information such as where and when smoking was permitted and how to get special leave to go beyond the fifty-mile radius of the fort once off-base privileges were approved. They would have one of these lectures on the Army way everyday for the first few weeks. Although some of the girls listened with rapt attention, Bett just managed to resist rolling her eyes and yawning with boredom.

I just can't wait until we go over the Army way of tying your shoes and brushing your teeth, she thought irritably.

Then it was time for their first class, which was on food preparation. Bett was probably only expressing the views of some other participants in the class when she blurted out, "Aren't we supposed to be getting women out of the kitchen?"

Helen, who was apparently ready to come out of her shell, chimed in, "Damn right. I didn't join the Army to cook. I could do that at home."

A rebellious mood was created and the presentation was not particularly successful. At lunch, Bett noted the lieutenant in charge speaking to Rains while gesturing in the direction of her squad's table.

At the exercise session before the next class, Rains walked among them as they were stretching. "Being in the Army is not an exercise in personal privilege. It is about learning to contribute your individual skills toward the advancement of the group." She stopped near Bett and continued. "Just because you don't find a particular class to your liking, you must allow for the fact that someone else in your squad may have been waiting for just that opportunity. We are here to build each other up and encourage every member of our family, not to let our own preferences negatively influence our sisters' interests."

At this Bett had a flash of regret, remembering Barb talking about how much she liked to cook.

Unfortunately, the afternoon class was on secretarial skills. Bett tried not to let the presentation of traditional roles bother her, but when the lieutenant presenting the material referred to the boss as *he* for the tenth time, Bett raised her hand. "When can we expect the boss to become a *she*?" The class roared with laughter and applause.

This time it was a private conversation with Sergeant Rains held in the hall after the rest of the squad had been dismissed. "I'm sorry, but at university we were expected to challenge pre-existing notions like that," Bett tried to explain.

"In case you haven't noticed, Private Smythe, you are no longer at Oxford," Rains said in what Bett had come to think of as her patient teaching voice. "And you must admit that the odds are considerable that most of these women will be working for a male boss at some point in their lives."

"Of course, Sergeant," Bett said, feigning agreement, "especially if we don't take advantage of this historic opportunity to try to change that."

"Do you intend for your stay in the Army to be a personal crusade for improbable causes or are you here to do something for your country?" Rains countered. Not waiting for Bett to reply she went on, "Because I must warn you, Private, if you continue on this path of disruption in your classes there will be consequences that you will not enjoy."

"Are you threatening me with some kind of retaliation simply for asking questions or giving my opinion?" Bett was incensed.

"I'm only trying to make you aware that in the Army there are measures which are designed to help mold recruits into part of a whole. On your next outburst, you will find yourself subjected to those measures." Sergeant Rains paused and rubbed her hand across her forehead, under her bangs. Adjusting her hat slightly, she continued, "I know you are an intelligent person, Private Smythe. You can understand that at some point I will have no choice. You must find the self-discipline to hold your tongue. Especially to these superior officers."

"Superior?" Bett muttered, loud enough for Rains to hear.

The sergeant sighed. "Dismissed."

Bett did manage to remain quiet during the next morning's munitions class, which was not a topic of particular interest to her but was well-presented by a dark-haired, thick-waisted lieutenant with an interesting accent. *Cajun?* Bett wondered. It seemed that the lieutenant's eyes came back to her frequently. At lunch, Bett noticed the same lieutenant talking to Rains but felt it couldn't have anything to do with her behavior. *Sergeant Rains does look displeased somehow,* Bett thought, but nothing came of it.

The afternoon class was about the Quartermaster Corps. As the major in charge droned on about facilities and labor, shop systems, excessive stockages, packing materials, and inventory control, Bett found it so boring that she fell asleep. She might have gotten away with it, except that she had a vivid dream in which Sergeant Rains was trying to wake her. She jerked herself upright, saying, "Oh, shite," loudly enough that everyone in the room heard, including the base commander, who was observing the squad. Colonel Janet Issacson was a no-nonsense woman with streaks of gray invading her wavy brown hair. Once the class was over, Bett was ordered to wait in an empty classroom next door, where she could hear Issacson questioning Rains on her disciplinary tactics to date. They then discussed her punishment.

"KP for a month and ten extra laps every day for a week." Colonel Issacson's somewhat muffled order didn't hide the brusqueness in her tone. "You said yourself that she's been warned. Maybe we can get rid of her after all."

Bett bristled at the words until she heard Rains's answer.

"Yes, ma'am," Sergeant Rains replied, her voice sounding more pensive. "In most cases I would agree with you. But I believe Private Smythe could become a good soldier if she wanted to. I'm not sure that KP for a month and extra laps for a week will make her want to."

There was a pause and then an almost-sad sigh. "Well, something is going to have to be done, Sergeant. Our enrollment is still down after that ridiculous slander campaign last year. This is bad for the morale of her whole platoon and her instructors, something we certainly can't afford."

"KP and laps for a week, but I'd like to assign her to do some additional tutoring with some of the squad members who are struggling," Rains suggested. "I think that would be a more productive use of her abilities."

Issacson cleared her throat, sounding as if she was ready to be done with the matter. "Very well, Sergeant. See to it and make it stick. If she slacks this, she's out. Sergeant Webber will take your people for the afternoon exercise."

"Yes, ma'am."

Well, at least she stood up for me...somewhat. Bett expected her sergeant to come through the door right away, but she didn't.

Time stretched out. Half an hour passed, then forty-five minutes. Bett knew better than to leave the room without permission, but she needed to go to the bathroom. Finally, just when she was about to give in to her bladder, Sergeant Rains appeared in the doorway.

Bett opened her mouth to ask, *Where the bloody hell have you been?* but the sergeant spoke first. "This is your first chance to practice the self-discipline that I spoke of, Private, unless you'd like me to come back later." Bett closed her mouth and crossed her legs. Rains waited a beat and then nodded. "Good."

After a stop at the restroom, they went to the parade grounds. Rains stretched out on the bleachers and watched the sky as her recruit ran. By the last lap, Bett's pace had slowed considerably.

The sergeant was standing as Bett panted to a stop. "You're not injured, are you, Private?"

"No, but I need to eat."

Sergeant Rains crossed her arms and raised her eyebrows. "Kindly address me as your officer, Private Smythe."

Bett breathed an exaggerated sigh. "No, Sergeant Rains, I am not injured. But since you asked, I am hungry."

"I think that you will miss dinner tonight, Private. But I will bring you something while you are doing your KP."

They began walking toward the mess hall. "How long is this KP going to take?" Bett asked.

Rains didn't answer.

Bett rolled her eyes and emphasized the name at the end of her question. "How long is this KP going to take, Sergeant Rains?"

"That depends on how fast you are at peeling potatoes, Private Smythe," Rains replied evenly.

They went in the side door of the mess hall, into a small area in the back of the kitchen. There were two buckets, a stool, and mounds of potatoes everywhere.

"You must be joking!" Bett sputtered. "There is no way I am peeling this many potatoes." Rains waited silently. "I'm serious, Sergeant Rains. This is too much, really." Bett was shaking her head.

"You may think so, Private, but you've been given an order. This is your evening duty."

"Well, thank you very much, but no thank you." Bett turned and started back out the door.

"Halt!" Rains's voice was knife's edge sharp. The tone made Bett stop immediately. Two MPs appeared in the doorway. "Escort Private Smythe to the stockade," Rains ordered.

The MPs came alongside Bett and maneuvered her out the door. Rains accompanied them across the grounds and up the steps of a small, squat building. They climbed five steps and went through the door into a hallway, which opened into an anteroom. Another MP, who was sitting at a small desk, rose as they entered. Beyond him, four very small jail cells—two on each side of the hallway— were visible. All were empty. Bett had been moving automatically, but she stopped abruptly when she saw the cells. The MPs stopped behind her, but Bett was trying to back up.

Rains spoke from behind the MPs. "Private Smythe, you disobeyed an order and you were deserting your duty. The punishment for that is a night in the stockade."

"Oh no, no, I can't," Bett said in a haunted tone of panic. As one of the MPs held her arms, the other took a set of keys from the MP at the desk and opened one of the doors. Bett began to struggle fiercely. There was pure hysteria in her voice. "No! No! No!" She turned enough to see Rains standing there. Pleading now, she cried, "Sergeant Rains, I can't stay in there. I can't. Oh my God! Oh God, no." She was beginning to hyperventilate. "Please, no. I can't. Oh God, please."

Sergeant Rains looked at Bett closely and saw her eyes rolling wildly, almost as though she were a spooked horse. *She is definitely not faking,* Rains realized. "Let her go," she ordered and Bett stumbled away from the open cell. Rains caught her arms carefully and the top of Bett's head butted against Rains's chest. Bett's eyes were closed and her breathing was still very fast and ragged. She was making whimpering sounds of fear. "You are claustrophobic?" Rains asked. In her NCO training, she had learned of various psychological ailments like this, most of which would disqualify someone from the service. Bett managed a slight unsteady nod.

Rains dismissed the MPs and walked Bett back outside into the fresh evening air. She was shaking badly and Rains was worried that her rapid breathing might cause her to faint. On the steps, she made Bett bend over and kept her head down for a count of five. Then Rains had her sit on the end of one of the low cement sidings along the steps, so that Bett's legs dangled off the front edge. "I'm going to loosen your collar, Private," she said, working down Bett's tie and undoing the top two buttons. Smythe was still gasping for air, her chest heaving. Rains knelt behind her and put her right arm around Smythe, resting her fingers on the breastbone, just below the opening of her throat. "Slow," she said softly. "Slow your breathing." Still ragged, but a bit slower, she judged. "Now try just one deep breath—breathe in...slowly...fully." Rains breathed with her. It took Bett two tries, but she finally matched Rains's respiration rate. "Easy...good. Now out slowly. Again. Good."

Less than fifteen seconds later, Bett's breathing was coming under control. Rains removed her fingers from Smythe's front, laying them briefly on her temple. Her pulse and temperature seemed to be returning to normal as well. Rains started to get up but felt Smythe begin to shudder again. This time it felt more like normal crying. Rains spoke gently, close to her ear, her hands very lightly on Smythe's shoulders. "Sh. It's all right. You won't have to stay in there. Come. We'll go back over to the mess hall."

Bett took in another shaky breath before giving a slight nod. Rains helped her up. Wiping her eyes as they walked slowly, Smythe was still shivering occasionally, even though the night was warm. Rains thought it was probably the last of the panic leaving her body, but she wanted to make sure there was no chance of shock. Unbuttoning her jacket, she slipped it onto Bett's shoulders. "There is nothing in your file about claustrophobia, Private."

Looking gratefully at Rains, Bett pulled the jacket close around her. "Thank you, Sergeant." She ran her hands over her face and her voice was small. "I lied. I didn't want anything to interfere with my enlistment going through. Are you going to run me off now?"

"No, not just yet. But is there anything else you need to tell me about?"

Bett sighed and stretched her neck.

Good, Rains thought. *She's moving more normally.*

Looking down at her hands, Bett had a little shyness in her voice. "Yes. I've never peeled a potato in my life."

Sergeant Rains looked away so quickly that Bett wondered if she was trying to cover her reaction. When she looked back at Bett, her face was serious as usual, though as they passed under a light, Bett thought she might have seen a little amusement in Rains's eyes. "Well, we are going to remedy that inexcusable gap in your education tonight, Private."

Rains settled Bett into the small potato-filled room with a plate of cold chicken, some fruit, and a roll along with a small glass of milk that she rustled from somewhere in the kitchen. While Bett ate, the sergeant carried in another stool, peeler, and two more barrels. She took her jacket back from Bett and hung it on a nail that was sticking out slightly from a window frame. Gesturing to it, she added, "The Private Rains Commemorative Coat Rack."

Bett giggled, but Rains kept her face neutral as Bett teased, "You can't mean that the fabulous Sergeant Rains was once a lowly potato-peeling private."

"Private Smythe, if you started now and really worked at it, I still don't think you could ever match the number of potatoes I've peeled in this very room. Now, this is how it's done..." She rolled up her sleeves and began the demonstration.

Bett had not noticed the size of Rains's hands before, but it was nothing for her to palm even the largest of the potatoes. The sergeant deftly swiped the peeler around and after a few quick strokes she tossed the potato into one of the barrels. "I think we'd better stick with the basic peeling technique for now. If you were more skilled, I'd recommend the difficult and technically advanced peeling, where you'll be able to trash the peel without letting it drop. This can save a good twenty-five minutes off your total time." She shook the peels from her hand into the other barrel. "Try it."

"I had no idea that potato-peeling could be such an art form," Bett mused, picking one up uncertainly.

"Henry David Thoreau said that the highest condition of art is artlessness," Rains replied. "I'm sure he must have peeled quite a few potatoes."

Bett laughed again but in her mind she was moving into a new level of appreciation for Sergeant Rains. *Not only is she smarter than I expected, she can be rather amusing and...unexpectedly kind. She could have left me screaming in that dungeon. I'm sure Sergeant Moore would have.* She watched Rains's hands work another potato and thought of how the touch of Rains's fingers had calmed her panic. Or was it that voice? *Low and almost lilting in its cadence sometimes. Where is she from?*

Rains's voice broke into her musing. "Come now, Private. I've done five potatoes and you haven't finished that one. Take off your jewelry and get busy. I'm not going to play Huckleberry Finn to your Tom Sawyer." She sounded adamant, but not angry.

"Yes, ma'am." Bett smiled to herself as she put her watch and rings into her pocket. She tried to work faster, but her mind kept interfering. What had that other WAC said? That Sergeant Rains couldn't even write her name when she joined up? Well, she was obviously able to read, since there had been two literary references in her last two sentences. Wearing just the shirt from under her WAC jacket, Rains looked thinner, although the muscles in her forearms flexed nicely as she worked. Just then Bett noticed that Rains was switching hands about every third potato and operating the peeler just as efficiently with her left hand. She was about to ask the sergeant if she was truly ambidextrous when Colonel Issacson came through the door. Rains dropped the potato and peeler and quickly stood at attention, saluting. Bett joined her a second later, but not before she detected an embarrassed grimace on Rains's face.

The colonel's perceptive brown eyes surveyed the scene: Sergeant Rains with her jacket off and sleeves rolled, obviously helping with Private Smythe's KP duties, Smythe's empty plate from the mess hall. "I understand there was a problem at the stockade?"

"Yes, Colonel. Apparently some information in Private Smythe's file was...incomplete," Sergeant Rains responded, sounding very formal.

Issacson's gaze lingered on Bett for a moment. Keeping her eyes fixed on the wall, Bett tried not to squirm. "I see. But things are resolved now?"

"Yes, ma'am," Rains stated firmly.

Bett wondered if she should say something and then decided that it would be better not to. She gave just the slightest nod of affirmation.

Colonel Issacson looked back at Rains. "Very well, Sergeant. Carry on."

Rains saluted again. Bett copied her. After Issacson left, Rains let out a breath as she turned and picked up her jacket.

"Have I gotten you into trouble, Sergeant?" Bett asked, genuinely worried.

"I shouldn't be here helping," Rains said, almost to herself, rolling down her sleeves briskly. "I should have reported in as soon as we left the stockade." She glanced briefly at Bett. "I'll be back to check on you later, Private."

Grabbing her jacket, she was gone before Bett could say another word. Bett resumed peeling, despite feeling somewhat forsaken. She thought about how Sergeant Rains had defended her to Issacson earlier and now had covered for her lie to the admissions board. *Of course I could become a good soldier if I wanted to,* she thought, somewhat crossly, but then checked herself. Perhaps she owed Rains's Army some benefit of the doubt. It was certainly a better option than going back to her family with her tail between her legs, admitting that she couldn't get through eight weeks of Army basic training.

❖

It was well after midnight when the sergeant came back. Bett had fallen asleep leaning against the wall with a potato in her hand. She had finished about three-fourths of the job. By the time Bett awoke, Rains had almost completed the chore. When she heard Bett yawn and stretch she said, "Sleeping on your post is a serious infraction, Private. You'll have another week of this if it happens again. In the future, you finish your duty assignment first and then you rest. You are dismissed."

Bett had made up her mind to try and be better about Army protocol. She cleared her throat and replied, "Understood, Sergeant. But aren't I supposed to complete this task myself?"

"Ordinarily yes, Private. But your emotional evening has taken its toll, I'm sure. For tonight only, I will finish your work. I don't want you thinking that you have an excuse for sleeping in class tomorrow. Dismissed."

Bett knew she shouldn't argue but she didn't want to leave things on a bad note. She nodded, but then bent and rested her hand carefully on Rains's forearm. It was lean and hard with muscle. She resisted the sudden urge to run her hand along the length of it. "I still want to say thank you. I appreciate the way you handled...well, everything."

Whether Rains turned to the touch or to the sound of her voice nearby, Bett wasn't sure. But for a moment their faces were close, and Rains's dark eyes searched hers with an unexpected intensity. Unable to venture even a guess as to what she was thinking, Bett wondered if Sergeant Rains always had her guard up, if there was a reason why she always seemed to maintain such distance. Then for one second, she thought she saw a change, a gentling of Rains's expression. Almost immediately, it was gone. Rains turned back to the potato in her hand and said, "Good night, Private."

Everything was quiet when Bett got to the barracks. She got ready for bed as carefully as possible, so as not to disturb her squad mates. Almost without meaning to, she touched the place below her throat where Rains's fingers had been before she fell asleep.

❖

As she finished the last potatoes and swept the little room, Rains went over the roller coaster of events that the night had produced. She had anticipated that Smythe would be difficult about her KP assignment and had the MPs standing by for just that reason. She had been prepared to let a night in the stockade make the significance of Army orders a little more imperative to a spoiled rich girl. But when the severity of Smythe's claustrophobia became evident, Rains had been fine with changing that plan. It was not in her character to injure someone without good cause, and the private's initial failure to peel potatoes didn't warrant serious psychological damage. Once

Smythe had recovered sufficiently to admit that she had lied about her claustrophobia, the way she had challenged her situation with, *Are you going to run me off now?* told Rains that she really wanted to stay in the Army.

Sergeant Rains's experiences with difficult recruits in the past had taught her that these types often said the very opposite of what they wanted. Those who would yell at her, *Why don't you just send me home, then?* really meant, *Please don't sent me home. This place is very different for me and I just need a little more time.* By her own manner even more than with her words, Sergeant Rains always managed to convey the same answer: *We want you here. There is time for you to learn. But you must show respect if you wish to be respected.* Then the absurdity in the way Little Miss Rich Girl had timidly acknowledged that she had never peeled potatoes had made Rains want to laugh. It had been quite some time since she'd had that reaction. Apparently Smythe had what some of the other sergeants called a quick trigger. She would lash out suddenly when upset, but she was quite manageable once that had passed. After the simple acts of getting Smythe some dinner and teaching her the most efficient way to peel a potato had created a familiar, almost friendly relationship between them, Rains had found herself relaxing, confident that she was getting Smythe on the right track. It was most unlike her not to think about reporting in, though, especially considering the critical nature of Smythe's presence here. Her report for Colonel Issacson tomorrow had better be thorough, but she felt that it could be mostly positive.

As she walked slowly toward her room, Rains considered that last moment when Smythe had moved to touch her arm. Instead of the crackling heat of their last contact, this was gentle, almost tender, and surprisingly…nice. And as Smythe bent to speak, her face was so close that Rains had let herself look, really look, into those blue-green eyes. There was almost always a time when Sergeant Rains took the measure of each of her recruits—where she would sense the proportion of their willingness or their cunning, whether there was fortitude or intelligence or deception or fear within them. These moments would come in their own unforced time and Rains knew how to wait. She'd already had that opportunity with Helen Tucker during their initial meeting. In those seconds of eye contact, Rains had seen Tucker's anger waiting just below the surface, ready to loose itself on a target. Beyond that, though, was pain. For the recent loss of her father or something more, Rains wasn't quite sure, but she understood both of those emotions all too well and had readied herself to absorb either. But Tucker had chosen to capitulate—that time—to what was being asked of her in this new environment. Rains was glad and felt hopeful that Private Tucker would find her place here, especially if she could find an outlet for those things that troubled her. She'd had a similar moment of assessment with Archer as well, and had been pleased by it.

In Smythe's eyes she had seen surprising depth of character, both a goodness of heart and an unexpected yearning, almost sadness over something lost or absent, which Rains would not have expected from the daughter of the forty-second richest man in America. And as Smythe had met her eyes willingly, had searched her in return, a warmth had kindled between them for a few seconds. Rains believed she knew why that had happened. Because while helping Smythe recover on the steps outside the stockade, in trying to model breathing more slowly for the shaky private, Rains had fully breathed in a scent—the mix of Smythe's skin, tinged with her soap, shampoo, and what must be a hint of some exotic perfume. The chemical blend that made Bett's own particular aroma was now lodged in her memory. Even Rains's jacket, after the short time that Bett had worn it, had enough traces of it to call her to mind. *Enough of that,* Rains ordered herself, *so now you know her.* The rest of her thoughts matched the timing of her footsteps as she mounted the stairs to her room. *Clear your head. Cool down. Tighten up.*

Chapter Four

That morning everyone in the barracks wanted to ask about Bett's KP. Bett only told them about the laps and the potato peeling. She didn't mention the incident at the stockade.

"Was Sergeant Rains really mean?" asked Maria.

"Well, not too much," Bett admitted. "She was tough on me about acting up in the classes and she's right, really. She made sure I had dinner, even though it was late, but then she left me with enough potatoes to sink a battleship."

"Do you think she's still mad at you?" Phyllis wondered.

"I'm not sure," Bett began slowly. "She's so difficult to read, and of course I couldn't just ask her. She's not cold exactly, but not approachable that way." She smiled at her squad mates. "You know, I haven't even been able to tell where she's from. Her accent isn't like anything I've ever studied and her cadence is so unusual."

"That's b-because she's an Indian," Teresa said softly. "Or at l-least half."

Silence filled the room. "What?" Bett said faintly. Her mind was picturing Rains's coloring. From the first day she had noticed that the sergeant's skin was the burnished shade of someone who spent a great deal of time outdoors, and she had such dark hair and eyes. After the time they'd spent together last evening, Bett was able to envision the finer points of Rains's appearance. Her nose and the shape of her face seemed more refined—well, more typically Anglo—and she had those marvelous cheekbones that made her face look almost chiseled. In the few Western movies she'd seen, American Indians were little more than caricatures. She was fairly certain that Sergeant Rains's solemn demeanor was based on the seriousness with which she approached her duty, not because of any cultural disposition. Then she recalled Moore's insult during the game—*motherless half-breed*. At the time, Bett had thought it was just something to say, but maybe it was true.

Teresa nodded. "There's lots of 'em in Oklahoma," she confirmed. "B-but she don't look the same as them. Must be another t-tribe."

"I think Tee's right." Maria's voice stopped everyone. "When I was little, some cousins of mine came to see us. They had moved somewhere up north, near Canada. Now that I think of it, one of the boys married a woman who looked somewhat like Sergeant Rains, black eyes with very long, dark, straight hair. They said she was a Sioux."

"Ooh, better hold on to your scalps, girls," warned Jo. "I remember reading about them in school. The Sioux were warriors, very fierce fighters. Other Indians were afraid of them."

"Good thing she's on our side," suggested Barb with a smile.

"Yes, but joking about scalps and other such rubbish is probably exactly why she doesn't go around talking about it," Bett said somewhat sharply. Jo dipped her head apologetically. "I'm sure she doesn't want to be called Chief or be asked where her feathers are."

Maria gestured angrily. "Yeah, or be called a mutt."

"Yes, just so," Bett concurred, looking fondly at Maria. "So we're not going to do any of that and we're not going to say anything about it to her unless she says something to us. Agreed?" Her gaze took in every member of the squad. They all nodded solemnly.

Bett tried not to be obvious about studying Rains at the officers' table after she marched them to breakfast. Her sergeant always sat on the end, facing the tables where the squad ate. From their first day, Bett had chosen a seat facing Rains and had observed that she appeared to listen, but almost never joined in the other officers' banter. Suddenly Rains dark eyes were on her, and almost reflexively, Bett smiled. Rains's eyes narrowed in puzzlement, and Bett became aware that the whole squad was looking at Rains. She cleared her throat loudly and all heads went back down to their meals, as if they'd all realized the same thing at the same time. Sergeant Rains rose and started toward them. "Uh-oh," Bett heard Jo murmur.

"Ladies." The sergeant was standing at the table. "Is there a problem?" Rains's eyes moved over the group. No one spoke. Her eyes moved back to Bett. "Squad leader, is there a problem here?" she repeated.

"No, Sergeant," Bett said. Rains did not move. She was obviously waiting for an explanation of the group stare. "We were just wondering...um..." Bett's normally agile mind deserted her. It must have been the late night. Rains's eyes moved over the group again. Not one head came up. Her squad mates were eating as if it was their last meal. Bett cast about for something that was different about Rains, other than her heritage. Suddenly she realized that Rains was one of the officers who was still wearing the old-style WAC hat, the rounded one with the stiff brim. Several of the others had on the newer, softer garrison style. "We were just wondering why you wear that particular kind of hat, Sergeant. Don't you think the other one is more comfortable?" Bett managed, at last.

Rains didn't answer for a few seconds. Bett worried that perhaps the sergeant did not believe her last-minute question was sincere.

"My hat, Private, is worn to cover my hair, in accordance with Army regulations," Rains finally spoke, her tone somewhat strained.

"But wouldn't the other hat do that just as well, Sergeant?" Bett was almost genuinely curious now. Then she felt Jo kick her under the table.

"No, it wouldn't," Sergeant Rains replied firmly. "Not my hair." She looked over the group again. "Parade grounds in one hour, ladies," she added, leaving the mess hall.

❖

For the second night of Bett's KP, Sergeant Rains let her eat dinner with her squad before meeting her at the door of the mess hall.

"You'll need to report to your KP duty now, Private Smythe."

Bett saluted smartly, with a touch of her own command in the answer. "Lead on, Sergeant."

Rains seemed to ignore the minor infraction and they walked back toward the kitchen. Once inside the little room, Bett sighed. "Will it always be potatoes?" Perhaps it was her imagination, but the unpeeled mounds seemed even larger than they had been the night before.

"That's not up to me, Private," Rains clarified. "The kitchen staff just sets out whatever they need done. Before the week is over, you may get to wipe tables and mop or just police the grounds and take out the trash. But don't get your hopes up."

"Yes, I don't see you as the type to lead a girl on with false promises, Sergeant." Bett grinned.

There was no answering smile from Rains. "I'll check on you later, Private."

"I was rather hoping you would," Bett said, inclining her head as she took off her jacket and put it on the nail that Rains had used before. "You don't even have to help this time, but I would love to have your company." Bett saw Rains draw back a bit, so she quickly added, "It just makes the time go so much faster." She heard Rains make the little grunting sound and wondered if it was something from her Indian background. They nodded briefly at each other and Rains went out.

Bett had taken off her jewelry and had stopped herself from looking at her watch at least ten times before her sergeant came back. Even though she had been listening for her footsteps, she heard nothing until the door opened.

Rains seemed satisfied to see that she was awake and working. "You're making good progress, Private."

"Well, Sergeant, I had an excellent teacher." Bett gestured toward the second stool that she had brought in and was pleased when Rains leaned against it without comment. "So I was thinking of your reference to *Tom Sawyer* last night. Is that your favorite of Mr. Twain's works?" She held her breath and worked diligently while Rains seemed to be debating whether or not to answer.

When Rains took her jacket off and laid it on the table which Bett had already cleared of potatoes, Bett just managed to hide her smile. "Where is the other peeler?" Rains asked.

"No, no. I told you that you don't have to help me this time," Bett assured her.

"I cannot sit idly by while you work, Private."

"Why not?" Bett asked. "That's what officers usually do anyway." As soon as the words were out of her mouth, Bett wanted to take them back. After a quick glance confirmed that Rains was not happy with her comment, Bett kept peeling without looking up again.

Finally Rains said, "Private Smythe, it is not your place to judge what most officers do or don't do."

Bett stopped working and dropped her head a bit. "Of course you're right, Sergeant. I apologize."

The sergeant rose and went out the door. Bett would have thought she was leaving except that Rains's jacket was still on the table. She was relieved when the sergeant came back with another peeler. They worked in silence for a moment, until Rains ventured, "Actually, I prefer *Huckleberry Finn* for content, although *Tom Sawyer* is an enjoyable adventure."

A wide-ranging conversation followed, from character analysis to historical context. Although Rains clearly had opinions and positions on whatever aspect of the novels they were discussing, she was a very careful listener, and there was usually a pause of up to a minute during which she peeled thoughtfully as she considered Bett's comments. Bett, who enjoyed lightning-fast verbal play that sometimes valued wit over substance, found that waiting for Sergeant Rains's reply forced her to slow her own thinking and listen better as well. Much more quickly than the night before, the potatoes were done. They were still talking as they left the mess hall, walking toward the barracks.

"So did you major in American Literature in college, Sergeant?" Bett asked, her most personal question of the night.

She watched as Rains's face took on a wary, more focused expression. "No, I didn't." Her drill instructor stopped walking, looking around as if just becoming conscious of where she was. "That will be all, Private."

"Sergeant Rains." Bett smiled and stepped closer, putting her hand on Rains's arm again. Rains stood very still. "I feel that I'm indebted to you again, for your time and your most stimulating conversation."

The sergeant stepped back, away from Bett's touch. "I have done you a disservice, Private. KP is not supposed to be enjoyed. You are supposed to be learning from your mistakes."

Rains's face was so serious that Bett couldn't help laughing. "But I have learned, Sergeant. I'll never think of *Huckleberry Finn* in quite the same way again."

Rains shook her head, turned abruptly, and walked away without another word.

❖

Rains was annoyed with herself. At the parade grounds she began running laps, trying to think through what had happened. *You were supposed to tighten up, not spend all evening talking to her,* Rains scolded. *You are not her classmate, you are her sergeant.* She knew the blame lay with herself and not with Private Smythe. Smythe just wanted to pass the time. What Rains could not understand was how she could have let the whole evening go by in conversation and never once have thought about leaving. Perhaps they were developing a level of mutual respect between them; she had readily acknowledged Smythe's intelligence, but now Smythe seemed to be genuinely interested in her thoughts and opinions as well. Rains wasn't usually swayed by such attentiveness, though in this case it seemed to be paying off in Smythe's improved attitude toward Army protocol.

In the years that she had been a sergeant, Rains had learned the importance of dividing herself evenly among her recruits. It was important to be fair, to be objective, and to be impartial. Even though Smythe was the squad leader, if any of the other girls suspected favoritism or that she was getting any special treatment, it could destroy the balance of camaraderie Rains always strove for with her groups. She thought about having Webber take Private Smythe to her duty tomorrow, but what reason would she give? *You'll just take her to her KP and leave,* Rains told herself. *Don't come back to check on her. She knows the routine now.* She ran two more laps, trying to get the sound of Smythe's voice out of her mind. She wasn't particularly successful.

❖

Bett was having trouble falling asleep, even though she was tired from KP and the long day. She kept thinking of things Sergeant Rains had said, finding little hints of her personality from their conversation. Clearly she favored the underdog in any situation. Several times Bett had started to bring up Rains's supposed Indian background thinking that it might lead to more discussion, but after the way Rains had reacted to her question about college, she was glad she hadn't been any more personal. Bett wondered if it was the Army that had made her sergeant so closed off, or if it was just her character. She speculated whether Rains's apparent aversion to being touched was part of that character as well.

The door to the barracks opened quietly. Bett's heart accelerated to an unexpected tempo. She was facing away from the door, so Rains didn't appear in her vision until after she had passed her bunk. She watched as the sergeant looked briefly over the sleeping forms and made her way back. Bett kept her eyes open, and when Rains made eye contact, Bett smiled. Rains didn't, but then she never did.

"You should already be asleep, Private," she said softly.

The sergeant was carrying her shirt; she was only wearing a sleeveless undershirt which clung tightly to her trim form and there was a sheen on her face and arms. When Bett raised herself on her elbow, she could clearly detect the outline of Rains's small breasts. After swallowing that observation away as quietly as possible, she whispered, "Why are you all sweaty? Don't tell me you have potato fever or some such."

There might have been another brief turning at the corner of Rains's mouth, but her voice was quiet. "I've been running. Now lie down before you wake everyone else up."

"Why are you running in the middle of the night?" Bett asked, lying back obediently.

"Go to sleep, Private Smythe." Rain walked toward the door.

Bett turned over to follow her, still whispering. "Can we talk about transcendentalism tomorrow night?"

Rains stopped and turned back. "No, Private. Our literary salon will give way to your solo KP duty from now on."

Bett stopped smiling. "Is that what you decided on your run?"

Sergeant Rains leaned closer to her bed, her whisper a little more severe. "That is the way it's supposed to be, Private. It was my error to let our mutual interests lure me into excessive conversation with you. It won't happen again."

They both looked down as Jo muttered something in her sleep and turned over on the bunk below Bett. When Bett looked back up, Rains was going out the door.

❖

Bett didn't say a word the next night as Sergeant Rains escorted her to the door of the mess hall. Good, Rains thought, this would be easier than arguing with her. There were no potatoes in the little room in the back. "Wait here, Private," Rains said.

Bett stood at ease.

"Trash only tonight," Rains said when she returned, leading Bett back into the main hall. She pointed at the various overflowing barrels. "Just police the tables, then dump these in the container outside, and you're done." Bett acknowledged the information with a short nod, but didn't answer. "Private Smythe," Rains said tersely, tiring of the silent treatment, "you should understand that I meant nothing personal last night. But I have a job to do and so do you. That is the reason we are here."

Bett's eyes flashed. "Oh yes, Sergeant. I understand completely. Another round of excessive conversation from you could cost us the war." She began dragging one of the heavy barrels toward the door.

Once again, Bett's sharp wit made Rains want to smile. Instead, she stepped over and took the other side of the barrel.

Bett's head snapped up. "I don't need your help, Sergeant."

"I know, I know," Rains answered, her voice somewhat more sociable than usual. "What you need is a conversation about transcendentalism."

"Don't flatter yourself, Sergeant. What I need is to finish this stupid KP and for my training on wireless coding to come up so I can get on with my life away from this bloody place."

They dumped the barrel in silence. "I'll leave you to it then, Private," Rains said, her voice flat as she walked away.

Five minutes later, Bett wasn't sure who she was more upset with, Rains or herself. She hadn't meant to be so ill-tempered but the sergeant's presumption and her self-possessed manner had just rubbed her the wrong way at that moment. She wondered if anything ever ruffled Rains's calm. She wasn't surprised when the sergeant wasn't around the mess hall as she walked back toward the barracks after finishing her duty, so she detoured by the track on the parade grounds, in case Rains was out running. She wasn't. When Bett arrived at the barracks, Sergeant Rains was there, talking with Helen and Tee. As their eyes met, Rains stood and signaled her over.

"Private Smythe, I believe Private Tucker and Private Owens would appreciate some assistance with the assignments from their classes." Helen and Tee were both nodding. "There may be others who will join you. This will be your duty for the next two weeks, understood?"

Bett looked up at Rains doubtfully. "You mean instead of KP?"

"Yes, Private. I believe your skills could be put to better use here." Rains had been nodding at Owens and Tucker, and now she looked down at Bett. "Unless you have some objection."

Bett tried, but Rains's expression was impossible to read. "None that come to mind, Sergeant."

"Good. I'll alert the kitchen." Rains started out and then stopped. "And your wireless class will be coming up in two weeks, Private Smythe."

Bett dropped her eyes. "Thank you, Sergeant." *When will I ever learn to mind my mouth?*

As Rains walked by, Jo called out from her bunk, "What's the play, Sarge?" The two of them often spoke in some kind of baseball language that Bett kept trying to understand.

"Turning two, Archer," Rains responded. Archer laughed as she always did.

❖

Their days settled into routine, the framework for Army life. After a few days, Bett no longer panicked when bright lights shone into the barracks windows and the first bugle call sounded at five forty-five a.m. Some days she would actually drowse until the cannon went off at six, when the flag went up and the band began to play. Like the rest of her squad mates, she learned how to be fully dressed in the fifteen minutes they had before reporting for roll call. After breakfast, they had another hour to clean up and organize themselves and their belongings before beginning a variety of exercises, drills, classes, and lectures that lasted the rest of the day. There was another company muster before dinner for a ceremony called Retreat, where the flag was lowered and the WAC band played the national anthem, followed by evening mess at five p.m. Undoubtedly, their new schedule was quite an adjustment for everyone, whether it was dealing with the ten-to-one bathroom ratio for only child Phyllis or the novelty of eating dinner at five p.m.

Sometimes there were additional lectures or meetings after the evening meal, but frequently they had that time to themselves, unless there were assignments from the day's classes or drills that needed to be practiced, which was often the case. Lights had to be out by nine thirty, but Bett, like many others, procured a good flashlight and would often continue to write letters, study, or read well after that time. At ten forty-five, Sergeant Rains, or occasionally one of the other sergeants, would come through for the last official bed check of the evening. If someone was not in their bunk, it was stressed, the MPs would be called.

Sergeant Rains conducted the morning exercises for the entire base, along with physical drills for each platoon. By the end of their basic training, all recruits had to demonstrate a certain level of fitness, which she would evaluate. The morning and afternoon classes were conducted by other specialists and were designed to help inform the recruits about different jobs that were available to them and to determine the ones for which they were best suited.

Since Bett had already made up her mind to work on the new wireless encoding machine, she was just biding her time. When she had expressed her interest in the recruiting office before signing up, she had been warned that her choice of specialty was the most difficult to get into. According to Maria, who had a distant cousin in the administrative office, the cryptography division hadn't taken anyone new for the last three rotations. Even so, Bett wasn't worried. From Kent Prep to Oxford, she had never failed to be chosen for something that she'd worked for. As much as she hated to admit it, she knew this drive for success was something she had gotten from her father.

Partly out of respect for Sergeant Rains and partly to avoid jeopardizing her chance at the wireless group by being labeled an agitator, she did manage to keep her opinions to herself and found that some of the lectures, like those on meteorology and photography, were actually quite enlightening. She felt herself settling in and began to feel sure she would be able to stick it out—to complete her basic training and prove to her family, if not herself, that she could do it. And she still had a score to settle with Herr Hitler.

In many ways, Army life reminded Bett of her boarding school days. Helen and Tee continued to struggle with some of the lessons and Bett was genuinely glad that Sergeant Rains had assigned her to help them. Bett enjoyed the process of education, although she had to work not to show her dismay at how far behind the girls were sometimes. She quickly determined that their deficiencies were not caused by lack of intellect, but because each of them had regularly missed long stretches of school when they were needed at home. Occasionally some of the other girls would sit in, usually Maria or even Jo. Bett kept the sessions informal enough that anyone felt welcome.

Bett thought that most of the members of her new family were really quite charming. There was none of the snobbishness and competition that there had been at Kent or Oxford. Only Irene Dodd remained aloof. She seemed unwilling or unable to find her place in the squad. The rest of them all seemed to take Rains's comments from that first day to heart, and they quickly learned how to steer clear of someone who was grumpy in the morning (Charlotte), how to keep their voices quieter after the first one went to bed (Jo), and who wrote letters home every day (Barb). Bett often saw Rains talking individually after drills with Tee, who was homesick, or running laps with Helen, to help her control her temper. And Bett acknowledged that Rains appealed to her intellect to help her fall into line. But not exclusively so, she thought, remembering Rains's calming touch and soothing voice when Bett had been in the throes of her claustrophobia.

Their sergeant's firm, even presence was a steadying influence on them all. Rains was the type who led by example, Bett concluded, watching her sergeant during morning exercise as their first full week was coming to a close. Sergeant Moore had returned to the base earlier than expected and her new squad had followed them onto the parade grounds that day, most of them cringing at her words and her tone. *I believe Rains genuinely wants us to be successful here,* Bett mused, *and not just because it looks good for her. Her leadership is not based on fear; it works because she respects us as much as we respect her.*

❖

That mutual respect grew even more the next Friday night as most of the girls were dressing for a trip to the NCO club for a special dinner. It was Maria's birthday and they were ready for an excuse to celebrate, or at least blow off some steam from the demands of their second week in basic training. Escorts had been arranged and even though Bett was scheduled to have her first squad leader meeting with Sergeant Rains that afternoon, she had promised to meet everyone there as soon as she was free. As the squad members were getting into their dress uniforms, Maria suddenly gave a sharp cry. "My grandmother's brooch. It's missing! My mother let me bring it for good luck and now it's gone."

Barb and Charlotte reacted first, gathering at Maria's footlocker. "Where did you have it? When did you see it last?" Their help with the search turned up nothing. In the meantime, Bett checked her locker. One of her rings was also missing, but Maria's tears made her wait to say anything.

"I'll go get Sergeant Rains," Irene Dodd offered, starting toward the door. Both Jo and Bett looked at her in surprise, as she had never volunteered for anything before. Then Jo turned a worried eye back to Bett.

Catching Jo's meaning, Bett acted instinctively as their squad leader. "No," she said firmly, and then added, "thank you, Irene, but I think Maria should go. She's the one who has suffered the loss so it would be less suspicious than if any of us left."

Irene frowned but couldn't seem to think of a reply. She slouched back to her bunk. Bett looked at Jo and then shifted her eyes in Dodd's direction, and Archer nodded, moving to a position where she could watch the older woman without being obvious. Irene looked around and then made a show of looking through her locker like most of the other girls were doing, as if checking to see if anything of hers was missing. When Maria returned with Sergeant Rains, the squad was shocked into silence upon seeing Sergeant Moore accompanying them.

The two sergeants stood stiffly at the doorway. "The Army takes matters like this very seriously," Rains stated, her expression grim. "Someone who steals from one of her sisters is not welcome in the WAC. We are going to make sure that the thief is no one from this squad before we expand our investigation." She glanced at Sergeant Moore who barked out, "Get out your bathrobes, ladies. Strip and put them on. You'll assemble in the latrine under Sergeant Rains's guard while I search your belongings for the missing item." The squad members stood in shock until Moore yelled, "Now!" Then everyone began to move at once as Sergeant Rains walked toward the rear of the barracks, where the bathroom was located.

She faced away from the girls as they changed, listening to Moore as she moved among them, insisting, "Move it. I said strip, ladies. That means naked, understand? Come on, honey, we don't have all night. Hurry up, hurry up—don't be so modest, you. Nobody cares what you've got under that robe. Let's go."

Rains turned back to face them as they began walking past her in single file into the lavatory area. Her eyes swept carefully over each one, as if gauging their responses. As Irene Dodd approached, Rains ordered, "Halt."

Bett, who was behind Dodd, winced, remembering when she had heard that tone before. Dodd's eyes didn't seem to settle.

"You need to empty your robe pocket, Private Dodd," the sergeant demanded, holding out the palm of her hand.

Private Dodd's hand moved as if to comply but instead she swung a clenched fist in the direction of Rains's head. Rains's movement was so quick it was almost imperceptible. In one motion she dodged the punch and maneuvered behind Dodd, her own forearm pushing Irene's head against the barracks wall hard enough that the woman's face was distorted. The arm that had been swinging at Rains's face was caught in the grasp of Rain's other hand, twisted so tightly behind her back that she screamed out in pain. The whole squad gasped, and Bett caught a glimpse of something very fierce in Rains's eyes before Sergeant Moore ordered them all back to their bunks, out of the way.

As Moore retrieved a brooch and a ring from Dodd's pocket, she advised, "You'd best apologize to your sergeant, Dodd, unless you want to go home with a other-than-honorable discharge *and* a broken arm."

"Fuck you, bitch," Irene Dodd managed to squeeze out from her pursed lips, followed by a groan of pain as she continued to struggle.

Oh God, Sergeant Rains, don't do it, Bett thought, fearing that Dodd's profanity would push Rains over the edge. The tension in the room was almost tangible.

But Rains's voice was dangerously calm. "It's not me you need to apologize to," she said as she pushed Dodd's arm just a little farther up her back and the struggling stopped. "It is your squad mates. You have violated their trust in you. You have disgraced yourself and failed your country. You have lost your place here and the chance to be something better than what you are." She turned the angry woman to face her fellow recruits, but Dodd's comment was directed at her sergeant.

"You can't do nothing to me," Irene Dodd insisted, breathing heavily as she looked back over her shoulder. "You can't prove nothing."

A sharp intake of breath was clearly audible as Rains released Dodd's arm abruptly and roughly turned her captive back to face her. Rains's fists were clenched at her waist. "You don't want to even think about what I could do to you." Her voice dropped to an intimidating whisper as she stepped very close and looked down into Dodd's face. The room was so quiet that everyone could hear the words she growled. "But you are a thief and therefore a liar as well, so I won't soil my hands by dealing with you any further. What has been proven is you are unworthy of being a part of this fine squad or of the distinguished Women's Army Corps."

Dodd couldn't maintain her defiance in the glare of Rains's eyes. Her gaze dropped, but her voice still tried for an indifferent tone. "So what?"

Rains's body tightened again but Moore nudged Rains lightly with her shoulder. "Stand down, Rains. Let's get this piece of trash into her uniform for the last time and move her out of here." Their sergeant took in a long, deep breath and stepped away as Sergeant Moore put the confiscated items in her hand.

The anxiety in the room went down a few degrees, but no one moved except Irene Dodd as she reached for the khaki skirt and blouse she had laid out on the bed. After she dressed, Dodd quickly threw a few extra things into her suitcase, but as she stood, Sergeant Moore grabbed it from her hand and threw it back on the bunk. "Nope. Not until we've had a chance to search it for anything else that doesn't belong to you." Dodd slumped, turned without a word, and kept her eyes on the floor as Moore escorted her out.

Barb acted first. She was closest to the disgraced woman's bunk, and as Irene Dodd passed where she was standing, she turned her back. There was no command, no order given, but each girl along the rows of bunks did the same. Rains watched with her jaw tight. Once Moore and Dodd had exited the building, Rains collected the suitcase and followed them.

Bett had been watching Rains very carefully and as soon as her sergeant began to move she called the squad to attention without a second thought. She wanted Rains to know that she approved of her handling of Irene Dodd. To Bett's thinking, Sergeant Rains had shown the proper combination of righteous anger and controlled contempt for someone who would take the value of something stolen over the opportunity for freely given, genuine comradeship and the chance to make a meaningful contribution to the war effort. Everyone quickly turned back to face the front and stood immobile.

❖

As Sergeant Rains walked between the bunks, she could feel a change. She thought she might sense fear or at least apprehension toward her from the women in the room. When she reached Maria's bunk, she stopped and cleared her throat, eyes sweeping around the room, glancing briefly on each face. "I want to apologize to you for my...my overly aggressive handling of Private—former Private Dodd."

A few of the girls looked at each other at her correction of Dodd's name and there were some murmurs of denial to Rains's declaration, but she held up her hand and it was instantly quiet again. "In the past I've had some...difficulty controlling my emotions, particularly anger. Sometimes in the heat of the moment, I still don't do as well as I would like. Even among the most enlightened of us, reaction sometimes triumphs reason, yes? But it is my promise to each of you to continue to strive for improvement in this area and to be very conscious of my responsibility to never bring shame to this squad, our platoon, or the WAC." She had come to attention as well and for a moment it was very quiet in the barracks.

The stillness was broken as Helen called out, "I think you did all right, Sergeant. If it had been me, I woulda decked her."

Some applause along with a widespread buzz of agreement followed this remark. Sergeant Rains turned to place the brooch in Maria's waiting hands, stiffening slightly as Maria grabbed hers and gushed, "Thank you, Sergeant. Thank you so much. You just—you don't know what this means to me."

Rains quickly extracted her hand from Maria's grasp, but her shoulders relaxed a bit. "You can thank me by not letting this incident cause you to lose faith in the rest of your squad or the WAC and what we are here to accomplish." Seeing Maria close to tears again, Rains moved a bit closer and her voice softened. "You are a very important part of who we are. Your sisters need to know that you are still with us. Can we count on you, Private Rangel?"

Maria looked around and her squad mates chimed in, unbidden, with words of encouragement. She took in a breath and straightened, wiping her eyes. "Of course you can count on me, Sergeant." She looked around and smiled, adding, "Why would I give this up? All I have at home is my grubby little brothers."

Everyone laughed and the mood lightened immediately. Jo took it from there. "All right, then let's get moving, ladies. We've got places to go and people to see!" And the noise level rose quickly as they all launched back into their preparations for the evening.

Rains inclined her head toward Jo and Bett as she opened the barracks door. Archer had said just the right thing at the right time—a trait of good leadership. And Smythe had shown initiative by calling the squad to attention, her first command as far as Rains knew.

"Good evening, Squad."

"Good evening, Sergeant," they chorused as Rains went out the door. She heard the movement and conversation rising behind her and nodded to herself. This was a very good group and they would be all right. Then she paused on the top step and looked at the ring in her hand, having forgotten it until that moment.

Private Smythe came through the door and stopped behind her, speaking quietly. "It's mine, Sergeant. I only discovered it was missing when Maria noticed that her brooch was gone. I didn't say anything before because I"—she glanced back briefly—"I thought her loss was more significant."

Rains looked more carefully at the centered diamond stone, surrounded by smaller emeralds. It was not a garish piece but she couldn't begin to calculate its worth. *Considerably more than I have made the last three years in the WAC*, she was certain. Smythe was waiting at ease, her eyes focused elsewhere. Rains was impressed that Private Smythe would put the sentimental value of someone else's property above the actual price of her own.

"Very good, Private," she said warmly, and Smythe lifted her chin a little, obviously pleased. Then another thought occurred to Rains. Although no one else had mentioned the disappearance of any jewelry, and there probably wasn't another person in the entire platoon who would be wearing a ring like this, she had no proof that the piece actually belonged to Smythe. It was always her goal to be fair and impartial. How would she react if circumstances were different and Irene Dodd had claimed the ring? The sergeant knew she had to ask. "But how can I know that this is yours?"

Bett shifted her position and her gaze as she lifted her palm to the level of Rains's eyes, fingers up, wiggling them slightly, her eyes alight with amusement. "Think of me as Cinderella, if you like." Rains didn't understand the reference, but she could see what Smythe was suggesting. Carefully, she slid the ring onto Bett's finger. As Bett tilted her hand forward to show the perfect fit of the golden band, her fingers closed lightly around Rains's thumb which had come to rest in her palm, effectively capturing her hand. Their eyes met and a slow smile crossed Bett's lips. "Well, Sergeant? Does the glass slipper fit? Am I the one you've been looking for?"

Bett had expected a snappy comeback about not being a prince or some such, but Sergeant Rains blushed deeply as she freed her hand, stepped back, and cleared her throat. "We'll have our first meeting next week instead, Private. Spend tonight with your squad. I think they will benefit more from your presence." She inclined her head in the direction of the administration building, where the forms of Sergeant Moore and Irene Dodd could be seen in the distance. "I have some other matters to attend to, anyway."

"Yes, ma'am." Although Bett was glad to be released from her duty, she also felt vaguely disappointed, realizing that she had been looking forward to the one-on-one meeting with her intriguing sergeant. She even felt oddly protective, as though she wanted to make sure that Rains was all right with everything that had happened. She had hoped that her joking comment about the ring would help the sergeant unwind a little, but she hadn't expected such a vividly uncomfortable reaction. Bett loved to tease and the stern Sergeant Rains had just revealed herself to be a very easy target. *I'll bet anger isn't the only emotion she has trouble with.*

Before Bett could think of anything else to say, Rains reached around her and opened the door to the barracks, motioning Bett back inside with the suitcase just as two male officers were coming into view. "Enjoy your evening, Private. Only be sure to change into more appropriate attire first."

Bett crossed her arms over herself and felt her cheeks flush as she recalled that she was totally nude underneath the short robe. Venturing a last glance, she thought there was just the slightest amusement on the sergeant's face.

"And please wish Private Rangel a happy birthday for me," Rains added, turning away into the evening.

❖

Walking toward the base administration office, Sergeant Rains became aware that in place of the rage that Irene Dodd had sparked in her were thoughts of the very delicate touch of Elizabeth Smythe's hand and the way her mouth moved into a smile. Several hours later, after arranging for the MPs to escort Irene Dodd to the stockade where she would await her court-martial, Rains was finishing the accompanying paperwork when it occurred to her to ask Sergeant Moore about Cinderella.

"My God, Rains, you must be even dumber than I thought," scoffed the older woman. Even though Rains now outranked her and they had worked well together on solving the theft, Moore never passed up the chance to put her in her place. Rains had long since become accustomed to Moore's attitude; it had never been anything different. "How can anyone get out of kindergarten without knowing that stupid fairy tale?"

In spite of Sergeant Moore's scornful tone as she told it, Rains liked the story very much.

Chapter Five

As the third week of basic training came to an end, Bett found herself thinking about her upcoming squad leader meeting with Sergeant Rains. Bett knew she hadn't been doing a very good job of keeping a low profile, as the sergeant had suggested on her first day. Besides being elected squad leader and making the mistake of speaking out during those first few classes—which still caused many of the instructors to keep an eye on her throughout their lectures—she had also become known among her squad for her generosity, buying Tee a new hat when hers had been ruined when it blew into a mud puddle during a sudden late-summer squall and springing for Phyllis's long-distance call home when her nephew was there on leave. She routinely made perfect scores on the assignments and examinations, but true to Rains's viewpoint, the rest of the squad seemed to take pride in her accomplishment rather than being resentful. Her success belonged to them all; she even heard Helen bragging to a girl from another squad about being tutored by the perfect one-hundred girl.

Since Irene Dodd's departure there was a new level of comfort among them. Bett's sewing kit had pretty much become community property, and everyone shared in the box of salt water taffy that came in the mail from Barb's sister. Even the laughter and teasing that followed various attempts at playing the harmonica that Charlotte's father had sent along were genial and good natured. And Bett had worked at minding her manners as well as keeping to Army protocol, so there had been no more KP.

Even so, she was aware that since that moment with the ring, Sergeant Rains seldom met her eyes or bothered to notice how well she was doing at putting on her gas mask or map reading or whatever task they were assigned for the day, even though Bett usually took a position toward the front during exercises and drills. Rains was generous with her praise to the others, though, Bett noted. Especially the timid ones like Tee and Maria. She wondered if Rains felt intimidated by her family's influence. She didn't think it was her intelligence or her education; Rains had more than held her own in the few intellectual conversations they'd had.

Still…Bett's thoughts drifted back to her early Oxford days, thinking of the rare professor who, upon finally accepting that she wouldn't offer any kind of ride on the Carlton coattails for her grade, made her work harder than anyone else in the class for the first-class marks she was so determined to get. And before that there were the upperclassmen in Kent Prep, her boarding school, girls so anxious that their own academic legacies continue unchallenged and unmatched that they sometimes made her life miserable when she had done too well in class. How much pleasure Bett took in seeing her name placed above theirs on the various plaques around the school. Sometimes she bested them before the upperclassmen had even graduated. And the biggest thrill there, like here, came in knowing that her father's money had nothing to do with her personal success. Did Rains expect more from her because of who she was? What would it take to please her? And why did it matter so much to her that she did?

It was after dinner and Bett was beginning to nod off in her bunk, drifting through those days at Kent, but in her dream Sergeant Rains was there in place of her old rivals, with Rains's name replacing hers on those plaques. Then the dream shifted suddenly and Rains wasn't her rival, but in place of Emma, her first love. Emma, who had taught Bett all about needing and hurting, whose smile could melt her and whose casual disregard would burn her. Once, Bett had thought Emma was everything she ever wanted, but in the dream it was Rains who reached out a warm, loving hand to touch Bett's face, her hair and then caress her breast. Bett wrapped her arms around Rains's strong back, pulling her closer. She moaned softly in anticipation as Rains's mouth moved slowly to cover hers, eager for the pleasure that would be shared between them.

"Wake up, Queenie." Jo's voice shocked her into consciousness. "Aren't you going to be late for your squad leader meeting with Sergeant Rains?"

"Oh God." Bett jumped off her bunk, trying to gather her wits. The dream had been so intense that she could feel a wetness between her legs. She hurried to the bathroom, then splashed some water on her face and straightened her tie. Still shaking her head to try to clear the unexpected feelings, she asked the room, "Does anyone have anything they want me to say?" Just a few negative sounds came back to her, with Jo calling, "Good luck!" as she went out into the warm Iowa evening. As she mounted the steps of the administration building, she realized that she had forgotten that stupid hat. It just never sat right on her wavy hair. And knowing Rains, there was no point in making an excuse; she would simply have another demerit. *How will I feel when I see her, after that dream?* The thought made Bett take a deep breath as she adjusted her clothing and ran her hands over her face. Then she tapped on the conference room door and opened it.

"Miss Carlton," a distinctly male voice boomed, "come in, come in." Bett stepped forward hesitantly as her eyes adjusted to the dimly lit room. "I hope you don't mind that Sergeant Rains let us sit in on your meeting today."

Bett found Sergeant Rains then, sitting toward the back, her dark eyes as impassive as ever. Or was there a hint of regret?

"No, sir," Bett said mildly, noting the odd feeling at hearing her other name.

"Good, good. This is General Foreman, General Hatcher, and General Rutherford," the speaker continued, indicating the other seated forms, each of whom nodded in turn. "And I am General Clifton, a great admirer of your father, as are we all." He waved his hand to encompass the group. More nodding.

"Yes, sir." Bett felt as though her voice was coming from someone else's throat, as if she were a ventriloquist's dummy.

"Sit, please." They all stood briefly as she did so, taking the chair he had indicated, directly across from Rains. "I hope you've found your treatment here to be satisfactory so far."

"Oh yes, sir. Just fine, sir." *They wouldn't be asking if they knew about me being taken to the stockade.*

"Good. Sergeant Rains has certainly given us a very positive report on your progress."

Bett thought she saw Rains dip her head just a bit. *She must have kept that KP off my record.* Suddenly it dawned on Bett how unusual it must be to have four generals present in a squad leader meeting. A warm glow of anger began to gather in her chest.

"Will you be passing that report on to my father, then, General?" she inquired, almost sweetly. Across the table, Sergeant Rains's eyebrows lifted.

"Well, I'm not sure that I'll be speaking to him directly," General Clifton began, "but we were asked to drop in and check on your satisfaction with the program thus far."

"Asked by whom?"

The generals chuckled, a bit uncomfortably. "Let's just say by someone who outranks us all."

"And what if"—Bett looked directly at her sergeant for a split second—"and I'm not saying this is the case, but what if I were not satisfied with the program?"

"Why then we would see to it that a transfer was put through immediately," General Clifton assured her.

"Or an honorable discharge," General Hatcher said encouragingly, "if you would prefer."

Bett shook her head slowly, unable to articulate anything more for the churning that had spread to her stomach.

"So we're given to understand that your primary interest is in wireless coding and transmission, Miss Carlton," General Foreman began, shuffling some papers. "And we'll see to it that you are transferred into that program immediately…today."

"Before I finish my basic training?" Bett's hands settled on the table in front of her.

"We hardly think that an Oxford graduate, and an honors graduate at that, needs to spend any more time in basic training," Foreman said.

"I'm just curious, gentlemen," Bett began, heavy sarcasm in her tone. "Is it the Oxford degree that gets me out of basic training, or is it my father's money?" She could see Rains's eyes narrow, as if surprised by the bluntness of the question.

Before they could attempt an answer, Bett continued. "And I'm surprised that WAC enrollment is down, if all of your recruits get such generous personal attention."

"Well..." Clifton began, but Bett had heard enough.

"Gentlemen," she stood and the men scrambled to their feet. Only Sergeant Rains remained seated. "You may tell my father, the president, and Adolph Hitler himself that I will continue my basic training, I will graduate with my platoon, and I will take whatever position I am considered qualified for at that time." Her voice reverberated in the small room. "And if that is all, I will take my leave."

"Rutherford," General Clifton hissed, "escort her back to her barracks. Try to make her understand—"

"I'll do that, sir, if I may." Rains's voice came through clearly, though mildly as usual, as she too stood, making her way around the table. "Private...Smythe may have some squad matters that she needs to discuss with me."

The men looked surprised, as if they had forgotten that she was there. Then they looked at each other uncomfortably. Finally Clifton spoke. "Very well, Sergeant." He removed a card from his jacket pocket. "If you should change your mind, Miss Carl...er... Private..." He offered it to Bett without finishing his sentence.

Without looking at it, she slipped it into the breast pocket of her jacket. "Thank you, sir." Bett saluted smartly and Rains followed suit. "Good day, gentlemen."

The two women walked silently down the hall and out into the twilight. After a few more feet, Bett began to giggle. She could feel Rains's eyes on her, but she couldn't help it. It was the mix of it all, the unexpected emotion of the dream, the obvious presence of her father's influence, and then the fun of running those tin-star generals around a bit. She tried to calm herself before the giggle erupted into full-scale hysterical laughter.

Sergeant Rains looked concerned as she glanced back toward the door. "Stop it, Private," she said gruffly. "That's an order."

"Is it?" Bett had been winding down, but the stern look on Rains's face made her start up again.

Hustling Smythe off the sidewalk and into the shadows between two buildings, away from view of the exiting generals, Sergeant Rains's voice was severe. "Don't you think they might hear you?" Bett could only shake her head as she caught her breath. Rains leaned around her to glance at the door again. "People in authority generally don't appreciate it when their special favors are refused. Your amusement will only make things worse."

Steadying herself with her hands on her hips, Bett raised her chin. "So are you suggesting that I do what they want?"

"Not at all," Rains answered quickly. "I think you did exactly the right thing." She paused to let her praise be heard before adding, "I just don't think you should laugh about it."

Meeting Rains's eyes, Bett asked, "Tell me honestly, Sergeant. Do you treat me differently because of who I am?"

"Of course," Rains replied. Bett frowned and looked away, feeling her resentment building again until her sergeant continued, "I approach each of my recruits a little differently because of who they are. Because of who *they* are, Private, not because of who their family is. Surely you understand the distinction?"

The emphasis in Sergeant Rains's voice confirmed exactly what Bett had observed in her treatment of their squad. Everyone valued for their individuality, even as they were learning to work together as a whole. Everyone had their different touchpoints through which Sergeant Rains—and therefore the WAC—found a connection. With her, it had been literary criticism; with Archer, it was baseball. But when they came together, they were 20th Company, 5th Regiment. Nothing else mattered. She nodded and Rains went on. "So explain to me your thinking to reject such a generous offer. I know it isn't because you are enjoying basic training so much." Bett saw that hint of a smile and she felt an answering grin inside herself. Then the sergeant's face became solemn again. "Aren't you aware that these men are in a position to make your time here very unpleasant? Any one of them outranks every woman on this base, including Colonel Issacson."

"Of course I know that," Bett answered, her voice sharp. "Sergeant, I've had the protection of money and the threat of that protection being withdrawn for my entire life. Would you rather I cried than laughed? Should I simply give in, rather than stand up to them? I certainly think that's what they would prefer, don't you?" She gestured toward the building they had just left, and then turned her gaze back to Rains, who was squinting uncertainly. "But don't you see that this is all about my father and the influence that he's acquired? It's not really even about me. It's about the contracts he'll be awarded or the write-offs he's getting." She sighed. "Obviously, his reach extends to the highest ranks of the Army and that meeting was just a reminder that I'm subject to him, even here."

The sergeant looked off in the distance for a moment, as if she was trying to see something far away. When her gaze returned, she still looked unsure. Bett asked, "You don't come from money, do you, Sergeant?" Rains drew back somewhat, but then shook her head once. Bett nodded in confirmation and spoke earnestly. "Which is why you don't understand. With my father, it's all business. When we first arrived, you spoke of family. Well, my family is more like a company. A company from which I tried to resign by coming here. But I'm still a commodity to him, still his product, and he's making sure I know it. Any imperfection, any deficiency, any sign of weakness—even here—and my value to him decreases." She looked down, thinking and added quietly, "Again." Taking a breath, she continued, "My father loves to quote Thomas Jefferson. *Money, not morality, is the principle commerce of civilized nations.* Well in that sense, my father is very civilized. And I am nothing but a commodity to him, and those generals are certainly his commerce, too." She slumped onto the grass, looking at her hands.

"Much of value in our world is not for sale," the sergeant announced, almost startling Smythe as she sat cross-legged, facing her. "And the most meaningful things in life have nothing to do with money."

Bett gave a doubtful shake of her head. "Everything has a price, Sergeant. My father taught me that."

"At times you remind me of a teacher I had once. Not your accent, but the way you put your words together." Bett raised her eyebrows. To her recollection, this was the first personal thing Sergeant Rains had ever volunteered to her. Even her sergeant's posture seemed much more informal as she leaned closer than usual. "She made me care about learning with her beautiful words, and by reading us the words of others." Bett was intrigued. Rains went on, looking into the distance again. "The one I liked to hear the most was Henry David Thoreau. He said, *Money is not required to buy one necessity of the soul.*"

Bett nodded as she recalled Rains quoting Thoreau that first night of her KP. It didn't fit with the image that she projected as a tough sergeant, but Bett already suspected that wasn't all there was to her. She took a ragged breath and lowered her voice. "Do you know why I chose to enter the WAC under this name?" Rains shook her head. After a few seconds, Bett's voice grew even smaller. "Because my father frightened me. When he couldn't talk me out of joining up, he convinced me that everyone would know the Carlton name and I would be a target for kidnapping, or at least extortion, because of our wealth. That no one here could protect me." She saw her sergeant's posture stiffen again and she added, "Of course, now that I'm here, I see how silly that was, but it's too late to change my name back now."

Sergeant Rains took Bett's hands in her own and Bett's eyes widened in surprise. "You don't ever need to be afraid here. I will keep you safe." As if realizing that what she had said sounded much too personal, Rains continued, "It is the job of all the officers to see to the security of our recruits. We take that responsibility very seriously."

Bett looked at her for a long moment and then lowered her gaze. "I don't know why I let him manipulate me this way. Even knowing that he's doing it doesn't seem to help. I don't think there's anything he wouldn't sacrifice to get his way. I know he doesn't care about what's right or what's true. He just wants to own everything, control everything. And somehow, he always does."

Rains watched as some of the light in Smythe's eyes dulled and her face saddened. *She needs to see another path.* Rains squeezed her hands gently, bringing Bett's eyes back to hers. "Private Smythe, regardless of what possessions your father may own or what persuasions he may be capable of, you must be guided by the spirit which belongs only to you." Her voice softened. "That is the truest, most beautiful part of yourself, and that is where your strength comes from. In your mind you may know something, but in your spirit is where you completely understand it. Facts you may memorize and recite, but that ring of truth, that awareness of the connections between all things, that consciousness of your existence as a vital part of this world—that is when you are feeling your spirit. Don't ever fear that someone can take that from you. You alone can decide if you wish it bought or sold. But I don't believe that is who you are or what you would want. I think you will always choose to walk your own path in your own way and that you will remain free, as all good things are."

Rains's tone was so sincere and her expression so intent that for a moment, Bett couldn't look away. The sergeant's eyes were kind, gentle, and almost…sweet. She couldn't recall anyone ever speaking to her about spiritual matters in this way and it drew her in, warmed her. Finally Bett looked back down. The sergeant's hands almost swallowed hers but they were gentle and warm with long fingers that tapered gracefully, like a musician's. The unexpected tenderness of Rains's gesture made something inside Bett feel touched, softened. She couldn't believe that she had talked so openly with this woman she barely knew, but it felt good to be honest about her feelings about her family, especially her father. She felt quite confident that her sergeant was not the type to go blabbing her business in the NCO club. *Being with Rains does feel safe,* she admitted. Remembering her dream, she took a deep breath and looked back up, wondering who Sergeant Rains was when she wasn't being a sergeant.

Caught up in the moment, Rains had spoken of such private matters because she hoped to make Smythe feel less intimidated, less trapped by the situation with her father. By taking Smythe's hands, Rains had wanted to move her away from what seemed to be her customary vision of herself as just one of her father's pawns and to emphasize that the WAC could give her the means to make her own way in the world. But when Smythe looked up with a hint of tears in her eyes, Rains realized there was too much emotion between them—emotion that was touching her, too. At first she thought that what she had seen in Bett's eyes were tears of laughter. But there was something else there, some deeper feeling that seemed to originate from where their hands were joined. Rains felt connected to the woman sitting before her with an intensity that was deep…and alarming. *What am I doing?* She released Bett's hands and stood quickly, shifting her mind back to the Army way. *You've said enough. Now back off*, she told herself, checking one last time that the generals were not in sight. *Right now.*

After a few seconds more, Bett seemed to recover her composure. "Why, Sergeant"—her voice took on Charlotte Jackson's Alabama accent—"what a delight to find that you are even more a philosopher than you are a literary scholar." She held out her hand and Rains automatically helped her up. Bett brushed the grass off her skirt as she continued. "And so gallant. Dare I hope your kind words mean I might be among your favorites?"

She's only teasing, Rains told herself, taking a breath. *Don't overreact. Girls like her have a name for this kind of talk. They do it all the time. It doesn't mean anything. It's only…* She was taking too long to answer and Bett's smile was widening. "There are no favorites, Private. I just take care of my squad members."

Bett tossed her head as if she was not the least bit convinced. "Well, I will certainly take your wise words under advisement. But will you still escort me to the barracks?" she drawled, stepping back on the sidewalk. They started walking again.

"Yes, but I would prefer it if you were speaking like yourself again," Rains bargained. Bett nodded, but it seemed a safe topic so Rains continued. "How can you take on someone else's voice like that? It's like you knowing where they come from. I still don't understand."

"You know how some people find it easy to recall things that they see? They can memorize images or poetry or street maps?" She smiled up at her sergeant. "Or quote readily from a favorite author?" Rains nodded slowly. "Well, I have something of an auditory memory. I can remember almost every voice, every accent, and every dialect I hear. It gets somewhat crowded in here." She tapped the side of her head with a fist. "Reproducing a sound is just a matter of letting my mouth repeat what my ears hear when I think of that accent."

Like imitating animal sounds when hunting, Rains realized, but much more complex because human voices were so varied. Smythe was looking ahead and Rains let herself admire the private for a few seconds. *She's not only beautiful, but also very clever.* Even knowing that she was veering back into a personal matter, the sergeant let curiosity get the better of her. "So can you tell where I come from?"

Bett stopped. By then they were only a few yards from the barracks. "Not precisely, no," she admitted, frowning slightly. "Sometimes I've thought Colorado, and sometimes Nebraska, but the cadence of your speech doesn't really fit either one." She looked at Rains full on. "Don't tell me though," she cautioned, finger up and almost touching Rains's lips. "I want to figure it out myself." Moving a half step closer, so that Rains froze from the nearness of her, Bett added, "I like a challenge, Sergeant. Don't you?"

For a moment, all Rains could register was a slow smile that drew her in like an embrace and those shining blue-green eyes that were part water and part sky. When she made no response, Bett winked and walked on into the barracks. Rains cleared her throat and turned casually, going back toward her own quarters. *Flirting.* That's what they called it.

❖

The next Monday afternoon finally brought the class rotation that Bett had been waiting for. In no time, she was involved in discussion with the officer in charge of the wireless coding system, a Major Ervin. But rather than challenging him, Bett practically turned the class into a one-on-one training session. Even after the class was over, their conversation continued until Ervin said, "You should come see our facility here, Private Smythe. It's in one of the off-base buildings in town that the Army has purchased. Do you have a car?"

"Sorry, no," Bett said, pleased to be invited. "Are you too far to walk?"

"Too far to get there, see the place, and get back by dinner," the Major replied. "I would take you myself but I have another meeting on the base in a few minutes. I could call my second in command, Lieutenant Foster or..." He looked out into the hall. Bett followed his gaze. Sergeant Rains was talking to an attractive auburn-haired woman in a captain's uniform who was leaning casually against the wall. The conversation was obviously not military in nature; Rains was gesturing with big circles and the woman was smiling with genuine interest. Something in the interaction pierced Bett with a stab of jealousy.

Ervin was saying something. "Excuse me?" Bett asked and Major Ervin repeated his suggestion that her sergeant could drive her over. Bett turned back to him and smiled warmly. "What an excellent idea. Could I go now?"

"Of course. Lieutenant Foster can show you around until I get back." Major Ervin walked over to Rains and Bett followed. "Sergeant Rains, could we have a word?" he asked. The redhead stepped away after giving Bett a quick glance. Ervin explained his request.

Rains looked a little concerned. "What time will she be through, sir?"

Bett's jealousy flared again. *She sounds as though she has important plans later.* A quick look confirmed that the captain was lingering down the hall. *Maybe even a date?* Unexpectedly, Bett's thoughts veered to questioning her sergeant's social life. Perhaps the serious manner, her low voice, even her aversion to casual contact might all be explained if she were...

Ervin looked at his watch and replied that she should easily be finished before dinner. He added that he would call Lieutenant Foster, to have him ready to show Bett around until he returned.

Sergeant Rains nodded, saluted, and replied, "Yes, sir. I'll get a Jeep now." She indicated the door to Bett. "Watch for me here, Private." Before she left, Rains looked back at the redhead and lifted her hand briefly. Bett noted that the woman watched Rains as she walked away before leaving by the other door.

When Rains pulled up in the Jeep, Bett made her wait until she saw Rains cut the engine and start toward the building before she walked out. "Sorry, Sergeant. I was in the restroom. I hope you weren't waiting too long."

"Hmm."

As they left the base and headed toward the cryptography building, Rains glanced briefly at the sky, saying, "I'm sure you are excited for this visit, Private, and I know this is your area of interest, but I hope you will keep to the schedule Major Ervin indicated."

"Why is that, Sergeant?" Bett asked, her tone innocent while her insides burned with unanticipated emotion.

"Because I have other responsibilities and I would prefer not to be waiting around all afternoon. I am happy to help you with this appointment but I am not a chauffeur."

Rains sounded a little testy. Bett replied in kind. "Well, Sergeant, I guess you sometimes have to follow orders just like the rest of us."

Bett noted that Rains glanced at her curiously, but she made no reply.

It was well after dinnertime when Bett came out of the building. The evening had cooled. Sergeant Rains had buttoned her jacket and was pacing along the sidewalk. Bett admitted to herself that she could have been through over an hour ago, and she almost felt sorry that she had deliberately kept Rains waiting for so long. But as she walked toward the Jeep, she saw a blanket, a thermos, and a paper sack in the back. It looked as if Rains had prepared for her date while Bett was inside.

"Private Smythe, why are you so late?" Rains asked, her eyes angry.

"There was a lot to see and I had a lot of questions," Bett answered, trying to sound convincing. Rains sighed and looked up at the twilight sky. "Did I interfere with your evening plans, Sergeant?" Bett asked in her sweet tone.

Rains looked back at her suspiciously. "Who said I had evening plans?"

"Don't you?" Bett indicated the blanket.

Rains dug her hands into her pants pockets and rocked back and forth on the balls of her feet for a moment, glancing at Bett from time to time. She looked at the sky once more and seemed to make a decision. "Fine," she said brusquely, and started the Jeep. They drove away from the base, Rains speeding a bit.

"Where are we going?" Bett asked, getting a little worried. Surely Rains wasn't going to drag her along on her date.

"Since you weren't able to keep to your schedule, Private, you're going to have to keep to mine," Rains replied as the city lights disappeared behind them. The air was cooling steadily and Bett shivered, crossing her arms over her chest. Turning off on a dirt road, the sergeant steered with one hand and reached into the back of the Jeep, grabbing the blanket and holding it out to Bett. She wrapped it around herself as they crested a little rise. Rains pulled off the road near some trees and turned off the motor. Silence and near-total darkness covered them quickly.

"Where are we?" Bett asked nervously.

"Just a place I know," Rains answered, picking up the sack and the thermos before getting out and walking briskly toward the trees. She looked back at Bett. "Do you prefer to stay with the vehicle?"

Bett got out and tried to follow Rains into the trees but lost sight of her almost immediately. "Sergeant Rains?"

A disembodied voice replied. "Over here."

Bett had no idea where *here* was. She took a few more steps, but it was so dark that all she could see was the Jeep. She decided she'd rather remain where she was than risk breaking an ankle walking over unknown ground. Making her way slowly back, she was about to get back into the Jeep when a hand touched her shoulder. Bett gasped.

"It's only me, Private." Rains's voice was quiet, but Bett could detect a little derision. "There's really no point in your being here if you're going to miss the show. Come on."

Bett's eyes had adjusted enough that she was able to see Rains's hand stretch out in the darkness. She took it gratefully and let the sergeant guide her through the trees to a part of the rolling hill that overlooked the horizon.

"Sit here." Rains pointed at the edge of a clearing. Bett did. Rains sat surprisingly close, leaning her back against the tree nearest to Bett.

The stillness suggested that there wasn't another soul around. Bett breathed in the clear evening air, getting over her jitters. "What are we doing here?" she asked.

"You'll see." Rains opened the thermos and poured, offering Bett the cup.

Bett sipped warily. It was hot tea, her nonalcoholic drink of choice. She smiled at Rains gratefully. "I don't suppose you brought dinner, too?"

Rains took a single sandwich from the paper bag and pulled it in half, handing Bett the bigger part.

"No, really, Sergeant, I was only joking." Bett knew it was her fault that neither of them had eaten. But Rains gestured with the sandwich half again and Bett's stomach convinced her to take it. Only one sandwich, she thought, feeling a little silly. She wasn't meeting anyone. Was that also relief she felt?

Her drill instructor pulled an orange from her jacket pocket, wagging it in Bett's direction. "Do you know how to peel one of these, Private Smythe?" she asked, one eyebrow cocked, her eyes light with amusement.

Bett was delighted. For the sergeant to display a sense of humor was unusual; for her to tease so personally was special. "Um"—Bett feigned uncertainty, taking the fruit and examining it carefully— "I'm not sure." She lifted her eyes, pretending to offer the orange back to Rains. "Perhaps you could show me?"

"Sure, having me do all the work seems to solve everything, doesn't it?" Rain replied easily and Bett laughed as she started peeling. When the fruit was divided, Rains topped off Bett's cup and leaned back against the tree again, eating and drinking from the thermos with a contented expression on her face. After a few moments, she sat up straight and looked out at the horizon. "Watch there," she pointed, and in a moment Bett saw a broad edge of light coming up.

"What is that?" she whispered.

"*Haŋwí*," Rain answered softly.

"What?"

"The moon," Rains said a little louder, as if she was repeating, but Bett knew it wasn't the same word she had said before.

As they watched, the light turned into a curve of whiteness. The moon seemed to be at least ten times its normal size, bigger and brighter than Bett had ever seen. She looked over at her sergeant, questions on her lips, but the expression on Rains's face quieted her. Rains looked almost reverent, and Bett didn't want to be an aggravation. As the spectacle of the rising moon continued, Bett unwrapped the blanket from around herself and moved close enough that she could put half of it around Rains. Then she leaned her head against Rains's shoulder.

"Stop that, Private," Rains said, shocked at Smythe's familiarity.

"No," Bett replied. Rains gathered herself to move away but Bett grabbed her arm under the blanket. "I promise I'm not going to do another thing but sit here with you like this, okay? Please, Rains. Don't you need to feel something earthly when you're watching this kind of beauty? I'm afraid I might float away if I'm not grounded."

Ignoring the more informal use of her name, Rains turned her eyes away from Bett. She didn't want to admit that she sat with her back against a tree for that exact reason. She didn't move or speak, trying to ease the tension in her body. Bett stayed very still, and after a bit, the sergeant returned her attention to the moon. It was an incredible sight, awing them both into stillness. Before too long, Rains became accustomed to the weight of Bett's head against her; it was a nice counter to the tree at her back. When Bett sighed and stretched her arm across Rains's waist, it felt secure, like a wrap holding her to the earth. A few minutes later, Rains began rocking ever so slightly, her chest vibrating as she hummed softly. When the big moon had gotten all the way up and was continuing its ascent into the sky, Rains turned her head to look at Smythe's face, so close to her own. Bett's eyes were closed, her breathing deep and steady.

Rains was moving Smythe's arm away from her when Bett mumbled, "No, I want to stay with you." Rains wasn't ready to leave but she was worried that the private would strain her neck sleeping at that angle. After a moment of consideration, Rains slowly lowered her until Bett's head was on her lap, her face up, making sure the blanket still covered her legs.

"Mm." Bett relaxed again as Rains brushed her hair back in a gesture that felt completely natural. In the quiet moonlight, Rains studied Bett's face with a leisure that she never had before. A person of such contradictions, she thought. Smart but silly; determined but lazy; capable but casual; beautiful... Well, there was no contradiction to that. There wasn't a male officer on the base who hadn't noticed Elizabeth Smythe, and many of the women knew who she was as well. It might have been the classic features of her face that drew casual attention, but Rains saw much more in her than that. Bett carried herself with a kind of stately grace, appearing almost untouchable, but when she engaged with someone, her wide range of emotions were very close to the surface—quite the opposite of how Rains conducted herself. The tone of Smythe's voice, her gestures, and the expression in her eyes could take any conversation from comedic to tragic, from biting to gentle, from noncommittal to intensely engaged and back again in seconds. Rains had experienced some of these personally, and what puzzled her the most was when Bett touched her or looked at her so searchingly or spoke to her with such warmth. *Surely she doesn't have a heart for another woman, so what is this emotion between us?* Rains asked herself. She still thought of it as flirting, but often Smythe brought a level of closeness to their time together that seemed like something more than silly girl play. Rains knew that the appeal had nothing to do with her command rank. It wasn't hero worship as sometimes happened with her recruits. She couldn't think of another private who was as argumentative or as likely to try to disregard an order.

Sergeant Rains rarely looked in mirrors other than to check the look of her uniform because she knew what she would see. Her face had filled out some since that terrible Nebraska winter but her cheekbones were still prominent, her forehead broad under her bangs, her nose straight, like her father's, and her eyes and mouth wide, more like her mother. *Beautiful* was not a word that would apply to her; her face was too angular for that. But there had been those who apparently found her attractive, whether for her face or her body Rains didn't know. And it didn't matter, because she had never let their attraction to her become mutual. She would admit that sometimes it felt flattering when someone's eyes lingered on her, but more often it was just a nuisance. A recruit would have to be ignored or redirected, another officer she would avoid or harden herself to. And even though a face or a figure might occasionally make her look twice, it was just easier to look the other way, to remain unavailable, to let opportunities for such connections fade. Several years ago she had been told by her healer to keep her heart ready and not give up, but Rains had found enough comfort in the routine and discipline of Army life, enough satisfaction in doing her job well and with pride. Until now. There was something about Elizabeth Smythe that made her bend the rules—not only the Army's, but her own.

Rains looked at the moon again. It was almost back to normal size as it made its way up into the heavens. She realized that she was still stroking Bett's hair. It felt full and soft in her fingers. Involuntarily, she thought of the other times they had touched: that first unguarded moment of electricity as Bett had brushed her arm when she offered to take the baseball bats, Bett's hand on her arm, her face close, when she was leaving KP, slipping the ring onto her finger, and the time after the squad leader meeting when she had taken Bett's hands. Each occurrence was uncomfortably vivid in her mind.

At least she was away from the base now, but to revisit those moments with Bett lying asleep on her lap was more than foolish. It was dangerous. Dangerous because she couldn't seem to break the connection that continued to develop between them. Dangerous because she wouldn't delude herself by pretending that she didn't find her time with Bett very…agreeable. Not Bett, Rains reminded herself sternly, trying to adjust her thinking. Private Smythe. Rains took her hand away from Smythe's hair. As if she was missing the touch, Bett sighed and turned, so she was facing into Rains's body. Rains fixed her eyes on the moon again. Gradually, she began to feel Bett's breath warming her pants. Rains closed her eyes until the warmth became a wanting between her legs.

"Private." She shook Smythe gently, though her voice was rough. "We must get back to the base. It's getting late."

A little groan of protest. Rains was going to shake her again, but then Bett's eyes opened. She sat up and faced Rains, smiling lazily. Rains felt an unexpected tug in her heart, which quickly turned to unease. Smythe's voice was soft with sleep. "I'm sorry, Sergeant. I haven't been sleeping very well in the barracks. I guess I'm still adapting to having so many roommates. Did I miss the rest of the show?"

"Yes. And you must wake up now. We need to go." Rains was trying to sound strict but wasn't sure she didn't just sound nervous.

Much to her relief, Bett yawned and rubbed her eyes. But then she leaned back against Rains's shoulder, her face close again. Rains felt her heart began to beat faster, but she carefully kept her breathing normal.

"You make a very nice pillow. Thank you for keeping me warm."

"That was the blanket, not me," Rains said, trying to get her feet under her so she could move away.

"Oh no," Bett insisted, yawning again and rubbing her head against Rains like a cat as she stretched her neck. "Perhaps you don't realize how much heat your body puts out. You're very radiant, like an oven."

"All right, Private, but I need to stand up now." Rains's agitation was growing. There had been entirely too much physical contact between them this night. She turned away quickly, stood, and stretched. Clearing her throat, she picked up the thermos and wrapped the orange peels in the sandwich paper before looking back at Bett.

Bett held out her hand and Rains helped her up. The bright moonlight made it easier to see, but Bett was still quite tentative as they started back toward the Jeep. Intending to hurry her along, Rain offered her hand again. Bett took it and guided it around her back, setting Rains's hand on her waist. She walked with her body close to Rains, a feeling that had already become much too pleasant.

"I want you to know that I'm aware of your efforts this past week, Private," Rains said, trying to sound more like a drill instructor and less like someone thinking about the curve of Bett's body. "You have been much less confrontational and very attentive in all your sessions."

"So was this my reward?" Smythe asked. Rains could hear the smile in her voice.

"No, no. This was just...coincidence. It just so happened that I already had the Jeep as you know, and I wanted to see this moon, and then when you were so late, I knew I couldn't get you back to the base and make it out here in time so I just...brought you." Rains was conscious that she was practically chattering and stopped as soon as they reached the Jeep.

Rains disengaged herself but Smythe made no move to get in. Instead she turned so they were facing each other. With the moonlight on her face, Rains thought she looked even more beautiful than usual. Rains realized she must have let something of her thoughts show, because Bett smiled knowingly and took Rains's left hand in her right, gently caressing the sergeant's bare fingers.

"I notice you're not wearing a ring, Sergeant. Is this an anti-jewelry principle on your part or are you truly not spoken for?"

Rains's hand gave a little jerk to escape, but Bett tightened her grip slightly and stepped closer, looking intently into Rains's eyes. There was no more resistance. She watched as Rains's lips parted slightly, and then her fingers began to respond, her thumb stroking Bett's palm. Bett saw Rains's eyes grow slightly unfocused and thought, *She's actually letting herself feel something, probably for the first time in a long time.*

Bett wondered if her stern sergeant would consider letting the beautiful moon set the scene for an erotic episode where she would guide Bett's hand down to cup her sex while she fondled Bett's breast that she'd surely noticed straining so nicely against her uniform every day at exercise. Wouldn't she bring her mouth to Bett's and taste with her tongue as their bodies crushed together...?

The bright moonlight dimmed suddenly and they both looked up. A cloud was passing over. Rains freed her hand, stepped around Bett quickly, and opened the door of the Jeep. She cleared her throat again. "Please get in the vehicle, Private." Her voice was deeper than Bett had ever heard it.

"Are you sure that's what you want me to do, Sergeant?" Bett tried, thinking that it had also been quite a while since she had felt something that pleasurable. Maybe things could get even more enjoyable, she thought, remembering Rains's deeply muscled arms. Oh yes, she acknowledged to herself without much surprise as she ran her gaze quickly down Rains's body, thinking of her heat and her gentle touch. She was definitely interested.

Rains gave one quick, definite nod and stepped back. Too bad. Smythe sighed as she got in and closed the door. For a moment Rains didn't appear on the other side. Bett looked around but couldn't see her anywhere, but she thought she heard pacing footsteps behind the Jeep.

Finally the door opened and Sergeant Rains got in. For a moment she just sat. Then she cleared her throat once more. "Again I have done you a disservice, Private Smythe. I was wrong to bring you on a nonmilitary outing. I should have taken us both back to the base when you finished at the cryptography building. I have acted most unprofessionally and I think I may have given you a wrong impression of myself."

"Please don't apologize, Sergeant Rains," Bett said smoothly. "I'm sure I haven't had a nicer time in recent memory. The moon was spectacular and you were wonderful company as always." She could hear that Rains's voice conveyed some anxiety, but she couldn't help giggling. "And don't worry. I'll still respect you in the morning." Rains started the engine and began driving without comment. Bett waited until they were back on the main highway before she said, "But you never answered my question, Sergeant." Rains didn't respond. "About the ring," Bett prompted. But the sergeant drove without speaking until they were parked by the barracks.

Then she turned to Bett, her face partly obscured by the nighttime shadows. "I have too many competing voices to answer you well, Private Smythe. And you may laugh, but I have no respect for myself right now."

Bett could hear the strain in Rains's voice. *Stop playing with her,* she told herself. *She's been nothing but kind to you.* Her tone turned sincere. "Sergeant Rains, I'm sorry for teasing you. But please don't be so hard on yourself. You haven't done anything wrong. Just because you let yourself feel something nice for once—"

Rains cut her off. "It is not my job to feel something nice. My job is to be your sergeant, not..."

Bett waited, but Rains didn't finish. After a few seconds she got out, came around, and opened Bett's door. At first Bett thought that she was being mannerly; then she realized that Rains was just trying to get her out of the Jeep without any further conversation.

"You are dismissed, Private." She shifted her feet, ready to be gone, and didn't meet Bett's eyes.

Bett sighed. She wanted very much to take Rains's hand again, to make her understand that the evening had been something delightful just between them and that a repeat or even something more would be most welcome, but she could see that the sergeant had withdrawn into her Army mode and wouldn't respond well. Still, she had to try. Standing tall, if not quite at attention, she risked a quick look at Rains's face. "For what it's worth, Sergeant, spending time with you has been the best part of basic training for me."

Rains did meet her eyes then, for just a second, and Bett even thought she might have seen that shadow of a smile. "I am most certainly doing something wrong then," she said and Bett giggled again.

The sergeant got back in the Jeep without another word and drove off quickly.

Bett went into the barracks and made up a story about being at a dinner with some of the officers from cryptography, which elicited many oohs and ahhs from Charlotte and Phyllis and Barbara. *Can't imagine what they'd say if I described what really happened,* Bett thought. *Which is, of course, one reason why Sergeant Rains reacted the way she did.* Once in her bed, she pretended to read while wondering about what had upset Rains more—spending the evening being close to someone or letting herself enjoy it. That was one thing Bett was fairly certain of...Sergeant Rains had enjoyed herself, at least for that one moment. *And oh yes, indeed,* Bett admitted, *so did I.*

As the squad leader, she was supposed to be in charge of the barracks lights when Rains wasn't there, but since Jo's bunk was the lower one, they had agreed that Jo would do it. When lights out gave her the closest thing to privacy, Bett felt free to replay more of the evening. It was true, she admitted, that she was finding Sergeant Rains increasingly attractive. Of course she had noticed Rains's lean, well-muscled physique almost from the beginning, but now she was being drawn by those few moments when she had gotten beyond Rains's carefully controlled leadership persona to an appealing mix of tenderness and depth of feeling. In that depth, Bett understood, there was much unknown in her sergeant, but she couldn't shake the feeling of something there she wanted.

In her past, just being ready for sex was enough to make Bett go after someone she found appealing—or even simply available. There was nothing like the chase. Bett smiled to herself, thinking of the many successful seductions she'd enjoyed in her first years at Oxford. Was it just Rains's inaccessibility that made her so enticing? No, there were plenty of women around her that were apparently unapproachable in that way, though Bett's experiences had made her believe that almost any woman could be had by another woman—at least on a one-time basis. She pulled her mind back to the fabulous moon and Rains's touch, which had been so sweetly appealing—as if she cared, like a mother or a sister or a best friend—that just thinking of it made Bett relax. But in that one moment just before the moonlight dimmed, there had been something more in the touch of their hands, something real, some intensity, something...Bett fell asleep trying to figure out how to describe that look in Rains's eyes.

❖

Rains returned the Jeep to the motor pool. The process seemed to take a long time. As she waited for the checkout, she noticed the mess in the offices, the rusted parts around the floor of the bays, and scattered tools. Nothing seemed very neat or organized, the way she expected things in the Army to run, but this wasn't her first negative experience in the motor pool. Finally, one of the privates who was still working brought her paperwork around.

She walked slowly toward her room. She didn't feel like running, but she didn't really feel like sleeping either. She wandered over to the parade grounds and sat high on the bleachers. The late-evening temperature was now even cooler and she started to wrap up in the blanket. Then it occurred to her that it had last been around Smythe's body. She brought the blanket to her face and sniffed... Yes, there it was, that scent that was becoming entirely too familiar. Only now it was also tied in her mind to the sound of that fascinating accent—*spending time with you has been the best part of basic training for me*—and the weight of Bett's arm around her waist, the sensitive touch of her fingers. Rains put her head in her hands and tried to work her way through her thoughts. Why was it Elizabeth Smythe, of all people, who was bringing out these feelings?

In their meeting before Smythe's arrival, Colonel Issacson had clearly stated her conviction that Carlton/Smythe had joined the WAC as a lark, and she had no business in the service. But in these first few weeks, Rains had seen something more in Private Smythe than a rich girl trying out a different life just for the fun of it. She showed a surprising determination to succeed and a genuine willingness to work with others, no matter their social status. Rains was fairly certain that Smythe would complete her basic training— unless that stubbornness or fiercely independent streak got her into serious trouble—and it now appeared that she would be awarded her desired position in cryptography.

All of that was well and good, but what of this emotion, this attraction between them? Why did her heart quicken when Smythe came into her field of vision on the parade ground or in the barracks? Why were the memories of the moments between the two of them the last thing she thought of at night? Straightening, Rains shifted her thoughts. None of these questions mattered. It would be a great deterrent to Smythe's training to allow her familiar manner to continue or to let the time between them be anything other than official business. Rains knew herself well enough to believe in her own integrity as a sergeant. Didn't she also have the strength to put her personal feelings aside and simply do what it took to get Smythe through her basic training? *It's no harder than being Lakota in a White world*, a voice inside answered her. Rains stood. Of course. All the passion of these confusing emotions that she was feeling was from the White world. She needed to turn back toward her Sioux heritage to find the balance. When she got back to her room in the officer's quarters, she burned some sage and chanted quietly for a while. When she fell asleep, she was feeling the cold of a familiar South Dakota landscape inside. She felt shielded again.

CHAPTER SIX

Rains's cool invulnerability lasted only until the next morning, when she gathered her squad as usual and marched them to the mess hall for their first meal of the day. It was her custom to hold the door for them, and the last two through were Smythe and Jo Archer.

"Thank you, Sergeant Rains," Bett said, going in first, but not before her eyes met Rains's for an instant.

"Did you see that moon last night, Sarge?" Archer asked.

"Uh, yes, I did, Private Archer," Rains replied hesitantly, wondering what Bett's glance had meant.

"That was something, wasn't it?" Archer said, as Rains followed them into the room. She gestured toward Bett with her thumb. "Queenie here missed it because she was having dinner with those guys from wireless."

It took Rains a few seconds to understand that Bett had made up a story so she wouldn't have to tell her squad that they had been together. She played along. "Ah, yes. How was your evening, Private Smythe?" Archer moved around them to get in the chow line.

"It was lovely, thank you, Sergeant." Bett smiled and deliberately adjusted the rings on her hands for a few seconds before bringing her eyes back to Rains. "I still have a few unanswered questions but I feel really good about my chances."

Rains raised her eyebrows.

"About getting in," Bett added.

Rains blinked.

"To the program, Sergeant," Bett clarified. "What else could you be thinking?" Her smile deepened and Rains felt the ice inside her crack.

She is shamelessly flirting with you in the middle of the mess hall. Before breakfast! Rains tried to find some semblance of authority in the midst an unfamiliar vibration that was running through her stomach. "It's good that you have confidence in your abilities, Private, but you must also know your limits. And the limits of those…situations…around you."

"Didn't you once say that you should always bring your best effort to getting what you want?" Smythe countered, obviously enjoying herself.

"I believe I said you should bring your best effort to what you do," Sergeant Rains said, shifting her weight as she rubbed her palms together, needing to do something with her hands since they seemed to have their own memory of touching that golden hair. "That may not seem like much of a difference to you, Private Smythe, but for me there is a vast gulf between what may be wanted and what is done."

Bett had stopped smiling, and in spite of having meant what she said, Rains was sorry to have caused the change in her countenance. She crossed her arms, strengthening her control. "If it is acceptable to you, I'd like to convene at the bleachers on the parade grounds for our squad leader meeting on Friday. At that time, I'd like your assessment of each squad member's progress so far."

Bett nodded. "Of course, Sergeant Rains." She entered the line without another word.

Rains turned away and went toward the officers' table. She was sipping her tea when she heard a voice behind her. "Thank you for the tip about the moon, Sergeant Rains. It was truly spectacular."

It was Kathleen Hartley, the auburn-haired captain she had been talking to yesterday while the squad had their wireless class. Hartley was a recent addition to the base, and there was something about her Rains liked. Even though she outranked her, Hartley never talked down to Rains or made her feel unimportant. "We had a great view from our place. It's a little ways outside of town, you know." Hartley knelt a little closer than Rains would have liked and her voice dropped slightly. "Maybe you could come out for dinner sometime, Sergeant."

Rains tried to control her surprise at the invitation, and then she reminded herself that Hartley was new. The others had stopped asking long ago. "That's very kind of you, Captain, but I don't go out much." *At all, actually.* Rains felt very awkward in social situations where there was no Army protocol to tell her what to do. She was not good at meaningless small talk.

Hartley stood, tilting her head. "Well, I hope you'll consider making an exception for us sometime."

Rains caught the use of the plural and wondered why. But she merely nodded. Hartley hesitated and then left to go sit at the other end of the table, where Major Wilson was waving her over. When Rains looked, she saw that Bett had taken her seat and had apparently been watching the exchange.

For the next two days, Bett stayed near the rear of the platoon for exercise and drills. She was gratified to see that Rains looked three times at the place where she usually lined up before her eyes found Bett in the back. Bett's mood went from being hurt by what Rains had said about the difference between wanting and doing, to being upset with her for talking with that captain again. Then she would be mad at herself for giving a damn either way. She couldn't seem to find a comfortable place for Rains in her thoughts or her feelings. Whenever she considered going into full-out seduction—*just have her and you'll get over it*—she would see the sergeant working with one of the other girls and could almost feel Rains's power as she gently molded them to the Army way...her Army way, actually.

Rains never criticized when she could praise. If a reprimand was absolutely required, she had a way of turning the tables so most recruits guilelessly corrected themselves. The more distressed or anxious someone became, the calmer and steadier Rains's manner. Much as she hated to admit it, Bett was pretty sure her practiced proposition for quick, raw sex wouldn't influence that kind of disciplined character. But what moved her the most were the times she happened to catch a glimpse of her sergeant walking unaccompanied across the grounds. Other officers almost always seemed to travel in groups of twos and threes, probably to seem more threatening to the new recruits, but Rains was always alone. She would salute, of course, and sometime exchange a word or two with others that she passed, but she never joined any group. Bett wondered if Rains was truly happy in her isolation or if she ever secretly wished to have company.

In spite of her high-society upbringing and her generally social nature, Bett also understood about the depths of a reclusive soul. Most of her last year at Oxford had been spent in solitary pursuits: researching, preparing papers, and trying to recover her whole self again. Sergeant Rains appeared completely self-contained, but Bett wondered if what she guarded so carefully was some kind of loneliness or loss. What settled in Bett was something beyond simple desire. Respect and appreciation, yes, but something else that she couldn't quite identify. Whatever it was, it also came with a keen sense of longing for Rains's company.

Just when she was beginning to wonder if Rains was going to ignore her for the rest of basic training, the sergeant stopped at her bunk early Thursday evening just before lights out. Bett was lying on her stomach, reading, and Rains's face was just a little above hers.

"Private Smythe, I wanted you to know that several instructors have commented on the improvement in Helen's and Tee's work. I'm aware you have continued to tutor them, even after your KP time was up, and I wanted to commend you for your effort."

Bett closed the book. "Why, thank you, Sergeant. I'm very glad to hear that. I must confess though, I've enjoyed working with them probably more than what they've gotten from my instruction."

Rains nodded. "Thoreau said, *We should seek to be fellow students with the pupil, and should learn of, as well as with him, if we would be most helpful to him.* I'm glad you have had that experience."

Bett smiled. *I've missed talking to you*, she wanted to say. She looked down at the novel in her hand. *Is that all there is to it? Do I simply like being around her? Will we just be friends?*

As if reading Bett's thoughts, the sergeant delayed there, brushing some imaginary dust off the frame of Bett's bunk. "What are you reading?" she asked.

"*The Age of Reason* by Jean-Paul Sartre. As you're a fan of philosophy, you might enjoy it. If you'd like, I'll loan it to you when I'm finished."

"Isn't it a library book?" Rains asked.

"No, I bought it." Sergeant Rains's eyebrows went up questioningly. "You see, I belong to a book club and they send me books each month. I can pay if I decide I want them or send them back if I don't, but I knew I'd want this one." She held the book out for Rains to take. Her bookmark was about halfway through.

"Can you already tell his premise?" Rains asked, examining the cover and flipping through the first few pages.

"Oh yes. Even though it's a novel, it's about his view of freedom. One of his notions is that ultimately a person's freedom is unassailable as it is fundamentally part of the imagination and so cannot be taken away or destroyed."

Rains continued looking thoughtfully at the pages. "If that view assumes that the person's mind is intact, I would agree up to that point." She turned to hand the book back to Bett who was still lying on her stomach, but now leaning on her elbows. Rains's eyes lingered in the V-neck of her pajamas for several extra seconds before she blushed and looked away.

Oh, that was much more than an accidental glance. Bett almost laughed to herself when she realized what the sergeant had seen. "Yes, the imagination is a wonderful thing, but sometimes reality can be even more enjoyable, don't you think?" she asked, her tone not entirely innocent.

Rains was saved from a reply when Jo's sleepy voice drifted up from the bunk below. "What in the world are youse guys talking about?"

"Would you consider that stealing second base, Sergeant?" Bett asked softly, thinking, *I wonder if you liked what you saw, Rains.*

Another night like the one with the moon and I might be willing to show you a lot more.

Rains cleared her throat and walked toward the door. "Don't forget your report for me at our meeting tomorrow, Private," she said, her voice a little huskier than usual. She put her hand on the switch. "Lights out, squad."

"Good night, Sergeant," they all responded.

❖

It was raining on Friday morning, but by the afternoon it had cleared off and there was a definite sense of fall in the air. There was talk of a VIP visit soon, so Sergeant Rains drilled her squad longer than usual. The First Lady had already been to Fort Des Moines, as had many other dignitaries and celebrities as well as the national press, but the Women's Army Corps always wanted to look their best for any visitor who might drop by. Bett thought all the marching was really a rather foolish waste of time, but she didn't want to make her squad look bad, so she tried to pay attention to Rains's commands and keep in step. When the afternoon was over, there was a line for the shower, so Bett decided to skip it and just go to dinner on her own. Arriving earlier than usual, she was the first one at her table, and she saw some different people at the officers' table, including the hefty dark-haired lieutenant who had done the training on munitions.

The lieutenant got up and came over. "You were in my class a couple of weeks ago, eh, Private?" she drawled.

"Yes, Lieutenant," Bett said pleasantly. "You did an interesting presentation."

"So, you thinking about munitions maybe?" the lieutenant asked, resting her ample hip on the edge of the table and leaning closer. "Would you like to see the rifle range?"

Even though the question was completely reasonable, Bett had the distinct feeling the lieutenant was actually suggesting something else. Before she could respond, she heard Rains's voice from behind her.

"Private Smythe has a meeting with me this evening, Lieutenant Boudreaux. If she wishes to take you up on your offer, it will have to be another time."

"All right, Rains, all right," Lieutenant Boudreaux said, getting off the table quickly and backing away a bit, waving her hands appeasingly. "Some other time, then?" she said to Bett.

"Thank you, Lieutenant, but I've rather got my heart set on going into wireless," Bett answered, turning to look at Rains. The sergeant was looking at Boudreaux with an expression so dark that Bett stood and put her hand on Rains's arm to distract her. "Shall we go, Sergeant Rains?" That Rains didn't even react to her hand told Bett that something was definitely wrong. Only after Boudreaux had turned and started back to her table did Rains's eyes turn to Bett. She nodded and her expression relaxed. Bett left her food sitting on the table and they walked out, toward the parade grounds.

"So tell me why I shouldn't go to the rifle range with Lieutenant Boudreaux," Bett asked lightly after they had cleared the crowds headed toward the mess hall.

Rains looked at her with alarm. "I hope you are not considering that, Private Symthe."

Bett had to smile; Rains took everything so literally. "Not for a moment. But I would like to know why you so obviously dislike her."

"By my judgment," Rains said after a brief pause, "Lieutenant Boudreaux is not a person of good character."

"In what way?"

Now there was a very long pause. They had reached the parade grounds, but Rains kept walking. Bett followed, wondering if her sergeant was ever going to answer.

Finally she looked at Bett briefly and spoke with an undertone of anger in her voice. "Lieutenant Boudreaux is a seducer of young women. I have come to know of at least three instances where this has happened or been attempted. The way I first found out was with a girl from my squad. This girl was genuinely interested in munitions so she had reason to spend time there, as when you visited the wireless facility, yes? She was also very young, barely twenty-one, and from a sheltered background. Boudreaux is in a position of power there, so I'm sure it was easy for her to…"

Seeing the anger in Rains's eyes, Bett nodded her understanding.

They had reached a large grove of trees on the far side of the base. Rains stopped walking and faced Bett. "I wouldn't normally speak of these things to a private, but she clearly had her eye on you after your class that day. You should know that she was also…uh… seeing another officer here, a good person who certainly had no idea of Boudreaux's other activities."

Bett felt her own anger well up. "So why didn't you report her? Or at least tell the other person what was going on?"

Rains shifted uneasily. "There is an unwritten code between officers. We prefer to handle such things among ourselves whenever possible. But when I confronted Boudreaux about this, I made it clear I would turn her in if something like that ever happened again."

"So what happened with the girl from your squad?"

"At first she was too upset or ashamed to explain what had happened," Rains answered. "Her encounter with Boudreaux was not the way she would choose to be with someone." She glanced at Bett again. "Do you understand what I mean?"

Bett considered this. "Do you mean that she wasn't homosexual?"

Rains flinched a bit and Bett could see she was uncomfortable with the term. "Yes."

"But that's not the point, is it?" Bett replied. "What happened wasn't about sex, it was about power, and that makes it rape."

The sergeant nodded with relief. "Yes, I agree with you, but I'm not sure if the Army would see it that way. In any case, I had begun to notice changes in the girl's behavior. She began to frequent the NCO club with a variety of escorts and was clearly drunk on several occasions. Her work and her appearance suffered. When I spoke to her privately, she finally broke down and told me everything. It took me a long time to convince her that what had happened was not her fault. Then I asked her if she wanted to press charges, but she was too frightened of Boudreaux and of an Army investigation. She asked me to just make sure that she didn't have to go back to munitions, and we decided she might enjoy meteorology instead. She is doing very well there."

Bett was still angry. "But Boudreaux got away scot-free."

"In terms of official punishment, yes," Rain replied, lifting her head just a bit. "But when I confronted her, I did so in the presence of many other officers. I believe her reputation here has been significantly affected. And it is my understanding that her... relationship...with the other officer also ended as a result."

"Good," Bett said. Then she glanced warily at the trees. "So what are we doing here, Sergeant?"

The area referred to as *the grove* by the WACs was a sizable corner on the far edge of the base that had been deliberately left in its natural state. There was little undergrowth, due to its occasional use for specialized training or even overnight bivouacs, but the good-sized shrubs and mature trees still lent a sense of wildness to the place. That feeling, plus its reputation as a place where illicit dates often occurred, made Bett wonder if she could possibly have misjudged her sergeant's intentions.

"I—I had planned..." Rains looked around and then flushed, clearly embarrassed. "But given our current conversation, I don't think..." She paced in a quick little circle and then looked back the way they had come. "No. No, I think we can get back to the mess hall and still get dinner if we hurry."

Bett looked at her curiously, unused to seeing her sergeant so obviously rattled. "Whatever is the matter?"

Rains ducked behind one of the trees and picked up a knapsack. "Let's go back."

Bett crossed her arms. "No. Not until you tell me what is going on."

Rains sighed and looked restlessly from side to side, not meeting Bett's eyes. "I had thought we might eat here where it's quiet while we talked about the squad. It's a nice evening and I like to be outside, so I brought some food. But having just talked about Boudreaux, I am seeing this idea in a different light and it doesn't look good. I wouldn't want you to think that I..." She let her gaze settle on Bett.

Bett smiled. "Do you mean I might think that you are trying to seduce me, like Lieutenant Boudreaux would?"

Rains glanced down for a moment, her uneasiness persisting. "After all, I am in a position of power over you"—she looked back at Bett with her almost imperceptible smile—"even though you often don't recognize it as such." Bett tossed her head. Rains's voice grew solemn again and her expression uneasy. "But there have been other occasions where we have been alone together. Some evidence might suggest something inappropriate—"

Bett cut her off. "Only someone who doesn't know you would think such a thing, Sergeant. Under oath or otherwise, I would freely acknowledge that I am the one who has initiated what little physical contact there has been between us. You have been the model of military decorum, despite my occasional efforts to the contrary."

Rains looked down, feeling her face grow warm. It made her nervous when Smythe's voice took on this flirtatious tone. *It doesn't mean anything,* she reminded herself. *It's just the way girls like her talk sometimes.*

Bett continued, "And other than a brief visit by Colonel Issacson to the mess hall, after which you left and were seen by others away from me, there is no evidence of our time together."

"Yes, well, I also wanted to thank you for not saying anything about the other night and the moon," Rains added quietly, still speaking to the ground, conflicted about exactly what she meant by that statement.

"So are you going to feed me, then?" Bett asked, hands on her hips in mock exasperation.

Rains cleared her throat, knelt, and began taking things out of the knapsack. She spread a blanket, took out plates and several containers of food.

Bett sat and let the sergeant serve her, smiling to herself about the irony of it all. *Clearly she doesn't realize how much I'd enjoy seducing her.* With the protection of her rank and her formal manner, Rains always managed to keep just enough of a wall between them. Bett decided there was plenty of time later for her to plot about how to get that wall down. For now, she would just let the evening unfold.

She looked at all the food. "Goodness, you must think you're feeding the whole squad."

Rains ducked her head a bit. "Well, the other night I didn't have much to offer you, and I've always believed that hospitality is very important."

"Did you fix all this?"

"No, we don't have kitchen facilities in the officers' quarters. I do like to cook, though I don't make anything fancy. A former squad member who works in the kitchen fixed this for me." She picked up an apple. "I thought the fruit looked especially good. Would you like this cut?"

Bett nodded and Rains reached around, pulling a knife from beneath the back of her jacket. It was a bright, broad blade, about five inches long with a beaded handle. Bett's eyes widened. "Do you always carry that weapon with you, Sergeant? It doesn't look like Army issue."

"Not always, but usually. And no, it isn't GI. It was my brother's and when I learned to use it well, he let me keep it. It's good to have a knife in the woods and good to know how to use one when you are by yourself." She finished cutting the apple.

"So how would you use it if someone was sneaking up behind you?" Bett asked, still staring at the blade. Rains turned and with barely a flick of her wrist sent the knife flying into the trunk of a tree fifteen feet away. "Remind me to always announce myself to you," Bett said faintly, as Rains got up to retrieve the knife. Bett watched as she smoothed back the bark after pulling out the blade and heard her say something softly before giving the tree a final pat. When she returned and sat, Bett cocked her head and asked, "What did you just do?"

After a slight pause, Rains said, "I apologized for hurting the tree and sent it healing thoughts."

"Do you think the tree felt pain?"

"Not in the way that we do, no. But at some primal level, I think all living things know when they have been injured. Therefore it is not our place to do so lightly. Thoreau said, *The squirrel that you kill in jest, dies in earnest.*"

"And have you killed many squirrels?" Bett asked, half teasing.

The sergeant grimaced. "Squirrel is not my favorite, but yes, I have killed some. For most of my life before the Army I hunted so I could eat and I have never taken a kill casually or without giving thanks for its life. To do so would be disrespectful of its spirit."

They ate in silence for a moment while Bett tried to imagine a life where you had to hunt each day or you would go hungry. She was genuinely intrigued by Rains's experiences and was about to ask about her Indian background when Rains said, "Oh, I almost forgot!" and produced two miniature bottles of Coca-Cola from the knapsack.

Bett laughed. "Where did you get those?"

"Last year the Coca-Cola Company made their one billionth gallon of syrup and they sent out cases to different armed forces locations. We got some here and I've been saving mine for a special occasion."

"I'm very flattered, Sergeant. How am I your special occasion?"

Rains looked a little uneasy again, but she nodded. "By my count you've gone an entire week without getting a demerit, something I never managed to accomplish. I think that's worth celebrating."

"Well, I'm all for that," Bett said cheerfully, "but did you bring a bottle opener?"

Rains's knife was still lying on her plate. She picked it up and pried the point under one of the bottle caps, steadying the bottle between her knees. The cap flew off as she flexed the knife and she caught it in her other hand on its way up.

Bett shook her head, smiling. "Now you're just showing off." Rains looked away for a second and Bett thought she might be smiling, too.

"Cheers," the sergeant said after she had opened her drink, clinking her bottle against Bett's.

"Oh, we must have something more profound for your special occasion." Bett thought for a few seconds. "Here's to learning the ropes without becoming unraveled."

"Very clever, Private Smythe." Sergeant Rains clinked again and took a small sip. Bett did the same. They were quiet for a moment. "I don't really like Coca-Cola," Rains admitted.

Bett laughed. "Neither do I. Too sweet."

Rains reached back into the knapsack and brought out the thermos. "Tea, then?"

"Lovely, thank you."

They ate quietly for a few moments, the silence easy between them. Why did food always taste better outside, Bett wondered idly, or was it the company? She let her gaze run over Rains's long body, coming to rest on her face, before acknowledging to herself that Sergeant Rains really was her favorite person on the base. She was very fond of the girls in her squad and she knew they liked her as well, but being around Rains was different in a way Bett still hadn't quite identified. Certainly there was a physical attraction, at least on her part, but there was also something else, something more. At times she thought there was a hint of her feelings being reciprocated, but the sergeant was so good about hiding her emotions that Bett wasn't completely certain, an unusual experience for her.

Just then, Rains looked over and Bett dropped her eyes. "Would you like something else?" the sergeant asked.

Yes, but I'm not quite sure what. Relationship-wise, she'd begun her time at Oxford with women who were nothing but desserts—sweet, but not particularly substantial. She was just coming off her serious scholar's ascetic diet of abstinence when she'd returned to Los Angeles. It had seemed that she was picking up with her previous tastes of uncomplicated sex and then she had joined the WAC and it was back to the diet. Smiling at her own mental metaphor, she concluded that Rains would probably be a full ten-course meal. "Not just now, thank you."

As the sergeant was putting away the plates and remaining food, she said, "I would like to ask you a question about your life, if you don't mind."

Bett was surprised but replied, "All right."

"Was it hard for you to go away to school? To be so far from your family for so long?"

Bett didn't know what she'd expected but this wasn't it. She gave the question some thought. "I'd have to say no, not really. Most of the families in our circle sent their children to boarding school, so it just seemed the normal thing to do. I never really got along that well with my family anyway, so it was probably a good thing we were apart for most of my life. The prep school I went to was excellent. I enjoy learning, and most of the teachers were intelligent, decent people who were genuinely interested in their subjects. And generally, the students were like me in most ways—girls from a certain class who were gone from their homes for an extended period, so we had a lot in common. By the time I got to Oxford, it was second nature to me to be away at school like that."

"But weren't you ever lonely? Or sad?"

"At times, of course. But it's always been easy for me to make friends. I suppose you could say that I just created my own family wherever I went." She smiled at Rains. "Rather like your Army life, wouldn't you say?"

"Hmm."

Bett arched her back, stretching. "I do hope to go back to England when this war is over."

When Rains stood abruptly and held out her hand to get Bett up, she wanted to refuse. "We're not going already are we?" Bett asked, reluctant for the evening to end.

"No, we're just moving," Rains answered, repositioning the blanket around the trunk of a tree. "Sit there." She pointed and Bett put her back against the tree. Rains sat alongside her, a quarter turn around the tree. Bett didn't like it that she couldn't really see Rains's face, but their shoulders were touching very lightly and that was nice. It was almost dark; just a few streaks of color from the sunset remained. There was a light but steady breeze. Bett relaxed, happy to be there with Rains. She didn't want to think about whether the sergeant had taken other girls here before her.

"Why would you go back to England? Why not stay here?" Rains asked, continuing the conversation. "I don't mean Iowa necessarily, but in somewhere in America. Don't you consider this country your home?"

"I think it's because I'm more my own person in England. Anywhere in America, I just feel like my father's daughter," Bett answered. "You must have some experience of that, Sergeant. Isn't it hard for you to go back home after being in charge of things here?"

"First, I am not in charge of things here. I am a very small cog in a very big wheel."

"You're in charge of our squad, and you command the whole platoon on the fitness drills," Bett argued. "And you evaluate every recruit on the base."

"Only to a point. A great number of people are above me in rank and could overrule me on anything at any time," Rains pointed out.

"All right, if you insist. But when you go home—" Bett stopped. Quickly she turned toward the sergeant and took Rains's left hand in both of hers. "Oh, I have a confession to make. Promise you won't tell. After all, I have my reputation to protect."

"What do you mean? What...confession?"

Bett could see by the sergeant's worried expression that she was dismayed by the sudden turn in the conversation. *And even more so that I'm holding her hand again,* Bett suspected. She managed to keep a solemn expression as she brought Rains's hand to her heart, causing Rains to blush again. When she spoke, she made sure to add some dramatic breathing effects so Rains could feel her chest rise and fall. "I'm giving up. Tell me where you are from."

Bett was sure she saw some relief in Rains's eyes and a twitch at the corner of her mouth. "Would you like a hint before you surrender?" she asked.

"I would love one," Bett said, keeping her grip on Rains's hand.

Rains reached behind her with her free hand and took out her knife again. Bett hoped that no blood would be involved in this hint, but then saw that Rains had the blade pointed toward herself. "Look at the handle," she directed. "What do you see?"

Bett let go of Rains's hand and took the knife so she could look more closely at the woven pattern that covered the handle. Finally she looked up at Rains. "Is that...a little snake?"

"Very good, Private. And based on that image, do you know what tribe's name was given to them by the Chippewa Indians?"

Bett had no idea, but she remembered what Maria had said about her relative who had married a woman that looked like Rains, so she guessed. "The Sioux?"

The Sergeant sat back a bit, nodding. "Once again, I am impressed, Private Smythe. Now I will truly test you. In what state was the Wounded Knee Massacre?" Bett shook her head and Rains pressed her. "Come now, surely your fine education didn't leave this out. The last battle of the so-called American Indian War, fought between the United States Army and the people of Sitting Bull? Where five hundred heavily armed troops of the Seventh Cavalry avenged their defeat at Little Big Horn by facing three hundred and fifty Sioux, all but one hundred and twenty of whom were women and children? Where they used their newest weaponry to murder over one hundred and fifty of these mostly unarmed men, women, and children? What Whites proudly refer to as The *Battle* of Wounded Knee?"

Bett lowered her eyes. She knew the history of the American Indian was filled with terrible treatment, lies, and injustices allowed by the American government and she could hear the anger in Rains's voice. "I'm truly sorry, Sergeant Rains," she said softly. "You are right that I should know, but I don't."

She didn't look but heard Rains breathe out. Her voice was calmer when she spoke again. "No, Private. I apologize for my tone. There is no reason for you to know that. It is not your history."

Bett was quiet for a moment. "But I imagine your people must feel very proud of the changes that you are bringing to that same US Army. You're part of a new era in American military history, which is bringing together women from all over the country and every walk of life. I'm quite sure that the armed forces will never be the same, thanks to the influence of leaders like you."

Rains glanced sideways at Bett. "That is good of you to say, Private."

"I'm not just saying it, Sergeant. It's the truth."

Uncharacteristically, Rains looked at Bett for a long moment. Bett wondered if she would ever learn to read the emotion behind Rains's eyes. "South Dakota," she said finally. "I was born on the Pine Ridge Reservation there but I've lived in many other places—Wyoming, Nebraska, Kansas, Colorado..."

"And now Iowa." Bett nodded. "No wonder I couldn't pin down your accent. Do you speak a tribal language also?"

Rains nodded and said something in Lakota that had been on her heart for days, watching Smythe's face for her reaction.

"What does that mean?" she asked, leaning forward with obvious interest.

"Roughly translated it means *We watched the moon*," Rains said, feeling uncomfortable about the lie to Smythe, and even more uncomfortable about the truth of it in any language. She stood and paced a bit, working to put herself back in command. "I would like to hear your squad report now."

Bett reacted to the finality in her tone as she stood, too, turning the knife so the blade was pointed toward her and extending it to Rains. Rains took the weapon and it disappeared behind her back. Bett looked away for a moment as if switching her thoughts to her new friends in the barracks. "Maria was quite taken with the medical presentation. I think she's leaning toward pharmacy technician and would love to go back to Texas. Tee wants to work in supply and stock here in our PX if possible. Helen is fascinated by the idea of driving those light trucks, so I assume she's willing to go anywhere." Bett paused and gave her sergeant an apologetic look. "Oh, and Barb wants to be a baker in spite of my poor attitude in that class. She too is willing to go anywhere."

Rains nodded. "Good thing someone wants to cook, since we all like to eat."

Bett's smile faded and she resumed her report. "The rest are still undecided, but there's still three weeks of presentations."

"You left yourself out," Rains pointed out.

"Well, you know about me," Bett said.

"But have you decided where you would want to work? Probably more than any other field, once you are accepted in cryptography you can write your own ticket. Although you should know that Major Ervin has told me that he would be thrilled to have you stay and work at the facility here." Rains stopped pacing and they were facing each other.

"What do you think I should do?" Bett asked, her eyes searching Rains's.

Rains answered, "My opinion has no bearing on the matter. You should go where your spirit leads you."

"Can't I ask your advice as a friend?"

"But we are not friends. I am your sergeant and you are a private in my squad. In a few weeks you will be gone to your cryptography career and I will be starting a new job here."

As the meaning of her sergeant's intial words registered, Bett's first reaction was to be offended, but then she had a sudden understanding of everything that Rains was saying. "And that's your life, isn't it, Sergeant? New recruits coming in every few weeks, transfers and assignments elsewhere for the previous group. You never have to let yourself become emotionally invested because you've chosen a life where no one stays around long enough for you to feel anything about them."

"You are out of line, Private," Rains said, her voice tight. "And you are wrong. I do feel for my squad members."

"But only to the limits of your job, Sergeant," Bett retorted heatedly, watching as Rains drew her hands into fists, clearly struggling to keep her composure.

"So what would you suggest, Private? That it would be possible to develop a deep, meaningful relationship with someone who is going to be gone in two months? Would a series of brief physical encounters make me a better person in your eyes?"

Bett opened her mouth to retort and then closed it. She lowered her eyes, thinking how *a series of brief physical encounters* described practically all of her relationships exactly. Was her interest in seducing the sergeant just her own way of remaining emotionally aloof? Was she hoping to stop feeling something deeper for Rains by just having a quick fuck, the way she had done so many times at Oxford? Bett wasn't sure what else to say, so she settled for the most obvious. "You're right, Sergeant, I am out of line," she said solemnly. "I don't know what it is about you that makes me lose control of my mouth sometimes. Will you accept my apology?"

To her relief, she saw Rains relax. "Yes, I accept your apology. And I will tell you what it is about me. You are not used to dealing with someone in authority who is as strong as you are, so you do battle with your sharpest weapon, which is your intellect."

Bett smiled weakly. "That's probably a much kinder assessment than I deserve."

"No, Private, it's an honest assessment. And if you ever learn to discipline that strength without losing your passion, you will be formidable indeed."

Bett looked back into Rains's eyes, knowing that whatever else happened, she would never forget how their blackness fascinated her. "Why are you being so nice to me?"

Sergeant Rains hesitated. "Sometimes those of us in command don't hear the truth as much as we need to, because others lack the courage to tell us. You spoke the truth about me. I know why I made the choice to be here, in this transient life without emotional attachment. But choices need to be revisited from time to time to see if they are still valid. Thanks to you, I will do that when I have time to put my mind and heart to it."

Bett felt another surge of admiration for Rains that she wasn't sure what to do with. It was more than the usual sexual attraction that she felt for certain women. She had been feeling that for her sergeant almost from the beginning, if she was honest. There was something deeply truthful and real about her, something genuine and almost lyrical about the way she spoke sometimes. "I would really like to have you as my friend, Sergeant Rains."

"There is a Sioux proverb that says, *Friendship between two persons depends upon the patience of one.* We may have to take turns being patient, Private Smythe."

Bett smiled warmly, not wanting to lose the intimacy of this conversation. "Now you're asking for another thing I'm not very good at."

"No false modesty now, Private. I have a feeling you are good at anything you set your mind to." Sergeant Rains shook out the blanket and folded it into the knapsack. She picked up the two bottles of Coke, stopped in her preparations, and stood thinking for a moment. She handed one to Bett and clinked again. "To the WAC," she said finally, "where the daughter of R. L. Carlton and the daughter of Last Moon find common ground in their dislike of Coca-Cola."

There were several surprising things in that statement, but it struck Bett as extremely funny, and she started to laugh. She heard Rains breathing out her airy chuckle and that made her laugh even more. Soon she had to sit back down and Sergeant Rains sat beside her.

"Are you all right, Private?"

Bett stopped laughing long enough to say, "I believe you've just summed up the high point of my Army experience in that one sentence." Rains looked away again and this time Bett was sure she must be smiling. Then her shoulders shook a bit and she covered her mouth. "Are you laughing at me, Sergeant Rains?" Bett asked with only amusement in her voice.

Rains shook her head and from beneath her hand she said, "Mine, too."

It took Bett a second to understand and then she started laughing again. She had to lie on her back and hold her stomach. When she looked, she saw Rains wiping her eyes.

Rains looked at Bett and shook her head again.

"What?" Bett asked.

"I have never known anyone who laughed like you do."

"In volume, tone, or frequency?" Bett asked.

"All of that," the sergeant answered, looking at Bett with an unguarded expression that seemed warm, almost tender. *This is a window into who she really is*, Bett realized. "I think you must have a good heart to laugh so freely."

Bett turned on her side and raised up on her elbow. Resisting the urge to pull Rains down beside her, she asked, "Did you know I was angry with you earlier this week?"

To Bett's delight, Sergeant Rains stretched out facing her, mirroring her posture. "I felt something was different with you, yes, but I didn't know that I had made you angry. What made you feel this way?"

"At breakfast after we had such a nice evening with the big moon, you completely rejected me in the mess hall, talking about the gulf between wanting and doing. Then not ten seconds later you had that redhead buzzing around you again."

Rains looked puzzled. "What redhead?" Bett watched her thinking until it clicked. "Oh, you mean Captain Hartley?" Bett raised her eyebrows as she saw just a flash of awkwardness cross Rains's face. "I hardly know Captain Hartley."

"But you find her attractive," Bett suggested.

"What? No. I mean, I don't know. I hadn't thought of it."

"And now that you do think of it?" Bett pressed.

Rains blinked several times. Stalling, Bett thought.

"I still don't understand why you were angry," she said after a few seconds.

"Yes, you do. I was angry because I could see she was attracted to you." Rains was shaking her head. "What did she talk to you about, Sergeant?"

"She thanked me for telling her to watch for the big moon."

"Is that all?"

Rains stood quickly. "This conversation is not appropriate for us, Private."

"Uh-huh," Bett said, in a tone that meant her point had been proven. She stood, too.

"There is no reason for this talk about attraction. I am in the Army and I intend to stay for some time. That—that way is not an option for me." Rains looked off into the trees, not meeting Bett's eyes.

"Even though there are probably several other officers on this very base, not including Lieutenant Boudreaux, who seem to be doing all right with being that way? They could be planning to stay in, too. It seems to me that if someone does their job well and keeps their personal business personal, then there's a place for them in the WAC."

"That may be, Private," Bett could hear her sergeant was genuinely upset now. "But I am not...comfortable with the deceptions required by that kind of life."

"But you are comfortable with deceiving yourself about how you feel?" Bett insisted.

Rains turned away and picked up the knapsack, holding it close to her body, almost like a shield. Even though she was still facing the trees, the tension in her quiet tone was evident. "You don't understand how I feel."

She hadn't planned to reveal herself this way, but it felt right to step closer and put her hands on Rains's shoulders, letting her body lean lightly against Rains's back, keeping her voice barely more than a whisper. "Yes, I do, Rains, because I feel the same way." She pressed closer, feeling herself soften into the firmness of Rains's body. Rains gasped. "I'm well beyond twenty-one and this is exactly how I would choose to be with someone. That was one of the things I learned about myself in England." *I want to be this way with you,* she was about to say until Rains stiffened abruptly, holding up her hand for quiet.

In the stillness that followed, they both heard it: laughter, male and female, coming toward them. Bett dropped her hands and stepped back. Sergeant Rains moved around her and quickly put the knapsack on Bett's back. "Follow me," she said in a low voice and started off at a trot. They ran out of the trees with Rains calling out a cadence. When they got in view of the couple, Rains slowed them to a walk. It was one of the male officers who taught the drafting class and a WAC that neither of them recognized.

Rains saluted. "Major Wilson."

The couple separated a bit as the man returned Rains's salute. "Sergeant Rains. Doing some overtime training?"

Rains inclined her head toward Bett. "This private has owed me laps since the first day of basic training. Today is payday."

Wilson laughed. "You never cut them any slack, do you Sergeant?"

"No, sir"—Rains continued walking past them, Bett following close behind—"no slack for the WAC." Wilson laughed again. "Have a good evening, sir."

"Sergeant." They saluted again.

Rains picked up the pace and Bett followed. As she ran, Rains heard Bett's words in her head. *I feel the same way.* Did that mean Smythe's flirting was real and was actually intended for her? In the previous weeks Rains had found herself enjoying their conversations, and yes, she could admit, there had been times when she'd acted differently than her usual reserved, detached manner among her recruits. She'd found Elizabeth Smythe interesting, intelligent, and temptingly easy to talk to. But now she considered that it had all been a sham, that Smythe had lured her in falsely, hoping to interest her in something she would not consider. Would not *act on*, she amended. Of course she was aware that there were those few women who had joined the WAC primarily for that purpose—to be with other women. Did Smythe think she was one of those? Was Smythe one of those? Sergeant Rains pushed these thoughts from her mind and concentrated on recovering her command presence. They stopped when they reached the parade grounds and Rains reclaimed the knapsack, speaking curtly. "This meeting is over, Private Smythe."

"Rains, I—"

Further incensed by the familiarity in Bett's voice, Rains cut her off, speaking curtly. "It's *Sergeant* Rains, Private. And if you are wise, you will keep your feelings to yourself, as I do. At least until you get back to Los Angeles or England or wherever you are going when you finish playing at being a soldier."

Bett seemed stung by the implication that she wasn't committed to the Army and she responded hotly, "Just because I have feelings doesn't make me less of a soldier, Sergeant. It just makes me more of a human being. You ought to try it sometime. Then you might not have to hide it if you want to smile or laugh or, God forbid, care about someone."

Rains wasn't prepared for the force with which the harshly spoken critical words struck her. Their eyes locked until she saw Bett bite her lip. Too late, she tore her gaze away, knowing that Bett must have seen something of her pain.

"You are dismissed, Private," Sergeant Rains said quietly. She turned and walked away.

Chapter Seven

An hour later, Sergeant Rains turned restlessly on her bed again. As always, she was grateful that even non-coms were allowed their own rooms within the officers' quarters so she could be by herself. Although she ate with the others at mealtimes, she never socialized with them, preferring to be outside alone in her free time. She knew they questioned why she chose to be apart and suspected they spoke badly of her for it sometimes, but it was worth it to have some distance, some space of her own.

Two unnerving incidents tonight, she told herself, trying to justify the turbulence in her body—Private Smythe's revelation about herself followed by the unexpected appearance of Major Wilson. Rains was certain her explanation of running laps was convincing; she had nothing to fear from that encounter. As it stood, Wilson had more reason to be worried, being seen near the grove with a WAC after hours. But things could have gone very differently. What if she'd given in to the significance of Bett's whispered words, to her intoxicating scent and the touch of her hands and the way she'd pressed her body close? Rains breathed out again, trying not to think about how her heart had surged with her initial impulse to turn and take Bett in her arms. Not Bett. Private Smythe. Someone in her command. A thought came, unbidden but strong. *She has awakened your spirit.* Turning again, Rains set her mind, as she often did, to finding answers for present dilemmas in the lessons of her past.

Her troubled contemplations led first to the memory of her mother's one and only reference to her daughter's possible future.

She couldn't have been more than six. In fact, it had been shortly before her mother's death, which had left her White father grieving in a dozen different jobs in almost a dozen different places, each place farther and farther from the tribe and each year deeper and deeper into his bottle. But on that day, Rains had been out playing with the boys of her age as she typically did. Whether racing, wrestling, or shooting the bow and arrow, she usually beat them all, and no one thought anything about it. Her mother was proud and loving and she must have managed somehow to explain her daughter's behavior to her father, because he never tried to prohibit her activities. She was accepted without question until that day when an older boy came around and warned her that no man would want a woman who was a better warrior than he was and suggested she learn to cook instead. The other boys had laughed and Rains left their games, her face burning with humiliation. After stopping along the way to give the matter some thought, she arrived at their house and announced to her mother that she intended to be a warrior, and if that meant no man would have her, so be it. Her mother listened carefully and then asked, "But who will cook the food you bring home and who will sew your clothes?" Rains had thought of this already and replied that she'd find another girl who was willing and live with her.

Rains's home was one in which their tribal language was still spoken, in spite of laws forbidding it and the threat of harsh penalties. So it was partly her mother's switch to English that had made Rains take notice of this moment. "Daughter," Last Moon said as she pulled her little girl onto her lap, "you are special to me because you are my own. And you know I had a powerful vision on the night you were born and so you have your special name." Rains nodded. She knew her Lakota name tied her to the Thunder Beings and so she was always conscious of the weather. She loved hearing that story, but as her mother went on, she realized they were speaking of something else. "But you should know if you choose such a life, others will see you differently as well."

She'd learned to copy her mother's quiet, thoughtful behavior when faced with something new or unclear. "How will I know what choice is right for me, Mother?"

Last Moon was silent for a time. "Such people learn to make their own way in the world," she said finally, giving Rains a comforting hug before setting her back on the ground. "When you are older, we will talk of this again."

Even now, there was always pain when she thought of how her mother was ripped from her by a death so sudden and so terrible that afterward, her childhood passed through many months in a void of internal emptiness. She had vague memories of drums and chants, of smoke and wailing sounds, of women crying and of small arms giving her a fierce hug, all of which were oddly comforting. But mainly she had sought a place where she wouldn't have to see that her mother wasn't there anymore. Within days of her mother's passing, she could make it dark inside herself, even with her eyes open; she could muffle the sounds around her until there was almost nothing. Blind and deaf with grief, her life during that period was almost like a plant's—growth without consciousness. At times she tried to find her way back to life, but those first years were a terrible dream from which she could only partially awaken.

After her father had taken them from the reservation, she gradually became aware of the two worlds in which she now found herself. At school the other children teased her for her different skin and her strange clothes. She was confused by their antagonism. How had she already made enemies of these people? Walking home with her older brother, she asked what to do to make peace. "Don't try to understand them," he advised. "And don't try to be like them. Doing either will only hurt your spirit. Stay strong in yourself and it will pass in time." The first few times that Rains forgot and spoke Lakota, there were beatings to remind her that she had to speak only English, her father's language. At some point she had become known by her father's last name, Lowell, and a first name she'd been given by a man who was supposed to be a holy leader—Faith. Still, she said her Lakota name to herself every morning and every night.

They'd kept moving as her father drifted from job to job. One evening she was startled into awareness by much yelling. She didn't understand all the words, but her older brother was pointing at the empty cabinet where the food was kept while her father sat at the table with a bottle. Rains had spent much of her time turning her emotions into nothingness, but she allowed herself to feel her brother's resentment at having to do so much of the work around the house and to know his worry that they had so little and were often hungry. Shamed, Rains understood that she had a duty to become more present and learn ways to help him. When the last moon appeared that evening, she crept out into the night, taking her brother's knife with her. She found a place where no one was, a field that had been left fallow far outside of town. Baring her thigh, she slashed across it, asking the pain of the wound to clear her mind and to release her from the pain in her heart. Her limp was practically unnoticeable as she made breakfast the next morning and cleaned up afterward, and her brothers' smiles soon made the ache disappear.

Each year, when the seasons brought the last moon of September, Rains repeated her ritual with the knife in her mother's memory. As she grew older, she added to her ceremony. She chanted remembered words and built a fire. She tried to recreate a dance that she had seen her mother do. The knife would come at the end of the night. Each new cut became a thin *osnáze*—a scar—and each brought her some new clarity. She learned to tell directions from the sun or the stars and understood how to keep time in her mind. Her hearing sharpened and her vision cleared. Whenever she wanted to evoke her mother's presence, to feel connected to her people, or to remember that she was a part of something bigger than herself, she would rub the patch of raised flesh that striped her leg. A week after she had made her sixth cut, she had felt for the healing before going to sleep, judging if she would be able to turn on that side without discomfort. That night she heard her mother's voice, although she could not see her face. *The fire, the dancing, the chanting—all those are good. We are already connected by blood and scars. You have one cut for each year we had together in this world. Let there be an end to it now.* Rains accepted her mother's words without question. She had what she needed.

Her older brother, who had been named Thomas by the same holy man, kept their mother's name: Moon. He was four years older than her, intelligent and quick, and Rains knew he would be a great warrior someday. She admired his strength and that he never used it on those weaker than himself. More than their father seemed able or willing to do, he ensured that they stayed together and survived.

Her younger brother by two years was given the name Nicholas, and his constant good nature and willingness to laugh were a gift to them all. Nikki was probably the best adjusted to their new world. His slight build and short stature made Rains and Thomas call him by a different second name: Small. He was devoted to Rains, and she made sure he kept up with her on her wanderings. Rains and Thomas both made a point of teaching Nikki all they could remember of the old ways, the language and the stories. He showed great promise as an artist.

Except for the time spent with her brothers, Rains kept entirely to herself. She had even managed to train each of her teachers not to call on her by giving them only apathetic silence in return, even in the face of punishment. Then, the year she turned thirteen, Jessie Olson walked into her school. She'd sat next to Rains and introduced herself, breaking into Rains's solitary world with her kindness and winning her trust with her confident goodness. Soon they were inseparable, playing and talking, making up stories together and acting them out. The first time Jessie took her hand, Rains felt something inside her soften. Since her new friend wanted to be a teacher, Rains agreed to play school, unexpectedly gratified when Jessie complimented her intelligence. Soon her heart felt like the sun had finally come out after a long, cold winter.

Then Jessie invited her for a sleepover, where she'd found herself yearning to comfort her friend as she'd learned that Jessie's life had its miseries, too. At bedtime, Jessie soothed her embarrassment about not having any sleepwear by getting into bed with her naked. A simple touch turned to a sweet caress. A first kiss became many more. With each new sensation, her body felt more and more alive. Through it all, Rains knew that she had finally found her place in the world and it was good. Good until the next morning when Jessie's mother walked in and found two naked girls wrapped in each other's arms. She'd let out a scream that Rains could still hear in her mind, a scream that would forever change her life and Jessie's.

Jessie's family took her away when they moved the next day. The agony of loss and the heat of rage were Rains's new companions as her itinerant life continued. When her mother had died, Rains had made the outside world disappear; after Jessie was gone, Rains learned to make herself almost invisible to everyone else. Whenever others in the Army told stories about their childhood, she had nothing to say.

When Thomas had finished high school, he'd left them to return to the reservation. As much as she missed him, Rains understood. She thought she might do the same thing, possibly even without graduating, until a new teacher—Miss Warren—took an interest in her. Miss Warren was so beautiful that Rains almost couldn't look at her, but it was her dedication to education and fairness with all her students that influenced Rains to stay after school for tutoring and catch up to her grade level. Steady doses of Miss Warren's praise and frequent smiles gradually brought Rains into the world again, and she most valued the times when Miss Warren read aloud to them. When the teacher introduced Henry David Thoreau as her favorite, Rains listened carefully. *If a man does not keep pace with his companions, perhaps it is because he hears a different drummer. Let him step to the music which he hears, however measured or far away.* Rains decided that Thoreau had a true spirit, and that his words were good for her to hear.

While she had no illusions about her relationship with Miss Warren, she came to recognize that what she'd felt for Jessie was coming to life again. On a rainy night when she'd walked Miss Warren home, she discovered that Miss Warren understood her better than any adult ever had. *You are a good person, Faith*, Miss Warren had told her. *You deserve to be loved.* That, and a copy of Thoreau's writings with the inscription, To Faith Lowell, *Being is the great explainer.* With love, Miss Vivienne Warren, were the gifts Rains carried as she left school for the last time. She was fairly certain that she would never see Miss Warren again and that thought started a pain in her heart that she sometimes still felt.

After spending the night with her past, Sergeant Rains slept through the first reveille. Webber banged on her door, yelling, "Are you sick, Rains? You never sleep this late." Webber's voice moved away, laughing. "Must be having some great dreams."

Rains realized she had brought the pillow down beside her and was cradling it in her arms. *Bett* was the name in her mouth. Rains had found the truth in her heart. It wasn't Smythe who had been false about her feelings.

❖

All the way back to the barracks that night, Bett debated what to do. Should she write an apology note to Sergeant Rains? If so, what should it say? Should she speak to her in person, try to get Rains somewhere alone again? Not bloody likely that would happen, not after she'd been such a bitch. Maybe she should find Rains's room and just show up one evening, try to talk to her there? No, she'd already heard a story about one disturbed girl who'd appeared in Rains's room uninvited, and the results of that had not been good. It didn't help any to replay their last conversation and realize that Rains's words about keeping her feelings to herself seemed to confirm what Bett had begun to suspect—that there was a mutual attraction between them.

Bett was not the least bit worried that Sergeant Rains would report her for what she'd disclosed about herself. If she didn't turn in Lieutenant Boudreaux, who had apparently assaulted one of her soldiers, Rains certainly wouldn't have a recruit discharged just for confessing to a particular sexual nature in a private conversation. Clearly, Sergeant Rains believed in the WAC and supported the women who were there with genuine committment. Rains's accusation that Bett was only playing at being a soldier was probably one of the worst insults she could give and was surely made to increase the distance between them…at least in Rains's mind.

As she'd feared, Sergeant Rains ignored her even more pointedly now than she had before. To make matters worse, at breakfast the next day, she saw Rains offer the auburn-haired captain a seat across from her at the officers' table. Not only did Bett have no view of her sergeant during the meal, but based on the animated movements of the captain's head, they must have been carrying on a lively conversation. The captain sat there again at dinner. Bett regretted ever mentioning the woman.

Bett wrote a note and folded it, decorating the outside of it like a bookmark. She had thought very hard about what to say. Not too much and not too little, she told herself. *I can't tell you how sorry I am for not being able to control my dullest weapon, which is my mouth. I only hope you can find it within yourself to forgive me. I sincerely appreciate all that you are doing to help me be a good soldier and a better person.*

She put the note inside the Sartre book and waited. It was Monday before Rains came to do an evening walk through the barracks. The sergeant moved so quickly that she was three bunks past before Bett could even look up. Knowing that Rains would have to pass her again to leave, Bett sat cross-legged on her bed and held the book on her lap like a gift. Sergeant Rains visited for a while with several of the other girls, including Helen and Tee, who were the best of friends now and seemed content to study together. They no longer asked for Bett's help, except on rare occasions. Phyllis wanted to know what other classes were coming up, so Rains went through some of the options. Listening to Rains's low murmur rising and falling in quiet conversation, Bett was lulled to sleep sitting up, her chin dropping onto her chest.

Then Rains's voice was very close. "You can't be comfortable like that, Private Smythe."

"No...please wait. I wanted—I'm so sorry—I wanted to give you this." Bett struggled to awaken and held out the book, trying to remember what she'd meant to say. "Please keep it, if you'd like. I want you to have it."

"All right." Rains took the book from her hands and gestured for Bett to get under the covers. "Thank you, Private. Get your rest now." Her voice was so soothing that it made Bett fall back asleep almost immediately. She had the impression that Rains's hand might have brushed very briefly across her shoulder as she moved past.

Her eyes closing, Bett barely had time to think, *How can she be so nice to me when I'm such a stupid little shit?*

❖

Sergeant Rains had begun watching Private Smythe circumspectly as she interacted with the other girls. She was friendly and pleasant to all of her squad members, but never more than that. She seemed to be closest with Jo Archer and they often laughed together, but there was no flirtation or even casual physical affection between them. Other than the times that she had been in a large-group instructional setting, Rains had never seen Smythe with individuals from the other squads, either. There was no indication that she was romantically involved with anyone, and given Smythe's looks, Sergeant Rains was sure she must have had plenty of opportunities.

Rains briefly considered that she might have misunderstood what Smythe had said to her in the grove. But there was no mistaking Bett's smile or times that she had met Rains's eyes with enticement; no misinterpreting the feel of Bett's hands on her shoulders, the alluring weight of her breasts pressing gently against Rains's back, the soft whisper, *This is exactly how I would choose to be with someone.* More importantly, there was no misinterpreting the way her own body had responded, betraying her at every sight of Smythe with a racing in her heart and a yearning that came from a place that Rains had closed off years ago. The sergeant almost wished that there had been evidence of Smythe having multiple affairs on the base or even a significant relationship with someone; that would have made it possible for her to put away those thoughts and dismiss the emotions Bett stirred in her. But that idea brought a different, almost worse kind of turmoil, one that made her feel tense and antagonized.

That night she dreamed of a time after they had been dismissed from morning drills. Smythe was walking quickly across the grounds, looking at her watch, and Rains was instantly consumed with the idea that she was meeting someone. In the way that it sometimes was in her dreams, Rains was aware that she couldn't be seen, so she followed Bett. Bett went into the PX and Rains slipped in quietly a few seconds later. In the PX of her dream there was only a post office, a soda fountain, and a large general store, which she recognized but did not think of as belonging on the base. She tried to sort out its rightful place as Bett rushed over to the post office counter. Standing near some shelves, Rains heard her ask, "Have I missed the last mail out?"

"No, you just made it," came the reply.

There were a few other WACs along the margins of the scene, but they were distant and faceless. Rains moved away, feeling very foolish. *Thinking about this woman is taking entirely too much of your time,* she admonished herself. Suddenly aware that her invisibility was wearing off, she turned her back to the exit route that she expected Smythe would take, thinking that she would be just another anonymous uniform. But a few seconds later, a warm caress on her back spread over her entire body and her pulse raced as she turned to meet Smythe's eyes and her smile.

"Sergeant Rains, I thought that was you. How lovely to see you." She glanced in the direction where Rains had been looking and her smile widened. "I wouldn't have taken you for one with a sweet tooth. May I buy you an ice cream?"

Rains hadn't even realized that she was in front of the soda fountain. Still flustered from the feeling of Bett's hand, she stammered a bit. "No, uh, no thank you, Private. I'm not allowed to accept gifts from members of my squad."

Bett's eyes danced and she moved a little closer. Rains felt her skin would not stop burning anywhere Bett touched, but without her touch, Rains feared she would freeze. Bett seemed unaware of this danger and was smiling in her mischievous way, perhaps thinking she had caught Rains off guard. She pressed her advantage. "Ah, we'll have to go dutch, then."

Rains knew this expression from hearing girls talk about their dates. Was that what Smythe was suggesting? For a moment the dream scene changed, and she saw Bett's beautiful face in candlelight, empty dinner plates between them, and then the flickering screen of a movie—something she had actually only glimpsed from outside the doors of a theater. Bett's hand was on the armrest of a padded chair and Rains felt herself reaching for it…and then they were back in the PX.

"Uh, no, Private, I'm not allowed to fraternize with enlisted personnel." She tried to step back but realized she was already against one of the shelves.

Bett's expression changed to one of exaggerated sadness, but her eyes were still laughing. "So many rules, Sergeant. I honestly don't see how you keep up with them all." Bett stepped as close to her as she could get without them actually touching, almost floating there as the very thin slice of air between them was filled with the perfume of Bett's body and her face filled Rains's field of vision. Rains found herself unable to look away, only falling deeper and deeper into those eyes.

"Just tell me this," Bett said softly, but with an undertone of such sensuality that the trembling Rains had been feeling in her stomach turned into a jolt between her legs. "If we were somewhere else at some other time, would you join me for an ice cream?"

If we were somewhere else at some other time… When Bett said the word *cream*, Rains saw Bett's lips as in slow motion, and for that moment, everything else and everyone else faded away. The desire to kiss that luscious mouth was so strong that she leaned forward until she could feel the space evaporating and it was replaced with the soft wetness of Bett's mouth. She had no idea that she'd answered until she heard the word in the air between them.

"Yes."

Then her hands were in Bett's hair and she could see the pulse throbbing in Bett's throat and it matched hers exactly. She knew that Bett could see into her, could see the desire so compelling that it couldn't be hidden anymore, and her hands were pulling, demanding, so when Bett's knees weakened, Rains held her up with her own body, and just that quickly, she was wet and throbbing with want. Bett's mouth wasn't moving, but her thoughts resonated out loud. *I want you. I want you naked, in bed. You said yes. Please take me somewhere. Take me.*

Just at that moment, the PA system crackled overhead. "Paula, please report to the cashiers. Paula."

Instantly, the PX came to life, filled with people moving around them. At any second someone would look over and see her with Private Smythe in her arms, their mouths still shining from a kiss that Rains didn't actually remember but that echoed all along her nerve endings. As Bett pressed her face into Rains's chest, the buttons of Rains's jacket seemed to open themselves the second Bett's fingers touched each one. Rains struggled to control herself. *No, no, no!* Her own breathing was harsh and shallow as she loosened her hold, making sure Smythe could stand on her own. As soon as she did, Rains sidestepped. "Please excuse me, Private. I must go now."

But she was still standing there, feeling almost too swollen to move, when she heard Bett's voice, sounding very disappointed and yet so alluringly husky that Rains knew Bett was unmistaken when she promised, "Another time and another place, then."

Sergeant Rains awoke with a very keen awareness that no matter her feelings, she needed to keep some physical distance from Private Elizabeth Smythe.

❖

On Thursday, Rains came to their table in the mess hall during dinner. "I'm sorry, Private, but I have a conflict during our meeting time tomorrow. Are there any urgent issues that we need to discuss?"

Bett's heart sank. She hadn't admitted to herself how much she'd been looking forward to another chance to be alone with Sergeant Rains, but now she felt it deeply. *Is she avoiding me on purpose?* She tried to think of a pressing matter, but there was only one: *I want to see you.* Rains cocked her head slightly and Bett realized she was waiting for an answer. "Uh, nothing really urgent, Sergeant." Rains nodded and started away. Desperate for something to keep her there, Bett blurted out, "Although Private Archer wanted to know how it is that you can keep your hat on through all the exercise we do."

Rains's gaze shifted to Archer, who was starting to choke on the drink she had just taken. Rains's ever-present and apparently immobile hat was actually a matter that the squad had speculated on frequently. Jo was desperate not to be the one to broach the subject, however.

"Whoa, Queenie, I didn't—" She coughed some more and Rains detected some movement under the table.

Bett smiled her most winning smile, but Rains's neutral expression had changed to a more intimidating squint.

"Is there anything else, squad leader?"

Bett was normally quick to make up a good lie, but the look in Rains's eyes told her she wouldn't get away with anything more. She ducked her head just a bit, hoping, "Not at the moment, Sergeant," would get her off the hook. Rains shot one quick glare at Archer, who gave her head a quick shake, and left without another word.

CHAPTER EIGHT

On Friday night, the barracks were bustling as many of the girls were getting ready for another night at the NCO club. Everyone had an escort, of course, but tonight there was also going to be a band and dancing. Tee declined, as always, but to everyone's surprise, Helen announced that she would be joining them. Jo had asked Bett twice if she wanted to go, but Bett couldn't seem to get interested in group drinking or gather herself for an evening of declining offers to dance or being pawed when she couldn't refuse any longer.

"Don't say no yet, Queenie," Jo suggested, assessing Bett's mood. "Just see how you feel after dinner."

How did she feel? As if she was waiting for the other shoe to drop, wanting to know that Sergeant Rains had read her note and forgiven her, worrying that Rains would come up with another conflict the next time they were to meet, feeling that there was a difficult problem she was working out. She found it hard to think amidst all the racket, so she decided to spend the time they had before dinner taking a walk around the base. As she walked, Bett considered her predicament. There was no one to turn to for advice. She didn't really know anyone on the base well enough to talk openly about an issue that could potentially put them both at risk, the mail was too slow to be of much help, and she certainly couldn't discuss the matter with a friend on a semipublic phone call at the PX. *I wonder who Rains talks to?* Bett pondered, and then remembered how Rains had asked her about being lonely when she was away at school. *Probably no one,* she decided.

She just happened to be walking by Officers' Row when her sergeant came out the door of one of the living quarters. Bett felt a funny little thrill, seeing Rains when Rains did not see her, and she began carefully following the sergeant, who seemed rather preoccupied as she headed across the grounds. Suddenly Rains turned and Bett realized they were at a gate. Bett waited in the shadows of the early fall evening while Rains signed out. Bett waited what seemed a safe interval and followed, and tried to make out what Rains had written on the ledger. It looked like the first word was *MEL* but she couldn't make out the second name. When her scrutiny of Rains's handwriting caused the MP to look at her curiously, she quickly wrote *MEL* by her name also.

"Are you meeting with Sergeant Rains at the restaurant?" the MP asked, glancing at the book. "Technically, she's supposed to escort you off base."

Restaurant? Bett glanced quickly again. She searched her mind for the acronym *M-E-L* but couldn't think of anything it could stand for. She smiled at the MP and leaned in a little closer. "Yes. I'm her squad leader, and it's my fault she's not escorting me. I'm running late. Please don't get me in any more trouble."

The MP sighed. "Well, you'd better get going. She's a few minutes ahead of you and it's getting dark."

Bett nodded and pretended to hurry away, but she didn't really want to catch up with Rains yet, so she slowed once she was out of sight of the gate. After a few minutes, however, she realized the folly of her plan. She wasn't that familiar with any of Des Moines, outside of the base, and the area of town she was walking through looked pretty rough. Many of the buildings were a bit run-down and even the streets looked poorly maintained. She squinted ahead, trying to see Rains's form in the darkness, but had completely lost her. At an intersection, she wondered whether Rains might have turned. *One more block,* she told herself, *and then I'll go back.* At the next corner, a fire was burning in a barrel and several older men stood around it. Bett was torn; should she approach them and ask for directions or avoid them? Would her WAC uniform give her some protection in either case?

One of the men called out to her, "Hey soldier girl, what you doing out here at this time of night?"

Bett inhaled and took a chance. "I'm meeting a friend at Mel's, but I've lost my way."

The man detached himself from the group and came toward her. "Mel's, huh?"

Now that she had stopped walking, Bett felt the evening chill. She shivered and crossed her arms around her waist, hoping she didn't look frightened, only cold.

"Don't the Army give you no coat?" the man asked, noting her movements.

"Yes, but I was running late and I accidently left without it. My friend is expecting me. Could you kindly direct me to Mel's?" Bett tried to strike the right combination of appreciation and urgency.

The man indicated that she should go a block right and two blocks left. "Mel's on your right-hand side at the far corner," he said. "But I think they closed already."

Closed? Bett wondered. She thanked the man and started away.

"Careful, soldier girl," the man warned. "Not everyone out here as nice as me." The men around the barrel began laughing and calling out playful insults. Bett waved and hurried on. After a block she turned left. There weren't many lights on and Bett mentally kicked herself for being so rash. If she couldn't find Rains or if Mel's was indeed closed, could she even find her way back to the base?

From the corner of her eye she saw a tall thin man come out of an alley just after she passed it. "Hey!" he called. "You got a dime, sister?"

Bett didn't answer but started to walk faster.

"Hey!" the man called again, and she could hear his footsteps following her. "I need a dime from you."

Bett looked back to see that the man wasn't far behind. She was trying to see if anyone was with him when hands grabbed her shoulders from the front. Without looking around she let out a little scream of shock and was beginning to struggle when a familiar voice asked, "Private Smythe, what are you doing here?"

Relief made Bett's knees week. "I got lost," was all she could manage, thinking she had never been so glad to see anyone in her life.

Sergeant Rains held her arms an extra second and then turned her to face the man who was approaching them. She kept her hands on Bett's shoulders, standing close behind her. "Do you have a dime?" she murmured to Bett.

"Yes."

"Give it to him."

Bett unbuttoned the pocket of her jacket where she routinely carried a few dollars and some change. The man stopped when he was close enough to focus on Rains. "Oh, friend of yours, Rainy?"

"Yes, Jimmy. She didn't know. We got it straight now."

Taking her cue from Rains, Bett extended her hand with the dime in it. "Sorry, Jimmy."

The man opened a mostly toothless mouth as he took the coin. "What's your name, sister?"

Rains answered for her. "This is Smitty." Then to Bett she added, "Jimmy is the toll collector on this street."

"Oh, I see," Bett answered, playing along.

Jimmy straightened a bit. "Next week will be thirty-five years on the job."

"How wonderful for you," Bett said, and she felt Rains tug just a bit at her shoulder.

"We've got to get going, Jimmy," Rains said. "We'll see you next time."

"Okay, Rainy," Jimmy said and turned his bleary brown eyes to Bett. "And no more running the toll, young lady."

"Yes, sir," Bett replied sincerely. "I certainly won't make that mistake again."

Jimmy nodded, satisfied, and moved back into the night. Rains dropped her hands from Bett's shoulders. Bett turned slowly to face her, knowing she was in big trouble.

"Explain to me how you came to be here, Private," Rains asked, her eyes boring into Bett with a mixture of concern and anger.

"I saw you leaving the base and I was trying to follow you," Bett said in a small voice, not able to meet that intense expression.

"Why?" Sergeant Rains demanded. "You know you are not allowed off base without an officer. And you have no business following me."

"I know, but I wanted to talk to you and you've ignored me for days," Bett blurted out. "When you canceled our meeting, I thought that maybe if I could catch you off the base we could talk like we did before."

"Anything I need to say to you I can say during drills, Private." Her voice was almost stern until she noticed that Bett was shivering. "Where is your coat?"

"I wasn't planning on being out this late. I just happened to see you and..." A little spark of argument formed as Bett looked at her. "You aren't wearing a coat either."

"Yes, but I am used to this climate and you are not," Rains replied and looked around. "As I am familiar with this neighborhood and you are not."

Bett nodded and looked down again. "I'm sorry, Sergeant. I know it was a stupidly impetuous idea on my part."

Rains seemed to waver for a second and then said brusquely, "Come on." She continued down the street but walked slowly enough to keep Bett close beside her. In the middle of the block, she guided Bett across the street and they continued to the corner, where a tiny sign that said *Mel's* hung from a darkened window. Rains opened the door and motioned Bett in behind her.

"Gracie?" she called out.

"Come on back, Rainy," came a distant answer.

Bett followed Rains past the room full of tables with chairs propped against them through a swinging door into a brightly lit and warm kitchen. The scent of food was in the air, although the area was clean. Sitting around a large, stainless-steel island was an older couple, both round and smiling. When Bett entered, their faces went blank.

"Who's this little piece of white bread?" the woman asked, a tinge of hostility in her voice.

"A private from my current squad," Rains said. "She's pretty smart, Gracie. I think she might be able to help us. And her writing is certainly better than mine, so she can help us fill out the forms if we decide to go that way."

Bett was very grateful that Rains didn't add anything about her being uninvited. Just then, her stomach growled loudly enough that everyone could hear.

The man started laughing. "Well, I guess we got to feed her no matter what else. You hungry too, Rainy?" He stood.

"Yes, Melvin. Thank you."

The woman pushed herself to her feet and they both began bustling around the kitchen. Rains began talking to Bett as if they were in the middle of a casual conversation.

"So like I was telling you, Melvin and Gracie have a good kind of problem, in a way. Sometimes they have too many customers, and there's no place for folks to sit," Rains explained, and Bett heard a bit of drawl and slang in her voice that wasn't usually there. "Folks sometimes take one look inside and just turn around and leave if they can't get a seat, even paying regulars. So we're trying to figure out about expanding. How much for the vacant place next door, how to knock down the wall between them if we get it, that kind of thing."

Bett nodded, genuinely interested.

Melvin left what he was doing at the stove to tell Rains, "Man say he want two thousand dollars for that space. Been empty since before the war. Two thousand dollars! That means we got to go to the bank and that's not good."

The sergeant shook her head. "It's too much, Melvin. You should offer him the seven hundred fifty you got, tell him take it or leave it."

Bett spoke for the first time. "You said sometimes there are too many customers. How often does that happen? What time of day? And what is your most frequent clientele? One or two people or larger groups?"

There was silence in the room. Gracie spoke, still sounding suspicious. "Where you from, honey?"

Rains looked away, running her hand over her mouth. Bett answered, "I'm from California, but I spent several years in England."

"She went to school there, Gracie," Rains filled in. "High school and college."

"Hmph," the large woman replied, her grunt a short cut-off sound of doubt, not like Rains's more drawn out, thoughtful sound.

"I'm asking because the first thing we need to know is whether or not your need for expansion is permanent," Bett explained. "Before you pay the man next door anything, you might be able to solve your problem at least temporarily with the space you have."

Melvin set down two plates of food. It smelled delicious. "We get a big rush at lunch, weekdays," he said, thoughtfully. "A lot of working men and some women, mostly ones and twos. Then dinnertime, it's more families—like four or five, sometimes more."

"We should look at how many you can seat now, see if there's any way to change the configuration of the room," Bett said, resisting the impulse to pick up her fork. "I have another idea too, but let's look at that first."

"No, you eat first," Melvin said.

"Oh, good." Bett smiled. "I was rather hoping you'd say that."

Melvin smiled back. Gracie looked at Rains who tipped her head in Bett's direction just a bit and raised her eyebrows. "Hmph," Gracie said again, but she didn't sound quite as hostile.

After eating, they looked at tables and counted seats. Bett pointed out that the round tables were a disadvantage, taking more space and unable to be combined for larger groups. They calculated that by cutting off the curves of their tables, they could fit five more one or two tops around the outside walls and then have room for more group tables of four, six, or eight in the middle.

"What else?" Rains asked, watching Bett's thoughtful expression as she examined the dining area.

Bett pointed to a small shuttered back area. "This is wasted space. You could make it standing room only, just attach a narrow shelf to the wall and let people stand to eat. You could probably fit five or six more people there. Also, there are probably some who would be willing to take their food away and eat it elsewhere, like at a park or back on the job. You could offer a few cents' discount on food taken out and that might save you a few seats."

Gracie was shaking her head, but Melvin said, "It might be worth it, taking off a little bit, if we ended up with more paying customers who stayed."

"Maybe you would only offer food to take away at your busiest hours," Rains suggested.

Bett smiled at her. "You're sounding like a businesswoman now, Sergeant." Gracie nodded then. "One more thing. I know we're getting into fall but there should be a few more good days yet, and there's also the option of using those barrels for heat until it gets really cold."

"For what?" Rains asked.

"Dining alfresco—out of doors—is very popular in Europe. Sidewalk cafés are where people love to gather and linger over coffee or a meal. I think you have enough room on the sidewalk outside here for several of those two- or three-seat tables. In the fall, spring, and early summer, I'd think those tables would be quite popular."

Gracie looked out the window. "I think you're right. Nice weather, folks would enjoy that."

"Is the next-door owner a local man?" Bett asked.

"Yeah. He live across town though," Melvin said.

"But when he learns you've been able to take care of your problem with these changes, at least temporarily, that may be the time to offer him a lower price," Bett suggested. "When you don't really need the place, you see? You're just trying to take it off his hands for him."

"College, huh?" Melvin asked, looking at her admiringly. He turned to Gracie. "Maybe Evie can go when she get out the Army."

"Don't get ahead of yourself, old man," Gracie said, laughing. "Let's see how all this work out before we start making college plans for everyone." She turned to Bett. "I gotta admit, you got some good ideas, little one. What's your name?"

"Please, just call me Smitty," Bett said, shaking each of their hands, "and I want to thank you for the best meal I've had in a long, long time." She was reaching into her pocket but Gracie stopped her.

"Your money's no good here."

Bett could tell this was not an argument she would win. "Well then, let me just say that it was a pleasure to meet you both."

She watched with surprise as Rains and Melvin embraced. *I guess she's not totally opposed to human contact.* "You bring her back sometime, Rainy," he was saying.

Gracie hugged Rains next. "I just might do that," Rains was saying, "if I don't court-martial her first."

The old couple laughed, but Bett looked away, knowing it was Rains's way of saying she wasn't forgiven for this trespass. "Give my regards to Evie and tell her she's missed," Rains added.

This perked Bett's curiosity even more. *Who is this woman Rains is missing?*

"We will. Careful getting back to the base, you two," Gracie said as she locked the door behind them.

Bett looked at Rains with hopeful eyes.

"We're running, Private," Rains announced and started off at a quick trot.

Bett fell in beside her. "Do we need more dimes for Jimmy?"

"No, Jimmy's gone down by this time of night."

They got back to the base much too quickly for Bett. When Rains signed back in she noted Bett's name under hers and gave her a look. Then she signed Bett back in as well. They trotted on toward the barracks. When they were about halfway there, Rains stopped. She turned to Bett, squinting, and rubbed her hand across her forehead, under her bangs, pushing her hat back farther on her head. "What am I going to do with you, Private Smythe? You consistently break rules and show no self-discipline whatsoever. KP had no effect...although that was actually my fault."

"Melvin and Gracie are such nice people. How did you meet them...Rainy?" Bett asked, unable to stop herself from smiling.

"If something had happened to you out there, you could have brought a lot of trouble to that community," Rains said seriously.

Bett's face became solemn. "I know you're right about that, Sergeant. Would it help if I promised never to do such a foolish thing again?"

Sergeant Rains sniffed as if she had grave doubts about such a promise. Bett smiled hopefully, watching as Rains's expression became more intent. *She has the most beautiful eyes,* Bett reflected for what seemed like the hundredth time, many of them in her dreams. Thinking of how often she'd been paid the same compliment, she wondered if anyone had ever said it to Rains. *I want to be the one to tell her,* Bett decided. *But not now. Not yet.*

"I would be remiss if I did not express my appreciation for your very good ideas tonight, Private," Rains said finally, "but that does not excuse your misbehavior. And you should know that you had better not ever call me by that other name again unless you want to run laps until you throw up."

"Yes, Sergeant," Bett said contritely. "But you can call me Smitty anytime. I rather like it."

Sergeant Rains ignored this. "Remember that you are not to leave the base until your basic training is completed. Another infraction like this and the result will be more severe than peeling potatoes, I promise you."

"But how will I know if my ideas for Mel's are working if I can't go and visit them again sometime?" Bett asked. She shivered again. The warming effects of the run were wearing off.

"When it's time, I will escort you," the sergeant replied. Bett smiled, wrapping her arms around herself. Rains shook her head. "And in doing so give you exactly what you want," she said, half to herself. She looked at Bett again, working to keep her expression stern.

"Thank you for not really being mad at me," Bett said sincerely.

"How do you know I'm not?" Rains answered, almost automatically.

Bett stepped closer, as she had learned to do with Rains who always kept a more than respectable distance between them. "I can read it in your eyes," she answered, using a gypsy fortune-teller's voice. "You have no secrets from me, Sergeant Rains."

Rains's mouth twitched. "If that were true, we would both be court-martialed, Private Smythe."

After a beat, Bett began to laugh. Sergeant Rains could be so unexpectedly delightful sometimes. Her complete lack of pretense was refreshing. Bett moved against her almost before she knew what she was doing, putting her right side against the middle of Rains's body, one arm around her waist, laying her head on Rains's chest. Had it been since Emma that just being with someone made her feel so good? *How I'd love to take this funny, sweet Rains and her warm body to bed with me. We'd have fabulous sex and then maybe I could just lie like this for a little while. She would hold me then, wouldn't she?* "Some things are worth the risk," she suggested by way of reply. She felt Rains's breath catch and heard her heart beating stoutly. *I can always pretend I was talking about the day I arrived when she let me guess where people came from.* Bett was about to step away, knowing she mustn't push her luck about getting back into the sergeant's good graces, when she felt Rains's arms come around her shoulders. It was as if Rains had read her thoughts about being held. Or perhaps this was the sergeant's version of taking a risk.

A low whisper close to her ear, Rains's voice was warm and not at all formal. "You really were wonderful tonight."

Bett was flooded with pleasure. Even making first-class marks in her hardest classes hadn't given her this feeling. She turned until their bodies were facing each other, putting her other arm around Rains also. She could feel the sinewy strength in Rains's body but her embrace was very tender. Was the sergeant breathing more quickly or was she imagining that? Bett couldn't help the little sigh that escaped her throat. *Oh yes.* It felt so good to be held by someone again. Or was it that it felt so good to be held by Rains? She tried to cover her reaction by saying, "Thank you for letting me be a part of it. Thank you for not telling them I wasn't invited." She swallowed. "And thank you for accepting my apology."

Rains's arms tightened just the slightest bit and Bett felt warmth pouring into her. Was that why it sometimes felt as though Rains's touch could melt her? "It's getting to be the time of year when evenings are cooler," the sergeant murmured, her low voice huskier than usual. "You might want to remember your coat the next time you are out late."

"I'd rather have you," Bett whispered, not sure if Rains would hear her or not.

There was just the slightest pause and then Sergeant Rains let her go and stepped back. She took a breath and cleared her throat. "You are dismissed, Private."

Was Rains's voice a little bit shaky? Bett wondered. She would have given half of her bank account to know what was in Rains's mind for those few seconds that they were holding each other. But she knew she shouldn't ask for any more—for tonight, anyway. She was already looking forward to her next opportunity to be alone with Rains. "Thank you, Sergeant. Good night."

Watching her walk away, Rains clenched her fists. *You put your arms around her! Right here in the middle of the base. That woman is a private from your squad and there was no reason to touch her that way.* Yet it had seemed inevitable somehow, as if there was some kind of chemical reaction between them that couldn't be contained. In spite of Rains's best intentions to keep her contact with Smythe to a minimum, something always seemed to happen to bring them together. And every time they were alone in each other's company, the feeling between them seemed to intensify. Fully aware of potential complications, Rains would tell herself to back away, to reestablish some detachment, but always Smythe found a way to cross the distance between them.

In the two years and three months that Rains had been a part of the WAAC and the WAC, she had never felt so drawn to someone. The fact was Elizabeth Smythe constantly surprised her. Or, Rains corrected, maybe it was her own reaction to Smythe that surprised her. At those ill-advised moments when they were alone together, a feeling would hit her with the same force as her rage, but instead of the quick flash of anger, it was an intensifying flame of desire. Could Rains truly not restrain herself, or had she, on some level, given herself permission to stop trying? *I'd rather have you*, echoed in her head. Was that true?

Knowing that sleep would be impossible just now, she walked over to the parade grounds, took off her hat and jacket, and began running. Not just her standard Army pace, but running as fast as she could. By her fifth lap she was breathing hard when Moore and three other officers walked by on their way back from Sweetie's.

"You'll never get away from whatever it is that way, Rains," an intoxicated voice called out. "You're running around in a circle, in case you didn't notice." The group laughed and moved on.

That's exactly right, Rain thought, slowing to a stop. *As if there's a circle that always leads me back to her.* She had gotten her hat and jacket back on when an unbidden idea came into her thoughts. *Is this something that is supposed to be?* When she consciously allowed herself to revisit the feeling of Bett's body pressed against hers, she could feel again the powerful pounding that started loudly in her heart before spreading all through her body. She shook her head but the movement didn't completely clear Bett from her thoughts. After a moment's consideration, she accepted that maybe nothing would ever completely clear Bett from her thoughts.

Still, no matter how good it felt, it was completely unacceptable. Even if Bett was willing, which she gave every indication of being, Rains could not in good conscience take part in a relationship of that kind. Because whatever connection they might feel now, this time would end and their separate journeys would continue. Besides, Rains admitted to herself, there was little chance that this closeness could be real, given the divide of their realities. And the main reality was that she was Bett's drill instructor, and she had no intention of violating the honor of that position. Ignoring the profound pang of sadness that accompanied her conclusions, she set her mind to what she most required of herself...some way to get control of these runaway emotions.

Chapter Nine

In the week that followed, Sergeant Rains gave absolutely no hint that anything unusual might have happened between them. The squad continued their training, but most girls had shifted their focus from simply making it through basic to planning for their future Army employment. Charlotte, whose worries about passing the physical fitness test had resulted in her losing at least ten pounds since their arrival, came late to dinner one night, excited that Rains had accompanied her to the rifle range that afternoon, since she was considering going into munitions testing. She mentioned that Lieutenant Boudreaux had not been available, but that she and Rains had an informative meeting with the second in command, a Sergeant Nash. Bett wondered if Boudreaux had deliberately avoided Rains or if it had been the other way around.

After exercise the next morning, Bett noted that her sergeant took Phyllis aside and they walked slowly toward one of the classroom buildings together, Phyllis talking and gesturing while Rains nodded. Bett knew that Phyllis was feeling anxious about her choice of duties; they had all talked with her about it. Phyllis was very interested in becoming a radio operator, but her scores in that class had not been particularly good. "I knew it!" Phyllis had agonized afterward. "I knew every single answer. I just panic when I take those stupid tests!" Bett watched Phyllis waiting nervously as Rains went into the building and came out a few minutes later with Major Seymour, who was the head of the department. After a moment of introduction, Rains walked briskly away, leaving Phyllis and the major in conversation.

And Jo had insisted on showing Bett page after page of the NCO's manual that Rains just happened to have at lunch one afternoon when she stopped by their table. The sergeant had been right, Bett realized, about success being better when it was shared. She felt absolutely no jealousy toward her squad mates, and no anger toward Rains for not including her in such a consultation. Her course was set, and the fact was she wanted something much more personal than job counseling from this woman.

Unexpectedly, the only shadow over their group came from Helen and Tee. Apparently, the two girls had experienced some kind of falling out, because they suddenly stopped speaking to each other or sitting together in classes or the mess hall. One Sunday after church, Sergeant Rains quietly informed the squad that Helen had left. "Private Tucker has qualified to attend the Motor Transport School, and she has volunteered to fill in a position at Fort Oglethorpe in Georgia." Turning away from Tee's teary eyes, Rains addressed the rest of the squad. "She'll return in time for graduation." No one moved. "Enjoy the rest of your day," she added and left the room.

Thinking she must feel deserted by her best friend, Bett hoped that Tee would find some comfort, as she did, in believing Sergeant Rains would always do exactly what she needed to do for her recruits. But Bett wasn't sure how she felt about the certainty that nothing about Rains's methods or her manner would change, even if she had any idea that Private Elizabeth Smythe couldn't stop thinking about her, day or night.

And the nights were definitely most troublesome, because after her brief moment in Rains's arms, Bett's sleep became increasingly restless with the sergeant almost always in her dreams. In addition to frequent erotic interludes, she often dreamed of running after Rains and usually awoke to find she had kicked at the blanket or even pulled the sheet off herself at some point. On one chilly night she awoke to the feeling of the covers being pulled back over her. A hand smoothed some hair out of her face. "Rains?" Bett whispered without opening her eyes.

"Shh," a soft voice answered.

"I dream of you all the time," Bett said softly, her voice still thick with sleep.

"You are dreaming now," came the reply.

When Bett opened her eyes, there was no one there. But she was tucked in under the covers.

❖

It was a beautiful September Friday, crisp and cool. They were doing a group quick march in formation with the whole platoon. Bett just happened to be in the middle of the pack on the outside edge where Rains was calling out their commands. Sometimes the sergeant would move ahead or behind her position to check on their alignment, but frequently she was walking right beside Bett. As they moved past the officers' quarters, Bett had a sense of being watched. Rains was in the back of the platoon at that moment so Bett sneaked a peek and saw a group sitting out on the officers' quarters porch. Among them was Sergeant Moore, who was glaring at her.

Looking had cost Bett her rhythm for a pace or two and she heard Rains call out from behind her, "Eyes front, Private." Then she heard Moore yell, "Yeah, Limey loser." Bett didn't look but she could hear Moore and the other officers laughing. She thought about sticking out her tongue but decided that using her middle finger would more accurately convey her message, so she just extended the position of her outside arm and made the gesture quickly. But she hadn't taken into account how much the motion of her arms helped her keep pace with the group, and a gap opened between her and the WAC in front of her.

"Dress that line, Private," Rains warned, but it was too late. As the WAC behind Bett tried to adjust her pace to Bett's change, the next girl back was unable to do so and she stumbled trying to avoid a collision. Rains brought them to a halt to the hoots and derisive calls of the officers sitting with Moore.

She turned the platoon to face the officers and kept them at attention as the jeering continued. No one moved a muscle as Rains walked up and down the line twice while the platoon suffered every insult that the officers could come up with. She then pulled Bett out and told Archer to run the remaining platoon members back to the barracks and then dismiss them for the rest of the day, giving them a rare afternoon off. Bett was quite sure that her cheeks were burning but she was able to keep her eyes on a distant spot somewhere while her sergeant stood in front of her.

"Private Symthe, you have embarrassed the entire platoon with your personal antics. Ten laps should help you practice some discipline."

What Bett most wanted to say sounded childish, even in her own head. *She started it.* So she kept her eyes forward and answered, "Yes, Sergeant Rains."

The rest of the group had quieted, but Moore's voice carried over to them. "Told you there'd be trouble with that one, Rains." Then, addressing the group around her again, Moore added loudly, "Takes one to know one, I guess."

"Let's go, Private," Rains said tightly and they began to run toward the far side of the parade grounds and away from the laughter following them. As they began their first lap, Rains added, "You keep pace with me, no matter what. Understand?"

Bett didn't, quite. "You're running with me?"

Rains slowed, nodding her head. "I'm not confident that you will learn this lesson on your own, Private."

Adding insult to embarrassment made Bett snap, "Oh, and you think you're qualified to teach me, I suppose?"

Sergeant Rains sped up, to a much faster pace than the group ever ran. With some effort, Bett caught up. Just as she was wondering how long she could maintain their current speed, Rains slowed again.

"I am surprised that someone of your education would need to have this explained to them, but clearly you are not used to being offended." Rains slowed almost to a walk and turned to look at Bett for the first time since they'd began running. "So yes, in this case I am qualified to teach you. When someone speaks of you unjustly, it reflects only on them—unless you respond in kind, in which case it reflects also on you." She waited a few steps and when Bett didn't respond, she added, "If you really intend to remain a WAC, you're going to have to have a much thicker skin. Your individual behavior will reflect on the whole organization, whether you like it or not." She resumed the regular step of a group march.

Bett followed Rains's changes of pace without saying anything for a time. She found she was unable to argue Rains's point and she wasn't sure she wanted to. Considering what Rains had revealed about her background, it was obvious she had had experience with injustice, and probably with insults as well. Bett was equally sure Rains wouldn't want to talk about it just now, so she decided to try a different tack. "Sergeant, may I ask you something?"

"You may ask, but I reserve the right not to answer," Rains said, speeding up.

Bett couldn't help smiling. *I think I'm detecting a pattern here. She speeds up for punishment and slows down for the lesson.*

"When did you join the WAC?" Bett asked.

"Is that your question?" Rains replied, surprised.

"Yes."

Rains relaxed the pace a bit. "I was in the first class ever. We arrived on July 20, 1942. And it was actually the Women's Auxiliary Army Corps at that time."

"Of course." They'd all gotten some background on the organization before they joined. "Your enlistment was quite historic, then. What was it like here at that time?"

"Very different. When the WAAC was created by the government, Fort Des Moines was not ready for the numbers who enlisted. The Army had planned for about twelve thousand total for the first year, up to twenty-five the second year, and so on. Instead, over sixty thousand women applied the first year. Our barracks at that time were former stables and many of the girls objected to the lingering smells. The building was drafty and they hadn't had time to pave the road, so we marched in dust or mud." She sniffed out a chuckle. "The coats they issued us were men's sizes, so they were big and long"—the sergeant paused to look at her own lanky frame—"even on me."

The image of Sergeant Rains being swallowed by a huge coat made Bett smile. "Given the conditions, it's surprising more of you didn't quit."

"No, there was a great sense of commitment, an awareness of the importance of what we were doing. This was even more true for women who enlisted, than it was for the country in general, I think. And I believe most of those who join still feel that. But those of us who were already in the WAAC had the option to leave when it was converted to the WAC. Fewer than twenty-five percent did. And the change was a good one. Many more job options opened for us."

While she spoke, Rains was running in different positions as well as at different speeds, sometimes behind Bett or on her left or ahead. Bett was beginning to feel the exertion when she heard Rains's voice from behind her. "You run well, Private Smythe. Have you ever raced?"

"Raced?" Bett tried not to pant.

"Yes." Rains was not the least bit winded. "Like track and field events in school."

"Oh. Not really. I was too busy studying. And certainly not distance running, like this. I suppose I'm more of a sprinter, actually."

"Are you fast?" Rain asked, coming up beside her.

Bett thought back to her childhood, how her brothers had never been able to catch her during their occasional games. She'd always been the fastest of her friends at Kent Prep and she recalled dashing across Oxford on numerous occasions to avoid being late for a tutorial. "Fast enough, I suppose. Why?"

"There will be an all-base race between squads and platoons on Friday. With each race, the winner advances, representing their squad in the next race. The winner of the final race gets a medal from the colonel. My squad has never won, and your group will be my last, so that's why I was asking."

Her sergeant's voice sounded a bit wistful. "Who won when you were a private?" Bett asked, thinking she could probably guess.

"I did. But after the ceremony I gave my medal to the girl I last raced against. She faltered near the finish or she would have beaten me." Rains looked away, as if remembering.

Bett could sense there was something more that Rains wasn't saying. After a moment, she asked, "What caused her to falter?"

Rains turned back and looked at her directly. "I believe that someone from my unit said something to her before the race. Like what Sergeant Moore said to you today, only much, much worse and more threatening. The other girl was in a colored unit, in the Nurses' Corps. They only let her race when I refused to continue without her participation." Rains lifted her head slightly. "That cost me laps for two weeks, and they haven't done it that way since. But it was the right thing to do. After that day, we became friends. Her name is Evelyn. That's how I came to know Mel and Gracie. She is their niece and was living with them before she enlisted."

Although Bett was intrigued by the account, it was the distant hurt in Rains's eyes that caused her to stop paying attention to their laps. *Those last words sounded almost...personal,* she thought.

But the sergeant seemed to detach herself from the story as she stopped, exactly where they had started, and announced, "That's twelve, actually. We'll walk a cool-down lap."

"So was your sergeant angry with you when you gave away the medal?" Bett wanted to keep her talking as their pace slowed.

Rains snorted. "I believe that is what they call an understatement."

"What was your sergeant like otherwise?"

"Like Sergeant Moore," Rains said briefly.

"Really? You have my sympathies. And I shudder to think that there are two of them out there."

Rains cocked her head. "I apologize. That seems unnecessarily deceptive on my part, but I answered the question the way you asked it. Sergeant Moore *was* my sergeant."

"Oh." Several things fell into place—Rains's sensitivity to the underdog girls, the way her strict formality could give way to a gentle nature when needed. Bett thought of how Rains had brought Sergeant Moore along when she'd had to deal with Irene Dodd. *She knows Moore's strengths and weaknesses and tries to be everything that Sergeant Moore isn't,* Bett thought. *And she succeeds.* "Then I sincerely apologize for today. You're quite right that I shouldn't have responded. But what did she mean by it takes one to know one?"

Rains seemed to be considering her answer. Her eyes scanned Bett's face for a moment as they walked along. "The Army was a different kind of life for me," she said finally, "as it is for you. But not the same kind of different." Bett nodded. Oddly, that statement made perfect sense. "Sergeant Moore and I didn't always see eye to eye on how I would fit into this new life. As you and I don't always see eye to eye on how you are fitting in here now."

"But, Sergeant"—Bett couldn't help smiling as she touched Rains's arm—"you know I like you and I believe you like me, too. I can't imagine you and Sergeant Moore had a similar relationship."

"Liking has nothing to do with it, Private. I learned to show respect to Sergeant Moore because she was my superior officer. And that is what I expect from you." As usual, she moved away and Bett let her hand drop. "Are you interested in the race?"

"But I don't know anything about that kind of running."

Rains eyed the distance to the bleachers. "Race me to the reviewing stand. If I think you can win against the other squads, I will coach you."

Bett took off like a shot. Rains closed in on her about fifteen feet from the bleachers and won, but not too easily.

"Fast and sneaky," Rains appraised her coolly. Bett was panting and grinning. "We can work the rest of this afternoon and tomorrow after lunch. The race is Monday. It's not a lot of time, but adequate if you are good enough."

Sergeant Rains took her back to the middle of the parade grounds. "The race is usually won or lost at the start. Your first five steps will likely determine the outcome, so we will look at this to begin."

She watched Bett through three practice starts, and then talked to her about footwork. During the process, Rains adjusted Bett's stance by gently turning her shoulders. Occasionally she would put her hand briefly on one of Bett's legs to draw her focus to a point about how to move. Bett was genuinely trying to concentrate, but every time Rains touched her, her body hummed as if caressed and she wanted more. More than once, she deliberately made a misstep so the sergeant would correct her with that firm hand. But after five more starts, Bett felt as though she actually understood what Rains was trying to show her and was able to move her feet consistently as the sergeant instructed. She hoped the next lesson would involve more touching. This kind of intimate contact with Rains was exactly what she had been craving.

She thought she was being too obvious when Rains said, "You seem distracted. I am probably talking too much. Let's run an easy lap and then we can talk about the finish for a moment."

Bett merely nodded and they trotted around the parade grounds. Bett almost didn't trust herself to talk, but she was still curious about Rains's initial Army experience, so she asked, "So when did you become a drill instructor?"

"That was the path I chose when I finished basic. As you have chosen to work in the wireless communication group."

"Why was that your choice? I would think after your experience with Sergeant Moore you wouldn't want anything else to do with basic training."

"Actually, it was my experience with Sergeant Moore that made me want to work with new recruits. Thinking of some of my own…difficulties, I thought I could be helpful to girls who might be having similar problems adjusting to their new life in the Army."

"But it couldn't have been Moore who suggested that to you."

"No, it wasn't." Bett could tell that Rains didn't want to go on.

Bett turned to Rains as they walked. "Look, Sergeant, I think you should know that I've never gone back to the barracks and talked about anything that's gone on between us." Bett couldn't help adding, "I'm very discreet."

Rains looked a bit uneasy. "I'm not sure what you mean, Private."

"I'm just selfish, if you want to know. I very much enjoy talking to you and I don't want to share our conversations with anyone else."

There was a pause and then Rains spoke slowly, as if she wasn't quite sure what she wanted to say. "I have often enjoyed talking with you also, Private Smythe. And I am glad that you are on our side."

"What?" It was Bett's turn to be confused.

"It seems to me that you are very good at getting information, so it's a good thing that you are in our army and not a spy."

Although her sergeant's mouth was still serious, Bett saw some amusement in Rains's eyes. Bett took a few more steps and then stopped. "You are teasing me, Sergeant Rains!" she said, laughing. "And I wouldn't have thought an unwilling subject like yourself would have noticed my clever interrogation tactics."

"Oh, I've noticed." Rains stopped also, her tone still light. "You are quite pleasant to be around when you are not arguing."

"Could I say the same for you?" Bett bantered.

"No. I don't argue. I'm just stubborn—according to those who care to analyze such things." The sergeant's answer interested Bett even more.

"And who would care enough to do such a thing?"

"The same person who recommended I become an officer," Rains answered with a deliberate tone to her voice.

"And of course, you're not going to tell me who that was."

"Not even under torture," Rains said, teasing again, but folding her arms across her chest in a pose of self-protection.

Bett could envision her ideal response to that. She would put her arms around Rains's neck and bring her lips so close to Rains's mouth that their breath would mingle. *There are many different kinds of torture, Sergeant,* she would say, waiting for Rains to kiss her. And she would. Although Sergeant Rains continually rebuilt the wall between them, it seemed a little less high each time. And even if Rains would not want to admit it, there was a special familiarity between them now. The sergeant would never have used touch to instruct her during the first weeks of basic training, and Bett was certain that she could feel Rains responding to her in increasingly physical ways. Knowing she possessed a certain beauty, Bett had complete confidence in her own appeal. She had never been turned down, particularly by someone she really wanted—at least not for long.

In real life, however, Bett knew that while she probably could get Rains to kiss her, she would get transferred out of the squad the next day. Or Rains would be so horrified by her own behavior she would never speak to Bett again. So she settled for just saying, "There are many different kinds of torture, Sergeant," and leaving it at that. She did sway her hips just a little more as she walked back toward the bleachers. Halfway across the field, she turned back. Rains was watching. *That's what I thought,* Bett confirmed to herself. "Are we going to talk about the finish?" she asked innocently.

"Oh yes." Rains cleared her throat and jogged over, drawing a line in the dirt with her foot. "Pretend this is the finish line. You need to practice staying in balance while leaning forward, because you want to lean across the line. Not fall, but lean." Rains made the motion. "Like you are running to hug someone, but your arms will be behind you, not in front."

They practiced the finish-line lean several times. Twice, Bett leaned too far and stumbled forward until Rains reached out her arm and caught her. Bett's momentum spun Rains a quarter turn until they were facing each other.

Bett giggled. "Why, thank you, Sergeant."

"My pleasure," Rains replied. But when their eyes met for just a second, Rains let go of her immediately.

It was starting to get dark as Rains watched Bett run again. "You have a nice stride. Swift and sure. My only correction is that you are bringing your arms up too high. Drop your shoulders. Relax." She ran along behind Bett and when Bett's arms came up too high, she touched Bett in the armpit.

Bett jumped away laughing. "Stop that, Sergeant."

"Why? Are you ticklish?" Rains asked in a devilish voice.

"Nooo." Bett sounded completely unconvincing, even to herself.

"Well, you'd better keep those arms down, or you will get tickled every time," Rains warned, wiggling her fingers.

"You'll have to catch me first," Bett said and sprinted away, using Rains's quick start method. *I think that actually does make me faster* she thought, but after a few yards she felt Rains's fingers slip into her armpit. Bett couldn't run at that pace and laugh at the same time. She stopped so abruptly that Rains ran into her and they fell to the ground. Bett was on her side, away from Rains who was still tickling her from behind. "Dress that line, Sergeant," Bett said, between gasps of laughter.

She could hear the chuckle in Rains's voice. "Keep those arms down, Private."

Bett wiggled away, turned over, and saw genuine laughter in Rains's eyes. For just a moment, the sergeant was looking at her with an expression that was relaxed and happy, though she still wasn't exactly smiling. Without thinking, Bett tucked a stray piece of hair back into Rains's hat and let her hand trace Rains's cheek as she said, "I really do like you, Rains. I hope you don't mind." She watched the expression in Rains's eyes change, deepen, as they seemed to connect with something inside. *Say it, Rains*, Bett begged silently. *Tell me what you're feeling right now.*

Rains's mouth opened just a bit before it dawned on her that she was lying on the parade ground just inches away from a private from her squad. Like every other time that she'd been with Smythe, the whole sequence of events had begun innocently enough, but somehow their conversation, their actions, even their physical contact had shifted into something much more personal. What if Colonel Issacson saw them? Rains judged that if conduct had to be explained, it must look bad. She was on her feet in a second, her face back to its usual firmness. "I apologize, Private Smythe. That was completely improper of me." She held out her hand.

Bett sighed as she let Rains help her to her feet. "As far as I'm concerned, you didn't do anything wrong, Sergeant. I thought we were just having fun."

"That may be, Private, but someone walking by might think differently." Rains tried to explain, but Bett was already moving away.

From over her shoulder, Bett snapped, "Well, who gives a damn what someone walking by might think?" as she started back toward the bleachers.

Rains caught up quickly, still uneasy. "Don't you know what happens to women in the service who are accused of such immoral conduct?" she hissed. "The Army may be lenient but they are not blind. There have been cases where certain women have been discharged—sent home with a blue ticket—immediately. Now you may not care about that, but I do. I told you that I may want to stay in the Army even after the war. I may want to go overseas before this is over. I'm due for a promotion. And I don't have a rich father to take care of me if I botch this up."

As soon as those last words were out, Rains knew she had said too much. Bett's expression hardened and her voice was like ice. "Don't worry, Sergeant. I'll make sure no one mistakes us for anything remotely resembling friends ever again."

"No, that's not what I meant—" Rains began but Bett had already reached the bleachers and was picking up her jacket. "I apologize." Bett was walking away very quickly. Rains felt a lurch inside; Private Smythe had good reason to be angry with her now, but she didn't want that. She followed, trying to think of what to say. "Wait. Please. I really am sorry. That was truly the improper thing. Not earlier. Please...Bett."

Bett stopped. She did not turn around, however. Rains came up close behind her, putting a hand on Bett's arm. Her voice was warm and sincere. "I was completely out of line on that remark. I know you are making your own way here, as I am." Smythe turned, her expression blank. Rains tried to continue, but she was flustered by Bett's coolness. "I—I—"

Bett cocked her head with her eyebrows up. "You what, Sergeant?" Waiting, she reached her right hand across her body to rub her left shoulder.

Rain seized on this. "I think you need me to take a look at that shoulder. The way you run, it must be sore."

"Don't press your luck with undue criticism, Sergeant. You'd better intend to give me a really good massage or I'm out of here," Bett warned, but there was less distance in her tone. She let Rains lead her back to the bleachers, where Rains put her jacket on the ground for Bett to sit on. Rains sat one row up and ran her fingers along the top of Bett's shoulder, feeling her trapezius muscle. She increased the pressure coming back toward Bett's neck, and Bett groaned involuntarily.

Rains stopped. "Too hard?"

"Oh no," Bett assured her. "Perfect." She undid three buttons and slipped her blouse past her shoulders, pulling her bra straps down with it.

Rains tried not to notice Bett's smooth skin or feel the heat coming off her body as she worked her fingers back out, stopping at a particular spot. "See? This is where it hurts from you bringing your arms up too high." She pressed in a little harder and worked in a slow circle.

"Ooh. I will pay you to do that every night," Bett said, and Rains felt her relaxing into her touch.

"No payment," Rains said, softly, smoothing out the muscle again. "It's just your turn to accept my apology."

"Uh-huh...but only if you do the other side, too." The anger was gone from Bett's voice, replaced by a tone as langorous as her body was becoming.

"Of course," Rains said, keeping her left hand where she had just worked and moving to the right side of Bett's neck with her right hand. As Rains worked her fingers across, she glimpsed Bett's firm breasts, barely covered by her shirt. Rains tried to block the idea of touching her there as well, as Bett sighed and leaned back against her, completely giving in to her touch. "That's right," Rains murmured, more than her hands responding to Bett's submission. She tilted Bett's head forward just a bit and began to massage the back of her neck.

"Oh God," Bett moaned. "That feels so wonderful."

"Good," Rains said softly, "because I truly didn't mean to hurt your feelings, Bett." Her hands moved along the sides of Bett's neck, stroking in smooth circles. "I like you, too, but I cannot tell you that. I cannot have favorites. I have to be impartial. It wouldn't be fair to the other girls if they knew."

"I told you, I'm very discreet," Bett mumbled, a flush of arousal spreading across her chest.

Rains worked her thumbs along the ridge of Bett's exposed shoulder blades with just the right amount of pressure. Bett's body was trim and firm but with very womanly curves. Listening to her little sounds of pleasure, Rains felt a pull deep inside. *I want to keep doing this. I want to touch her all over. I want to...* "Stand up," she said gruffly, with her hands back on Bett's shoulders.

"No." Bett didn't want to move, unless it was to pull Rains on top of her.

"Come on. I need to move your arms while I check your shoulders again." Bett could hear that Rains was trying to sound official. Stepping down to the ground to help Bett rise, the sergeant slid her arms under Bett's shoulders. "No tickling, I promise." As they moved together, Bett was almost too relaxed to stand alone, so she leaned her full weight back against her sergeant's body. Her hips fit just at Rains's crotch and they moved gently there as she tried to keep her balance. Bett felt Rains's breathing quicken as she rested her head on the left side of Rains's chest. She knew Rains was looking at the visible swell of her breast and at her hard nipples pushing just at edge of her lowered blouse. She moved her hips again until she heard a sound of desire come from Rains's throat. She began to arch, stretching to make Rains's hands move over to her breasts. *Oh yes, Rains, please...*

When Rains's hands moved, though, they were on the backs of Bett's shoulders, and Rains had managed to move a step back. "Don't turn, Private," she said roughly.

"Why not?" Bett asked, still breathing deeply, trying to think of what else she could do to make Rains touch her again.

"I cannot look at you now. This cannot happen." The sergeant held Bett off with one hand and picked up her jacket with the other. "This cannot happen now," she repeated and ran off into the deepening night.

Bloody hell. Bett fixed her bra and buttoned her blouse. She had to sit for a few moments before she was composed enough to walk back to the barracks. Once there, she showered and tried to read until lights out. It was hard to believe that even though the time with Rains had caused her to miss dinner, she wasn't a bit hungry. Not for food, anyway. She was having trouble concentrating on anything else, though; her mind was more interested in revisiting the afternoon. She chatted a bit with Jo and Phyllis, asking about their Saturday afternoon off, complaining halfheartedly about her punishment. Rains did not come through every night anymore, and Bett was not surprised that Sergeant Webber appeared for CQ.

After lights out, Bett turned restlessly on her cot, waiting until she heard regular breathing all around her. She knew she would have to release the tension she had been feeling since her encounter with Rains or tomorrow would be impossible. She lay on her back, slipping her right hand inside her pajama bottoms, and began to masturbate. With her left hand she cupped her breast, playing with the nipple the way she had hoped that Rains would do, while gradually working the fingers of her right hand faster between her legs. All she could think about was Rains...her warm hands, her strong fingers, that one minute when they were on the ground and she had looked so relaxed, and that sound she'd made when she had felt Bett's hips against her. Yes, that was very good. Bett could play that moan in her head, knowing that no matter what Rains said or did, it was happening for her, too. Rains's arms tightening around her that night after Mel's—yes, that was nice. Her low voice murmuring, *You really were wonderful tonight* and *I like you, too...*

Now she was almost as wet as she had been earlier that afternoon when Rains had run away from her. As she imagined how Rains would kiss, Bett tried to make sure that her breathing did not get too loud, but it was difficult. She enjoyed being vocal during sex, but she knew one of her squad members could wake at any time. Her pace quickened as the tingling sensations began to spread outward through her body. Then another thought came into her head. *What if Rains was doing the same thing in her bed in the officers' quarters?* A vision of Rains's strong body, naked and straining against her own hand, pushed Bett over the edge. She came hard, shuddering quietly but thinking, *Oh yes, Rains, yes. Now you come for me.* She pulled her pillow down beside her and lay on it as she fell asleep, wishing for Rains's body.

Bett's brief pleasure turned to worry when Sergeant Webber arrived again to march them to breakfast. Rains was not in her usual place at the officers' table. Even though it was Saturday, they had already been scheduled for another morning of marching. Several of the girls expressed the opinion that if a VIP was coming, it had better be Clark Gable to make the extra practice worthwhile. When Webber dismissed them for lunch after conducting their drills, Bett went quickly to the mess hall. As she reached for the door, she looked back and thought she saw Rains's tall form in the distance, talking to someone. But the sergeant did not appear for lunch, either. Bett ate lightly and hurried back to the barracks to get changed, hoping that Rains would not stand her up for their second round of coaching. She had started over toward the parade grounds again when she heard someone call her name. Looking around, she saw Jo Archer coming toward her.

"Sarge told me she would be coaching us this afternoon for the race tomorrow. I see you're ready to go."

Coaching *us*? Bett asked herself. *That must have been Archer that Rains was talking to. That's how she is going to deal with what happened yesterday, by having someone else there.* But she did like Jo, and it wasn't the New Yorker's fault that she'd spent the night dreaming about being in Rains's arms. "Great," she said, hoping she sounded genuine. "The more the merrier."

Rains was sitting on the very top row of the bleachers, watching as they arrived. She told Bett to take a lap while she showed Archer some of the quick start moves that she had showed Bett yesterday. Bett noted with some satisfaction that Rains didn't seem to be touching Archer quite as much as she had touched her. When Bett finished her lap, Rains had them run three races against each other. Archer won every time. Somewhat reluctantly, it seemed to Bett, the sergeant told Archer to take a lap. Rains looked at the ground until Archer was out of earshot. "You are not running with any heart today," she said finally, not really meeting Bett's eyes.

"Were you afraid to be alone with me?" Bett asked, disregarding Rains's criticism.

"No, I am not afraid, but I thought it was best this way," Rains said, still looking away. "I told you how it is for me, with my position in the Army. You are under my command. This"—she gestured back and forth between them with her hand—"is not right, Private. Ours cannot be a…relationship…like that. I am your drill instructor."

She's thinking of Boudreaux, Bett understood, studying Rains's profile. She looked tired. "Didn't you sleep last night?" she asked softly, both of them watching as Archer ran around the far turn.

Rains finally looked briefly at Bett. "Not much," she admitted, turning as Archer continued coming toward them.

"Can we still be friends, at least?" Bett asked, hoping to keep Rains's gaze on her.

"I don't know," Rains answered, a little sadly, Bett thought. Then she asked, "Can you beat Archer?"

"Are the two related?"

"I'm trying to change the subject," Rains stated, looking at her hands.

Bett had to laugh a little. "You're not supposed to announce that, Sergeant. You're supposed to be more subtle."

"I was never very good at duplicity," Rains said, shrugging. "If I want you to know what I am thinking, I will tell you."

Bett looked back at Rains as Archer ran up, panting a bit. "I'll try."

"You'll try what?" Archer asked.

"To beat you this time," Bett answered.

Jo grinned. "Easy to say, hard to do, Queenie."

"Remember what I told you, Private Smythe," Rains said in her voice of authority while, much to Bett's surprise, she put her hands on Bett's shoulders—from a respectable distance, of course. "Keep your arms down. Relax your shoulders."

Bett won the next two races. The third was too close for Rains to call. "Take another lap, Smythe." Rains worked with Archer on the finish lean that she had showed Bett. Bett noted that Rains never caught Archer, though probably it was because Jo never leaned too far forward. *Perhaps that is the secret to winning in tomorrow's race,* Bett thought. *Use a bigger lean at the finish.* She wanted to ask the sergeant, but when she got back, Rains dismissed them, saying, "It's almost time for dinner. Take an easy run back to your barracks and take a warm shower immediately. Not too hot." She nodded encouragingly. "Good work. I like both your chances tomorrow."

Archer ran off, saying, "I'll beat you to the shower, too, Queenie."

Rains was sitting back on the bleachers. Bett sat beside her, a little distance away. "I couldn't help noticing that you weren't at breakfast or lunch today. Will you be at dinner?"

"No," Rains said shortly. "I am fasting today."

"You are? Why?" Bett asked automatically.

Rains eyes shifted into the distance. "For personal reasons, Private. And please don't interrogate me about this."

"Just tell me...is it because of me?"

"No," Rains shook her head. Her eyes swept briefly over Bett. "Although it would be nice if that would help."

"Well, why then?" Bett pressed.

Rains's voice was unusually heated. "It is not your place to ask me these things. You are a private and I am a sergeant. I have dismissed you. Please return to your barracks."

Bett stood, her tone defiant. "I wasn't asking you as a private. I was asking you as a friend."

Rains leaned back against the next row of the bleachers and looked at the sky. She sighed deeply and her hand rubbed slowly on her thigh, a gesture Bett couldn't recall ever seeing her make before. Her quiet answer sounded forced. "My friend would hear me when I asked her not to interrogate me. My friend would see that I just want to sit here alone for a time while the sun goes down. My friend would not force me to say that this is the day that my mother died and I am fasting to honor her memory."

Bett brought her hand to her mouth. "Oh, Rains, I'm sorry. I'm so, so sorry. I'll go."

Rains said nothing. Bett walked away, with her head down. She felt terrible but there was no way to repair what she had done. *She's right, damn it. I wasn't being a friend. I was being nosy, and thinking everything was all about me. She's made it clear how she feels. Instead of still trying to seduce her, I should try to actually care about her.* As she turned toward the barracks she could still see Rains, just a speck, back on the top row. *If I could win tomorrow's race for her, maybe she'd forgive me.*

CHAPTER TEN

"Come on, Queenie," Jo exhorted when they returned to the barracks after breakfast. "We've got to stretch and you know Sarge will want us to be the first squad at the race. Think you can beat the Bronx Bullet when it counts?" she asked, pointing proudly at herself.

"I doubt it," Bett said, laughing. "I was never much good at sports, though I did take dance all through my childhood, and enjoyed that."

"Ooh." At the exclamation, they all looked at Teresa, surprised, since she rarely initiated conversation and had spoken even less since Helen had been gone. "M-momma and I went to Oklahoma City once when I was l-little. I don't remember why, only that we passed by a ballet school and she let me look in for a minute. I guess there was gonna be a show, because they were playing music like I had never heard, and the girls were wearing tiny little dresses that practically floated when they moved. And when they started dancing…" She stopped, a dreamy expression on her face. "It was so pretty."

"Ballet!" Jo snorted. "How can you call this dancing?" She hopped around in imitation of pliés and jetés. As the other girls laughed, she landed off balance and crumpled to the ground in obvious pain. Grabbing at her leg, she cried, "Oh damn, my knee."

The others rushed over to her, just as Rains entered, looking crisp and official as usual in her khaki pants, jacket, and hat. "This squad is due on the parade ground now—" she began, but seeing the group gathered around Jo, her orders cut off abruptly. She made her way to Jo and knelt beside her. "Let me see," she said to Jo, and took the injured knee between her hands. As Jo wiped her eyes, Rains felt the area gently. After a moment, she turned and ordered, "Jackson, Ferguson, Rangel, Kendrick, get Private Archer to the infirmary."

The four attempted to pick Jo up in the fireman's carry that they had recently learned. She tried to brush them off, arguing, "I can walk, I just—"

"Private Archer," Rains said, her calm voice cutting through the squabble, "your squad members would greatly benefit from practicing this technique."

And that's as close to please *as you're ever going to get from an officer,* thought Bett, as she nodded at Archer in support.

"Oh, hell, all right." Archer submitted. As the four lifted her, she amended, "I mean, yes, Sergeant."

Rains straightened. "I'll check on you soon, Archer." As the group passed through the door, Rains turned and surveyed the remainder of her group. Her eyes stopped on Bett. "What happened here, squad leader?"

"We were talking about ballet, and she was just being silly," Bett explained. "She was imitating a dance move and landed badly."

"Ballet?" Rains questioned, and looked around to see the others nodding in agreement. "Why—?" She turned back to Bett with a stern expression. "Private Smythe, when the other members of your squad return, bring them to the parade ground, on the double."

For the first time, Bett understood the wisdom of not looking your commander in the eye. *She thinks this is my fault, and maybe it is.* She snapped to attention. "Yes, Sergeant."

By the time the squad reached the grounds, other groups were already competing. Sergeant Rains was nowhere to be seen, but Sergeant Webber conducted their races. Knowing how much Archer had been looking forward to participating in the event, Bett ran harder than she ever had. They ran in groups of five, and much to her surprise, she defeated everyone in her group, and then defeated the winners of the other squads within her platoon.

There was to be a break before the final interplatoon competition began, and Bett sat on the ground, exhausted. *This may be it, Archer.* Maria had brought her some water and Phyllis supplied a damp towel that she had covering her head. Bett hadn't really been listening to the girls' excited conversation, but she noticed when things got quiet.

"I guess Your Highness thinks she's pretty fast, huh?" said a vaguely familiar voice.

Bett pulled the towel back from her head to see Sergeant Moore standing beside her. Bett didn't have the energy to think of a witty response, so she just pulled the towel back over her.

"On your feet, Private," Moore ordered brusquely.

Bett considered this order and what would happen if she just sat there instead. With a patient clearing of her throat, she stood, pulled the towel off, and straightened.

Moore looked around Bett's squad members who were also standing at attention. "The rest of you birds, beat it."

Everyone hesitated, obviously reluctant to leave Bett alone with Sergeant Moore. Bett felt a warm appreciation for their loyalty.

Moore's face reddened as she glanced around. "Dismissed, Privates."

The group drifted away, although only as far as the next platoon group, keeping their eyes on their friend Bett and Sergeant Moore. Moore stood with her back to them. "I've got something for you, Private," she said in a strange tone. She reached into her pocket and then hesitated. "Where's Rains? I thought she'd be here giving you a rubdown or something."

Bett resented almost everything about this comment, but the mention of her sergeant's name kept her calm. "I believe she's seeing to an injured squad member at the moment."

Moore's eyes scanned the infirmary in the distance. "Oh yeah, here she comes now. Good. Then I'll go ahead and give you this." She handed Bett a telegram.

Bett wondered about the timing of this delivery. Was it even a real telegram or was it just a ploy to shake her concentration? She took it without looking and put it in her pocket. "Thank you, Sergeant."

"Shouldn't you read it now?" Moore asked.

"Are you giving me an order, Sergeant?" Bett responded.

Hostility flared on Moore's face. Then, checking the distance that Rains had yet to come, she tried for a more moderate attitude. "Why no, Private. It's not an order. I just thought you'd want to look at it right away. You know, so your mind wouldn't be elsewhere. I would think you'd want to make sure that everyone in your family is okay before you do a silly thing like run a race."

Just as I thought, Bett assured herself, *it's a trick to make me lose.* "Thank you, Sergeant Moore," she replied, straightening again.

Moore waited. Bett continued standing at attention. Moore realized she had been dismissed and gave up the evenhanded tone. "You're not gonna win anyway, you know," she snarled. "Have you checked your competition? The girl from my platoon is almost as tall as Rains and fast as the wind."

As if Moore's words had summoned her, Bett saw that Rains had reached the parade grounds, accompanied by Jo, who was wearing a cumbersome-looking knee brace and a big smile. Moore snorted and walked away.

"Way to go, Queenie!" Archer congratulated her. "You're just lucky I wasn't there to knock you off in the first round," she added as Bett met her with a hug.

"I'm so sorry, Jo. And I'm afraid this is the last gasp for me." Bett smiled at her. "I know you could take on all comers, but I believe I'm done. Unless you have some secret advice to help me win."

"You want to win for Archer and for your squad," Sergeant Rains said, glancing briefly at Moore's withdrawing form, "and that is good." Her voice deepened with intensity as she added, "But this race you must run for yourself. Not just with your legs, but with your heart. Do that, and I know you will win." She put her hands on Bett's shoulders and squeezed.

Their eyes met for a second and Bett smiled. She knew what Rains was reminding her of. Or was it something more? *I really want to win for you, Rains,* she wanted to say. The rest of the squad was gathering back around her. Bett felt strangely energized. Rains gave her a nod and stepped back from the group.

"I will be one of the judges in this race, so I will be at the finish line. Webber will start you. Good luck, Private Smythe."

When she was out of earshot, Jo spoke up. "You know, Sarge really is okay. She sat there the whole time they were examining me, just kinda humming a weird little song." She lowered her voice. "I guess it was some kind of Indian thing, but it helped me calm down, just hearing it."

"So are you going to be all right?" Phyllis asked.

"Oh yeah. It's just a sprain so I'll need a couple of days with this getup. I get out of exercise too, for a week, and then I have to check back with the doc." She turned to Bett. "Rains asked me to tell her what happened again. I told her it wasn't your fault, that I just ain't no ballet dancer."

Everyone laughed. Bett looked around at her friends—her family, Rains would say—feeling the ties between them deepen. A whistle sounded and a voice called, "Runners to the line."

Archer touched Bett's shoulder and said quickly, "When I was little and we raced in school, I used to imagine something I really wanted at the finish line, like a bicycle or a doll. And I would tell myself if I could get there first, I would get it. Maybe you could try that."

Maybe I could, Bett thought, looking toward a tall form at the finish line.

❖

At the presentation of the winners' medals, Bett's gold was awarded to her by the base commander as the squad cheered loudly. Sizing her up as she hung the ribbon around her neck, "Private... Smythe, isn't it?" Colonel Issacson asked, clearly knowing who she was.

"Yes, ma'am," Bett saluted, realizing too late that by winning, she had again strayed from remaining incognito.

"Well congratulations, Private," Issacson continued. "I'm sure you've made your squad and Sergeant Rains very proud."

Bett tried to sneak a quick glance at Rains, who was standing in her usual place at the head of the squad, but the late afternoon sun was in her eyes. Thinking back on Archer's advice, Bett was not completely sure what her sergeant's reaction would be if she knew Bett's true motivation, or if the sergeant suspected that the best part of winning for Bett had been how Rains had stepped forward to catch her as she almost fell while hurling herself across the finish line. Rains had let them spin around once to slow Bett's speed, whispering, "Well done, Bett," and Bett's arms had gone tightly around Rains's neck as she answered, "I did it for you." To the colonel, she only smiled and said, "Yes, ma'am."

After she was dismissed from the reviewing stand, Bett walked directly to Archer and hung the medal around her neck. The girls started to cheer, but Rains immediately called them to attention and led them in saluting Bett as she walked back to her place among the group. Archer was blushing but kept looking at the medal with an expression of wonder. When Bett got to her space, she glanced back at the reviewing stand and saw Colonel Issacson frowning at Sergeant Rains. *Does she suspect that Rains told me about her race? Am I giving away too much about our time together?* Bett wondered, but the deed was done. When they were dismissed, the cheers started again.

Bett was almost too tired to go to dinner after her hot shower, but her squad members convinced her that she would feel better after she ate. It was true, even though she was frequently interrupted during the meal by congratulations from well-wishers. The area around her table was so busy she couldn't even see over to where Rains was always sitting. For once, she felt fairly confident that Rains would come through the barracks later, so she didn't worry about it.

As she got ready for bed, she was replaying the day one more time in her mind when she remembered the telegram. Not wanting to alarm the others, she quietly retrieved it from the pocket of her dirty exercise clothes, placing it in the pocket of her robe before starting toward the door of the barracks.

"Where are you off to, speedy?" a drowsy voice asked.

"Is that my new name?" Bett smiled at Jo's sleepy form, still wearing the medal over her pajamas. "Well, I like it better than Queenie. I'm still a bit keyed up, Jo. Thought I might get some air before I"—she adjusted her accent to pure American—"hit the sack."

"Don't be late for bed check," Jo cautioned with a yawn. "You know the Sarge will be here to tuck us in pretty soon."

"I'll just be a moment," Bett assured her and stepped through the door. In the light of the barracks porch, Bett could just make out the choppy letters of the telegram: *Kent Prep bombed. Casualties unknown. More to come.*

It was signed by William Prosser, Emma's brother.

❖

Rains looked at the medal hanging around Archer's neck. *I'm proud of you, Smythe*, she thought, deciding that this would be all right to say personally when Smythe returned. Rains assumed she was in the bathroom. After making her way through the barracks and waiting another five minutes with no sign of Smythe, Rains checked the restroom. Not a sound. Rains moved quickly back to the empty bed.

"Archer!" She gently shook her awake.

"Sarge?" She seemed a little blurry from the pain pill the doctor had given her for her knee.

"Yes. Where's Smythe, Archer?"

"She's not here?"

"No. She's not in her bed or anywhere else in the barracks. When did you last see her, Private?" Rains demanded, as Archer yawned and her eyes closed again.

"Um, I dunno, just before lights out, I think. Something about too excited to sleep...and getting some...air." In less than five seconds, Archer had drifted off again.

Rains scanned the room again, as if Smythe might suddenly materialize. When she looked back, Archer was snoring softly. She began her search methodically, first around the outside of the barracks, and then expanding it to the buildings between there and the mess hall. She'd taken one of the camp's emergency flashlights and shined it wherever she thought it wouldn't be noticed. Twice, she called out Smythe's name softly. Finally, she walked out toward the parade grounds and stood quietly, listening. Breathing in the night air, she turned toward the race course, where the makeshift finish line had been. Something...a faint sound, a rustling...and a familiar scent?

Rains turned off the light and walked quietly, letting the soft sounds guide her. Smythe was sitting against a barrel that had marked one boundary of the race, with her head buried in her arms.

"Private, what are—" Rains began heatedly but stopped when Bett lifted her tearstained face. Rains was so undone by her devastated expression that she dropped to her knees. "What is it, Bett?" she asked, her fingers touching Bett's hand very lightly.

In response, Bett handed her a crumpled telegram, but there wasn't enough light for Rains to read it, and she didn't want to give their position away with her flashlight. Rains slipped down beside her and sat, cross-legged. "Can you just tell me?"

Bett took in a ragged breath. "Bloody Nazis," she managed to say, breathing in a sob. Rains squeezed gently. Bett didn't seem to notice. She wiped her nose on her shoulder, repeating more strongly, "Bloody Nazis. They hit Kent Prep, my boarding school, with one of their rockets. An all-girls school. What kind of military target is that, I ask you?" She shook her head, and her face twisted with sorrow as she started to cry again.

Turning to face her, Rains slipped her arms around Bett's heaving shoulders. Bett gave in willingly until her face rested on Rains's chest. Above the occasional catch of her breaths, Bett could hear a low humming sound and she felt them rocking together, ever so slightly. She felt the evening breeze, cool on her tears. She felt the vibration from Rains's throat, the soft sounds completely foreign to her but still soothing somehow. Her crying slowed. She felt the solidness of Rains's arms holding her, the very soft touch of Rains's hand resting in her hair, moving ever so slightly. Then the sadness pushed its way through again. She allowed herself another thought of Emma, of the wide stairways and dark-paneled classrooms, of girls' laughter and those damned plaques. Could it really all be gone? Tears started again as she felt such profound loss. Kent Prep had been her home for all those years. *This dreadful war. How much longer can it go on? How many more lives will it cost?* Finally, she breathed two deep shuddering breaths, and leaned back to raise her head. Rains released her at once. The humming stopped.

Straightening, Bett sought to compose herself. "I'm sorry, but I simply couldn't stay at the barracks. I couldn't seem to stop crying and I didn't want to upset everyone else. In fact, I'd rather not tell anyone, at least until I know something more."

Rains nodded, her eyes sad. Bett wondered if concealed grief was something else she completely understood. "What else did the telegram say?"

"Casualties unknown." Bett looked hopefully into Rains's face. "My—my best friend from school, Emma, she works there now in administration. Her brother sent the telegram. Perhaps there was some warning. They may have evacuated." She felt her lip begin to tremble again.

Rains reached into a pocket and offered her a handkerchief. Bett uttered a choked laugh in spite of herself as she took it.

"Oh God, you really are gallant, aren't you?" Bett asked, wiping her eyes.

Rains looked away. "I don't know what you mean."

"Chivalrous." Rains shook her head. "Brave, heroic."

Rains grunted and stood quickly. "You must be the brave one now. We need to get you back to the barracks. It's late and you need some sleep. There is nothing more to do with your grief tonight." She held out her hand and Bett took it and held on even after she was on her feet.

"I want to thank you, Sergeant," she said almost shyly. "You've been most kind. I know I don't deserve your compassion, but I very much appreciate it." Not quite ready to look into Rains's face, she eyed the tear-dampened cloth of her jacket. "Oh, I hope I haven't ruined your uniform." She began trying to dry it with the handkerchief. Rains grabbed her arm abruptly and Bett realized she had been rubbing against her sergeant's breast.

"Let's walk," Rains said thickly. She still had hold of Bett's wrist, so there was little choice. They walked silently, Rains's long stride hurrying Bett along. After a few steps, Rains's grip had softened, and Bett managed to slide her hand into the sergeant's large, warm palm. "Could you slow down a bit?" she asked softly. Rains's long stride faltered for a moment and as Bett drew even, the sergeant was looking at her with an expression that was almost pained. "It's all right," Bett added, daring to give Rains's hand a soft squeeze. "I'm just not quite up to military haste tonight." The sergeant turned away without comment but slowed her usual quick pace to an easy stroll.

Letting Rains lead them, Bett closed her eyes for a few seconds, but images of familiar buildings exploding amidst fire, smoke, and screams came toward her again, as from a distance, and she trembled. Rains pulled her closer, cradling Bett's hand with both of hers, the length of their arms touching, matching her walk to

Bett's exactly so their bodies moved together. Bett felt the comfort that was being offered and she took it gratefully, leaning her head against Rains's side and feeling absolutely no resistance. She let the warmth and sweetness of contact with this good woman fill her, let the depth and kindness of Rains's heart drive the horror of war away...at least for this moment. She sighed and Rains squeezed gently, as if she knew what Bett had chosen and approved. For a few sweet moments that was all there was, until she felt Rains lift her slightly and she realized they had stepped onto the sidewalk and were turning toward the barracks. Breathing in, Bett felt eased and strengthened, and she had just raised her head when a Jeep rolled down the street and turned toward them.

A male voice called out, "Who goes there? Stop and be recognized."

Quickly dropping Bett's hand, Rains stepped forward into the headlights. "Sergeant Rains escorting Private Smythe back to barracks." A flashlight shone from the darkness, sweeping over Rains and settling on Smythe, whose robe was somewhat askew, revealing clinging silk pajamas.

"What's going on here, Sergeant?" asked the voice, with a suggestion of a leer.

Rains stepped sideways, taking up the light and shielding Bett. "Private Smythe has had some bad news from home, Corporal. She needed some time away from the squad. You understand." She stepped closer to the Jeep. "Is that you, Lutz?" she asked in a slightly more familiar tone.

The light switched off. "Yeah, Rains. It's me. Okay, finish your business. But you'd better hurry, 'cause Crowley's on the next patrol." Bett could hear his voice drop to a serious mutter. "Can't believe that bastard's still here."

Rains pointed toward the barracks. "We're right there, Lutz. Thanks"

"So are we even?" Lutz asked, hopefully.

Rains gave a scornful snort. "Not even close, brother."

The Jeep's engine started. "Carry on, Sergeant," came the fading voice as the vehicle rolled away.

Rains turned to her, and Bett thought she was angry until she felt her robe being closed gently around her and the belt tightened. "Let's go," Rains ordered and directed Bett a little more quickly toward the building, her hand on the back of Bett's shoulder. They walked to the silent barracks, their voices low.

"Have I gotten you in trouble?" Bett asked miserably, turning back to Rains at the steps that led to the door.

"No, but we were lucky. Some of the other MPs aren't as decent as Lutz." In the dim light, Bett could see a worried look come over Rains's face. "And we do look a little…"

"Disheveled?" Bett supplied.

Rains grunted. After another quick glance at Bett, her chin lifted. "You know those pajamas are not regulation issue."

"Regulation issue pajamas are scratchy and stiff."

"That's not the point, Private," Rains retorted, but Bett saw the encouragement in her eyes.

"That's exactly the point, Sergeant." Bett raised her face to look at Rains, feeling the beginning of a smile inside. Then she took a shuddering breath.

Rains extended her arm and slowly brushed Bett's cheek with a delicate touch. "Sleep," she ordered.

She had started to turn away, but Bett caught her sleeve. Quickly slipping her arms around Rains's neck, she stretched and kissed her lightly on the cheek. "Thank you again for being so… understanding," she whispered into Rains's ear.

Rains stood very still. As Bett quietly opened the door to the barracks, she thought she heard the word *gallant* like an echo, but when she turned, Rains was gone. Her last thought before she drifted into sleep was for the telegram, but all she could feel in her hand was a soft white handkerchief.

❖

The next day was back to the routine, although it seemed to Bett that their sergeant worked them a little easier than usual. Twice she found Rains's eyes on her; the second time Bett gave just the slightest nod. *I'm all right,* she tried to say. She thought she got a quick nod in return, although she couldn't be sure. Rains didn't really look at her again, though.

On Tuesday, Helen returned from her specialized school at Fort Oglethorpe in Georgia. By the next morning, whatever problem had soured her friendship with Tee seemed to be resolved and harmony was restored. Everyone seemed to be taking a deep breath for the home stretch of their basic training.

Bett had taken to carrying Rains's handkerchief in the pocket of whatever she was wearing. After several days had passed and the sergeant made no mention of it, Bett decided it was a gift. Almost a week later, she was holding it folded in her hand when she felt the soft pressure on her bed of someone leaning across her while bringing up the covers. Then there was just the lightest touch on her cheek, so faint she almost might have dreamed it, except for the way her body reacted. She turned toward the source, keeping her eyes closed.

"Oh, Rains," she whispered in a voice soft with sleep, "it could be so good."

"Shh."

Bett snuggled into the pillow, hugging it as she sighed softly, and Rains felt the sigh rush through her like a warm wind. The press of emotion moved into her thoughts until she imagined herself there beside Bett; she was the one Bett curled against, the one Bett held close. She almost stumbled as she turned to leave, forcing herself away from the place she most wanted to be. Despite all her resolutions and all her best intentions, Rains had to admit that she was unable to keep herself from crossing the line she had always kept between her true self and her recruits, and knowing the impropriety of it didn't seem to help either. Something about Elizabeth Smythe erased all such lines and kept the steady calm that Rains had carefully created inside herself in a constant state of upheaval.

Rains had given herself a firm talking-to after their first embrace, but then had given herself permission to pull up the covers on Smythe after deciding that she would have done the same for any of her recruits. Now it had turned into spending an extra moment just watching Bett sleep when Rains was there on the pretense of looking in on the rest of the squad. She'd come in late on her restless nights, having convinced herself that no one else—especially Bett—would know, certain that allowing herself that one unguarded moment would help her maintain better control during the day. But now she had touched Bett, twice. The first time, admittedly, Bett's hair had fallen forward onto her face, but this time…a caress on the cheek for no reason except to feel her skin.

Running didn't help, chanting didn't help; she had lost the cool dispassionate place where she could stay clear of such feelings. Every time she dug in and tried to resist, Bett slipped past her defenses with the skill of a warrior, found her, and pulled her closer. Now her blood raged inside her each time her memory took her to the moments she had been with Bett, especially those times they had touched. She couldn't avoid her own mind that replayed over and over the warm feeling of Bett turning into her arms the night they had been at Mel's, the sensuousness of Bett's hips leaning into her by the bleachers, and the sweetness of holding her as she cried about her school.

But it was when she had seen the indomitable spirit in Bett's eyes during the race that Rains understood why she hadn't been able to shake the physical attraction. Because in those seconds before Bett flung herself across the finish line, Rains saw all she truly had to offer—and the steadfast resolve and bold courage that propelled Bett past her competition in a race she had no business winning touched Rains's core. Elizabeth Smythe was a special woman, and at that moment, Rains simply couldn't let her fall. She'd spun them to dissipate the impact of their bodies, but when Bett's arms had come around her neck and she'd whispered in Rains's ear, that touch and those words had fused the bond between them. Now there was almost no controlling the body that seemed virtually unknown to her, the one that burned and throbbed and ached for something she couldn't ask for, that she would never have. Sergeant Rains steeled herself all the way back to her room. *No more late-night visits. You can do this. Leave her alone. She'll be gone soon enough anyway.* She actually welcomed the pain that accompanied that last thought. Pain was her most familiar companion in matters of the heart.

CHAPTER ELEVEN

B ett thought about her conversations with Sergeant Rains while passing the time in classes she didn't care much about and found herself fascinated with the question of how a Sioux Indian came to be a sergeant in the Women's Army Corps. One afternoon when they had some free time, Bett used the arrival of a new batch of recruits as cover to slip off base unnoticed and found the town library. Its rather limited collection made her long for Oxford's incredible resources, but she found a few things worth reading to improve her woeful knowledge of American Indian history and culture.

It was only when she reached to turn on a reading light that Bett thought about the time. "Bloody hell," she muttered when she looked at her watch. "I've missed dinner and the gates will close in ten minutes." They had been told over and over about the procedure for signing out with an officer, and the penalty for an unauthorized leave from base was severe. Rains had even warned her personally after Mel's. Other than attending classes and drills, she would be confined to the barracks for the remainder of her basic training and would have KP every night.

To make matters worse, as she struggled to the base after a twenty-minute jog across town she suffered the indignity of being made to wait outside the gate until her drill instructor came to claim her. She put her face in her hands at the news. Sergeant Rains was not going to be happy with her...again.

"Oh, cheer up, honey," said the MP at the gate. "Who's your sergeant anyway?" Upon hearing Bett's brief answer, he rolled his eyes. "Oh, you're all right then. She's easy. Not like Moore or even Webber. You'll probably just have to do the KP, not even lose your liberty." He rang the officers' quarters from the tiny guardhouse.

Bett looked at his nametag: Crowley. She vaguely remembered hearing his name in some connection with a warning…the other MP, the night Rains had brought her back to the barracks after she'd gotten the news about Kent.

After a brief conversation, Crowley hung up the phone. He looked Bett up and down. "Yeah," he continued his train of thought, "some of us think Rains is a little too sweet on her girls. You know what I mean?"

Bett knew she had to be careful in her response, for Rains's sake. She also sensed that Crowley was the type of man who she might be able to manipulate by her looks. Putting on her most winning smile, she leaned toward him, thinking she had really not spoken enough for him to wonder where the Alabama drawl had come from. "Well, she's been pretty strict on us, but I'm sure she's not as tough as you, Corporal."

"Ha!" Crowley laughed, but it sounded almost threatening. Bett tried not to recoil as he stepped nearer to her and put his rough hand under her chin. "She just needs what the rest of you broads need. A good fu—"

"Private Smythe!" Rains's usually smooth voice rang out sharply. Crowley's hand dropped and he turned toward the sound. "This is your second major infraction this week."

Although her expression was serious as always, as Rains approached the gate, Bett could tell from the sergeant's body language that something else was wrong. She straightened to attention and watched as Rains seemed to circle Crowley cautiously, rather than walking directly up to him.

"You sure got here in a big damn hurry, Sergeant," Crowley growled.

Rains assessed Bett quickly. She seemed satisfied and answered, "Just in the neighborhood, Corporal."

"Unusual for one of yours to come in so late, Rains. I thought you taught 'em better than that." He brazenly looked Bett over again, sneering. "Guess this one just couldn't resist meeting her honey for a little romp."

"No, this one's our scholar, Crowley," Rains answered evenly. "I'm sure she just stayed too long at the library."

It took a large measure of Bett's willpower not to let her mouth drop open. *Did I tell anyone where I was going?* She tried to remember.

"Library," barked Crowley. "That's rich." He opened the gate and Bett stepped through and stood beside Rains. "See ya around, Chief. Don't take any wooden nickels."

Bett heard Rains exhale slowly.

"Corporal," Rains said tightly, watching as Crowley returned to his post inside the guardhouse.

Then Rains wheeled around, walking away so fast that Bett almost had to trot to keep up with her. She knew if she waited for Rains to speak first, they would be back at the barracks, and she wanted a chance to explain to her privately.

"Sergeant, I truly am sorry—"

Rains rounded on her. "Being sorry isn't enough, Private. You are the squad leader. You are supposed to be setting an example for your group."

Bett recognized this Sergeant Rains. She was pure Army, and as strict as she'd been during the first week of basic training. Bett dropped her head a bit in response to the truth of this. "You're right, of course, and I shall apologize to them as well," she said. "And as for Corporal Crowley, I just thought if I charmed him a bit—"

"Crowley is not a man to be charmed. He is not a man to be reasoned with. He is a man to be avoided. Do you understand?" Rains spoke heatedly. When Bett didn't respond immediately, Rains abruptly took hold of her arms, her voice almost fierce. "Do you understand me, Private?" she repeated urgently.

Bett wondered what the history was between those two.

"Yes, Sergeant. I understand," Bett replied clearly, and Rains let her go and begin walking quickly again. "Wait," Bett called, but

Rains kept going. Bett had to run several quick steps to catch up. "Sergeant Rains, please wait."

Rains stopped and sighed. She turned. "What is it, Private Smythe?"

"Did you know I really was at the library?"

"It is my business to know the whereabouts of my squad members. Especially those with a habit of disobeying regulations."

Bett could tell by her tone that Rains was still mad. She tried to lighten the mood. "Well, then, I wish you had come and gotten me before I was so late. Then we both would have been spared that encounter with Corporal Crowley."

"You may be accustomed to having servants whose role it is to tell you when you have to be somewhere, Miss...Carlton," Rains said through her teeth, and Bett startled at the use of her real name, "but that is not my job."

"That's not at all what I meant—" She tried to interrupt, but Rains didn't stop her lecture.

"You don't have much time left to learn how to stay out of trouble in this Army, and you won't find that lesson in a book. You must develop it within yourself. You must start acting with some self-control and discipline. You cannot just disregard the rules you don't like or disobey orders and think you can outsmart us with your costly education." With barely a glance at the evening sky, she added, "Especially if an honors graduate from Oxford can't even tell time." Rains stopped and breathed deeply, trying to rein herself in.

The criticism hurt, and a dozen possible retorts flashed through Bett's mind. After the briefest moment, she asked only what she really wanted to know. "Why are you so angry with me?"

Still flushed with emotion, Rains stepped uncharacteristically close and looked into Bett's eyes. "Because you are too smart to act so foolishly. Because you are too beautiful to be so reckless. Because my life here was simple and caring about you has made it complicated—" Rains stopped short again, as if she realized that she had said too much.

She cares about me. Bett knew better than to smile. Instead, she put her hands gently on Rains's arms. "Crowley is simply arrogant, while you are a skilled leader and a visionary."

Rains mouth opened but no sound came out. She cocked her head and swayed slightly toward Bett, as if she might catch the words again, reverberating in the night. Bett heard her breathe again. She wished that it was not so dark, so that she could see Rains's face.

The sergeant straightened away from Bett's touch. Breathing in, she cleared her throat. "Other than your classes, you are confined to the barracks. I will speak to you further on Friday at our squad leader meeting in the administration building, Private," she said shortly and disappeared into the darkness.

❖

Rains slowed from her run as she approached the colonel's office, trying to get herself under control. The colonel was well-known for her late hours, and this was not the first time Rains had found her working well into the evening. Delores, the weary receptionist, barely had time to nod to her curt, "She in?" before Rains gave a knock and was in the colonel's door.

"Sergeant Rains," Colonel Janet Issacson said, rising. "Whatever is the matter? Please, sit." She gestured but Rains remained standing stiffly, saluting.

"Ma'am, I need a transfer from this squad," she said, without preamble.

"Is that a formal request, Sergeant, or are you just expressing a wish, like, I need a million dollars?"

When Rains didn't answer immediately, the colonel sighed. "Hell's bells, Rains, you know I transferred you there when we got word that Carlton girl was coming." Apparently detecting the slight reaction Rains made at the mention of Bett's name, Colonel Issacson asked, "Is that it, Sergeant? Is the Carlton girl being difficult again?"

Rains inclined her head. The colonel sat heavily. "I knew it. I knew her kind just wouldn't fit in here. And it's not the education. We have lots of women with college degrees. It's the money. Her class. Whatever. Oh, I checked on her, little Miss Moneybags, yes, I did." The colonel was on a roll now. "I don't care if she's a Carlton or a Rockefeller or whatever. She wasn't barging into my outfit without me knowing something about her. I couldn't get through to anyone at Oxford, but I called that high-class British boarding school of hers weeks ago. Outstanding student, they told me. Awarded this and that. But when I asked about discipline…" Issacson paused. "There was something there. Something they weren't telling me." She looked back at Rains. "That's it, isn't it? She's still undisciplined, isn't she? Not up to Army standards?"

Rains knew she shouldn't have come. Turning to Janet Issacson had been simply an emotional reaction and now she was trapped by what she couldn't say. "Yes, ma'am. That's it."

"Well dammit, Sergeant Rains, you were pretty undisciplined yourself when you came in. Can't you handle it? I mean, I've seen you smooth out some of our roughest characters and then work for hours with a girl who can barely read her name. What did Carlton do this time?"

"She came in late from an unauthorized off-base, ma'am." As the colonel began to raise her eyebrows, Rains added, "Crowley was on duty and I…"

A discerning expression crossed Issacson's face and her voice softened. She glanced down at some paperwork on her desk. "All right, Rains. I understand. I was going to call you in anyway. Crowley's transfer came through. His last day here will be…October sixth, graduation day. I'll be informing him this Friday."

Rains nodded. She wondered if Lutz knew.

"So don't let this girl get to your head," Issacson said, by way of dismissal. "Just give her some extra KP again or have her run some more laps or something and she'll snap to, won't she? You've got less than ten days and then she's someone else's problem."

"Yes, ma'am. Thank you, ma'am." Rains saluted. Walking toward her quarters, Rains thought wryly, *She's not only in my head, she sees my spirit.*

Then the image of Crowley touching Bett's face rose in Rains's mind. She felt the familiar rage uncoil deep inside as she remembered finding Crowley with Jennifer Lutz that night she had come back late from an unsanctioned visit to Sweetie's. Jenny's life had been sheltered, and she joined the WAC to have some freedom and some fun. Although completely inexperienced, she tended to act a bit wild, and her brother knew it. Because she was the little sister of a popular MP, it wasn't unusual for officers to look the other way at her occasional infractions. Even though she was in Webber's squad, he'd asked Rains to keep an eye on her. When Rains heard Webber complaining that Private Lutz had missed CQ again, she'd gone to the guardhouse. Crowley had Jenny in a chair with her blouse half undone, and his hand across her mouth told Rains that his other hand between her legs was not her idea, as he had later claimed. Rains had stormed in and punched Crowley in the side of the head so hard that she cracked two bones in her hand. She couldn't get Jenny to rise before he recovered enough to turn on her with an animal fierceness and would have done some serious damage had she not pulled her knife and held him off. In the series of accusations and counteraccusations that followed, Crowley and Rains were both put on probation, although both were allowed to continue in their jobs. Before Jenny Lutz got dismissed from observation the next day, she drank half a bottle of cleaning fluid from a cart outside her room and got sent home with a discharge other-than-honorable once she was well enough to travel.

Having reached her quarters, Rain sat on her bed with her eyes closed, trying not to think about what would have happened if she had caught Crowley trying the same thing with Bett. She knew with complete certainty that she would have gladly killed him. She felt the wolf inside her growl.

❖

Their morning rotation that next day was in the motor pool. Bett took an immediate dislike to the lieutenant in charge, although she couldn't say why, exactly. She just didn't understand why some of the officers had to be so arrogant and belittling. Their attitude reminded her of her father, Bett realized. She didn't fare too well in assembling the greasy engine parts, but since she knew that working there was not her goal, she wasn't concerned about it.

Walking back to the barracks to get ready for lunch, Jo limped alongside her and asked, "Do you think I'd make a good drill instructor, Bett?" She was obviously thinking ahead. The commissioned and noncommissioned officers' training was their afternoon rotation.

"Why, Jo? Is that what you are thinking of doing?"

Jo looked a little embarrassed. "Yeah, maybe. I read over that NCO manual that Sergeant Rains let me borrow and…I think I could do it. Plus, I kinda like the way Sergeant Rains handles herself…and us. I was thinkin' that with a little practice maybe I could be like that."

"I think Sergeant Rains sets a fine example of leadership, Jo. You should talk to her about your interest. I'm sure she'd be glad to recommend you," Bett said sincerely.

"Aw, I don't want to bug her."

"Not at all, Jo. I think Sergeant Rains is genuinely concerned with helping all of us find something that really appeals to us. And I think you'd make a fine NCO." She squeezed Jo's arm and added playfully, "Just don't expect me to salute you." Jo grinned. Then Bett thought of something else. "Jo, have you ever heard Sergeant Rains come in really late at night to check on us?"

""You mean after CQ, even?" Bett nodded. "Nah," Jo said after a few seconds' thought, "but I'm a pretty heavy sleeper. A tank could drive through the barracks and I probably wouldn't wake up."

Sergeant Rains was sitting off to one side at the front of the room during their officers' training class but she was not a speaker. The class was held in a large presentation room and the entire platoon was present. Rains had changed into her deep olive-green dress uniform and looked very striking. Bett tried to keep from staring at her, but since she wasn't particularly interested in the presentation, it was hard not to. Rains mostly kept her eyes down, occasionally nodding at something the presenter, Captain McGinnis, was saying, but Bett had a clear view of her profile. As always, she wondered if it was true what Teresa had once said, about Rains keeping a braid under that ever-present hat. She imagined tracing her fingers along those amazing cheekbones and that strong jaw, speculated again on how Rains's mouth would taste. She envisioned how Rains's hips flexed as she ran and wondered what it would be like to have those hips moving between her legs while feeling those long arms holding her again. Trying to tamp down the rush of her arousal, Bett regretfully acknowledged to herself that her failure to seduce Sergeant Rains was due to the fact that Rains's character was too strong for her, and that was a first. Of course, that strength only made her more desirable. Once, when the sergeant cast a quick glance at her squad, Bett had to pretend to be taking notes for fear Rains would be able to read her thoughts.

At the end of the presentation Captain McGinnis asked Rains to stand. "As many of you know, Sergeant Rains is rotating out of this duty. Eight days from now, after her squad graduates along with the rest of this platoon, she will assume new tasks and responsibilities... most of them a lot easier than working with new recruits, I would imagine."

Everyone chuckled appreciatively, but Bett was processing a thought: *A little more than a week and I might never see Rains again.* At the beginning of basic training, it had seemed as though eight weeks would take forever, but suddenly their time was almost up. Bett's mind sifted through the many things she and Rains had talked about, and the way Rains always seemed to rescue her from her own foolishness or from others' bad intentions. Wouldn't she miss that as much as their almost nonexistent physical relationship? In her heart she knew, in spite of everything that the official Sergeant Rains kept telling her, that they had become friends...and they could be more.

Then everyone was standing at attention as the base commander walked toward the front. She and Rains saluted each other and then Colonel Issacson added a ribbon to those that Rains was already wearing. They shook hands, and the colonel said something that only Rains could hear, getting a nod in return. Bett sensed a genuine affection between the two women who, from all appearances, couldn't be more different. Rains's squad could contain themselves no longer and cheering broke out. Jo yelled, "Speech!" and others picked it up. Rains shook her head but the cheers and calls continued. Finally Issacson got everyone seated and quiet and looked expectantly at Rains.

Rains stood before them, staring at the floor for a moment. When she raised her head and began speaking her voice was quiet. "When I first came to the Army, I was lost. I had no vision for my life or any means to understand my place in the world. With the discipline of order in my daily routine, the Women's Army Corps has helped me find direction inside myself. For that, I will always be grateful." Rains nodded at Issacson, who smiled broadly. "But lately I have begun to observe that order, once incorporated into oneself, doesn't always need to be the scale by which everything else is weighed."

She cleared her throat and her words became more certain. "Recently a friend said to me that the influence of women would change the United States Army forever, and I began to consider if I believed that to be true."

A friend, Bett heard, surprised. *That was me.*

Rains went on. "What can women bring to make a difference, if we have the same system of command, the same basic code of conduct, wear uniforms like the men—" Rains looked at her dress skirt and added, "Well, not exactly like, of course. But if we model our ways on the men's Army, how can we influence any change?

"I'm sure I speak for most of us here when I say that although I honor the system of leadership the Army provides, I am not a man and I do not aspire to be one. For what I have seen in my life is that the ruling men who have brought us to this place in time have done so with their desire to destroy and to conquer. I do not want to be led by those forces, nor do I wish to cultivate them in myself.

"As a species, we live in this tension: societies need rules while individuals need freedom. For the last decades, we have leaned heavily on our rules to guide us through dark, uncertain times. It is my hope those times will soon be over, and we can be more willing to embrace the chaos of freedom, because that is where creation starts. So what will we create in the space that the vast death and destruction of our age has left behind?"

There was total silence in the room. Even Colonel Issacson was transfixed. The sergeant's voice grew in passion.

"What most women know in our hearts, even if we never verbalize it, is that the best in us comes from our relationships. Women have such amazing capacity to nurture and grow, to create and to build up—in ourselves and in others—and we must not turn away from that power. We here came together from very different places and vastly dissimilar lives and formed bonds that will never be broken. We share this with our brothers in arms. So we must lead them to this lesson: the relationships that connect us throughout our brief lives are deeper and stronger than we can imagine, for truly all people are part of our family and the whole world is our neighbor. For those men who still wish to conquer, let them conquer their fear of seeing this truth; if they wish to destroy something, let them destroy the obstacles of injustice and need that separate us. All humanity is on the same journey. We must be able to greet each other along the way without fear. Our men will be at their best when they allow themselves to walk with us on this path.

"These thoughts brought me to realize that changing the Army is not what we as women should aspire to do with our newly found influence...we should change the world." Rains focused on the faces before her, and met each eye as she spoke slowly. "No matter how far your reach or how wide your grasp, each of you can offer the best gifts of life, every one of you can share the treasures of love, and all of us together can make a world of peace."

Bett's eyes were filled with tears. She knew without looking that everyone else in the room felt the same way. *Life, love, and peace. There isn't really anything else that we could want, is there?* In the silence, she heard Helen's voice say with great emotion, "Amen, sister."

Then the platoon rose as one and began applauding. It was different, somehow, from a cheering, congratulatory applause. It was the applause of people who had felt something move in themselves, and who wanted to commit to continuing that movement.

Sergeant Rains just looked at them for a moment. She blinked a few times, seeming just a bit confused at their reaction. Then her eyes cleared as they found Bett, and that now-familiar ghost of a smile crossed her face. Bett made a decision. *I can go to Washington, DC or New York anytime. For now, I'll work here, with the cryptographers in Des Moines.* As soon as the thought became conscious it felt so right that she couldn't wait to tell Rains. But by then half the platoon was standing around her, so Bett slipped outside through a side door, waiting between the classroom and Rains's quarters, planning to catch her there. After waiting impatiently for what seemed like much too long, she caught Jo leaving the building.

"So Sergeant Moore had started yelling 'Traitor! She's advocating treason!' from the back where she had come in to watch, but none of us could hear it at first for all the applause and talking," Jo explained as they walked across the base. "Then Issacson was the one who had to pull Helen off when she was punching Moore in the face once Moore came to the front with her bullshit." Jo grinned. "I didn't know Helen had it in her, but she was like a little Joe Lewis, and you know none of us were going to get in the way of Sergeant Moore taking a beating. Anyway, then the MPs came and I know Helen's in the stockade and I think Rains and Moore and Issacson are all in the colonel's office."

Bett followed Jo into the mess hall and got some dinner for Helen. She found Helen none the worse for being held in one of the tiny cells. "How long will you have to be here?" Bett asked, trying not to shudder at the memory of almost being forced into the exact same place when she'd tried to duck out of KP.

"I think it's supposed to be a week, but Rains might be able to get me out sooner once they clear this mess up," Helen said. Then she motioned Bett closer to the bars. Bett leaned in reluctantly. "But I know I got at least two good punches in, and that's worth two weeks to me." She grinned. "That redneck bitch has had it coming since our first day, Bett. She was awful to every one of us, remember? If it hadn't been for Sergeant Rains, I'd have probably spent a lot more time in here...or just got sent home. When Moore started talking that way about her, I—I just couldn't take it."

Bett nodded. "I know Sergeant Rains appreciates your support, Helen, even if she disapproves of your methods."

"Yeah, she'll probably say something just like that," Helen said, digging in to her meal. "Thanks for this." She stopped and looked at Bett again. "And thanks for all your help, too. Next to Sergeant Rains, you're the reason I've made it this far. I know Tee would say the same. You're all right in my book."

Bett smiled as she stood, thinking how right Rains was in what she had said about relationships. If someone had told her seven weeks ago that she'd be good friends with the daughter of a coal miner..."You're all right, too, Helen." She lowered her voice, looking at the MP on guard duty at the end of the hall. "And don't tell anyone I said so, but you did exactly what we all wanted to do." Helen grinned again. "I'll try to check on you before breakfast tomorrow," Bett said, turning. "Now I'm going to see if I can find out what's going on with Sergeant Rains."

On her way out, she passed a very worried looking Teresa Owens, heading inside. "She's fine," Bett assured her. "But she'll be glad to see you, I'm sure."

By the time Bett got to the administration building where the colonel's office was located, all the lights were out and everyone seemed to be gone.

When she finally got back to the table at the mess hall with her own dinner, Rains was nowhere to be seen, but Jo was still there, talking with some of the other girls from the platoon. She had more news. "The colonel doesn't want to bring charges, but Moore won't shut up about this treason crap, so Issacson's gotta call in some brass for a hearing tomorrow. We're all going to testify for Rains if we can. I think she's confined to quarters for now."

"Put me on the list of people who want to testify, Jo," Bett said, finishing her meal quickly. "I'll see you back at the barracks later."

She went back to the cafeteria line again and the first server looked at her suspiciously. "Ain't you been through here already?"

❖

There was a WAC MP posted outside the officers' quarters, but Bett smiled at her and the MP nodded, letting Bett pass without comment. Once inside, she looked down the hallway that led past several doors. There was also a stairway toward the back. She didn't know which room was Rains's and hoped she wasn't upstairs. Only one door was open—a bedroom at the very back of the building. Bett walked there quietly and looked in. Rains was sitting on the floor with her eyes closed. Her back was against the wall, and a bundle of herbs with an acrid tang was burning on a ceramic plate in front of her. Bett walked in and set the tray on a small chest of drawers as Rains looked over.

"I am not the least bit surprised to see you here, Private Smythe."

Bett smiled. "Am I so predictable?"

Rains tamped out the burning herb and stood. "No, I would not say that. But maybe I've just gotten used to being surprised by you."

"Well, that's no good," Bett replied, tidying the tray. "If you're used to it, it can't be a surprise."

Rains nodded. "You have a point there."

Bett tried not to be obvious about looking around, but she had already seen that the room was very sparsely furnished. "Don't you have a chair in here?"

"No, it's a bedroom. I only sleep here. If I want to sit, I sit on the floor, as you saw."

"But how will you eat?"

Rains looked at the contents of the tray from behind Bett. "Stop fussing. It won't be the first time I have eaten standing. Or the last, I expect." She put her hands on Bett's shoulders, her low voice softening. "It was good of you to bring this, Private Smythe. And I am glad of your company." She squeezed gently and let go.

Rains had never said anything like that to her before, and her words, and the touch, made Bett's heartbeat race. She cocked her head, trying to act casual. "You must be really desperate to say such a thing."

"Actually, there have been very few times when I wasn't glad of your company. Sometimes I would have liked more notice is all. But for now, I am tired of being in my own mind."

Bett turned, speaking somberly. "What's going to happen to you, Sergeant?"

"I have no idea."

"Well, what does Colonel Issacson say?"

Rains took a bite of a roll. "Would you mind if we talked about something else?"

Bett knew well that when Rains said this, she meant it. "We could try. What did you have in mind?" Bett couldn't believe she could say this without a flirting tone, but it seemed to be happening.

"What's the weather like tonight?" Rains asked, tasting her soup.

Bett didn't want to admit she had paid absolutely no attention. She tried to think of how it had felt on her walk over. "It's fine."

"Meaning you really don't know," Rains teased.

"Meaning I had other things on my mind, like trying not to spill all of your soup." Bett couldn't quite pull off sounding offended.

"Thank you for that. It's good. I'm hungrier than I thought I would be."

"I took some to Helen, too," Bett said, before she realized that she was drifting back to talking about the day's events.

"Would you prefer to sit?" Rains asked, as if it had suddenly occurred to her that Bett might not be comfortable. "You can use my footlocker if you'd like."

Bett strolled across the room and sat. "Aren't you worried that I'll ask you about your décor?"

"I don't think my décor merits a single question," Rains countered, "but feel free to look."

Bett already had, noticing several stacks of library books, each of which had various bookmarks in them. "You certainly are a reader."

"I think you already knew that."

"Yes, I suppose I did," Bett murmured, seeing the Sartre book on the nightstand closest to Rains's bed, her folded note still in it. She looked around to see nothing on the walls and nothing personal on any of the surfaces. Everything visible was neat and tidy but the room was almost bare. "You're right. I can't think of a single question except to wonder why there is almost nothing of you in here."

"I'm right here," Rains said, wiggling her fingers in a wave. "I am not found in some little trinkets." She finished the brownie and sighed. "I must admit to a weakness for chocolate. Did you know that or was I just lucky in your dessert selection?"

"I wasn't aware of any weaknesses on your part, Sergeant."

"Hmm. Then you haven't been paying attention, Private."

There's something different about her tonight, Bett thought. *She's more relaxed, almost playful somehow. Just when I want to talk seriously about her situation, she's bantering with me.* "Sergeant, I'm sorry but I just have to say something."

"Just one thing?" Rains asked, her eyes shining with amusement.

"One thing about today."

"Ah, that. Well, you held out longer than I expected you to, actually."

Bett stood and crossed her arms. "You are teasing me and I am trying to tell you something honestly."

Rains nodded amiably, her tone lightheartedly sympathetic. "I know that can be difficult."

"Fine. Then I won't tell you I thought your speech was amazing, that you said the most beautiful, important words I've heard in… forever, maybe. Your vision was so inspiring I—"

A knock on the door frame cut her off. Rains looked over. The MP was standing on the threshold, trying not to look into the room. She cleared her throat. "Excuse me, Sergeant Rains, but your curfew starts in ten minutes. If you are through eating…"

"It's okay, Nix. Thank you. My squad leader will be leaving now." Rains gestured in her direction.

The MP hesitated as though she wanted to say something else, but turned sharply and left.

Rains looked to Bett. "You should go, Private. Thank you again for the food." She took in a long breath. "Perhaps I could repay you by taking you back to Mel's for dinner sometime before we go our separate ways." She gestured haltingly. "Just so you can see the progress they've made."

Bett couldn't hide her smile. *I can't believe she's finally asking me out.* Then she put it together differently…all the changes in

Rains's behavior. *She's not planning on fighting the charges. She's giving up.* Her smile vanished and her tone became stern. "Oh no, you don't, Sergeant. You're not walking away from this. Tell me you're not going to let that awful Sergeant Moore get the best of you."

"Well, she is correct," Rains said, shrugging. "I am advocating treason, by some measures. I stated that I will not be led by those currently ruling and I favor all people living together in harmony. We are presently at war, as you recall, so those remarks could easily be construed as sedition."

"No, no. We all understood what you meant by the forces of death and destruction. Everyone is sick of this war, Sergeant, sick of what it's cost us all, the toll on the whole world. It's easy to see that we can't keep doing this to ourselves. No one with half a brain would ever see another war as a solution to our problems. You were right. Human beings have got to change."

Rains tried to explain. "It's one thing to say that socially or even politically, as civilians in private. But for a sergeant to say it to a platoon suggests some kind of reactionary overthrow of our military system, apparently."

Bett said nothing for a moment. Then her tone was sad. "So this must be the weakness you spoke of. You want to have your beliefs, but you're not willing to fight for them. You try to slip in a little piece of free speech on the sly and then you don't have the guts to defend it. Yes, I must not have been paying attention to have missed that. You'll stand up for others because it looks noble but you won't stand up for yourself because it's too hard."

Rains looked shocked. "Wait just a minute, Private—"

Bett picked up the tray abruptly. Now she was angry enough to cut Rains off. "No, that's fine. I'm just glad I found out now, before I agreed to work with Major Ervin. I might as well go to Washington where I'm sure I can find some other spineless weaklings. And you can go work for Mel where you can settle for serving take-out orders instead of giving orders that would show some kind of real leadership."

Bett could see Rains was frowning in the one second she dared to look, but nothing more was said as she left the room. On the outside steps of the building, the MP's words stopped her. "Rains was my sergeant and I was her squad leader about a year ago."

Bett was still angry but she tried to respond reasonably. "This must be a difficult situation for you, then."

Nix seemed eager to talk. "Yeah, but it's worse for Sergeant Rains. See, there was a girl in my squad that they said was an antiwar agitator, based on some letters that she wrote and stuff she said around the base. Sergeant went to bat for her, convinced she was being wrongly accused, but then the girl made up some stories that got Rains in trouble, too. Like saying she was in on it. The girl was discharged other-than-honorable and Sergeant Rains barely got to keep her stripes. All that stuff went in her file, and that's the main reason why she hasn't been promoted." Nix looked at Bett. "You ever been to one of those hearings?"

"No, but I've volunteered to testify on Sergeant Rains's behalf if needed."

"Well, watch yourself," Nix recommended somberly. "Those lawyer-officers are tricky and then some. They'll have you saying *no* when you meant *yes* and then crucify you because the right answer was *maybe*." She shook her head. "I don't envy Sergeant Rains having to go through that again. She probably feels pretty beat up right about now."

And I've just made that worse, Bett told herself. Setting the tray on the steps, she asked, "Could you give me just two more minutes?" and ran back into the building without waiting for an answer.

Rains's door was closed but Bett went in without knocking, leaving the door slightly ajar. The lights were off but she could smell that Rains was burning some more of that herb. From the bed, she heard Rains sniff the air twice and her voice sounded distant. "Bett?"

Bett moved closer by sound as her eyes adjusted to the darkness. "As usual I said all the wrong things, but I said them for the right reason. I want to know that you're going to fight this. I want to know that you'll still be here in two weeks or two months or two years. I want to know that you're the person I think you are."

There was a creak of springs as Rains got up. Her voice closed the distance between them. "And who are you to ask me this?"

Bett could only see Rains in silhouette from the light that filtered through the window shades. She didn't see the outline of Rains's hat or of her uniform shirt or pants. Bett swallowed hard as she couldn't help wondering what else Rains wasn't wearing. She ventured a little closer. "I am the stupidly hot-tempered, spoiled, and stubborn private who has come to realize that she doesn't want to leave where you are until"—she took another step—"until I...until we—"

Rains's fingers were on her cheek—firmly, almost possessively—and Bett closed her eyes. Everything seemed so concentrated in the half darkness; she felt blood pounding through her veins and warmth building around Rains's hand. Her heart was beating so hard she thought the MP could probably hear it.

"So you would really choose not to go to Washington? Or New York? Or England?" Rains's compelling voice sounded very close but Bett couldn't move.

"Yes. I've decided to stay here." Bett could feel the heat from Rains's body. She wanted to lean toward her but was afraid she'd lose her balance.

"Why?" Rains's hand moved slowly to Bett's neck and the warmth followed. "Is it for me?" There was the slightest rustle as Rains shifted her position and then Bett felt the soft cloth of Rains's undershirt brush against her face. Then she could feel skin and knew her forehead was in the vee of Rain's T-shirt, between her breasts. She pressed in, feeling as if she'd been given truth serum.

"Yes," she answered, without hesitation. "And for me. For us."

Rains ran her other hand across Bett's hair and tilted her face up. Bett couldn't see her expression, but she could feel the intensity in Rains's scrutiny. "I am a warrior. I will always fight. You misunderstood about my weakness. It is you."

Bett was certain that Rains was going to kiss her then and she parted her lips in anticipation, wanting that and so much more. She wanted to run her fingers through Rains's uncovered hair, ready to give Rains anything she asked for, but there was a knock on the door frame and Rains jumped as though electrified.

Nix's voice came from out in the hall. "Uh, Private? You have to leave, ma'am. I'm sorry, but Sergeant Rains is under curfew."

Rains brushed the top of Bett's head with her cheek. "Go now," she whispered very softly, "and don't come to the hearing tomorrow. I'll need to concentrate and you make that very difficult."

Bett didn't even know when she had put her arms around Rains's waist but she almost couldn't turn, not realizing that she had to let go first. "I know you'll win," she said back over her shoulder, shuffling almost blindly toward the light from the hall.

"I already have," Rains said. Bett closed the door. Nix was waiting in the hallway, eyes fixed out the front door. Bett managed to thank her for the time.

"Sorry I couldn't give you any extra." She glanced at the upstairs floor. "You never know when Moore will come back and there would be hell to pay if she caught you in there."

"Sergeant Moore lives here, too?"

Nix's eyes shifted and she looked concerned. "Uh, can you forget I said that?"

"Absolutely, Nix. And thanks again."

After reassuring the squad that Sergeant Rains was doing fine, Bett fell into a deep, dreamless sleep. The next morning Sergeant Webber led them through their muster and everyone changed into their dress uniforms after breakfast. Bett made the excuse that she was too nervous to be in the hearing but told them to send someone for her in the barracks if she was needed. She spent the time writing another round of letters telling everyone about her decision to remain in Des Moines without adding many details about why, except to her two best friends to whom she only hinted that she had a very good reason for staying on, knowing they would read between the lines.

"The hearing was a joke, really," Jo told Bett later. "See, no one had an exact transcript of Rains's speech, 'cause it was all unplanned. So it only took four or five of us to tell our version of it, contradicting whatever Moore was saying, and you could tell the brass wasn't interested in pursuing it."

"And do you know who our best speaker was, Bett?" Phyllis added. Bett shook her head. "Jo. She did a great job." Phyllis turned to Jo. "I could tell Sergeant Rains was really proud of you, Jo."

Jo's face was a bright red. "Aw, it musta been hanging around with Queenie here that did it."

They had some time before lunch, so Bett went by the PX, where there was another telegram waiting for her. She hadn't thought about it, but Emma's brother William had sent his messages to Elizabeth Carlton, not Smythe, which was probably why Moore had such a strange tone in her voice when she had brought the first one, and why this one hadn't been delivered to her immediately. William had sent the news that there had been only four deaths in the bombing, two girls and two of their teachers. Sad, but almost a miracle, considering how bad it could have been. Bett sent a reply, thanking William for the news and inviting him to visit her in Iowa if he ever made it over to America. She sent her love to Emma as well, but as she signed her name she knew it was Rains who occupied her heart now.

CHAPTER TWELVE

Sergeant Rains had come to appreciate many things about the Army over the years, but she knew she would always hate the paperwork. She would rather do hours of KP or run an extra fifty laps around the parade grounds, but neither of those were options just now. Spending an afternoon and evening under house arrest and another morning at a hearing had put her badly behind schedule for the end of this rotation.

She was working in the conference room of the administration building because it had no windows to distract her, which was practically the only way she could force herself to get the job done. Her hands hurt from hours of trying to make her writing legible. She was hungry and thirsty, since she had missed lunch. The only good news was her squad's progress was outstanding, and it looked as though most of them would get the assignments they had requested. Technically, their basic training was now over, and they would spend the next week in smaller group classes, attending advanced lectures for their specialties, except for Helen, who might have to graduate a week behind them if she wasn't released from the stockade in time to join Webber's squad to make up the classes she'd missed. She sighed, and was making a note to speak with Sergeant Moore, when she heard a knock on the door.

"Come," she said, feeling very grouchy as she flexed her hand.

Bett stepped into the room and the air seemed to change. Rains had thought it was just someone else to interrupt her and wasn't prepared for the verbal sparring that frequently occurred when she and Private Smythe were together. Not to mention the internal corporeal war Rains knew she was losing, and had been ever since she watched a beautiful blond recruit stand up to Sergeant Moore on her first day on the base. She had sent Bett word through Jo Archer that due to the upheaval of the past two days, the squad leader meeting for this week would be canceled, but somehow Bett had found her here.

It hadn't been a lie; Rains had to catch up on entirely too much paperwork. But it was also true that she knew she had no business being unaccompanied with Private Smythe again. She had spent much of the night thinking about their times together throughout basic training, and she had recognized that not a week had gone by that she hadn't managed to spend some extra time with Private Smythe, alone. On the record, everything looked legitimate enough—squad leader meetings were a prescribed part of a sergeant's duty—but Rains knew better. There had been the night she had taken Bett to see the big moon and the night Bett had followed her to Mel's, both of which were entirely inappropriate outings. She forced herself not to think about what would have happened between them in her room if Nix hadn't knocked.

As Bett smiled at her, Rains felt something else that was unusual for her: nervous. In the nearly three years that she had been in the Army, she had never met someone who could make her feel less in control than Elizabeth Smythe. Almost everything about her made it impossible for Rains to keep her guard up, and worse, Bett seemed to know it. All right. Rain gathered herself. *I've walked into commanders' offices before when they were writing,* Rains thought, *and sometimes I've had to stand for several minutes before they even acknowledged me.* She decided not to be that harsh, but to act as she thought Colonel Issacson might act.

"Oh, Private," she said, tiredly, "I need just a moment more with these reports. Have a seat"—she gestured to a chair across the table—"and I'll be right with you."

"Certainly, Sergeant," Smythe replied pleasantly, totally ignoring Rains's gesture as she closed the door and sat in a chair right next to her.

A whiff of her wonderful scent drifted over. *Ignore it*, Rains ordered herself sternly. She tried to continue with her work but saw Smythe watching her write. She tried to shift her body slightly away, but Smythe moved with her, still looking.

"What?" Rains snapped, losing all semblance of formality.

"Did you know you have very large hands, Sergeant?" Bett asked smoothly.

"Of course I know I have large hands. They're my hands, aren't they?"

"Have you always written with your right hand?" Rains kept her left hand in her lap as she wrote, and she used that hand to mirror everything she wrote with her right. It was the way she had finally managed to coordinate the two sides of her brain to make her writing more easily read.

"As long as I have written, I have written with my right hand," Rains replied with exaggerated patience. "In my schools, you were punished if you wrote with your left hand, so yes, this is how I write." She flexed the hand in question, trying to work out the stiffness. "So if you are through with your personal questions—"

"Oh no, Sergeant," Bett interrupted teasingly, "I have dozens, maybe hundreds of questions for you."

Rains rubbed her forehead, closing her eyes. She had practiced to herself, over and over, what she was going to say to Private Smythe at her next opportunity about attending to her duty, about maintaining self-discipline, but every bit of it had gone out of her head the minute Bett had walked in the door. Trying for a convincing response, Rains scrubbed her hand down her face. "Has anyone ever told you that you have no respect for authority?"

"Dozens, maybe hundreds," Bett answered again, laughing as she leaned closer. "And I'm just getting started."

"Well, that needs to stop right now." Rains stood and paced to the other side of the table, shaking her pencil in Smythe's direction. "Stop asking me questions about my hands or my handwriting. You must not...you need to take yourself and your job more seriously."

"Why, when you take it seriously enough for both of us?" Smythe stood also and moved toward Rains from the other direction.

Rains had been flexing the pencil between her fists; when it snapped with a pop, she threw it on the table angrily. "My, you are a bear today, aren't you?" Smythe asked, her eyes dancing.

Rains couldn't believe what she had just heard. Was it possible Smythe learned something about the spirit guides during her library expedition?

She must have looked apprehensive, because Smythe went on, "I know I'm always apologizing to you, Sergeant, but you are really so easy to tease. Please forgive me," she added, moving another step closer. She smiled again. "Although your squad did have one more question about that hat..." She trailed off, not really expecting a response when Rains yanked off her hat and threw it on the table. A braid of raven hair fell almost to her waist. Bett drew in her breath, moved by the way Rains's appearance suddenly changed. She looked younger, and very stunning. Bett gazed at her face, thinking Rains was much more a woman than a sergeant with her hair down. A vision of Rains naked, with her long, unbraided tresses trailing down her body, made Bett moisten her lips with her tongue.

Suddenly, Rains closed the distance between them. "Why are you the only one who asks me these things? Why are you the only one who talks to me this way?" There was frustration and a little desperation in her voice. She didn't ask what was really in her mind. *Why do you make me feel this way?*

They stood facing each other. Smythe answered, "I think the other girls still feel a bit afraid of you."

"While you, obviously, do not."

Bett linked her fingers through Rains's, as if to keep her from escaping. "Fear is about the last thing I feel for you, Sergeant," she said softly and stretched to place a light but lingering kiss directly on Rains's lips.

At the touch of Bett's mouth on hers, Rains's eyes closed with the sensation of complete stillness inside her. The frustration and anger dissolved completely, like a question answered. When she thought to look, Smythe was still very near, looking at her with a combination of shyness and expectation.

"Well, say something," Smythe finally said.

Rains felt her mind begin to work again. "You can't," she began, her voice hoarse, "you can't do that again." She cleared her throat, watching Bett's face sober at her words. "You are a soldier in my command. That is a...a sacred thing. I, we, cannot, not while— not until..." She couldn't finish but stood, hoping Smythe would understand, that she would know what she wasn't saying.

"Ah yes, your gallantry again. I suppose I do have to respect that." Bett mused, secretly relieved by Rains's unfinished encouragement. "But I only have one more week before graduation." She smoothed the new ribbon on Rains's jacket. "What then?"

It happened so quickly Bett couldn't say how, but suddenly Rains's arms were around her and Rains's mouth was kissing hers intently, warm and urgent. Bett wrapped her arms around Rains's neck, and their mouths explored each other eagerly. The fierce longing that Bett had been feeling for weeks exploded into desire as the sergeant moved one hand to cup Bett's hip and draw her closer. She moaned willingly and pressed her chest up into Rains's until their shirt buttons clacked together. Something, perhaps that sound, made Rains break the kiss, and when she rested her cheek on Bett's hair, they were both breathing rapidly.

"My God," Bett said after a few seconds, "that was beyond everything I ever imagined. And now you're going to tell me we have to stop?" She felt Rains's head nod against her. Slowly, reluctantly, Rains held Bett away from her. Although Bett could see her struggling for control, she couldn't resist running her hand down Rains's black braid one time. *And this is more beautiful than I imagined as well.* "Well, if you're going to kiss me like that," she said gently, "you're going to have to tell me your first name. I can't very well go around thinking, *Oh, Sergeant.*"

Rains almost smiled. "Gale," she said.

Bett seemed surprised. "Well that's very nice—"

"Like a strong wind. *G-a-l-e.*"

"So your name is Gale Rains?" Bett put it together. "But that's wonderful. Is that the translation for your Indian name?"

"More or less," Rains said. "It should really be just Rain, but when I enlisted in the WAAC they wrote it with the *s*, and I just let it be." Then was a moment where they could only look at each other; their breathing matched as it slowed gradually.

"I told Major Ervin I was going to stay here, in Des Moines, after graduation," Bett said finally, unable to look away from Rains's eyes, "working with their wireless encoder. But I don't have to report for another week until they finish some enhancements to the equipment."

Rains nodded again, seemingly willing her hands not to move back to Bett's body by clenching them into fists.

"So I've found living arrangements off base, a little house." She smiled to herself, wondering what the sergeant would say if she knew how readily her colonel had approved this move—even granting her official permission to go off base and finalize the deal. *Issacson really wants to be rid of me.* Instead, she raised her brows and asked the more important question, "Will you...will you come see me?"

Rains surprised herself by being able to speak almost normally. "I would like that." She knew she needed to say something else. "And I thank you for understanding and for not...for not..." She paused. "For waiting." Rains saw in Bett's eyes what they both knew. The edge of control was very thin between them, and Bett could have easily pushed them both over with just one more touch, maybe just one more word. Trying to find her voice as a sergeant again, Rains added, "I commend your self-control."

Bett smiled ruefully. "Well, don't count on it for long, Sergeant." She ran one hand through her hair, pushing it back behind her right ear, and Rains closed her eyes, unable to watch the familiar gesture. "I take it this will be our last squad leader meeting," she remarked.

"Yes, I think that would be best," Rains said softly, running her hand over her face again before opening her eyes. "You can speak to me during exercise if there are any problems."

"I already know of one big problem." Bett sighed, catching Rains's hand and kissing the back of her palm very softly. "But I think it will be solved in a week or so." Rains swallowed hard and Bett saw her start to lean closer, saw her eyes darken, and sensed that Rains would reach for her again. As much as she wanted more, wanted it right this second, she knew Rains was right. For something real to come of this, they needed to move beyond their official roles as sergeant and private. For the first time in her life, Bett made the decision to wait. She turned very quickly and opened the door. Rains's deep groan probably passed as a throat clearing sound to the corporal walking down the hall outside. "Thank you, Sergeant," she called back over her shoulder.

She almost thought Rains wasn't going to answer as she began pulling the door shut. Just before it clicked, she heard, faintly, "Thank *you*, Private Smythe."

❖

That night Bett had a vivid dream of her time at Kent Prep, and of Emma. At first she was merely watching herself on her first morning at her new boarding school—a frightened ten-year-old sitting in the headmistress's office with her father, so desperate to make him proud. Then the sounds of girls' voices in the hallway turned her head and she watched a group going up the stairs. They returned her look with expressions of curiosity, disdain, interest, or indifference. Some were holding hands or had their arms around each other. Bett looked away, and the dream scene shifted. Now she was among the girls, holding hands happily and skipping with two others as they made their way to class. One was Emma, the most beautiful girl Bett had ever seen. Then it was just the two of them, alone in one of the dressing areas, standing side by side in front of a mirror, comparing: Bett's wavy blond hair to Emma's very curly brown, Bett's green-blue eyes to Emma's soft brown. Emma was taller, but Bett stronger, and Bett challenged Emma and they wrestled and she pinned Emma's arms and straddled her, victorious, until Emma rose up and kissed her and she let go in shock and Emma ran laughing...until Bett caught her easily. She got another kiss for her effort.

And then, she was on the phone with her father.

Emma says she'll have a title someday, she said to him, unable to stop smiling at the vision of Emma dancing in the hallway outside. *Can I have one, too?*

You already have a title, he snapped. *Rich.*

In her dream, the click of the phone turned into the click of a door latch and Bett walked through, older and returning to school after one summer back in California. Suddenly everyone was laughing at her when she tried to hold hands with Emma because they'd reached some age, some barrier and there was to be no more physical contact, even though Bett still wanted it so. Luckily no one else seemed aware that she had this need, this desire, and so they all remained friends in and out of class, studying, while Bett learned to control her emotions. She desperately wanted to be satisfied with the casual brush of Emma's shoulder as they walked to class together or a silly touching of toes when they stretched out on opposite ends of the big couch in the common room. She tried to imagine a future with Emma—with them both working in London, perhaps, and sharing a flat—because she didn't quite know how to imagine a world without her.

Then her dream flooded with music. They were at a dance with boys from the Hadbury School. Bett smiled and danced every time she was asked, but not one of the boys ever made her feel the way she did with Emma. Bett watched herself avoiding those boys with more adventurous hands and offering a simple kiss to those who were nice enough not to press her, not to embarrass her with declarations of undying love or not to try and arouse her with coarse suggestions of lust. A sharp hurt tore her heart as Emma danced close with one boy, and Bett took a cup of punch from an unseen hand in the hopes of soothing the hot ache in her stomach when Emma returned holding another's hand after a walk in the darkened garden, her lipstick smeared and a dreamy smile on her face.

The dream shifted from the dance to Emma's home, Werborne Manor. Bett stopped going back to the States for holidays, but Emma's parents and her handsome brother William made her feel like family. In the darkness of her room she listened to the creaks and moans echoing as the big old house seemed to expand, until finding Emma's room felt like making her way through an endless maze. She was never so grateful as when Emma opened her bedroom door and her bed to Bett's knock that first night, and each time she prayed that Emma would never wonder why, after all these years, she was still afraid to sleep by herself there. She never rested well when sleeping with Emma, of course. Because she had to wait for Emma's breathing to become regular and slow before she could move closer, hoping that Emma would throw a dreaming arm across her or that she could pretend to do the same, and then to watch for the lightening of the sky in the morning as a notice to move away.

At the sound of someone announcing her name, she was back at school. She had done well—the best in her class—and Emma was hugging her and Bett was happy but longing for something...more. Then it was the last holiday from school—Easter—with graduation coming in just two short months, and they were together at Emma's house as usual and it might have been the wine they were allowed to have with dinner, the champagne toasts with dessert to celebrate their upcoming graduation, that gave Bett the courage to put her arm around Emma while they were both still awake and kiss her neck and her back until Emma turned over and said into Bett's eyes, *I know you want this—more than I do*, and they were kissing and touching so wonderfully. Soft lips, warm downy hair, wet hot soaring falling shuddering closeness that Bett never wanted to end. Her fears for the next night vanished as Emma—even though she drank more wine with dinner—took the lead this time. And even though Emma's passion felt almost like anger at times, Bett responded to her every wild move, every rough touch, and every hard kiss. Then, just as suddenly, it was over. In the Prossers' big black car on the way back to school, Bett tried to reach across the seat for Emma's hand. Emma moved away, putting her hand in her lap as she looked out the window for a moment. She turned her head back to check the mirror, checking for their chauffeur's eyes, and then she whispered, *No, Bett. Never again. I can't. I'm sorry.*

Then she was on the bench outside the nurse's office, sobbing. A week had passed and she couldn't stop the feelings, like being slowly cut into pieces by a dull knife. There must be something they could give her, something that would make her like the others. Something to make this horrible suffering go away, the wanting... and the shame. She knew she should be ashamed because no one knew what had happened between her and Emma, which meant Emma hadn't said anything, Emma, who never kept secrets well. This must be completely unlike a matter of casual gossip, something too awful to tell. As if proving the point, a classmate, Catherine, passed by. *What's wrong with you then, Pratt?* she asked disinterestedly, and Bett realized that she couldn't tell her, couldn't ever tell anyone, and she pushed by on her way outside to run, run through the drenching English rain until she accepted there was no cure for what was wrong with her.

When Bett awoke on her bunk, she realized the rain of her dream was actually tears. She dried them with the soft white handkerchief that she had clasped tightly in her hand. The truth was that dozens of other women over eight years and thousands of miles from Emma had not completely healed her. Would Gale Rains want such damaged goods? Then she thought of the times that she had seen through Rains's formal veneer to the glimpses of sadness and pain in the depths of her eyes. Perhaps Rains had personal reasons as well as official ones for keeping herself unavailable. Burrowing into her pillow the way she always did when thinking of Rains, she decided, *All right, Rains. I'm willing to try it again, if you are.* In the last stages of her deepest sleep, just before reveille, she was certain she heard that low, melodic voice whispering close to her ear, *Oh yes.*

❖

Rains remembered a story she once heard from a tribal elder about a place where time went backward. Sometimes she felt she was in that place now. She worked with the platoon as usual during morning exercise, but it took two days before she felt she had garnered the restraint to visit the barracks, knowing she would have to see Bett lying on her bed and smell her scent as she passed by. She forced her mind to concentrate on the accomplishments of her other recruits, and she felt a warm pride especially for Charlotte, who had passed her fitness test with flying colors, and especially for Teresa, whose stutter had improved tremendously.

When Helen was finally scheduled for release from the stockade, Rains heard the squad members planning a reunion lunch. Maria was showing off the small trophy she'd acquired and how she'd reworked the base to include Helen's name and the date of her fight, September 28, 1944, with big letters below that read *TKO*. There was much laughter and teasing but everyone expected that Helen would be very pleased with her memento.

They were well into their celebration when Sergeant Rains entered the mess hall with Sergeant Moore. The bruising around Moore's eyes was starting to fade but she still wore a bandage on her nose. They stopped by the squad's table, and Moore snapped her fingers and said in a loud voice, "Get my food, squaw."

Rains stiffened and stepped closer to her. "I have told you this before, Sergeant. That word does not mean what you seem to think it does. It is extremely offensive, and such abuse was not part of our arrangement."

Sergeant Rains's voice was tight and low, but Bett heard her response. For a few seconds, Moore looked like she might argue, but Rains's eyes never wavered from hers and finally, the ruddy-faced woman looked away.

"I'm getting hun-gry," she sang in a taunting tone, and there was laughter from the officers' table. Rains turned away without another word, picked up a tray, and begin loading it with food. Moore sauntered over and sat with the rest of the officers, a few of whom, Bett noted, were grinning widely. One man, a major, even moved closer, patting Moore on the shoulder as he sat. A few more looked offended and two women—both captains—got up and left the table.

Jo turned to Bett with a shocked expression on her face. "Why would Sergeant Rains be waiting on that woman?"

There was a moment of silence as everyone else tried to come up with a plausible explanation. Then Tee's quiet voice filled the void. "For Helen. She's doing it so Sergeant Moore won't p-press charges." She glanced at the group and then focused on Helen. "To get you out in time to graduate with the rest of us."

Helen stared at her. "What? How do you know that?"

Tee looked down as she took in a breath. "I overheard them talking one day when I was coming to see you. And Sergeant Rains has to clean Moore's room." She leaned in and her voice quieted. Those farthest away leaned toward her. "Even the t-toilet."

As everyone else shivered in disgust, Helen started to stand up, her fists clenched. "Oh no," she began, fury on her face. "This is not going to happen."

Several pairs of hands pulled her back down just in time to avoid being seen by several officers who looked over at the sound. "Helen," Bett said in a sharp whisper, "it's already happening. You getting in more trouble again now will only make things worse."

Helen's expression gradually calmed. She looked around at the rest of the squad. "Okay, okay. You're right, okay? But what do we do about it?"

Bett looked around quickly. Rains was almost through the line. "I've got an idea," she said, and everyone looked expectantly at her.

While the officers were busy hooting and hollering as Rains approached with Sergeant Moore's food, everyone in the squad except Helen and Tee got up quietly and went through the line again. Rains waited at Moore's side while she made a big production of tucking in her napkin and preparing her silverware. Before she could take a bite, however, the other half of the officers' table began laughing. Marching as best they could while carrying trays, the entire squad approached, with Bett calling out the cadence from the rear. Jo led, and when she reached her shocked sergeant, she called out, "Please be seated, ma'am."

Rains looked around uncertainly and then went to her usual seat at the end of the table without a word. Following her, Jo set down a tray with every salad option on it. "Compliments of your squad, ma'am."

Rains stared at the food for several seconds, and Bett was sure the corner of her mouth twitched. "Thank you, Private Archer."

Jo stepped aside, making room for Barb, whose tray carried every type of bread available. "Compliments of your squad, ma'am."

"Thank you, Private Ferguson."

Each person followed, bringing meats, vegetables, and soups of every variety being served. The entire mess hall was watching, with laughter and growing applause following each presentation. Finally, when the plates in front of Rains stretched across most of the table, Bett approached with a tray of desserts—but only those containing chocolate. Rains covered her mouth with her hand as Bett repeated, "Compliments of your squad, ma'am," but she couldn't cover the genuine laughter in her eyes.

In spite of having cleared her throat, Rains's voice sounded slightly strained as she replied, "Thank you, squad leader."

The applause had started up again but it died quickly as Helen walked toward the officers' table. Worried that Helen would lose her temper again, Bett had specifically told her not to participate, even leaving Tee to keep her company. She wondered if she ought to intercept her, but Helen marched past Sergeant Moore without the slightest glance. Stopping in front of her sergeant, she came to attention. Extending the trophy, she said, "Compliments of me, ma'am." Before Rains could reach for the object, Helen turned and faced the room, holding it over her head. "It says Sergeant Rains, *BSE*. That stands for Best Sergeant Ever." She turned back and lowered her voice. "I guess we both know it ain't likely, but if there's ever, ever anything I can do for you, you just ask, all right?"

Rains gave the same, slight nod as Helen placed the trophy on the table. "Thank you, Private Tucker."

❖

The last days of basic training were hectic, as always. Post-training work assignments had been given out, and now the specialized training classes the recruits attended meant they were seeing each other much less during the day. But that evening, with only two full days before graduation, the squad was unusually scattered.

Rains was in one of the small offices in the administration building, working to finalize travel arrangements for those who would be working at other locations after graduation. When she'd marched the squad to dinner earlier, she'd noted Bett's absence but she didn't even bother to mark down a demerit. Even the Army wasn't going to entirely change Bett's headstrong ways, apparently. But Bett would be here after the others were gone. She'd given up trying to suppress the pleasure of that thought. *Bett will be here. We'll have time to figure out—*

In the distance of her mind, Jessie's voice echoed. On the night of their sleepover, Rains had been so astounded by all the new ways her body was feeling that she had almost panicked. Jessie, sensing her nervousness, had stopped her tender caresses, telling Rains not to worry, saying they'd have time to figure all that out. But Jessie had been wrong. Was she wrong now? After a quick glance at the room clock, she stood, fighting a little snake of fear trailing down her back. Though it was a bit early for CQ, she told herself there might be some questions, some last-minute details to be attended to.

Harold Lutz met up with Rains as she was walking quickly toward the barracks. "Did you hear the asshole is getting transferred out next week?"

"Yes," Rains said. "About time."

"Word is, he's not taking it too good. I heard he was talking especially bad about you. Like, blaming you."

"I'm not worried about Crowley," Rains said quietly. "He doesn't want a fight. He is a coward."

"Or not a fair fight," Lutz agreed. "He's the type that tries to win by taking away something you care about, not playing you face to face."

At that, Rains felt the snake become a shaft of dread that passed through her back and into her heart, where it lodged with the sharpness of an arrowhead. "Will you check on my squad, Lutz? I'm going to the guardhouse."

❖

Through the guardhouse window Rains could see that Crowley had Bett gagged with her hands tied behind her in the same chair where he had assaulted Jenny. She thought she detected a red swelling on Bett's face, too, as if she'd been slapped hard, and there was a deep scratch on Crowley's cheek. Rains tried to quiet the hammering beat in her ears, to think of the best approach, of how to get Bett out safely before putting her knife in Crowley's heart. She flattened onto the ground as he came to the door. There was no cover, but the guardhouse was on a slight rise, and it was dark enough that she was confident she wasn't seen.

She heard Crowley's voice call out, "Hey, Chief! You out there?" Then to Bett: "Don't you worry. Geronimo will be here soon. Then we're gonna settle things once and for all." He sounded as though he'd been drinking. Good, Rains thought as she crept closer, still working out her next move. But then she heard him say, "So in the meantime, let's you and me get better acquainted, huh, sweetheart?"

In an instant, Rains was in the doorway. "I'm here, Crowley. Let her go. This is between you and me."

"Oh, fuck no, Chief. Me and your little soldier here, we're gonna have some fun and then it's your turn." He waved his pistol at Bett. Carefully, Rains begin to move into the tiny room.

"That's far enough." His voice sounded almost normal and Rains stopped immediately. "You think you're gonna get me shipped off to the front? I almost made it through this whole war safe and sound just watching you twats parade around, and now you're sending me out to die on some fucking island or something?" Spittle flew from his mouth and his head shook wildly.

Never taking her eyes off him, Rains reached up and took off her hat. Crowley watched dumbfounded as her braid tumbled out. Loosening her tie, Rains undid the top two buttons of her shirt while saying in a seductive voice, "Come on, Crowley. We can work this out." She thrust her hips toward him in a provocative motion as she undid two more buttons, her firm flesh shimmering through the gap. "I'll talk to the colonel. Say it was all a mistake." Crowley's mouth was open and he swayed slightly. "Wouldn't you rather start with some nice red meat?" She ran her hands up to her breasts and reached around to her back, pulling out her shirttail. Then the knife was in her hand and before he could react, she was behind him with the blade at his throat, her free hand holding the pistol to his side. Crowley tensed and the gun fired, the bullet striking the floor. Bett struggled to get free as acrid smoke spread throughout the small space.

Crowley tried to move away and Rains dug the point of her knife in until a thick drop of blood materialized on his neck. Her voice sounded almost exactly like before, but the message was very different. "That's right, Crowley. That's what I want." Her voice became a growl. "An excuse to cut your fat White throat." He stopped struggling. For the first time, Rains looked at Bett. "Are you all right?" she asked, and Bett nodded emphatically. Rains slid the blade from the side of Crowley's jaw toward his Adam's apple. The drop became a thin line of blood. "Did he hurt you?" Rains asked, almost more to Crowley than to Bett.

Bett shook her head, concerned that Rains wasn't really looking at her. What she had seen in Rains's eyes the night that she had dealt with Irene Dodd was nothing compared to the wild viciousness in her expression now. *She is going to kill him,* Bett realized. Unable to make her muffled words heard, she struggled frantically to free her hands. Rains slid the blade a little farther across, and the blood on Crowley's neck began to drip. "But he wanted to, didn't he?" The blade finished its journey to the other side of his jaw. "He likes to hurt women." Her voice was menacing now.

"Naw, Rains, naw. It wasn't nothin' like that." Crowley begin to babble, his voice higher with fear. "I was just mad...because of the transfer, you know."

"Shut up, Crowley," Rains growled. She moved the dagger up his face past his ear to the edge of his hair. The bead of blood followed. "Or I'm going to have my first scalp in ten years. And it's going to be yours."

The pistol clattered to the floor.

Harold Lutz came into the doorway, holding a rifle. "All right, Crowley. You're gonna spend your last week here in the stockade. And maybe the rest of the war, too."

Crowley looked almost relieved. But Rains didn't move away and the knife went in a little deeper. Crowley whimpered.

Bett had finally gotten her hands freed and she had the gag off at last. "Rains, it's okay." She gently touched the arm that held the knife. "Stand down, Sergeant."

Without releasing her captive, Rains turned slightly toward Bett's voice. Bett pressed close to her, hoping her whispered words would break through the rage. "The battle is over, Rains. You've won. I'm fine. I'm here. It's all right."

Rains turned and sheltered Bett close to her chest and held her tightly—not bothering to button or tuck in her shirt or put her hat back on. Lutz got the bleeding corporal out and the medics arrived to take Bett to the infirmary. Bett was shaky but not crying, although if Rains hadn't been holding her, she wasn't sure she would still be standing.

❖

Bett gradually awakened to hospital sounds and morning light. Seated in a chair that she had moved right next to the bed, and where she had apparently spent the night, Rains held Bett's hand; she was bent at the waist so her head rested on the bed in the crook of her other arm, folded near Bett's knee. Not wanting to wake her, Bett lay very still and studied the side of Rains's face. She thought again how much younger Sergeant Rains looked without her hat, with that gorgeous braid trailing down her back. Her bangs hanging over her eyes were somewhat ragged, and maybe that was what made her look like a little girl who needed a haircut. In sleep, her features were relaxed and sweet, with none of her guarded, severe expressions. Bett was ready for the day when she would see Rains actually smile. More than anything, she wanted to be the one to make that happen.

Suddenly, Rains gasped and sat bolt upright, looking alarmed. Bett squeezed her hand and watched Rain's eyes gradually focus, as if she'd come from a long way off. Then she noted something different in Rains's expression. She looked at Bett now, full on, with no inclination to look away or shutter her emotions.

"How are you feeling?" Rains asked, stretching her shoulders but still holding Bett's hand.

"Like I'm quite ready to get out of here." Bett smiled, sitting up in the bed. "You didn't have to stay all night, you know." Bett had tried for a casual tone but wondered if the sergeant had any idea how comforted she was by seeing Rains beside her when she awoke.

"Well, I will say," Rains replied, sounding serious as always, but her eyes had turned bright, "if that's what they mean by sleeping together, I'm rather disappointed."

It took Bett a few seconds to process this uncharacteristic remark, and then she broke out into a rush of laughter. "Oh my God, Sergeant. I'm not sure I've ever heard you make a joke before. Especially one so risqué." Rains grunted as if in disagreement, but her mouth turned up a bit as she turned her head from side to side, stretching her neck. "What if I absolutely guaranteed that you wouldn't be disappointed the next time?" Bett asked coyly. She moved Rains's hand toward her breast and was leaning forward as the sound of the nurse's voice came down the hall.

"I hear you, Sergeant. You come out here and leave that girl alone. You got some business with me now."

"Where are you running off to?" Bett asked, releasing Rains's hand regretfully and settling back onto her pillow.

Rains reached for her hat on the night table and Bett watched with great interest as the sergeant wound her braid to fit under it and settled the hat on her head. The plait started high on her head and now she wound it to fit under the cap, allowing only the thin line of scissored hair on her neck to show beneath it. "I had to make a deal in order to stay with you. And now that you're awake, I'll have to fulfill my part of it."

"I hope you didn't sell the family jewels or some such. I'm quite fine, really."

"No, just agreed to go for some treatment." In response to Bett's quizzical expression, she added, "Apparently Crowley's pistol shot caught a bit of my leg. Either that or it was a splinter ricochet."

A shadow crossed Bett's mind at the mention of Crowley's name, and she grabbed Rains's hand again and put it to her lips. "I knew you would come," she whispered, closing her eyes. "You're much too gallant not to save a lady in distress."

Rains cupped Bett's cheek with her other hand. "I want—I want you to know you can count on me, Bett. If you ever need me, I want you to call for me. Call with your heart and I will hear you. I will come anywhere, anytime." Giving Bett's hand a soft caress before releasing it, she stood and walked stiffly toward the door, buttoning her jacket as she went. As she moved away, Bett could see the dark stain of dried blood down the side of her left pant leg.

❖

Bett sat anxiously in the waiting area until Rains was released. She saw the sergeant taking a few painful steps down the hall, grimacing as she adjusted her weight to compensate for the work that had been done on her leg. Then she saw Bett and lifted her head, walking toward her normally.

"Don't you try to fake it with me, Sergeant," Bett said in an angry tone. "And if you ever take a wound like that again and then sit around all night with some woman, there'll be hell to pay, I can assure you." Rains's expression turned so worried that Bett had to look away. Then she stepped as close to Rains as she dared and whispered, "And if you knew how hard it was for me to keep from kissing you right now, you surely wouldn't have put me through it."

"Sorry," Rains mumbled, looking uncertain, and Bett realized they might have given her something for the pain.

"Come on, then."

She put Rains's arm around her shoulder and led her limping out the door as the nurse's voice followed them. "Wouldn't take no crutch. Oh no. Gotta walk out herself like some war hero or something."

"Are you hungry?" Bett asked as they made their way across the compound. "The mess hall has just started serving lunch."

"Probably should eat," Rains mumbled. "Shot's making me feel sick." She stopped for a minute and Bett could see her lips moving as if she was saying something over and over again.

"What is it, Rains? Do you need something?"

Rains took some deep breaths. "It translates to *stay strong*. My brother and I used to say it to each other when we were tired or hungry on our hunts. Stay strong."

Bett nodded in understanding and she touched Rains's cheek briefly. "You are strong, Sergeant. You're the strongest person I know."

Sergeant Rains straightened somewhat and turned her eyes to Bett's. "Then you should get to know yourself better," she suggested, and Bett smiled.

They started walking again. When they reached the mess hall, Bett opened the door and helped Rains up the steps. "You go on," she said, thinking that they probably shouldn't enter the room together, especially with Rains leaning on her. "I'll be right behind you."

Rains was no more than five limping steps into the room when the call went out. "Attention!" The entire mess hall stood as one, saluting. Rains looked around in confusion for a moment. Bett watched proudly from just outside the doorway. She knew this was the WAC's way of honoring their own, of acknowledging a special deed. *And you deserve it, my dearest Gale,* Bett thought as Rains took a breath to gather herself, straightened, and walked normally to the officers' table. Once there, she executed a sharp military turn and returned the salute. Everyone sat. Bett walked in after counting slowly to one hundred, and her squad led off the cheering. The officer's table joined in. Rains startled at the noise, looking around for the source of the celebration. When her eyes found Bett, she gave a single nod. Bett couldn't help letting a smile spread across her face. Rains looked away as one of the other officers asked her a question. Bett sat happily with her friends, thinking she had never in her life wanted anyone more than she wanted Sergeant Gale Rains. And never in her life had she been so sure that someone was worth waiting for.

❖

Graduation was held on a wonderful fall afternoon. The band played and every platoon paraded around the grounds, showing off their marching skills to the officers, VIPs, and proud parents. Bett was not the least bit surprised that no one from her family was in attendance. She knew how they felt about her participation in the WAC, but she found she honestly didn't care. She was proud of what she'd accomplished and that was enough. Bett knew that Rains's leg must still be hurting her, but the sergeant gave no sign. She wore the olive uniform skirt and jacket, for the second time that Bett could remember, and the dress WAC cap with her braid tucked back inside, of course. After their marching was over, Sergeant Rains stood, along with the other sergeants, through the rest of the ceremony, awarding Private First Class designations to some of her recruits, many of whom would be leaving Fort Des Moines to take up postings at Army locations around the country. Sergeant Rains said her good-bye to each with a handshake and a few words, accepting excited embraces from a few—after saluting first, of course. Bett did not hug her, but when they shook hands, she winked and slipped a piece of paper into Sergeant Rains's palm as cleverly as a spy. It was the address of her new house in town—near the library, naturally. Rains slipped it into her pocket with great care.

After all the recruits had received their awards, and everyone had been seated, the colonel announced a special citation. "Created by the Congress of the United States on July 2, 1926, the Soldier's Medal is awarded to any person of the Armed Forces of the United States or of a friendly foreign nation who, while serving in any capacity with the Army of the United States, distinguished himself or herself by heroism not involving actual conflict with an enemy," Janet Issacson read, and when she called Sergeant Rains's name, the cheers started up again. Rains stood very straight as she received the medal, pinned to her uniform by Colonel Issacson. "There will have to be an inquiry," Issacson said as she shook Rains's hand, softly enough that only Rains could hear over the cheers, "but we wanted to give you this in front of your squad." Her eyes shifted to Private Smythe and back. "You'll be on paid leave for a week. It's just a formality. And when you get back, we'll talk about your promotion."

"Yes, ma'am. Thank you, ma'am."

After dismissal, it was a madhouse. There were so many parting hugs being given that Bett lost track of Rains after she walked down the platform steps. She was about to give up and get her things from the barracks, when she glanced back one last time and caught sight of a familiar form in front of the reviewing stand. *That looks like my father, but it can't be.* She turned back into the tide of bodies, pushing her way forward. When she reached an open space, she saw what she'd never thought possible—Mr. R. L. Carlton talking to Sergeant Gale Rains. Quickly, she was close enough to overhear them.

"So I understand I owe you a debt of gratitude, Sergeant," her father was saying. Although his back was to her, she could hear the hint of contempt in his voice. She was quite sure that she could have predicted the disdain in his reaction after being informed that his daughter had been rescued by an Indian. An Indian *woman.*

"Not at all, sir," Sergeant Rains replied. Then, perhaps sensing what Bett knew to be in his tone, she added, "I just did what any red-blooded American would have done."

"Be that as it may," her father said, the double meaning of Rains's words apparently lost on him, "I would still like for you to have a token of my esteem." His hand stretched out with a fan of hundred-dollar bills.

Bett stepped forward, smiling uncertainly. "Father, I had no idea you were going to be here today."

"Elizabeth, don't misinterpret my presence. I'm sure you can imagine how I feel about this escapade and your mother agrees," her father said to her curtly. "You have finished your training here and proven your point. Now I am here to take you back to California." He seemed unaware that he was still holding out the money.

"No, sir," Rains said, and father and daughter looked back at her in surprise. She indicated the bills. "I couldn't, sir." She glanced at Bett expectantly.

"Oh, come now, Sergeant," her father insisted, exasperated. He took Rains by the wrist and pressed the money into her hand. "I know you're not getting rich on Army pay."

"*A man is rich in proportion to the number of things he can afford to let alone*," Rains quoted, easily breaking his grasp and letting the money drop to the ground. There was an awkward pause. "Congratulations again, Private Smythe." She met Bett's eyes for another brief second. "Sir," she nodded to Bett's father, who regarded her as if she were an insect he was about to crush. As she walked away, each long stride showed some blood seeping through the bandage under her skirt.

"I'm sorry, Father," Bett said, not the least bit apologetic. "I'll be staying on here. I have a job to do." *I'm not running away*, she told herself with certainty as she turned to follow Rains, not even telling her father good-bye. *I'm running toward.* "Wait! Oh God, Rains, wait."

Chapter Thirteen

Three days after the graduation of her last squad of WAC recruits, Sergeant Gale Rains walked off the Fort Des Moines grounds bareheaded, wearing her jeans, a red flannel shirt over her white T-shirt, and her moccasins—the exact outfit she had arrived in over two and a half years ago. She carried a few other personal items in the used knapsack. The wound on her leg was healing well; now it was just covered by a large Band-Aid, and she was ready to walk.

But as she went through the streets of the town, it became apparent that her uniform had been a part of her most recent version of invisibility, at least for the people of Des Moines for whom the ladies of the WAC were no longer a novelty. Now, in her own clothing and her braid hanging down her back, she drew stares from almost everyone she passed. She stopped in front of a storefront window and tried to see what they saw. She was tall and lean. Army food had filled her out some from the undernourished high school girl in Miss Warren's class, and the constant exercises with her squads had kept the muscle in her arms and legs defined. Her coloring was different from most people in this part of the country, and her braid was nothing like the common hairstyles that ladies wore. Was that all that people really saw? What did Bett see? In that moment, Rains noticed her shirt cuffs were a bit frayed and her jeans had been laundered so much that they were a white-blue. She looked up and saw that she was in front of a Western clothing store. She went in.

As she picked out a few items, she felt almost elated at the experience of buying herself something new with her own money. After she paid, she wore the satin shirt she'd found and her new jeans and boots out of the store, carrying her old wardrobe in a store bag. For a few blocks she walked proudly, not caring if people stared at her or not. Then she remembered Thoreau: *Beware of all enterprises that require new clothes.* Her new boots began to hurt. She found a park with a public restroom and changed back into her old clothes, carefully folding the dressier outfit and putting it in the shopping bag. *Another time,* she told herself. *Bett will like what she sees or she won't.*

When she finally found the address that Bett had given her, a group of moving men were driving away, leaving one box on the porch. The door was still open, but she rang the bell anyway. "Please come in and bring everything to the back room," she heard Bett's voice call. Rains carried in the large box high on her waist and it hid her face.

Bett saw a body in jeans carrying a box into her house; she'd seen that all day long. It wasn't until Rains passed by her that Bett saw her braid. "Sergeant Rains! Good Lord, is that you?"

Rains put down the box and turned to face her. Bett looked her up and down in shock, her mouth just open a bit. "You look...you look..." It was not like her to be at a loss for words. "You don't look a bit like yourself," she managed, finally.

"Actually, I do," Rains said calmly. "I look exactly like myself. This is how I looked for most of my life. What you know is only how I've looked for the last two and a half years."

Bett could not stop staring. She felt almost like she was in the presence of a stranger. Wearing jeans and flannel, her former drill instructor looked even younger and wilder, somehow.

Rains lifted her chin and asked, a bit tightly, "Would it make you feel better if I went back to the base and put on my uniform?"

"No, no, of course not." Bett was embarrassed. "Let's just— let's sit and talk a bit, shall we?" She started toward a sofa which was piled high with boxes.

Rains remained where she was. "So this is your house?"

"Yes, uh, yes. Let me show you around." Bett couldn't understand why she was suddenly so nervous, but she really wanted Rains to like the house, to be impressed even. She gave a quick tour of the two-bedroom, two-bath home that had a dining room and a small breakfast area in the kitchen, but only a large den instead of a formal living room. "And I have a telephone now, look," she said, pointing to the black apparatus, hanging on the kitchen wall, to the left of a small breakfast table and two chairs.

Rains frowned in the phone's direction, unable to imagine what kind of strings had been pulled at what expense to get Bett such a device so quickly, now, with the war on. She had not enjoyed the few phone conversations she'd had. She'd found it quite disconcerting to speak with someone while not being able to read their facial expression, their eyes, or their true intentions. She turned back toward the den, her eyes moving over everything. "Big," she said. "My whole family lived in places the size of just this room."

"See," Bett said, "in some ways I feel I don't know very much about you at all, and I'd like to."

Rains walked over and looked out onto a cement patio and a small fenced backyard. "Is this where your dozens, perhaps hundreds of questions come in?"

Bett laughed. "Yes, unless you suddenly take it upon yourself to start blabbering away about your life, which you haven't seemed particularly inclined to do, so far."

"Hmm," Rains grunted, still eyeing the fenced yard. She could hear a dog barking in the house next door.

"For example," Bett picked up, hands on her hips, "what does that sound you just made mean? Does it mean *okay* or does it mean *forget it* or does it mean *stop your bloody running on, woman*, or what?"

Rains stopped looking outside and turned her gaze back to Bett, who had a smudge of dirt on her left cheek and hair escaping in all directions from under the kerchief she wore. She was dressed in a dirty white long-tailed man's shirt with the sleeves rolled up and worn black slacks. She was barefoot. Rains thought she was absolutely gorgeous. Breathing in, she walked back toward her, allowing herself to feel the goodness of seeing Bett again. "Just now it means that I would like to get to know you better also." She gently took Bett's hands and turned them over, looking at the dirty palms and then back up into Bett's eyes. "But perhaps we should talk while I help you clean up."

Silly, Bett told herself, *Rains isn't the type to be impressed by material things. She believes in actions.* "Oh, Rains," Bett said, and threw her arms around Rains's neck. "I'm so sorry. I don't know what's gotten into me." When she felt the warmth of Rains's body, she knew it was all going to go just as she'd dreamed.

Rains's breathing deepened and her hands moved gently on Bett's back, almost as if she were reading Braille. Bett's nipples hardened in response and she hoped Rains could feel them. They held each other for a long moment. Bett felt her body fitting into Rains's in a most delicious way. *This is what I've been waiting for,* Bett thought. Just as she lifted her face, the doorbell rang.

"Bloody hell," Bett murmured, dropping her head back onto Rains's chest. She sighed as she stepped back and walked toward the door. "It's just this mess that's making me anxious. I'm terrible at organizing but I'm worse about living in such a shambles."

Bett signed for a small package and carried it back into the room, tossing it hopelessly on a pile. She returned to where Rains was standing and placed her hands on Rains's chest. "I know my home isn't currently up to Army standards, but you won't give me KP, will you, Sergeant?" She leaned in and brushed her lips across Rains's.

"Hmm." Rains seemed immobilized by the kiss, even though it was different from the kiss they'd shared in the conference room, which had been intensely passionate. This time, Bett kept her lips light and sweet and moved away so quickly that Rains hadn't really kissed her back.

"Which means you wouldn't dream of it, right?" Bett batted her eyelashes so exaggeratedly that Rains breathed out her now familiar chuckle.

❖

Sergeant Rains needed every bit of her considerable organizational skills to make any semblance of order in Bett's house. On their break for lunch, Rains asked, "You said at boarding school they called you Pratt. What did they call you at Oxford?"

Bett was flattered. "Do you remember everything about all of your recruits?"

"Hmm."

"I'll take that as a compliment, then. Well, things at Oxford were much more formal, of course, so in class it was Miss Carlton."

"But your friends at school," Rains persisted. "What did they call you?"

Bett's mind flashed back to her first week at university, where she'd developed a kind of self-identity, learning there were other women who felt like she had toward Emma. Her desires might not be acceptable to the wider world, but at least they were genuine. She barely remembered the first girl—*Jillian?*—only recalling how good it had felt to be touched again. But then she'd panicked, jolted by a desperate need to get away before she felt something deeper and got hurt again. She'd seen other women, briefly each time, only wanting some release, something to fill the void. And now? Bett looked at Rains. Now that the strangeness of seeing her sergeant in civilian clothes had worn off, she found her even more desirable. If she had felt this kind of attraction in the past, she would have dragged whoever into the bedroom—boxes be damned—had her way and then sent them off before the night was over. But she couldn't imagine Rains taking part in a story line like that. *Is this something different? Is this something more?*

Rains was looking at her curiously. She was taking too long to answer.

"Um, they mostly just called me Bett."

Rains contemplated this. "Bett is not enough for you," she said after a moment. "You are so much more. Your name should be more."

"Like what?" Bett asked, pleased by the assessment.

"Right now I don't know you well enough to say."

"But you'll let me know?"

Rains nodded. "What will you call me now?" she asked. "Here in your home?"

"What do you want me to call you?" Bett asked, amused at the question.

Rains moved closer and took Bett's hands again. "Let me explain. I believe that words have meaning and names have power. In my life, I almost lost the tribal family name that is a big part of my identity. And my language is also very important to me. It's the glue that holds my culture together." She freed a hand and touched Bett's mouth very gently. "When it is just you, speaking to only me, call me Rain—without the *s*." Her own mouth turned up a bit. "To anyone else I would be Gale Rains. Though I must admit I have never had a recruit say *Sergeant* quite like you. I can hear your laugh in the middle of it."

Bett smiled at this last remark, but her mind was on what Rain had said about her identity and her language. She knew she might not ever completely understand, but she wanted Rain to know she had heard her. Hoping she was posing the right question in the right way, she asked, "How do you say your real name, your...tribal family name, Rain?"

Those black eyes searched hers for so long that Bett thought she wasn't going to answer, or maybe she had taken offense at being asked. Perhaps Rain was deciding if she was worthy of knowing something so personal.

Just as Bett thought she might have to look away, that she wasn't prepared for such scrutiny, Rain answered, her words slow and almost fierce. "All I have is my childhood name because I wasn't with my people when I came of age. But my mother always told me that my name was special, and it suits me." Rain spoke her tribal name, and to Bett it sounded like poetry, or a prayer. "In English it would be Wind and Rain."

Bett felt like she had been given a gift. She repeated the unusual sounds with great care, first in her head, then out loud, trying to match the accent and cadence that Rains had used. Reaching out her free hand, she touched Rain's cheek softly. "Wind and Rain, I want to apologize to you for acting so strangely when you first arrived, and

I want to tell you that I like the way you look." She brushed Rain's bangs back out of her eyes. "I like it a lot." Rain's eyes seemed to deepen, reminding Bett of that moment they had fallen together on the parade grounds. "May I ask what you are thinking just now?"

Rain's answer was deliberate, as if she was just formulating the words as the thoughts became clear. "I was thinking how I..." She swallowed again. "How I missed you these last three days." She nodded, as if relieved to have admitted it. "It was dreary not seeing you or hearing your voice every day. I was thinking that I am glad to see you." She gently squeezed Bett's hand back. "I am very glad to see you."

Bett felt that funny flutter of her heart that only Rain seemed to bring on. Could she be any sweeter? She wanted to kiss Rain right then, to start and not stop, but instead she resorted to teasing as she often did to cover her feelings. "But don't you miss all of your squad members, Sergeant? Mightn't you be helping any one of them with packing or unpacking, or getting them settled in their new position?"

Rain seemed to consider this. "I might," she admitted, and then looked over at Bett with a slight crook of her mouth. "But I wouldn't at any point be holding their hands." She stood and pulled Bett up with her so quickly that Bett wobbled a bit and Rain caught her arms to steady her.

"Good," Bett said when she had her balance, looking seriously at Rain. She added, "Let's keep it that way, shall we?" When Rain nodded, Bett settled for another quick, light kiss on the lips and repeated, "Good."

After they had gotten back to work, Rain began thinking about how it was for her in Bett's house. It seemed to be a good space, even a little familiar, maybe a bit like being in Miss Warren's house. At least she didn't feel uncomfortable or terribly out of place, and she hoped nothing would change during the upcoming evening.

Trying not to focus and what might happen between them, she thought about Bett herself, watching her from the corner of her eye, the way she had done so many times on the base. Her expressions, the way her body moved, how her words echoed in Rain's head long after they had been spoken—all of these things pleased Rain beyond any normal measure. At one time Bett had said that she wanted them to be friends, so perhaps that was part of what was happening, now that they were away from the base and working out how to be together as something besides sergeant and private. But eventually the boxes would be empty and the day would be over and then she felt there would come a time when something more could happen between them. She had felt this possibility for weeks now, every time she looked at Bett, every time they touched. But then Rain would find herself almost undone with a wash of competing emotions—excitement, nervousness, desire, apprehension...Clearing her throat, she got herself a glass of water and brought one back for Bett as well.

"Are you all right?" Bett questioned, coming over to stand near her as she accepted the drink.

"Fine, yes," Rain answered, puzzled. "Why do you ask?"

Bett moved a little closer. "One thing I think I've figured out about you is that you often clear your throat when you're nervous or upset. I just don't want you to feel either of those things with me." Smiling as Rain blinked in surprise, she stroked Rain's cheek softly. "I hope you know I care for you as I believe you care about me. But nothing is going to happen here that we don't both want. All right?"

Their bodies were not touching, but Rain took Bett's hands and clasped them between hers in the narrow space separating them. Her expression softened. "Thank you for saying that. You are kind and good, and I am happy to be here with you."

Looking into Rain's eyes, Bett wondered how such simple words could affect her so profoundly.

By early evening, the most immediate unpacking process was all but finished. After wiping down a figurine which she put on the end table, Bett happily surveyed the room, seeing the furniture neatly arranged and her things artfully displayed. It was beginning to look like a home, her home. She stood and walked over to where Rain was putting plates in a cabinet. "I don't know how to thank you." She put her arms around Rain's waist, standing behind her with the side of her face pressed into Rain's back. She felt Rain's braid where it lay alongside her own hair. It felt solid and strong, like the woman who wore it. She remembered the only other time she had touched it, how she'd wanted to run her hands down it again and then take apart the woven strands and let Rain's hair fall loose. In this, as in all of her more recent fantasies about Rain, they were naked. The vision was temptingly erotic, and a shiver of desire ran along Bett's spine, settling between her legs. She pressed in a little closer, thinking how she had liked having Rain here today, even beyond anticipating having sex with her.

She'd been so looking forward to having her own place, to finally having some peace from all of the noise and bustle of the base and some privacy from all of her squad mates, and yet she'd found herself unexpectedly lonely and restless the first three nights in her new home. Bett found herself ready for some company, and Rain, who made no demands and seemed to have no expectations, fit the bill perfectly. Additionally, Rain seemed so much more relaxed than she ever had on base and she was easy to be with in a way that belied what Bett knew to be a rather powerful personality. They had worked together well and their conversations, which had been mostly about unpacking, had been enjoyable.

Now the sergeant turned in Bett's arms so they were facing each other, her face very serious. "I think you should know something." Bett leaned back in and Rain enfolded her. Rain sighed and a little sound of pleasure escaped.

Bett sighed her own sound of contentment. "As long as it's not about you leaving tonight or some rubbish like that." *Because I have big plans for you, Sergeant.*

"No, it's that I don't think we will finish this unpacking tonight. Unless you want to work in the bedroom after dinner."

"I certainly was planning to," Bett said, breathing against Rain's chest as she traced her hand down Rain's tight stomach. "But probably not in the way you mean."

Rain didn't move away, but she gave a sort of choked cough, which probably meant she was even more uncomfortable than when she cleared her throat. Bett suppressed a laugh, realizing suddenly that it was very possible Rain was less experienced than she was in that area. Perhaps that was one reason why she'd resisted Bett's advances for so long—she was uncertain of exactly how to proceed. Bett thought of something she'd been meaning to ask. "How old are you, Rain?"

The sergeant drew herself up a little taller. "I am almost twenty-one now," she said boldly, and then lowered her voice, "but the Army thinks I am almost twenty-three."

"You lied to the Army about your age?"

"Yes, and I am not proud of that." Rain dipped her head slightly.

"Then, why?"

"To get into the WAAC program."

"And you couldn't just wait?" Bett asked, trying to put the pieces together.

"It's a long story and one I may yet tell you, but for now let me say that I just needed to enlist right then," Rain answered, with a tone of finality in her voice. Then she cocked her head and asked, "How old are you, Bett?"

"I'm twenty-five. Does that bother you?"

"Bother me? Not at all. I just would never have guessed you were so old."

Again, Bett detected a smile in Rain's eyes, although not quite on her lips. She reached out to tickle Rain's side but Rain caught her hand and kissed it. "You must know I am teasing you now," Rain said easily.

Bett wasn't really offended. Actually, the role of a slightly older seductress was rather intriguing. At school, she'd usually been the youngest in her class, so this arrangement might be a really fun change of pace. Thinking to move the evening in that direction, she pulled Rain toward the refrigerator. "Well, shall we get cleaned up and see about getting something to eat? It'll only be leftovers from what I had last night, is that all right?"

"I could cook"—Rain opened the door and shook her head at the all but bare space—"or maybe not." She gestured at Bett.

"I think a visit to the grocery store is in your future." She looked toward the backyard. "But not tonight. A storm is coming."

Through the kitchen window, Bett could see the sun was starting to set in what appeared to be a clear sky, but she didn't pursue it. "Fine," she said, emptying some food into a container and putting it in the oven. "But for now, let's get ready to eat or my stomach will start growling and I'll be embarrassed."

❖

Rain showered and washed her hair in the guest bathroom. *I'd have you in with me, darling, but I fear that dinner would waste away in that oven, all alone*, Bett had said. She'd been horrified to learn that Rain was content to wash her hair with soap, so she brought in some shampoo and conditioner, as well as body lotion, making Rain promise to use it. The fragrances seemed familiar at first, but then different on her own hair and skin. Rain put on her new dark jeans and, after considerable thought, her new white satin shirt with the gold fringe. Not wearing a T-shirt under it made her feel just slightly indecent, and more than a little bit excited. As she combed out her hair, leaving it down to dry before she braided it, it occurred to her that other than today and the very first day they had met at Bett's induction, she had only seen Bett in her uniform.

Still barefooted, she moved quietly toward the master bedroom. Bett was coming out of her bathroom in a black silk slip, her head turned as she put in a second sparkling earring. Rain saw the swell of her breasts along the top of the clinging material and the shapely curve of her thighs where they disappeared under the thin fabric. She held her breath.

Bett looked over, surprised. She took in Rain's appearance for a moment with a little smile on her face and then said, "Oh no, Rain. I can't have you sit at my table looking like that." Rain stood still, but her eyebrows knitted with worry. Bett crossed the room, meeting Rain's gaze as she ran her hand through Rain's loose hair, thinking, *Here is half of my fantasy already*. "I won't be able to pay our meal the slightest attention. You look astonishing."

Standing this close, Bett could read Rain's smoldering desire and she had to close her eyes for a few seconds. She couldn't remember the last time she had seen such undisguised hunger on a woman's face. Rain breathed in Bett's scent, intensified by the warmth of the shower, and slowly moved her hands up Bett's arms until her shoulders. She ran her fingers along the top of Bett's slip, just above where the fabric began. Her touch was achingly gentle, but Bett could feel the heat in her caress. She shuddered with the sensation and put her lips to Rain's while she put her hand on the thick fabric of Rain's jeans, just at the crotch. Rain moaned deep in her throat and slowly pulled the slip and bra straps down Bett's arms, stopping just short of revealing her breasts. Pressing herself against Bett's hand, she moved her mouth to the newly revealed flesh, kissing tenderly and slowly across Bett's body. Bett put her other hand in Rain's hair again, ready to guide her mouth to her nipple.

"Oh yes," Bett said in a whisper, close to Rain's ear. Rain's warm, soft lips felt exquisite on her skin. *Possibly less experienced,* she thought, *but not inexperienced.* This was going to be all she had imagined, and more.

A buzzing sound made them freeze against each other, breathing shallowly, quickly. The sound continued.

"That must be my timer," Bett managed to say, finally.

"Your what?" Rain asked gruffly, as Bett released her.

"To let me know the food is ready," Bett explained. She felt Rain start to draw away and stopped her with hands on Rain's shoulders. Taking a deep breath, she looked imploringly into Rain's eyes. "I'm sure I'm stretching your patience to the absolute limit, but could you take care of that, darling?" She looked down at herself. "I seem to be a bit…indisposed." Rain cleared her throat, but didn't move. "I'm so sorry. Really. You don't have to do anything but just turn off the oven. Please?" Bett added. Rain turned without replying and walked down the hall. Bett said to herself, "I should have just let it burn."

❖

They had their leftovers in the dining room, talking of Bett's squad members and what they might be doing, Bett making Rain blush deeply when she suggested that the girls would never guess what the two of them were doing. After she did the dishes, Rain stepped out onto the patio and Bett followed. "It's not like me to spend all day inside," Rain remarked.

"Well, you were outside when you arrived this morning," Bett offered. She moved beside her, thrilled when Rain put an arm around her shoulders and drew her closer. Rain was breathing in deeply and Bett followed her gaze into the sky to a line of dark, threatening clouds almost directly overhead. The first raindrops fell, and Rain guided her quickly back inside as the sky began to open up. A torrent of water poured off the roof and the wind pushed some of the water toward the door.

Rain's hair was still loose down her back but now it seemed to almost sparkle as tiny droplets of water shone in the light. Beneath the damp white satin shirt, her slightly erect nipples were clearly visible. Bett felt the familiar ache between her legs that Rain had caused for weeks now. A booming clap sounded very close by. Bett was about to ask Rain how she'd known about the storm when something in Rain's expression told her there weren't going to be any more questions tonight. Just answers.

A thick lightning bolt ripped through the sky, just beyond the backyard. The electricity blinked out as a tremendous crash of thunder shook the house. Bett stepped into Rain's arms, and the storm began.

Much later, when she had her analytical mind back, Bett actually let herself think about the difference between being with Rain and the other girls she'd had sex with. With Rain, there was no pretense, no posturing. She was never timid or hesitant, although she could be very gentle. She never asked if Bett liked one thing or another. She didn't have to. From the first time they touched in the darkness of the bedroom, Bett's body told Rain everything she needed to know. With Rain, everything was immediate; she was so completely in the moment that Bett lost all sense of time. There wasn't any need to worry about what was going to happen later, tomorrow, or next week, because there was only now.

They were naked in bed, facing each other, kissing eagerly, deeper and deeper until Rain raised up on her elbow and Bett lay on her back. Rain's mouth was on her body then, not just kissing but tasting her down her chest and onto her breasts and then onto her belly and along her side. Her mouth was so warm and soft and her hands were touching and pressing on places on Bett's body that made her breathe harder, her legs, her breasts, the backs of her shoulders, and little sounds of pleasure came with every breath. Bett laid her hands on Rain's back under her long hair and pulled her closer, closer. She had been waiting so long for this that it simply wasn't possible to wait any more. *Now, please, touch me now*—but before the thought was even finished, she felt Rain's long fingers glide across the wettest part of her. The sensation was almost electrifying and yet so sweet and she was ready to move and pressed herself harder against Rain's fingers as they slid to touch every part and quickly found the most responsive, the part that made Bett arch her back and rock her hips faster. *So good, so good...* Rain was breathing hoarsely, moving with her, and Bett stopped moving and let Rain take her and Rain didn't stop, couldn't stop, as Bett's cries changed into tones of needing and having and Rain's other hand moved up her belly and squeezed her breast and her teeth grazed the side of Bett's neck. Bett's arms tightened desperately around Rain's back and her head went back as she cried out through waves and waves of shuddering release, and a thousand streams of tingling radiances passed along all the pathways of her body until there was nothing left to be but still, and breathing, and feeling Rain.

Rain's hand. Still there. Not moving now, just tenderly holding her together. Bett's breath slowed as the throbbing against Rain's fingers grew weaker, fainter. When Rain did move her hand, Bett murmured with just the slightest protest, or regret. Then in one motion Rain lay back and pulled Bett alongside her, head on her shoulder. Bett pushed her leg across Rain's thigh so she could press against her there, and Rain's head dropped slowly, her lips sliding over Bett's hair. They slept.

It might have been hours or maybe only minutes later when Rain moved slightly and Bett came completely awake. It was still very dark except for the occasional flashes of lightning and she could hear a hard downpour outside and thunder echoing around the area. Bett could feel a current pulsing between her and Rain. She kissed Rain's face very sweetly and heard a very faint breath of enjoyment. She moved her mouth to Rain's ear and whispered, "Rain?"

"Um?" Rain swallowed.

Keeping her face very close to Rain's, Bett began to run her hand up and down Rain's chest, between her breasts and down to her belly. She felt Rain's lashes brush her face as her eyes came open. Bett moved to touch each breast very lightly, letting her finger dwell a bit on each nipple until they began to harden.

Rain cried out her approval, and Bett felt Rain's body begin to move. Rain's mouth found Bett's with all the passion and desire of their earlier meeting. Their breathing quickened together, and it was as if they had never stopped, would never finish. Bett extended her reach farther down Rain's body, moving along her hips and then back to her belly, and then down, combing her fingers through the soft hair there. Rain's mouth was open on Bett's and their tongues were touching as they tasted each other. Then Bett licked up the side of Rain's neck and a deep, almost chuckling sound came from her throat. She moved to do the same on the other side and Rain's body writhed and Bett turned her hand so the heel of it pressed against the wet folds between Rain's legs and she spiraled gently. Rain's hand came into Bett's hair and tightened along her scalp. Bett pressed again, a little harder, and Rain's body jerked against her, with an urging noise now coming from her throat. Bett turned her hand again so that her fingers were poised at the place where she could feel the heat, feel the flesh begin. She put her mouth on Rain's breast as she slowly slid her fingers down, slowly caressing the swollen flesh, stopping just at the place where Rain's body opened. Rain was so slick with wetness that it felt like moving across priceless silken fabric. Rain's breathing was getting louder and her hips were pressing forward in response to Bett's every movement. Bett let her teeth run across Rain's nipple and moved her mouth to the other breast, as she moved her fingers just a little faster. Rain's motions were urgent now and Bett bit very gently on her nipple, and Rain exhaled a long quivering breath as her back came up off the mattress.

When Rain's breathing had slowed enough, Bett moved her hand, exploring. She could feel that Rain was still very hard, so she touched just there with only the pads of her fingers. Rain's body stiffened at once, and Bett thought she might try to move away, so she put her hand flat on Rain's chest and kissed her deeply. Rain was running her hands across Bett's back, and when the kiss ended, she breathed very close to Bett's ear, pressing the side of her face against Bett's head. There were no words, but only sounds of pleasure and want. Bett began to move her fingers very fast, much faster than she had before, but very lightly. She heard Rain's breath catch. For a long moment it was like they were both looking for something, until Bett whispered into Rain's ear, "Yes, Rain. Yes." Then Rain's head turned toward her and her body bucked and a series of her cries flew out into the night.

Bett stretched out on her side, her body running the length of Rain's, and put her arm across Rain's waist, feeling incredibly contented. Rain was completely limp. Bett snuggled under Rain's shoulder and after a moment, Rain's arm fell across her back.

Barely opening her mouth, Rain's low voice said, "I can't move."

"Don't," Bett ordered as she pulled the covers back up. They slept. The storm clouds passed by and a sliver of moon appeared.

And then Rain was moving, and Bett was on her back again and Rain settled her body between Bett's legs. Her forearms were on either side of Bett, holding herself just off the bed, and she slanted above Bett until their bodies touched there once, twice, three times, and Bett felt a wave of delicious need roll up from inside her. In a very different voice, almost like a warning, Rain breathed huskily, "I can't stop."

"Don't," Bett commanded again and Rain was kissing along her throat and biting her with little nips that set off sparks of pleasure at each point. She bit around the fullest parts of Bett's breasts while they ground into each other, moaning together. When Rain kissed down Bett's belly and felt Bett's hands on her shoulders, she slid her body away and down the bed, moving her hands until they were under Bett's hips. Rain's fingers dug into the muscles there, while she pushed her breast into the hair above. Bett trembled, her hands squeezing Rain's arms. Lifting Bett's hips as she moved down to kiss along the insides of her thighs, Rain caught Bett's truest scent, the sweet musky interior of her, and she breathed deeply, enraptured. She lowered her mouth onto Bett's eager wetness, caressing with her lips, wanting to taste everything. Somewhere outside herself, she heard Bett saying her name and she began to stroke with her tongue.

Bett felt each millimeter of movement as something deeper, as something in her that Rain's fingers hadn't found began to open. Rain's tongue was soft and firm, and so sweet and so insistent and every second she felt herself drawing closer to the edge, to the place where she would fall. She knew she was calling out, matching each time that Rain tasted her again and again, and her hands grabbed Rain's empty pillow and then Rain pushed in a little deeper and a little faster and the last conscious motion that Bett could make was to pull the pillow onto her face to muffle her scream of surrender that seemed to go on and on until she landed safely in Rain's arms— the most perfect place she had ever been.

Later, there was a suggestion of first light.

For someone so strong, Rain was enticingly soft and yielding when Bett lay full length on top of her. She took Rain's wrists in her hands and pushed them over her head, a spontaneous gesture that she found unpredictably exciting. While she could have easily twisted loose, Rain made no attempt to free her hands from Bett's grasp; they both knew Bett wouldn't want to go very long without letting Rain touch her again. But for now, Rain responded to the sliding of Bett's body on hers by rising and falling, rolling against her, the moans in her throat urging Bett, begging. An unfamiliar force rushed into Bett's core and her hands and her mouth had to have Rain, to possess her, to own her. But before she let go of Rain's wrists, she bit her twice on the neck, hard. Not hard enough to break the skin, but enough to make Rain call out, two sharp, urgent, imploring sounds that made Bett move down Rain's body pressing her own breasts against her and following her body's movement with a trail of kisses. She returned to gently, very gently take each of Rain's hard nipples into her mouth, just rolling her tongue over each, just finishing each with a kiss. Now Rain was making sweet, trembling moans and Bett moved again, stroking each leg, feeling the incredible muscles there that were straining and rolling against her hand. As she stroked the inside of Rain's thigh, her hand brushed against the soft, damp hair between Rain's legs and Bett lost control.

She lifted Rain's hip with one hand and slid into her with the other and at first it was just her own elated cry in the night as Rain gave only a sharp gasp in her ear. Bett stopped moving for a second, the sound echoing in her consciousness but the meaning unclear. When she felt Rain soften around her, she understood it was another yielding, and she pushed her fingers slowly deeper into the hot, incredible softness wrapping close around them. Rain put her hand on Bett's arm, keeping her inside and moving her in the way she wanted. When her spreading wetness began to flow out over Bett's hand, Bett felt her own blood throbbing and pushed deliberately now, exulting when Rain's hips began to follow the rhythm of each thrust. Rain's arms were around Bett's back again and her breathing had begun to match Bett's movements, which made Bett move faster. She wanted Rain breathless, wanted her desperate, wanted those arms which were tightening around her now, Rain's hands pressing into Bett's back until she could feel the nails on each finger there, and until she could feel Rain's sex contracting around her fingers, until she could feel herself throb, until she put her forehead down on Rain's chest and felt Rain push back against her, forcing, with two long keening wails which meant she had lost control, too, and that was what Bett wanted as she collapsed onto Rain's body and they rose and fell, panting fiercely, still together.

Bett kissed Rain as sweetly as she could when she began to slide out of her. She felt just the slightest shudder and then the cool air on the dampness of her fingers. She remembered the first gasp from Rain's throat then and looked down at her in the lightening room. Rain's eyes were barely open and her focus was far away. "I didn't hurt you, did I?" Bett asked softly.

Rain's lips curved into a little smile. "No. You were wonderful. I..." She trailed off for a few seconds and then cleared her throat, though she still spoke quietly. "I've not had any experience quite like that, as you could probably tell."

As Rain's meaning became clear, Bett felt a weight settle on her chest. She'd wanted Rain so much—had she been too wild or rough? "Oh my God, Rain, are you sure you're all right?"

Rain turned until they were lying side by side again. Bett was almost quivering with worry, but Rain could only manage a soft shushing sound as she rubbed her cheek softly against Bett's face, nuzzling her and soothing her. As her worry subsided and Bett's mind began to work, she understood Rain's implication. She was—technically, at least—a virgin. *Had been a virgin*, Bett corrected herself and felt a wry smile spreading inside and across her face. *The smile of a rotter*, she scolded herself, *deflowering an innocent maiden*, but she couldn't stop smiling, even as she felt Rain's body going slack in her arms and heard her, with a final deep vibrating sigh, say something in Lakota.

"What, darling?"

The warmth of Rain's presence and her steady breathing had almost lulled Bett to sleep when a low whisper translated for her. "You have won me."

CHAPTER FOURTEEN

It was very bright and very chilly in the bedroom. The storm seemed to have brought in the first really cold weather of the fall. They were sleeping close together, in a tangle of arms and legs. As Rain shifted her position slightly, she felt Bett's arms tighten around her and heard Bett's sleepy voice ask, "Where are you going?"

"Nowhere," Rain assured her, putting her face close.

There was a pause. "Good," Bett said shifting slightly with a sigh, though she sounded no more awake. "I'll go with you." Rain's mouth pulled into a slow smile.

The phone rang. Rain startled up, but Bett pulled her back. "Leave it," she whispered.

Rain started to fuss about the phone, but Bett stroked her hair and snuggled back close to her and Rain decided she'd rather not. She moved her thumb in a widening circle on Bett's shoulder, thinking of the last forty-eight hours and how the connection between herself and Elizabeth Frances Pratt Carlton Smythe had now become deeper and stronger than with any other human being in her entire life, outside of her family. She knew she should be careful, knew she should pull back and evaluate the situation, try to find the balance in it, but somehow she just couldn't bring herself to withdraw. Instead, she took it all in and let herself be filled with the silken texture of Bett's skin and the perfection of her shape, with the scent in the air that was of them both, with the way her own body seemed only partially hers now, part of it in Bett's power, and the way she wanted to take Bett's body for herself, to have it over and over again. And somehow, that was all as it should be. Any other way of being in the world seemed very far off, and Rain was content to let it stay that way.

In spite of her completely relaxed and totally fulfilled—for the moment—condition, Bett's stomach was telling her that a cup of tea and something to eat might make things even better. She'd always thought that her mother's long-standing arrangement of having breakfast brought to her in bed was impossibly indolent, but at this moment the idea was quite appealing. But mostly she just wanted to look at Rain, thinking they were entirely different people to each other now. Rain's eyes seemed a bit lighter than usual. Her look was soft, still quite relaxed, with nothing of the sharp, guarded expression she had worn for all those weeks on the base. *That's it,* Bett thought, *she looks vulnerable.* Bett wanted to say the perfect thing, express just the right sentiment to let Rain know she was safe, that everything between them was incredible, and that she would never hurt her. *Hurt her!* Bett remembered Rain's shy confession. She touched Rain's face gently and said, "Darling, are you all right?" She looked toward Rain's crotch. "I had no idea—I mean, I'm so sorry about—"

Rain cut her off with a light kiss. Her voice throaty, she said, "Was there anything I did or said to make you think I didn't want you or that you did something I didn't like?" Bett smiled in remembrance of their passion, almost embarrassed, and she shook her head. Rain went on, more clearly. "Bett, don't apologize to me for what you feel, and don't apologize to me for what you make me feel. If you want to apologize if you spill some milk or burn the toast, fine. But I trust I'll never be sorry for anything between us from now on."

In a wash of emotion, Bett felt tears close to the surface. Rain's presence in her life had been relatively brief, but she had a way of bringing Bett to a level of feeling that was previously unimaginable. Last night had been absolutely incredible, and the equally amazing thing was that Bett was thrilled to wake and find Rain still beside her. She wasn't panicky or anxious, she was…blissful. *My God, what an extraordinary woman she is.* She eased her arms around Rain and held her very tightly, her heart soaring as Rain responded to her immediately. There was just the slightest trembling, but she wasn't sure which of them it was. Finally, Bett murmured into Rain's neck, "If I promise not to spill the milk, would you like some tea?" She could feel Rain smile again.

They rose reluctantly, into the chill air, with a few complaining sounds. As Bett watched Rain, feeling uncharacteristically uncertain, Rain stepped closer and offered her hand. Bett smiled as she took it—*she's such a charmer*—and they walked into the kitchen hand in hand.

The whole house was cold. Rain lit all the gas burners on the stove and they had their tea by the open oven, wrapped in some of Bett's extra blankets and standing very close together.

"Does your fireplace work?" Rain asked, looking into the den.

"As far as I know," Bett replied. "But I haven't any wood." Noting Rain's expression, she added, "Well, don't look at me like that, you know I only just moved in."

"I'll go out later and get you some," Rain offered.

"What makes you think that I'm going to let you out of my sight for that long?" Bett asked, putting down her tea and slipping her arms around Rain with her head on Rain's chest. *Out of my bed for that long is what I should have said.* Rain's body felt so good, so solid and inviting, that Bett felt a renewed surge of need. Rain's arms encircled her, returning the embrace. Rain moved her hands ever so gently along the lines of Bett's back. When she heard Rain's breathing quicken, heard that slight hum of pleasure, she pressed in closer, rubbing her cheek against the soft flannel of Rain's shirt. The thought flashed through her mind, *If every morning-after feels this good, I have certainly missed something.* Then she heard Rain's voice whisper her name, soft and low, and she knew that no one else would ever have felt like this. They were swaying very, very slowly, as if they were moving to a distant, delicate breeze. This was what she had wanted, had yearned for all those weeks on the base—to feel this connection with Rain, to have her close and welcoming. Rain's heartbeat in her ear was steady and strong, and Bett's heart heard an assurance that Rain felt the same way about her. It had been a long time since Bett had listened to her own heart. She didn't think she had ever listened to someone else's.

The phone rang again. It was hard to ignore, since it was right in front of them, and Rain sighed. "Go on. I'm going to take a shower. But don't be surprised if I secretly disconnect it later."

Bett moved away reluctantly and answered. Her expression changed to one of delight and she exclaimed, "Darling!" as Rain shook her head and headed to the bathroom.

❖

When Rain came back into the room, Bett was off the phone and finishing her tea. Rain was shaking and her teeth were chattering. She was wearing only a towel and her skin was so pale it was almost gray.

"No hot water," she managed to say.

Bett rushed down the hall to the linen closet, grateful they had unpacked her imported comforter and some extra blankets, and wrapped them around Rain as she stood by the oven. She rubbed briskly on Rain's arms and shoulders and back, trying to get more circulation, but it didn't seem to be helping. Rain had her head down and was still shaking violently. Finally, in desperation, Bett led her to the couch, took off Rain's towel and her own gown and robe, and used the blankets to make a kind of bedroll. Throwing off the back cushions so there was more room, she got Rain into the blankets and slipped in on top of her, wrapping the comforter on top of them both, almost covering their heads. Now that she was closer, she could hear Rain making some little noises in her throat as if she was struggling hard against something. Bett pulled Rain's arms around her own back and pressed into her, whispering, "You don't have to fight this, Rain. Let me…"

Rain let Bett's words resonate in her mind. *You don't have to fight this…let me.* Underneath the cold, she felt a deep tiredness. She was drained from weeks of fighting her feelings for Elizabeth Smythe, from weeks of pushing herself to exhaustion physically in the hopes that she might fall asleep without tossing and turning through her thoughts of Bett's scent and her eyes and her hair and her body and her voice and...herself. She felt some of the tension go out of her shoulders; until now it hadn't really occurred to her that she could indeed stop fighting. And then what? Could she just let Bett care for her; could they be that way for each other?

An involuntary groan escaped as Rain felt Bett's breast brush against her mouth. Her lips reached for its lush fullness eagerly, sucking very gently on the small, tight nipple. As wonderful as it felt, it wasn't quite like last night. Not urgent, just...comforting. Her breathing slowed and the trembling subsided.

After a minute, Bett stretched to stroke Rain's neck and cheek, her hand now caressing Rain's breast. "That's better, sweetheart. Can you tell me what happened?"

Rain was no longer shaking but her voice wasn't quite steady when she finally explained, "I was thinking of you when I got in the shower. Just expected the water to get warmer, but my mind wasn't on it."

Not nearly as cold, but not quite back to normal, Bett assessed, running her hands down Rain's sides, missing the warm body she associated with her former sergeant. *It's like her pilot light has gone out.* "I'm sure Dr. Freud would say your subconscious mind was just trying to figure out a way to get me naked in your arms again." Bett heard a faint chuckle. She offered her other breast to Rain who sucked with the same delicate movements of her lips, a soft hum of contentment coming from her throat. As Bett gently massaged Rain's other breast, she could feel new warmth kindling between them. *Better.* Melting dreamily into Rain's growing heat, she added, "Personally, I think it was a brilliant idea." Rain's lips had stopped moving; her breathing was growing slower, pulling Bett under with her.

Bett hadn't meant to fall asleep but when she moved, she felt herself waking. Rain tightened her embrace, quickly shifting them both until Bett was pinned against the back of the couch. Rain was up on her elbow again and Bett knew she wouldn't be able to get up unless Rain let her. Normally such lack of control would have made her uncomfortable, but as she looked into Rain's face, she knew she was truly captured by those dark eyes, and at this moment, she wasn't the least bit worried. Rain's warmth was back; as her hand moved slowly over the curve of Bett's hip, around to her bottom, and up to the dip in her waist it left a trail of heat. At Bett's waist Rain's hand paused, moving so very slowly back and forth at the curve there three times, as if confirming some previous memory of measurement. Bett, who had never been much of a morning person, felt a rush between her legs. *Oh yes.*

Rain began to move up toward her breast, her hand stretching as she caught Bett's hardened nipple in the web between her thumb and forefinger, her mouth opening ever so slightly in remembrance as her eyes lost their focus. She let her thumb slide across the erect flesh and on up to Bett's shoulder and Bett's eyes closed. Still moving firmly, yet carefully, Rain traced a line that only she could see from the roundness of Bett's shoulder across and up her neck to the jawline. Both of them were breathing more hoarsely and Rain's hand jumped to lightly trace Bett's eyebrow with her middle finger, down her face and over to her ear where she leaned in to speak, her voice a haunted hush. "I have had this dream so many times these past weeks. Tell me—are you real? Is this true?" She couldn't speak yet of the way it felt to be with Bett in this place, of the hope pounding inside her when she looked into Bett's eyes or of the wanting in her body that had been appeased last night but was now simmering anew, just below the surface of her skin. She needed to get some understanding, some sense of Bett's feelings and where her heart might be.

For a few seconds, Bett couldn't speak. How was it that Rain could say things that touched her in ways that no one ever had before? The idea that her impenetrable Sergeant Rains had dreamed of her, had wanted her this way…naked, helpless…made Bett catch her breath and a throbbing started in her core. "I think I'm becoming more real every moment I spend with you, Wind and Rain." Bett knew better than to use Rain's real name lightly. She meant it. Shifting slightly, she continued, "And as for true…" Before she could finish the thought, her stomach growled loudly. Rain blinked in surprise. "I guess that is the truth, warts and all." Bett laughed, self-conscious and embarrassed, but trying to play it off lightly.

Now Rain stroked her there, on her belly, but it was a different touch, more purposeful. "Oh no, Bett. No. There is nothing negative here. Your body is…" Rain searched but no exact word existed in her mind. She settled for one she had heard Bett say before, indicating she was well pleased with something. "Lovely." Her lips curved up shyly. "And truthful."

The smile that Bett had been waiting to see softened Rain's face, relaxing her features into an elegant loveliness that made Bett want to keep her close. She embraced her warmly, thinking to take Rain's hand and put it between her legs to show her another truth, but she thought the sergeant might be shocked. And clearly she would need some sustenance before long. So she took Rain's hand from her stomach and kissed it. "I don't suppose you'd be willing to cook for me?"

"It would be my pleasure." As they started to move, Rain stopped and took Bett's face in her hands, her voice deep and earnest. "I want to thank you. Thank you for giving me back my fire." She kissed Bett's forehead tenderly.

There it was again. That special way Rain had of expressing herself that was unlike any of Bett's previous acquaintances. *That must be one of the reasons why I find her so interesting.* "My pleasure," she echoed and they smiled at each other.

Rain stood, arching her back and shoulders in a way that made Bett think of a cat, and began searching around for her clothes. Bett found it amusing that Rain was so blasé about walking around naked, especially compared to the tightly buttoned, uniformed Sergeant Rains. She certainly didn't mind the view, observing how certain movements made Rain's muscles roll beneath her skin, marveling at how such an angular body could be so smooth to the touch. *But she's too thin,* Bett worried, deciding she would make sure Rain ate well while they were together. For enough money, extra ration coupons could always be had.

❖

Bett stayed cocooned on the couch for a few moments while Rain began cooking, but she soon missed the warm haven of Rain's body. The house seemed even colder. She dressed quickly and held out one of the blankets to Rain, saying, "Keep this around you, darling. I'm worried about you catching a cold." Bett took one as well and sat at the little breakfast table watching Rain.

After Rain made eggs and toast with the last of the groceries on hand, they ate, still wrapped in their blankets.

"What are you thinking?" Bett asked, after a moment.

"I was thinking of home," Rain said quietly, looking away. "We spent a lot of time wrapped up like this in winter. Sometimes there wasn't much heat."

Bett was quiet, waiting to see if Rain would say more. She knew so little about Rain's childhood. After a moment, she leaned to touched Rain's cheek gently and let her hand go through Rain's hair. Rain seemed to pull herself back. She took in Bett's appearance with a little smile that gradually grew into a twinkle in her eyes. "But I must admit, I did expect more amenities from a Carlton household."

Bett gave a surprised laugh and then acted offended.

Rain's smile faded. "Actually, I find this quite luxurious. But it will be even colder tonight." She stood. "I've seen a man with a truck selling firewood, when I've been in town. Maybe I can find him when I go out to buy groceries." She added, "I'll be fine. And I'll see you again very soon."

Rain braided her hair and left the house without another word, dressed in almost everything she had brought.

About an hour later, Bett heard a strange sound, a ringing, cutting sound, at regular intervals. She looked through the kitchen door window and saw a neatly stacked pile of logs along the side of the house. Rain was on the little porch, wielding a bright ax, splitting some of the logs into kindling. Bett watched the beautiful form, the economical motion of Rain's swing. As if in slow motion, she felt Rain's hand slide down from the ax head, heard the edge whisk the air with the quickness of a breath. When the log split, Bett felt a carnal joy. It was physical perfection, erotic exactness happening right outside her door, courtesy of the woman who had come into Bett's life as Sergeant Gale Rains and who had become the person Bett most wanted to see, the person she most wanted to have in her home, in her bed, in her life.

When Bett opened the door, Rain walked over, breathing a bit from the exertion of her work and said, "I found the firewood truck." She presented the blade horizontally. "He had an extra ax to sell, so this is my housewarming gift to you." Her eyes were fixed searchingly on Bett's.

Just that second, Bett could envision a younger Rain, one who had gotten so little from her difficult life but who was still willing to give. *Where did she find this goodness, this decency, in the midst of this pitiless world?* She felt admiration, and a strong sense that there was much that Rain could teach her about a life of courage, of integrity. But at that moment she mostly felt protective, like she wanted to hold that sweetness and shield her from sadness. She closed her eyes for an extra second and knew another truth. She could be falling madly, hopelessly, desperately in love with Wind and Rain.

"Rain," she began, not taking the axe. "I want to—"

"Bett"—Rain moved back a step—"your house needs warming. Let me build a fire and we can talk inside." She put the ax against the back wall of the house and returned to where Bett was standing.

"Can your fire wait one moment?" Bett asked. Rain nodded. "Good," Bett said, "because if I can't touch you right this second, I think I might explode." She put her arms around Rain and the quick response let her know that Rain had been feeling the same thing. They didn't kiss, but held each other through several deep breaths. Rain rubbed her cheek across Bett's hair and Bett tightened her arms, pleasure in her sigh.

❖

The fire felt wonderful. Bett couldn't remember the last time she had sat in front of a real fire since she'd returned from England. Of course there was rarely need for one in Los Angeles. They sat on the floor, very close to the heat, facing each other. Between them were some remnants of the cheese and apple and crackers that they had nibbled on while the flames caught.

"I have been thinking that I should apologize for teasing you about your family's wealth," Rain said solemnly. "I've experienced being judged as someone poor, but as I've gotten to know you, I can see the rich are judged, too. Perhaps by a different standard, perhaps even a stricter one since they seem to have so much. I believe that you, Elizabeth Carlton, are walking a difficult road to becoming your own person, even as you fear falling short in the views of others just as much as anyone, maybe more. You want to stay out from under your father's shadow while staying true to who you are and how you were raised. This is a narrow trail. I think you may have had many"—Rain hesitated just for a second—"friends, but there are also those who would like to see you fall from your own path and return to your father or even descend into a place of regret...or shame."

Suddenly Bett's mouth was on hers, kissing her as much as she could, kissing her face, her throat, even the front of her shirt, and crying at the same time. Rain held her and returned her kisses, tasting the salt and telling her, "No, Bett, please don't cry. Shh. It's okay. Shh."

At length, Bett was lying quietly in Rain's arms. She couldn't believe she had become so emotional, but the things that Rain had said and the way she had said them were so perceptive that she had simply been overcome. She knew she would have to sit up to continue their talk, so she did, leaving Rain's embrace after one last sweet kiss.

"My darling, I don't think even a doctorate from Oxford would prepare me to match your eloquence, or your insight. You've come so far in your life, and you've made your journey with decency and bravery. I thought of all the qualities you have that I and others admire—you are steady and good, you don't complain, and you lead by example. I think you have probably seen the bad in some people, but it's still not the first thing you look for. I think you've always been a seeker. I think you've found your answers where you could, and you could certainly have done worse than Henry David

Thoreau. As I understand it, his philosophy is one of simplicity, of finding harmony with nature and human beings, and I think you've always yearned for that in your life."

Rain had drawn her knees up to her chest and was rocking slightly. Bett plunged on. "I know you've had your heart broken. More than once, I think. I saw it the very first time we were alone and I looked into your eyes. Do you remember? After my first night of KP?" Rain nodded. "I was thanking you and you looked at me and I could see the wall you had up, the way you were protecting yourself and how you had no intention of letting anyone come close. Sometimes I can feel your pain in the way you hold me. But I can't, in all my thinking, imagine who would have been fool enough to hurt you. Because I think you are the most wonderful person I've ever met. I couldn't be more proud of you, Rain, or happier that you are here, together with me now."

They began to kiss and undress each other very slowly. Bett knew she would need to be gentle with Rain after last night. They brought their couch bedroll onto the floor in front of the fire. She turned Rain onto her stomach and sat on her bottom, rubbing Rain's shoulders, thinking she would give her a massage. But the heat coming from Rain's body and the way her own crotch began pulsing as she rocked herself back and forth was too fantastic for her to maintain control for long. She leaned down and began kissing the warm, smooth skin of Rain's back, letting her breasts brush lightly along as she moved toward Rain's shoulders. Rain began to moan and move under Bett's mouth. Bett put her mouth close to Rain's ear and whispered, "You like that, don't you?"

Rain didn't respond with a recognizable word, but the way she stirred as Bett softly kissed her ear was answer enough. She turned Rain back over and set herself between Rain's legs, her hands rubbing circles on Rain's chest and down to her breasts. Rain was breathing heavily and her eyes were closed until Bett said, "Look at me, Rain. I want you to see me."

As soon as she saw Rain's dark eyes open, she put her opened mouth between Rain's thighs, taking her in with a single motion. The surprise and delight in Rain's cry made Bett think that this too might be something new for her. Each time she worked her lips, she brought her tongue a little farther out until she felt Rain's hands slide off her and heard them hit the floor.

"Bett," she heard Rain say, although her voice was much more highly pitched than usual. It sounded like she was begging, which made Bett slide her tongue all the way out and begin a caressing motion up and down the length of Rain's opening. Rain's hands hit the floor again and she moaned. "Bett, I can't..."

Oh yes, you can, was in Bett's head. *And you will. Right now.* She centered her tongue on Rain's thrusting body and increased her pace until Rain's hands came off the floor and buried themselves in her hair, digging in, clutching at her, and the sound was like a passing gust of wind, screaming and then sighing.

As Bett began making her way up Rain's now tranquil body, she kept her thigh between Rain's legs. Head on Rain's shoulder, she gave Rain as much time as she could before she asked, "No one's ever done that to you either, have they?" Rain tried to move but Bett pressed herself on top of her. She could just feel Rain shaking her head. "Good," Bett said, "then you'll always know it's me."

"It's always been you." Rain's whisper was hoarse with emotion. "It's only been you." Bett closed her eyes and let the words fill her.

The places where their bodies touched seemed to simmer with desire. When the fire popped loudly a second time, Rain lifted one knee slightly and Bett began to move slowly against her thigh, still lying stretched out on Rain's body. As her arousal pulsed slowly, she wondered if this need would ever be satisfied, and if their passion for each other could become more than physical. She worried that she might no longer be able to pull back from the edge she could feel herself approaching—not just the building of her climax, but the place where everything would change and her heart would no longer be her own. Rain raised up slightly and put her hands on Bett's thighs, shifting her over so she was straddling Rain's narrow hips and the wetness of Bett's body came into contact with Rain's tilted pelvis.

Still stretched out on Rain's body, Bett moaned a short "Oh!" and then Rain positioned her hands on Bett's hips to make her repeat the motion. When Bett began moving on her own, her next cry stretched out longer. She was moving steadily, loving the feeling of sliding her body against Rain's.

Then Rain said, "Look at me, Bett."

Bett pushed herself up to a seated position, leaning back slightly so she could see Rain's face, which caused the sensations growing inside her to increase. Her body fit into Rain's just at the place where she needed her release, and then Rain's fingers traveled up to Bett's breasts which made Bett move faster. She couldn't help opening her mouth to pant at the pace of her movements. Rain held Bett's breasts, squeezing gently, occasionally running her thumbs over Bett's nipples. Then Bett had to close her eyes again, her head tipping back as her body began to shudder. She let out a long, slow groan and fell back on top of Rain, who grabbed Bett's hips and pushed into her just a little harder until the shuddering finally stopped.

After a few minutes, Rain rolled Bett onto her back. Bett felt Rain's hands brush the hair back from her face, and then Rain's lips brushed the hollow in her throat, her hair pooling softly on Bett's chest. Bett didn't want to open her eyes, but her mouth moved into a smile.

Then Rain's voice, back to its normal deep tone, was in her ear. "Tell me," Rain demanded.

Bett knew what Rain was asking. "Only you." She breathed. "Always you." The edge was gone. She knew she was lost...and found.

❖

A few hours later, Bett opened her eyes, instantly aware that Rain wasn't beside her. Looking around, she found Rain sitting up, watching her with one of those unreadable expressions on her face.

Bett sat also, anxious, coming fully awake almost immediately. "What is it, darling? Is something wrong? Please tell me."

"It's that," Rain replied. "What do you mean by *darling*?"

"It's just a term of endearment, Rain," Bett said, relieved at the simple question. "Like sweetie or dear. Something to say in place of someone's name. I'm sure I picked it up at school."

Rain shook her head. "I asked it wrong. I meant, *who* is darling?"

"Why, you are, of course." Bett smiled.

Rain didn't. "But not only me," she persisted. "Just this morning I heard you say this to your friend on the phone. It sounds the same. Is there no difference in your mind between them and me?"

Bett was beginning to understand. "Yes, there is a world of difference, of course."

"But how am I to know, when it is the same word? How should others who hear you say this to me know that it is not the same as what you say to them?"

Bett moved closer and took Rain's face in her hands. Looking into her eyes, she said, softly, "Tell me what you want, Rain. Don't ever be afraid to do that. If you'll tell me what it is, I will move heaven and earth to give it to you."

The unreadable expression changed as Rain's eyes focused on the promise that lay waiting between them. She took a breath. "I want a word that we use just for us. Something that neither says to another."

Bett nodded, feeling the intention of Rain's words resonate inside her. "I would like that, too. Did you have something in mind?"

Rain lifted her gaze, thinking. Bett's words had already made their way into her heart: *heaven and earth*. She thought, *That is what you are to me, Bett. The beauty of the stars above me and the solid world in my arms.* Taking in Bett's scent, the feel of her skin, the look in her eyes just now as she waited, Rain searched for a word that would confirm the goodness that was between them, wanting something meaningful for them both. After some challenging conversations with the base chaplain during her own basic training, she'd read the entire Bible. The beautiful expression from the Song of Solomon where a lover described the one for whom she'd waited sounded right, and true. She spoke the word aloud. "Beloved."

Bett closed her eyes, feeling the deep well of emotion that Rain opened up in her. *How like my gallant sergeant to find a lovely, old-fashioned word like that.* She opened her eyes and blinked to clear them. "That is perfect, Rain," she said, taking each hand and kissing it. "You are indeed my beloved."

About the Author

Jaycie Morrison is a second generation native Dallasite who is also in love with Colorado and now splits her time between the two. She lives with her wife of twenty-eight years and her ten-year-old blue heeler. As a youngster, she and her friends entertained themselves making up and acting out stories featuring characters from popular TV shows or favorite bands—lots of action and a little romance even then! A voracious reader, she always wondered what it would be like to write a book and found that once she started, it was almost impossible to stop. Her first novel, *Basic Training of the Heart*, begins a series that combines her love of the written word and of history.

Books Available from Bold Strokes Books

Basic Training of the Heart by Jaycie Morrison. In 1944, socialite Elizabeth Carlton joins the Women's Army Corps to escape family expectations and love's disappointments. Can Sergeant Gale Rains get her through Basic Training with their hearts intact? (978-1-62639-818-4)

Before by KE Payne. When Tally falls in love with her band's new recruit, she has a tough decision to make. What does she want more—Alex or the band? (978-1-62639-677-7)

Believing in Blue by Maggie Morton. Growing up gay in a small town has been hard, but it can't compare to the next challenge Wren—with her new, sky-blue wings—faces: saving two entire worlds. (978-1-62639-691-3)

Coils by Barbara Ann Wright. A modern young woman follows her aunt into the Greek Underworld and makes a pact with Medusa to win her freedom by killing a hero of legend. (978-1-62639-598-5)

Courting the Countess by Jenny Frame. When relationship-phobic Lady Henrietta Knight starts to care about housekeeper Annie Brannigan and her daughter, can she overcome her fears and promise Annie the forever that she demands? (978-1-62639-785-9)

Dapper by Jenny Frame. Amelia Honey meets the mysterious Byron De Brek and is faced with her darkest fantasies, but will her strict moral upbringing stop her from exploring what she truly wants? (978-1-62639-898-6E)

Delayed Gratification: The Honeymoon by Meghan O'Brien. A dream European honeymoon turns into a winter storm nightmare involving a delayed flight, a ditched rental car, and eventually, a surprisingly happy ending. (978-1-62639-766-8E)

For Money or Love by Heather Blackmore. Jessica Spaulding must choose between ignoring the truth to keep everything she has, and doing the right thing only to lose it all—including the woman she loves. (978-1-62639-756-9)

Hooked by Jaime Maddox. With the help of sexy Detective Mac Calabrese, Dr. Jessica Benson is working hard to overcome her past, but they may not be enough to stop a murderer. (978-1-62639-689-0)

Lands End by Jackie D. Public relations superstar Amy Kline is dealing with a media nightmare, and the last thing she expects is for restaurateur Lena Michaels to change everything, but she will. (978-1-62639-739-2)

Lysistrata Cove by Dena Hankins. Jack and Eve navigate the maelstrom of their darkest desires and find love by transgressing gender, dominance, submission, and the law on the crystal blue Caribbean Sea. (978-1-62639-821-4)

Twisted Screams by Sheri Lewis Wohl. Reluctant psychic Lorna Dutton doesn't want to forgive, but if she doesn't do just that an innocent woman will die. (978-1-62639-647-0)

A Class Act by Tammy Hayes. Buttoned-up college professor Dr. Margaret Parks doesn't know what she's getting herself into when she agrees to one date with her student, Rory Morgan, who is 15 years her junior. (978-1-62639-701-9)

Bitter Root by Laydin Michaels. Small town chef Adi Bergeron is hiding something, and Griffith McNaulty is going to find out what it is even if it gets her killed. (978-1-62639-656-2)

Capturing Forever by Erin Dutton. When family pulls Jacqueline and Casey back together, will the lessons learned in eight years apart be enough to mend the mistakes of the past? (978-1-62639-631-9)

Deception by VK Powell. DEA Agent Colby Vincent and Attorney Adena Weber are embroiled in a drug investigation involving homeless veterans and an attraction that could destroy them both. (978-1-62639-596-1)

Dyre: A Knight of Spirit and Shadows by Rachel E. Bailey. With the abduction of her queen, werewolf-bodyguard Des must follow the kidnappers' trail to Europe, where her queen—and a battle unlike any Des has ever waged—awaits her. (978-1-62639-664-7)

First Position by Melissa Brayden. Love and rivalry take center stage for Anastasia Mikhelson and Natalie Frederico in one of the most prestigious ballet companies in the nation. (978-1-62639-602-9)

Best Laid Plans by Jan Gayle. Nicky and Lauren are meant for each other, but Nicky's haunting past and Lauren's societal fears threaten to derail all possibilities of a relationship. (987-1-62639-658-6)

Exchange by CF Frizzell. When Shay Maguire rode into rural Montana, she never expected to meet the woman of her dreams—or to learn Mel Baker was held hostage by legal agreement to her right-wing father. (987-1-62639-679-1)

Just Enough Light by AJ Quinn. Will a serial killer's return to Colorado destroy Kellen Ryan and Dana Kingston's chance at love, or can the search-and-rescue team save themselves? (987-1-62639-685-2)

Rise of the Rain Queen by Fiona Zedde. Nyandoro is nobody's princess. She fights, curses, fornicates, and gets into as much trouble as her brothers. But the path to a throne is not always the one we expect. (987-1-62639-592-3)

Tales from Sea Glass Inn by Karis Walsh. Over the course of a year at Cannon Beach, tourists and locals alike find solace and passion at the Sea Glass Inn. (987-1-62639-643-2)

The Color of Love by Radclyffe. Black sheep Derian Winfield needs to convince literary agent Emily May to marry her to save the Winfield Agency and solve Emily's green card problem, but Derian didn't count on falling in love. (987-1-62639-716-3)

A Reluctant Enterprise by Gun Brooke. When two women grow up learning nothing but distrust, unworthiness, and abandonment, it's no wonder they are apprehensive and fearful when an overwhelming love just won't be denied. (978-1-62639-500-8)

Above the Law by Carsen Taite. Love is the last thing on Agent Dale Nelson's mind, but reporter Lindsey Ryan's investigation could change the way she sees everything—her career, her past, and her future. (978-1-62639-558-9)

Actual Stop by Kara A. McLeod. When Special Agent Ryan O'Connor's present collides abruptly with her past, shots are fired, and the course of her life is irrevocably altered. (978-1-62639-675-3)

Embracing the Dawn by Jeannie Levig. When ex-con Jinx Tanner and business executive E. J. Bastien awaken after a one-night stand to find their lives inextricably entangled, love has its work cut out for it. (978-1-62639-576-3)

Jane's World: The Case of the Mail Order Bride by Paige Braddock. Jane's PayBuddy account gets hacked and she inadvertently purchases a mail order bride from the Eastern Bloc. (978-1-62639-494-0)

Love's Redemption by Donna K. Ford. For ex-convict Rhea Daniels and ex-priest Morgan Scott, redemption lies in the thin line between right and wrong. (978-1-62639-673-9)

The Shewstone by Jane Fletcher. The prophetic Shewstone is in Eawynn's care, but unfortunately for her, Matt is coming to steal it. (978-1-62639-554-1)

A Touch of Temptation by Julie Blair. Recent law school graduate Kate Dawson's ordained path to the perfect life gets thrown off course when handsome butch top Chris Brent initiates her to sexual pleasure. (978-1-62639-488-9)

Beneath the Waves by Ali Vali. Kai Merlin and Vivien Palmer love the water and the secrets trapped in the depths, but if Kai gives in to her feelings, it might come at a cost to her entire realm. (978-1-62639-609-8)

Girls on Campus edited by Sandy Lowe and Stacia Seaman. College: four years when rules are made to be broken. This collection is required reading for anyone looking to earn an A in sex ed. (978-1-62639-733-0)

Heart of the Pack by Jenny Frame. Human Selena Miller falls for the domineering Caden Wolfgang, but will their love survive Selena learning the Wolfgangs are werewolves? (978-1-62639-566-4)

Miss Match by Fiona Riley. Matchmaker Samantha Monteiro makes the impossible possible for everyone but herself. Is mysterious dancer Lucinda Moss her own perfect match? (978-1-62639-574-9)

Paladins of the Storm Lord by Barbara Ann Wright. Lieutenant Cordelia Ross must choose between duty and honor when a man with godlike powers forces her soldiers to provoke an alien threat. (978-1-62639-604-3)